THE LADIES OF BEVERLY HILLS

By Sharleen Cooper Cohen and published by New English
Library

THE DAY AFTER TOMORROW
REGINA'S SONG
THE LADIES OF BEVERLY HILLS

THE LADIES OF BEVERLY HILLS

Sharleen Cooper Cohen

NEW ENGLISH LIBRARY

First published in the USA in 1983 by Delacorte Press

First NEL Paperback Edition September 1983

NEL Books are published by
New English Library,
Mill Road, Dunton Green,
Sevenoaks, Kent.
Editorial office:
47 Bedford Square,
London WC1B 3DP

Typeset by PRG Graphics Redhill
Printed in Great Britain by
Cox & Wyman Ltd, Reading

British Library C.I.P.

Cohen, Sharleen Cooper
    The ladies of Beverly Hills.
    I. Title
    813'.54[F]   PS3553.04278

ISBN 0-450-05615-5

This book is dedicated to the 'Ladies' in my life whose friendships have meant so much to me . . .
And to Ellen G. Ruderman, Sandi Gelles-Cole, and Elaine Markson for sustaining, nurturing, and inspiring.

Acknowledgments

To the many people who graciously gave me their time and advice so that my quest for accuracy could be met, I am extremely grateful. They are:

Ronald Harrison Cooper—Novak, Cooper & Wohlgemuth

Barbara Gordon, M.S.W.

Sam White

Peter Metzler

Neil Tucker

Joel Nall

Myra Cochnar

Franklin Kissane—State Bar Association of California

Ronald Gordon—Buchalter, Nemer, Fields, Chrystie & Younger

Edward Brown—Cohen-Brown Management Group

Alice Fisher

Michael Cohen—Buchalter, Nemer, Fields, Chrystie & Younger

Judy Brand Leaf

Jacques Purris—Bache Halsey Stuart Shields Inc

Don Blyth—American Civil Liberties Union

Karl Sussman—Cantor Fitzgerald & Co. Inc.

Glynn Mays—Commodity Futures Trading Commission

Mark Young—Commodity Futures Trading Commission

Rose Gorta—New York Mercantile Exchange

Jim Parese—American Savings Bank

Lawrence Ellis—First Interstate Bank

Michael Douglass—Searchers Investigating Co.

Lee J. Beck—Searchers Investigating Co.

Sally Rumbley—Guild Mortgage Co.

Norman Cohen—Buchalter, Nemer, Fields, Chrystie & Younger

Robert E. Blythe—Sherman and Nordstrom

Jerry Spielman—Merrill Lynch Pierce Fenner & Smith, Inc.

Jay Zagar

Robert M. Eller—Loeb and Loeb

Edwin G. Pryor—Merrill Lynch Pierce Fenner & Smith. Inc.

Vincent J. Conway—Merrill Lynch Pierce Fenner & Smith, Inc.

And my deepest appreciation to my husband, Martin L. Cohen, for his devotion, invaluable assistance, expertise, and love.

Who is rich? He who rejoices in what he has.

The Talmud
Midrash Avot 4:1

BOOK I
Dreams

Chapter 1

PHYLLIS TREMBLED with excitement as she stood in the dining room of the guesthouse adjacent to the English garden where her wedding ceremony was about to take place. She parted the lace curtains to peek at the arriving guests, but her usually tranquil hands were shaking so in anticipation of this glorious day that she had to let go of the curtain and clasp her hands tightly. There was too much emotion to contain. Electricity coursed through her body and she felt incredibly alive. She was getting married today; she was committing herself to the future, to womanhood.

In a moment of quiet reflection she bowed her head and gave thanks to God. 'Please bless this union,' she prayed. 'I am in your hands.' Her inner faith always brought her comfort, yet still she trembled.

How she wished with all her heart that every second of today could be lived in slow motion. From here on in every second must be guarded, photographed, preserved, so she could possess her precious moments as well as cherish them. She would not hurry, she would fight the urgency inside that made her blood race with anticipation, but on it raced. If only these last remaining moments before the wedding could be suspended in time, could be savored and enjoyed as one counts and touches each pearl on a long, graduated necklace; if only one could hold on to life's special moments and not allow them to tick so swiftly away, but like the oyster's perfect creation keep them on a string long enough to notice the glow of rosy color, long enough to feel the size of each sphere, the tiny flawed indentation

13

where the oyster has left its mark. But even if time did pass in fleeting, often unnoticed moments, she could still hold a special joy within, a sense that everything delicious in the world would soon be her feast. And that tantalizing knowledge, that overwhelming excitement, transported her above the mundane, because soon, only moments away, she would become Mrs Peter McKintridge. How could one young woman deserve such happiness?

Final curiosity overcame her trembling and she parted the curtains to look out.

It was a painting by Monet.

The grounds were awash with pastel colors on a background of emerald green made fragrant by an acre-sized rose garden. The garden was directly adjacent to the McKintridge estate guesthouse where she stood and Phyllis could smell the scent of roses wafting through the open window. At the end of the rose garden was a large expanse of lawn bordered by a pond complete with weeping willows, live swans, and a quaint wooden bridge à la Giverney. On the other side of the lawn was a terraced hillside ablaze with blankets of flowers, some grown in hothouses just for this occasion. Azaleas, camellias, peonies, hydrangeas, and ranunculus grew in colorful profusion, while at the base of the hill was a border of low flower beds filled with pansies, sweet pea, sweet william, and candytufts. The ceremony would take place under an arbor between the hillside and the pond, which was covered in a wild tangle of Cecil Brunner roses all in bloom. Mother Nature's only improvement on this setting was to make the temperature a perfect seventy-five and to give the air a slight breeze freeing it of smog.

Even though the main house was too far away to be visible from the guesthouse, Phyllis could feel its presence. The huge, French-style mansion hovered over her wedding day the way it hovered over Beverly Hills, magnificent and imposing like an enormous god looking down on his worshipers.

14

Guests were milling about, others were already seated; ladies in garden hats and flowing spring dresses added to the impressionistic landscape. Here and there Phyllis could see famous faces among the family and friends come to see her wed. She saw the minister approaching the podium, stopping to chat with some of his parishioners, and she knew that it was nearly time. Strangely enough she felt calmer than she had all day. It was the waiting that had been the most difficult. Now there was only joy to anticipate.

In the living room of this five-bedroom house where she waited for the sound of *Lohengrin* to begin, her bridal party was assembled, looking demure and feminine in their rose-colored dresses trimmed with antique lace. Her own bouquet of lilies of the valley, stafonoitis, white baby roses, and tiny white orchids was in its box in the refrigerator surrounded by crinkly green tissue. Her shiny, golden hair was curled at the ends and hung down her back as she always wore it; only today the two front sections were caught up on top of her head into a knot of braids and curls festooned with ribbons and baby's breath. She had only to place her veil over her hair to complete the picture. And what a veil it was. Yards and yards of tulle, appliquéd and trimmed with antique lace, every delicate twist and twirl made by someone's expert hand.

Her dress was a vision of seed pearls and Irish organdy trimmed with handmade antique lace. The throat and yoke were also lace, revealing the cleavage of her soft round breasts. There were fifty-three covered buttons up the back of the dress, and fifteen at each wrist. The dress contained eighty yards of fabric in the train, and it cost eight thousand dollars.

She was wearing a bit more makeup today than usual: a touch of pink color on her cheeks and lips, a dash of azure shadow above her gray-blue eyes, and an extra dollop of lapis lazuli mascara to give her eyes that wide-eyed glow. Her perfume was Joy, the cameo at her throat belonged to

Grandmother Anhalt, her shoes were from Charles Jourdan, and of course the three-carat diamond ring was from Tiffany.

Gracefully she let the curtain fall into place before someone spied her taking a preliminary peek. And then her heart gave an authorized jump as she thought about what would happen tonight when the wedding was over. She and Peter would spend their wedding night at the Bel-Air Hotel in the Presidential Suite and they were finally going to make love. Peter had been with other girls before, but she was a virgin, a rare phenomenon in this day and age, an oddity, sometimes even an embarrassment. Not that it had been easy for her, especially over the past year of her engagement. Many times she had come close to giving in to her desires. She was twenty-four and very passionate. Her body cried for fulfillment as much as anybody else's, she masturbated and fantasized, and often dreamed of sex sometimes to an obsession. But her virtue was inviolate none the less. All through college her friends teased her about it; fraternity boys asked her out as a challenge to see if they could be the one to score. But Marla Gilbert and Vicky Feinstein, her two closest friends, didn't tease her, and her high school sweetheart, Matt, and her college boyfriend, John, had respected her wishes and not tried to coax her too much. But she had not kept herself chaste to impress her friends; she had done it to fulfill an ideal she had formulated for herself years ago and would endure any discomfort to maintain. Denying herself the pleasure of intercourse was a small price to pay for being the kind of person she wanted to be. For she wanted to be able to say to her husband on their wedding night: 'I am yours, my beloved: no one else has known me.' Sometimes she thought she was being perverse, sometimes merely stubborn, and often she suspected it was fear that kept her chaste. For in putting off sex for such a long time she had made it far more important—and far more frightening—than it ought to be. But when she gave herself the benefit of the doubt, she realized she had merely set a goal for herself that placed her apart from others—not above them, only apart. And it was this knowledge of her own strength of character that kept her going when it was difficult to do so. Now, having reached this moment, and knowing what it had cost her, she had no regrets.

Voices interrupted her thoughts; she could hear her friends in the next room. Vicky Feinstein's rose above the others; she was exclaiming over the wedding gifts on display in the main house. Phyllis thought it a vulgar tradition to display one's gifts, but her father had insisted, so she acquiesced as she always did when Felix insisted. It was as if her father needed to show Mr McKintridge—*Belson*, she reminded herself—that his grandson wasn't marrying a woman without means. Not only did she think it a vulgar tradition, but it was inconvenient to transport all the gifts from her parents' house to the McKintridge estate by armored truck. The gifts had to be cataloged, guarded, and arranged in the trophy room, but none the less it had been done. Her mother worried herself into her usual state of near inebriation because of her concern over theft and breakage of the expensive items, constantly checking to see if everything was all there. But of course it was safe. The McKintridge estate was a fortress and Belson had an entire staff of servants, forty-five in all.

'Did you see that solid gold silverware for twelve?' she heard Vicky saying. 'Ye gods! And the Waterford crystal and Georgian silver. I counted thirty-two silver platters. Phyllis could open a shop. David Orgell must be *having* himself over this wedding. She's received three complete sets of Pratesi linens, and two Porthault. And the Anhalts gave her and Peter the down payment on a three-hundred-thousand-dollar condominium on Elm Drive. Can you believe it? Phyllis is the first one of us to own her own home. And in Beverly Hills no less.'

'The condo cost two hundred and fifty,' someone said, but Phyllis didn't recognize the voice. And then Vicky again. 'They're taking a three-week honeymoon at Kapalua Bay. The only vacation I've had in years was four days in Carmel and it was foggy the whole time.'

Phyllis smiled at Vicky's *kvetching*. She didn't mean half the things she complained about.

Phyllis heard Marla Gilbert's voice shushing Vicky. 'Phyllis might hear you,' she cautioned. 'You know she'd be as happy to go to Carmel as Hawaii. And no matter how many fabulous gifts she receives, she'll never be spoiled.'

Dear Marla, Phyllis thought, *always jumping to defend.* She hoped Marla was right about her: she didn't want to be spoiled, or take for granted all the special advantages she possessed. She certainly didn't feel entitled to the incredible gifts she'd gotten. She too was awed by their lavishness; for newlyweds to own their own condominium was embarrassing. But her greatest fear was not that she couldn't handle her new acquisitions—she could do that easily—nor that she might lose them—that she could handle also—but that perhaps they wouldn't make Peter happy. And her only goal in life was to make Peter happy.

She wanted to give him lots of children, the sooner the better, unless he didn't want them, and she wanted to cook him wonderful meals, unless he'd rather eat out, and she wanted to make love to him any time he'd let her, unless he'd rather make love to her. Whatever Peter wanted was what she wanted. She was going to give him all the security and close family life he'd lost when his parents and sister were killed in a plane crash. Her heart ached for him every time she thought of what he must have suffered to be ten years old and the sole survivor of a plane crash that killed his entire family. He'd awakened in a hospital to find the only people he had left in the world were his grandparents. His grandmother wanted him to stay at home but his austere potentate of a grandfather packed him off to boarding school at the first available opportunity. Of course Phyllis didn't blame Belson; his wife was ill and he had done what he thought was right for Peter. After his grandmother died, Peter never lived at home again until he graduated college and went to USC Law School.

Phyllis thanked God every day for giving her Peter to

love, but most of all she thanked her father for introducing them. Felix had gotten to know Peter at the Los Angeles Country Club when Peter was in law school, and they had developed a very special friendship. Peter came to rely on Felix as the father he had never had. They played tennis doubles together and golf, and for years Felix's conversations were peppered with mention of 'the McKintridge boy'. Phyllis chuckled to herself remembering how she'd refused to meet him. She was going with John Aames at the time, and after they broke up, she'd immersed herself in the graduate business program at Claremont. There had been no time for dating or romance until finally Felix overruled her protests and invited Peter to dinner.

Had it been love at first sight? No, Phyllis thought, not exactly love, but in many ways something more important. It had been *like* at first sight. She had liked Peter's shy soft-spoken mannerisms, his sincerity, and the kindness in his smile. It amazed her that anyone as handsome as Peter could be so sentimental, and it overwhelmed her to see tears in his eyes when she told him she loved him. At first she'd had to contrive ways to see him because of his reticence to approach her. It seemed he wanted to make such a good impression on Felix Anhalt's beautiful daughter that he was too much of a gentleman. It was she who took the initiative, who made tennis dates with her girl friends at the club when she knew he would be playing there. She was the one who studied at the courthouse law library in hopes of running into him (it worked twice), and she even invited him to a play at the Music Center, telling him they were her parents' tickets. Actually she'd paid scalpers' prices, and when Peter found out they weren't her parents' seats, he overcame his shyness and started asking her out. There was something in his attitude toward her that made her feel cherished. And they both shared an idealization and reverence for love.

To say that she was impressed with him was putting it mildly; she was smitten. Not only did he have ambition and drive to succeed on his own even with his family's wealth, but he treated her father with awe and deference, and that touched her. She'd never seen anyone as anxious to please as Peter was to please Felix. He even looked at her father in the same adoring way he looked at her, which only demonstrated how much Peter needed a family. Of course she too always deferred to Felix; he had such a command of everyone around him and impeccable judgment. Phyllis learned early in life not to question him. And when Phyllis realized how much Peter cared about her father, that's when she began to love him.

The momentous day she declared her love they had gone walking in Ferndale Park and stopped to sit on a bench overlooking the stream. It was a warm autumn afternoon; the air felt heavy with expectancy.

'I have something to tell you, Peter,' she said, solemnly turning toward him, not letting even a smile lighten the importance of her words.

Alerted by her tone, his light-brown eyes flicked to hers and she saw a fleeting expression of tension as though he were afraid. She took his hand to reassure him. 'It doesn't matter if you return my feelings,' she paused, 'but I wanted you to know that I love you.' Her words hung in the air and that moment she knew she was saying something irrevocable.

'You love me?' he said incredulously, as though he hadn't heard her correctly. His disbelief caused something inside of her to turn over and she wanted to envelop him in an ocean of love, to repair all his hurts and pains, and she felt more love for him than she'd ever felt for another human being, as though every ounce of her had been awakened. It was so bittersweet it made her ache. 'I've never known anyone as kind and as giving as you are, Peter, or someone I enjoy being with as much as you. And even if you don't love me, it doesn't matter, I have enough love for both of us.' And then she let her smile break through, that perfect smile that displayed sparkling white teeth, made dimples in her cheeks deepen, and had won her the title of best smile in her senior class both at Beverly

Hills and in her college sorority. Her smile was so broad she beamed rays of love all over him.

Peter gazed at her in amazement. 'Nobody's ever said that to me and made me believe them.' And that's when she saw his eyes fill with tears. He looked away quickly, down at his hands, embarrassed by the emotion that was flooding his face; his hands were a pale reddish color around the cuticles and there was a fluff of fine brown hair that curled at the wrists. Something about his hands made her feel even more tender.

He looked up again. 'I want you so much it scares me,' he said, searching for the exact, honest expression of his feelings. Everything he did, he did with honesty. 'But how can I show you?'

'Just be as happy as I am.' She laughed, her words spilling out. 'Because I'm absolutely joyous. I feel as if I were skipping down a garden path lined with roses in bloom, or throwing pebbles into a sparkling mountain lake and watching the ripples widen, or racing a baby colt over a meadow of wild flowers with a shaggy dog barking at my heels and a blue sky full of billowy white clouds overhead. That kind of joyous.'

Peter's eyes sparkled through his tears at her descriptions. And there was a look of such longing on his face to feel what she was feeling that she wanted to throw her arms around him and crush him with hugs and kisses, but she was embarrassed because there were people walking by.

And then he too started to smile, infected by her joy. But smiling with joy seemed so new to him that it made her sad. 'I don't deserve you,' he said. 'And I don't know if I can be worthy of you.' His words caught in his throat. 'I don't know how to love; but I want to.'

And this time tears came to her eyes and she was overcome with such a rush of love she didn't care who saw her put her arms around him and hug him to her. 'You'll learn, darling Peter,' she whispered. 'You'll learn.'

Phyllis's reverie was interrupted by a knock at the door and she felt her heart leap to her throat. Her mother entered, carrying her veil. 'Is it time?' she asked.

Audrey Anhalt nodded and approached her daughter, the white lustrous folds of the veil blending with the ecru and rose lace dress she was wearing. Phyllis thought her mother looked beautiful; her saffron-colored hair was wound into a chignon and tendrils of soft curls framed her still lovely face. Only the red rims of her eyes and the icy coldness of her hands as she handed the veil to Phyllis revealed the emotion she was feeling today.

Phyllis took the veil and approached the mirror over the buffet, then she lifted the pearl-covered headpiece and pinned it to her hair while Audrey arranged the yards of tulle down her back. The veil made all the difference—transforming her from a nervous young woman into a radiant bride. She loved what she saw and hoped Peter would too.

She heard her mother sigh. 'You look so beautiful, dear.'

Phyllis smiled. 'Where's Dad?' she asked, gazing at herself through a haze of white.

'Waiting right outside. Everybody else looks beautiful too, all the attendants. And Peter is so happy. Both of us were nearly crying together.' Audrey leaned toward her to help arrange the net over Phyllis's face and Phyllis caught a whiff of her breath.

'*Mother*,' Phyllis said with alarm, staring at Audrey, whose eyes locked with her own. 'You promised, not today!'

Audrey's lower lip trembled from the rebuke. 'I've only had one glass of champagne, darling. Just to steady my nerves. After all, this is a special day. I'll be all right, don't worry.'

Phyllis stopped herself from letting panic engulf her and studied her mother's face for the truth. Perhaps for once her mother would be in control of herself. From all the signs it seemed as though she would be. Phyllis relaxed a bit and took her mother's hand, squeezing it with all her might, as much to give courage as to receive it. 'Everything is going to be perfect, isn't it, Mother?' she asked anxiously.

'Don't worry,' Audrey repeated.

And Phyllis nodded with relief. Everything was all right. 'Oh, Mother, will my life always be as wonderful as it is today?' she asked. 'This is the happiest day of my life.'

'I pray that it will always be this happy, darling,' Audrey said, smiling through misty eyes. 'But even if it isn't, you have everything in the world, and it's only going to get better.'

Chapter 2

'A PREGNANT matron of honor is ludicrous,' Marla said to Larry. 'I'll feel ridiculous waddling down the aisle with all those people watching me.' They were waiting with the rest of the wedding party in the entry hall of the guesthouse for the procession to begin. In front of them were the brides-maids, flower girls, and ushers. Behind them was the bride. Marla sighed as she looked at her own pear-shaped image in the entry-hall mirror. The rose-colored organza brides-maid dress floated about her like the petals of a giant hibiscus trying to be pollinated by a reluctant bee.

Larry stood next to her with his legs apart in his rented tux, twisting the studs in his ruffled shirt and admiring himself in the same mirror. No seventh-month bulge in his womb. 'It's a bit late for regrets when the wedding is about to start,' he said.

Marla suddenly felt like crying.

'You look fine, honey,' Larry said, trying to make her feel better. 'That dress is a good color for you with your dark hair and light complexion.' And then he laughed. 'But you do look kind of like a big pink lampshade.'

She laughed with him in spite of herself. 'No sympathy from you, right?'

'If you hold your bouquet in front of you, no one will even notice.'

'You will,' she retorted, but he was admiring himself again and didn't hear her. He seemed so unattainable standing there, so out of reach even though they were married—as though if she embraced him he would disintegrate into thin air, or by the mere act of reaching for him he'd elude her like a mirage, always a step away. Had she ever felt they belonged to one another? Felt their fusion as one being the way she felt fused with this baby cuddled beneath her ribs? Why did she bother to reach out at all? Her invisible connectors were raw at the ends from being bluntly cut by his self-possessed scissors. And yet she still longed for him the way she always had.

As if to punctuate her depressing thoughts, she saw he had the beginning of a hard-on. It couldn't be for her. He hadn't been excited by her during her first pregnancy, and this second time was no exception. She could just imagine what he was thinking about, some little secretary, no doubt. But she wouldn't ask him. she would not!

'What are you thinking about?' she asked, hating herself the minute the words left her mouth. He started guiltily.

'Nothing.'

'Is that what you call this?' she reached down between his legs and ran her hand over his erection.

He moved away. 'Hey, don't do that here. Someone will see.'

'I must be driving you wild with my alluring, hourglass shape, right?'

'Don't start, Marla,' he snapped.

She turned away to hide the sudden pain that gripped her, trying to protect that vulnerable place inside that hurt whenever Larry got that expression on his face of repugnance that annihilated her self-esteem. If Larry didn't make her feel so unattractive with his comments about big lampshades or baby elephants she'd be willing to walk nude down the aisle of Phyllis's wedding and proudly display the life growing within her. But he couldn't resist making comments and she couldn't help feeling ungainly. She'd even offered to drop out of the wedding party. But Phyllis swept away her insecurity. 'You're dearer to me than anyone in the world; there would be no wedding without you.' And that settled that. At least Marla had felt loved and comforted by Phyllis, if not by her own husband. How could anyone be as good as Phyllis? She turned around to look at her childhood friend standing with Mr Anhalt in the living room behind them. Phyllis blew her a kiss and Marla responded with one of her own; Phyllis was so exquisite she took Marla's breath away, and today she was glowing with happiness.

Did I ever feel like that? Marla wondered, turning back. She and Larry had been married for four and a half years— technically they were still newlyweds. Wasn't it too soon to feel the goodness slipping away? Maybe she expected too much from him, or too much from marriage. What the hell did she expect? *Just love*, she thought. And in that moment she felt that longing again to hold him close, to find the special feeling between them that had drawn them together, that had made her choose him out of all the rest. He had certainly not been reluctant then. He had pursued her relentlessly for two years before they got engaged. In fact she had been the reluctant one. She would have given anything right now to have him want her like that again.

Larry leaned toward her so no one else would hear him, interrupting her thoughts. 'There's something I've been meaning to tell you.'

She looked up, alerted by his tone, suddenly very concerned about what he was going to say.

He paused, finding it difficult to go on. 'I've made a decision about the Michaelson firm,' he said carefully, watching her reaction.

Her heart gave a fast, staccato beat. 'What did you decide?'

He was defiant. 'I'm turning them down.'

'But why?' Her voice rose an octave and increased in volume until she realized where they were and lowered it again. 'They made you a wonderful offer, thirty-five thousand a year and no overhead, compared to the eighteen five you've been making with the Real Estate Board.' She felt as though the narrow promontory on which she was perched had just been engulfed by the tide and waves were lapping at her ankles.

'I knew you would say that,' he said, throwing his hands up in the air. 'Don't you understand, it's not just more money I want. I want to have a future too. I just can't be stuck in some cubbyhole of an office working on sections of huge cases while the action passes me by. I'm not a corporate man. It's been torture for me to swallow the bureaucratic bullshit I've had to put up with at the Real Estate Board. But now I've got two years' experience; I've got credibility as a real-estate expert and I've made good contacts. Damn it, if I have to work nights selling cars to pay our bills, I'll do it. But I won't work for a law mill!'

She tried to keep her composure, but inside she felt panic. The baby was due in three months and they had five hundred dollars in the bank. Their rent was six hundred a month, the hospital bills would be at least thirty-five hundred—that's what it had been when Lori was born—and she hadn't bought herself any new maternity clothes. They could barely make ends meet and yet they lived in one of the richest cities in the world surrounded by constant reminders of what they didn't have. And now she'd have two babies and no steady income. Two babies' colds to worry about, two screen beds to drag down the duplex stairs to the carport and into the car, two diaper bags, and two children to carry. With thirty-five thousand a year they could afford an occasional sitter, or a cleaning woman now and then. He just didn't understand how trapped she felt sometimes, how disillusioned. Her life wasn't going the way she'd planned either. She hadn't thought motherhood would be so hard. Sometimes she felt terribly frustrated.

Taking care of infants was not why she'd studied so hard in college to learn the relationships of spatial objects, or the interplay between positive and negative space, or how to superimpose images on film to evoke existentialism, or how to assemble everyday materials into a kaleidoscope of expression so intricate that her professor termed it a tone poem of visual art. It won her second prize at the UCLA student art exhibit during her junior year. She wanted to get back to a career in design and put all that knowledge to work. She wanted to be challenged, fulfilled, not merely exhausted.

But in a two-bedroom duplex with a new baby to care for and one on the way there was no time to paint or draw or design. And her brain couldn't free itself long enough from the responsibilities of motherhood to have any creative thought. Lori's constant needs came first. *Just give it time,* she told herself. *Be patient.* It wasn't as if she didn't adore the child, derive great pleasure from her. It was just hard sometimes to be so confined. And now Larry, whom she depended on for support, both financial and emotional, was letting her down.

'What *are* you going to do?' she asked finally.

His voice was tinged with excitement. 'I'm going to open up a private law practice in partnership with Peter McKintridge. He's offered to cover three fourths of our overhead for a while until we establish ourselves and I'll reciprocate by taking only one fourth of profits until I can pay my share; then we'll split fifty-fifty. We've rented space in the bank building on Wilshire and Camden,' he added guiltily.

She stared at him in shock. 'When did all this happen? How could you have made a decision like this without discussing it with me?' Tears of betrayal stung her eyes.

'Please keep your voice down,' he begged, looking around.

'I don't care who hears!' she insisted, but she lowered her voice. 'I'm part of this marriage too. I'm your partner first, before Peter. This affects me.' She was about to unleash on

27

him, but she saw that tightening of his jaw, that narrowing of his eyes that said defiantly, 'You want to fight? Just go ahead and try it. You'll be sorry, because I fight dirty.' And she retreated.

'How are we going to live, Larry Gilbert? Just answer me that? What profits are you going to split? You haven't got any clients.'

'Peter's taking a few with him when he leaves his firm,' he said defensively, 'and we'll get more.'

'A few?' she exclaimed. 'Peter has nothing on his own. Even his own grandfather uses other lawyers. I know because Phyllis told me.' She was incensed, but with great effort she controlled herself. 'First of all, when a young lawyer goes into private practice he usually finds someone as a partner who can help him get started, or carry the financial burden for a while. Not someone who's even more of a novice than he. Peter needs you, not the other way around.'

'Shhh!' Larry said, his face coloring.

She lowered her voice again, which had risen with the intensity of her objections. 'Peter is a sweet guy and I love him, but he's a lightweight in everything except brains,' she whispered. 'He looks to you for an opinion on when to sneeze. He emulates you, he admires you, but he isn't your equal, Larry. Not nearly,' she insisted.

'That's where you're wrong,' he whispered back. 'Peter knows everybody in this town. He belongs to the "inner circle"; he knows the people with real money, he has the social connections. And look who he's marrying. Phyllis's father is no slouch. He'll throw tons of business our way. I know it.'

'How can you be so sure?' she asked.

'It's great to know you have so much confidence in me.' He glared at her, and then his face softened.

'Aw, baby,' he said. 'I'm sorry I didn't tell you about everything; I was afraid you'd say no. I couldn't fight the world and you too. This is a major step in my career. I just didn't want to hear you nagging me.'

How she hated that word. It cut her to the quick when he said she was a nag. It was his term for dissent.

'Trust me, Marla. This is something I have to do. I've got to make it on my own, you know I do.'

She just didn't know what to say to him, how much would be nagging, and how much was her right to object. It was true, how he earned his living and who he wanted as a partner was his own choice, but she should have been consulted. She was so damned scared. She pictured them being evicted for nonpayment of rent, the hospital hounding them for bills; what if there was a physical problem with the new baby, God forbid, and the bills went even higher? And yet part of her was proud of him, proud of his nerve. Larry's overabundant ambition, his desire to attain everything in life in a hurry, was what drew her to him. Still, she was the sensible one; someone had to balance his eagerness.

'Why don't you take a salaried job for just a year or two, until the baby is old enough to go to day care and I can go to work? It's not too much to ask, is it?'

'Don't nag me again, Marla,' he said, his temper flaring. 'This was a difficult decision to make. I'm not taking it lightly, but I'm sure of what I'm doing.'

'But I'm not,' she said, in quiet contrast to his anger. 'You present me with a *fait accompli* and say "take it and like it". I need some reassurance.' She reached to put her arm around him, but she had to turn slightly to the left to position her belly so she could get close to him. He stiffened and she felt repugnant again. She wanted to sink into herself and disappear. *Damn this pregnancy!*

He pulled away. 'Peter's waving to me,' he said. 'We'll talk about this later,' and he left her side to join the other ushers who were about to walk down the aisle.

Marla felt the tears coming and fought them back. *Not now*. This was a happy occasion. Here they were at the McKintridge estate, California's version of Buckingham Palace, complete with its own prince and a princess. Every famous movie star in Hollywood was here today and she was going to have a wonderful time if it killed her.

As if to say, 'It's okay, Mom, I'm still with you,' the baby gave a large wiggle and a knob came pushing out of the skin of her stretched belly and skittered across from right to left. Could it be an elbow, or maybe a knee? What a miracle to have that live person inside of her. *I'm sorry, God,* she thought, *don't damn this pregnancy.* The baby's movement gave her a sense of comfort and she patted it back and clutched her bouquet as she waited for her turn to walk down the aisle.

The irony of being where she was and feeling as she did had not escaped her. She was the only married (and pregnant) attendant in the wedding party. She was the authority, the shining example of what today's ceremony was all about. And the only thing she felt right now was uncertainty and inadequacy; marriage was very difficult.

Just then she caught a sight of her reflection again. Except for her round-eyed, tense expression, she looked better than she felt. Her cheeks glowed with cosmetic blush-on, her eyes were still their violet-blue color, the short, straight nose in the middle of her face didn't detract from the overall effect, and even her hair was thick and lustrously dark, in spite of being pregnant. *Smile, Marla,* she thought. *Show them your flashy-white teeth.* She gave herself a small smile. It was a definite improvement. If only Larry thought so. Well, if he wouldn't pay her attention tonight she'd find someone who would. Maybe Phyllis's father, Mr Anhalt, would dance with her. He always made her feel good about herself and he was gorgeous besides. And as for Larry, they would finish their discussion later. She would tell him all her objections and then he would probably do exactly as he wanted anyway. But, as he said, she would have to trust him. She had no other choice.

Chapter 3

VICKY'S HEART was pounding so hard she didn't think she could actually put one foot in front of the other to walk down the aisle. *If only I were tall instead of five feet two*, she thought, *I wouldn't be the first bridesmaid in line.* But she was first in line, and as soon as the flower girls threw all their rose petals on the red carpet and reached the podium it would be her turn.

Relax, Vicky, she told herself. But she was terrified.

A sea of people sat on either side of the long red carpet, their attention focused on the procession, their necks craning to get a better view. Vicky felt their scrutiny as a palpable entity and forced herself to look straight ahead. *Don't think about them.*

Peter and Larry and the ushers were in their places under the rose arbor, their faces masked by solemnity. She longed to do something outrageous to break their composure like lift her skirt and moon this illustrious audience. *That's why you're still single at twenty-six and Marla and Phyllis are married*, she told herself. *No respectable man will have you.*

She reached up for the umpteenth time to touch the teased and lacquered curls piled on top of her head. This hairdo didn't flatter her small face but it gave her an extra three inches of height so she loved it. She had fine straight hair that never held a curl and today's coif was attached to her head with a thousand hairpins. By the end of the evening she would have a roaring headache but that was the price of fashion. And tonight she needed to look great. Tonight Vicky Feinstein was going to rub shoulders with

31

the fancy folk. In only a few moments every one of those rich, beautiful Beverly Hills people would be looking at her and she wanted to knock their eyes out. If only this dress were more form-fitting. It did nothing for her great body and her tiny waist, or her perfect size 32B breasts, or her legs that were slender at the thigh, tapered at the ankle, and muscular from all the athletics she performed. She had a great brain too (thank God for small favors), for she wasn't beautiful. Cute was more like it. Her big brown eyes never missed a thing, she'd had her nose done when she was sixteen by Dr Leaf, one of the best, her eyebrows were plucked by Aida Grey, and she gave herself Juliette Marglen manicures, but kept her nails just short of Barbra Streisand's. Yet here she was waiting for her cue with shaking knees and a quaking heart.

There were reasons for her fright. Most of her former high school classmates and their wealthy prominent parents were here tonight and she was afraid they would give her the same vacant expression she'd always gotten when they learned she lived *south* of Wilshire Boulevard instead of *north* of Santa Monica. 'And what does your mother do?' they'd ask, expecting to hear that anyone with a name like Reena Feinstein must be a television producer or a psychologist. And Vicky would cringingly admit: 'She works at I. Magnin in designer dresses.'

The eyebrows would come down a notch, the smiles would diminish, and a look close to pity would shoot across their faces. 'Oh, *that* Reena Feinstein . . . Know her very well . . . Couldn't face a fall season without her.' And Vicky would be dismissed; the daughter of a saleswoman in a department store. Those memories made her teeth hurt like the sound of screeching chalk on a blackboard.

But meeting her old friends and antagonists wasn't the main reason for Vicky's unease. It was being at the McKintridge estate again to attend Phyllis's wedding. Her best friend, Phyllis, maid of the golden countenance, Princess Grace of North Roxbury Drive, was marrying Peter McKintridge, and Peter had been Vicky's first love, the first boy she'd ever had sex with. They'd done it on a lounge chair by the pool of this very estate one hot July night ten years ago.

Vicky had met Peter at Sorrento Beach on a Saturday three days before the fateful night. He was a member of the Jonathan Club and she was one of the peons who sat by lifeguard station seven. She had watched him for an hour as he sat alone with a single backrest and a book. He was handsome but remote, with reddish brown hair, a straight classic nose, a cleft in his chin, high cheekbones, and a slight build, not too muscular, but not too flabby either. He was definitely someone out of a romantic novel. Whenever he went into the surf, Vicky went too, flirting like mad to get him to notice her. Finally he did. They swam together for a while and walked all the way to the Santa Monica pier and back before she got him to ask her out. Up close he was even better looking than from far away. He had a slight case of freckles across his nose and forehead.

She could hardly contain her excitement. Vicky Feinstein from South Peck Drive was going out with the richest boy in Beverly Hills.

And he was so sweet; she really liked him. Kind of shy and not given to small talk, but she had enough small talk for both of them. He was smart enough to be interested in Heidegger and Kant, and told her things even she didn't know. Besides, Stanford didn't accept dummies. After Stanford he would go to Harvard Law School. His grandfather expected it. The way he said that made it sound like an edict.

That was the first Saturday Vicky had taken off from work all summer. The other kids from Beverly went to the beach every day, unless they were in Europe or Hawaii with their parents. But not Vicky. She had to work every summer and weekends during the school year to pay for her clothes and pocket money. And if she didn't get a scholarship to college she wouldn't go, because her mother couldn't afford to send her. But she'd get her scholarship. She was real smart too.

It had been worth it to work two extra days for one Saturday off. She'd gotten a suntan and a date with Peter McKintridge.

What had possessed her to go through with it that night? she wondered. Had it been Peter's money, or his social status? Or had she really fallen in love? She thought she had. She'd come home from the beach in a romantic haze and written Peter's name over and over on a piece of her best stationery, linking it with her own. Vicky McKintridge, Mrs Peter McKintridge. What a substantial sound it had. And her mother's reaction was typical. 'A date with *the* Peter McKintridge? You don't mean it? Oh, Vicky—Belson McKintridge's grandson? Do you know what they're worth? Millions. *Millions!* I don't believe it. My daughter going out with Peter McKintridge. Do you like him? Of course you do. He's a lovely person. And you know what I always say . . . ' Vicky mouthed the words with her: 'It's as easy to marry a rich boy as a poor one.'

Of course all those elements worked on her psyche as she talked herself into being in love with Peter. If she'd stopped to think about it she'd have realized he wasn't the kind of boy who usually attracted her. She liked the smart alecks who made wisecracks and had cocky attitudes. She could always give them their money's worth.

It was a beautiful night. Enough stars to pepper the sky with glamour. They went to dinner at the Brown Derby and though Vicky lived a few blocks away from Rodeo and Wilshire, she'd never been inside the restaurant. They ate tournedos of beef and Caesar salad, and afterward they sat in the projection room in Peter's own house and saw an Elvis Presley movie that hadn't been released yet. Vicky was in heaven. The seats in the enormous screening room were large and plush, dwarfing the two of them. And after the movie a servant brought them champagne and chocolate fondue out on the terrace. Vicky had never had more than one glass of champagne at a time, and had never seen fondue before.

34

Both of them went to her head.

She felt dreamy and in love, and very tender towards Peter, who described to her how he lost both his parents in a plane crash when he was ten and had lived with his grandfather during vacations when he wasn't in boarding school. But even with all his possessions he seemed lonely to her.

They took a walk down by the pool, and when Peter took her by the shoulders and turned her around to kiss him, she felt there could be no more perfect setting for love than this starlit night, even if she waited the rest of her life. And there could be no more perfect person than this remote, rich young man with the tragic past.

That was why she found herself underneath Peter's thrusting body, with her white cotton dress from Jax up around her waist, and her feet in their white sandals from Chandlers dangling from the imprint of the tufted buttons of the lounge pad, while Peter deftly but without finesse pushed his penis into her virginal vagina.

As soon as she had proven nonresistant, it had happened very quickly, even before she could figure out what the hell she was doing here. She wasn't enjoying it in the least; it was awkward and strange and embarrassing. She was about to push him away when suddenly the lights above them in the trees and around them in the bushes and below them in the pool came blazing on, blinding her with a painful shock. It felt like a bucket of ice water had been thrown in her face. She gasped and looked up to see the face of Peter's world-famous grandfather burning into her retinas. Belson's arms were folded across his chest and his face was a nasty shade of red as he yelled the question she'd been asking herself over and over for the last ten minutes: 'What are you two idiots doing?'

Her first impulse was to make some smart remark, but she was really too mortified. Even wiseass Vicky hadn't been able to say, 'What does it look like, Grandpa? We're balling, that's what.' Instead she threw Peter off of her, pulled on her panties, and fought with all her might not to burst into tears. Her heart was pounding in her chest so violently she felt like a fox cornered by a pack of baying, snarling hounds. What a way to lose your virginity. It was enough to make a person give up sex for life.

How austere Belson McKintridge had looked, glowering at her. She'd hardly known her own father; he had left when she was just a child, and at that moment she was glad. If this was what fathers were like, if this was how they made you feel, who needed them.

'I'll take you home, Vicky,' Peter had stammered, his eyes glued to the flagstone decking.

'Not so fast,' Belson had insisted. 'I want to know something about a person who would behave this way, who would take my generous hospitality and turn it into filth! What is your name, young lady?'

'Vicky Feinstein,' she whispered.

'*Fein*-stein,' he'd said, dripping sarcasm on the first syllable, the Presbyterian puritan and the soiled Jewess. She'd wanted to crawl into a hole and disappear. She'd wanted to cry.

No. She'd wanted to die.

'Does your father know what you're doing? Does your mother know what kind of a girl you are?'

Vicky could see in some part of her brain that Belson McKintridge, the ex-movie star, was milking this scene for all it was worth. But she was too frightened and too ashamed to do anything about it. She remembered a line from an old Fred Astaire – Jane Powell song: 'We never had a mudder, we was too poor.' But she didn't use it. She just hung her head and hated him, hated the shame he made her feel. He was one righteous prude. Hadn't he ever done anything in his life to be ashamed of?

Her mother would kill her, absolutely kill her. Her reputation was ruined. That was something else her mother had always told her, besides the part about marrying a rich boy: 'If ever you allow a boy to take advantage of you, Vicky, you can expect him to tell everyone he knows every sordid detail. That's the only reason he's messing with you at all, so he can have something to brag about. And don't ever fall for that old line about blue balls; or I need you so much, Vicky; or I'll only put it in a little bit.'

She should have listened. Why hadn't she listened? Now she'd never marry a rich boy. She'd spend the rest of her life on South Peck Drive and never be good enough to be mistress of any house north of Santa Monica Boulevard.

Terrible, sorrowful sobs came bursting out of her six-teen-year-old soul to wrack her body, while a helpless Peter muttered, 'Don't cry, Vicky.'

But Belson interrupted with another scathing remark. 'She ought to cry for the cheap way she's behaved. And so should you, Peter. Is this the thanks I get for devoting myself to you? For taking you in, for allowing you to turn my home upside down with your cheap friends? I'm only glad your mother isn't alive to see this.'

Vicky heard Peter gasp; she guessed he was as ashamed in front of his formidable grandfather as she was. Belson McKintridge sounded like an ultraconservative member of the Supreme Court, or the last word in moral rectitude.

Why don't I die, she wondered, *right here, right now?* And to make matters worse, she could feel herself bleeding. A small, warm trickle of hymenal blood came through her white nylon panties and dripped inside the expensive dress she'd saved for weeks to buy. She could feel it running down her newly sunburned legs to her white patent-leather sandals. Life was too cruel to bear.

'I'll take you home, Vicky,' Peter offered again.

'No, thank you,' she said, turning to walk away with dignity. She was certain he wouldn't let her go by herself. After all it was one o'clock in the morning and very dark out. But when Peter didn't come after her, she stopped and turned to look back. He was sitting on the lounge chair with his head in his hands and Belson was standing above him, still glaring at her.

'Well, what is it?' Belson asked, his tone implying, *You made your bed, now lie in it.*

'Nothing,' she replied meekly, and somehow found her

37

way around the estate to the front of the house.

It was a long way home from the top of the highest hill in Beverly Hills all the way down Foothill to Lomita, and across Lomita to Camden, and down Camden through the tall buildings of the business district to Wilshire, and then over to Peck Drive. She was very frightened and tried to contain her fear when passing cars slowed down to see if she was available. She walked by Saks on the way, not noticing the new fall clothes in the windows that she couldn't afford. And finally she arrived at her apartment.

Her feet were raw and bleeding, but at least the blood from her broken hymen wasn't so obvious. And her mother wouldn't believe that a boy as nice as Peter McKintridge, from such a fine family, could have refused to drive her home after she refused to sleep with him. Vicky must have done something, Reena insisted over and over, questioning her for details. Reena could not allow herself to believe that story.

Vicky knew otherwise. Peter was weak. He should have defended her in front of his grandfather. But for some reason he couldn't. Did it have something to do with her? Was she really not worthy of any respect? Whatever the reason, she would never excuse him or his grandfather. She arrived home at her mother's apartment detesting Belson McKintridge with her entire being and vowing that some-day, no matter how long it took, she would get even with him.

But that wasn't the end of it. Peter came to see her the next day and apologized while she cried. Then he put his arms around her and told her he really liked her and wanted to see her again. That in spite of what happened he did respect her. That was all she needed to hear and she forgave him. She told herself that he hadn't behaved out of weakness, that he was just being respectful of his grandfather. And though she knew she would never forgive Belson, she agreed to see Peter whenever he wanted. She should have known he had only come to her out of guilt, that his gentleman's code of ethics determined his behavior. But she didn't know him well enough then to know that he was not only assuaging his guilt but that he was as starved for affection as she was.

Their romance, such as it was, lasted through Peter's sophomore year whenever he was home for school vacations. They groped one another in parked cars and occasionally in the pool house on the estate, but that was risky because they were keeping their relationship a secret from Peter's grandfather. Vicky didn't mind keeping it a secret: she didn't relish another run-in with Belson, and she imagined their love to be like Romeo and Juliet.

In April she missed her period.

Peter failed all his midterms worrying about her. And she was stuck. Here she was, a senior in high school with her whole life ahead of her and a mother who demanded a shotgun wedding. Reena wasn't about to let Peter off the hook. Never mind that Vicky knew Peter wasn't the man for her, never mind that he was a gentile with an anti-Semitic grandfather. He was rich, wasn't he? Never mind that Vicky was terror-struck at the idea of being a teen-age mother and wanted to go to college more than anything in the world. Reena insisted! The two young people should elope.

And then Belson found out.

That was the worst night of Vicky's life.

Belson McKintridge came raging into their apartment, his face so red the veins in his neck were straining to pop. He threw five hundred dollars in cash down on the Formica table and glared at them, a maddened animal ready to charge. Vicky had never see that much money all at once and she'd never seen anyone in a rage before. 'If you don't get rid of that bastard in her womb'—he pointed at Vicky—'I will use every ounce of influence against you, woman,' he said to Reena. Vicky felt a sickening familiarity at the scene. 'I'll have you fired from your miserable job. I'll have you run out of this state. I'll make you sorry you ever heard the name McKintridge.'

Reena was trembling. All her plans were being destroyed. Her lifelong dreams for her daughter were being cruelly snatched away. 'We can sue you too,' Reena said, her voice barely audible. She knew the law concerning sex with a minor and the requirements of paternity support. Vicky was amazed at her mother's gumption, but she was horrified at the idea of a lawsuit that would examine the details of her sex life. Nor did she want to spend her youth vindictively pursuing Peter through the courts or being part of a scandal that would never fade from the memory of this insular town.

Vicky picked up Belson's money and agreed to an abortion. In 1964 that was a frightening choice.

'And you will never see my grandson again,' Belson demanded. 'Is that clear?'

It was, and she never did, not romantically anyway. But she did write Peter a note two weeks later to let him know she'd miraculously gotten her period. Like many teenagers she was notoriously irregular. Peter wrote her back and told her to keep the money.

Then years later when Peter started going with Phyllis, she and Peter made their peace; after all they now had their affection for Phyllis in common, and they found they could be friends.

The minister gave Vicky her cue and she stepped shakily forward. Her absurd fear was that Belson would stand up and denounce her in front of all these people as the girl who in her youth seduced his grandson in their cabana. What could she say in her defense? That she'd learned her lesson and would never venture out of her class again? That now she was a respectable woman, a teacher at the prestigious Southwick School for girls, that she graduated UCLA summa cum laude? Big fucking deal. She still detested Belson McKintridge and supposed that he still detested her. To him she would always be Vicky *Fein*-stein with the sarcasm on the first syllable, and not good enough for North Beverly Hills.

Chapter 4

BELSON MCKINTRIDGE sat ramrod straight in the first row of guests; behind him sat aisle upon aisle of relatives and friends. There were 450 people here today to see his grandson wed, some of whom he didn't know, others whom he knew but detested, and all of whom knew him. They would have seen his famous face in any of the thirty-odd films he had starred in when he was younger. But even if they hadn't seen his films, his six-foot-three-inch frame was unmistakable, with its broad athletic shoulders and the full head of white hair, which at the moment was probably blocking some smaller aunt or uncle's view of the ceremony. But Belson didn't give a damn whose view he blocked; part of being the host at these overpriced affairs was having the best seat in the house.

He tried to concentrate on the ceremony taking place before him, but he was too aware of Felix Anhalt seated across the aisle. The sight of the man made Belson's Scottish temper flare. How ironic that life had thrown them together again after all this time, and how strange that a lovely creature like Phyllis could be the daughter of someone as socially incompetent, as vulgar, as crude, and as beneath contempt as her father. If it weren't for Felix, Belson would have been totally delighted with his grandson's choice of a bride. Her father was her only unfortunate flaw.

Belson noted the look of adoration in Phyllis's eyes as she stared at Peter while the minister spoke about commitment and sharing life's goals. How amazing it was that

41

someone as uninteresting as Peter could have attracted such a prize as Phyllis. Peter couldn't possibly appreciate this girl; he was primarily a milquetoast, as his father, James Randall, had been. And even though Peter took the McKintridge name for himself as a gesture to please his grandfather after his parents were killed, he had never lived up to it, and never would. Belson supposed Peter's young bride wouldn't notice how boring Peter was, and how easily controlled. Not at first anyway. But the truth of it was, Belson thought, that Peter had a sickness at his core that manifested itself in weakness of character and lack of backbone. The boy exasperated him, annoyed him, and above all disappointed him, and the disappointment was the bitterest of all because he was Belson's only heir. He'd inherited none of Belson's panache or charisma, and Belson only prayed marriage would make a man out of him. He sincerely doubted it. Peter had always been merely average, never distinguishing himself in any way. The only extraordinary thing he'd ever done was to marry Phyllis.

Belson went over the details of the reception in his mind; he had paid a great deal of money so everything would be first class. Following the ceremony, the guests would be served hors d'oeuvres in the Grecian garden adjacent to the reflecting pools, their fountains alive with bubbling, spraying water. And then at sunset dinner would be served in formal tents that had been erected on the McKintridge nine-hole mini-golf course. After the lavish party Peter and Phyllis would take themselves off on their Hawaiian honeymoon and Belson would get back to business, which at the moment wasn't going so well.

The ceremony caught his attention again and he thought what it would be like to be young and in love again and not encumbered by the prejudices and inhibitions that had bound him in his youth. He thought about how Phyllis would be on her wedding night. He could just see her—nervous, slightly trembling, or delighted and lost in wonder, her lovely head flung back in the kind of elegant sexual transport that only a young woman of her quality could display. Her lips would be parted and moist, her long lashes closed and fluttering over those incredible blue-gray eyes, and the tips of her young pink breasts would be reaching out for . . . love. God, he wished he were to be the one to crush them between his aging lips. How that would restore his youthful vigor. Even now he could feel himself getting excited. Not bad for a man of seventy-five. But Peter would probably fuck up this first night of sex for Phyllis the way he fucked up everything else in his life. But then no one, least of all Peter, could initiate Phyllis into the wonders of sex as well as Belson could have. When Peter confided in him that his bride was a virgin, Belson ached to be the one she had chosen and not his fop of a grandson. But one couldn't thwart the passing of time, and after all he had had plenty of women in his day, and plenty of virgins too. He liked them best when they were really pure, the younger the better.

He glanced sideways at Phyllis's mother, Audrey, a pale, older version of her daughter with only a hint of the striking beauty Phyllis had become. He hated to admit it but Phyllis had inherited most of her good looks from her father.

Belson always enjoyed watching the girl when she was unaware of his scrutiny. Her long blond hair swayed when she moved and there was a studied elegance in the way she held her head. Her high cheekbones always seemed to glow with a natural color and her nostrils were delicate, adding a fine dimension to her sculpted nose. It fascinated him to see them flare now and then when she smiled. But her eyes were the best part of her. Sometimes they were dark gray, and other times light and clear as white wine when they reflected amusement or serenity. But always they shone with delight when she saw something that caught her fancy.

And her body couldn't be faulted either. Her shoulders were slender, tapering into a perfectly formed back and waist that appeared both vulnerable and enticing. Her breasts were high and round, her legs were long and well shaped. She was the stuff of poetry, the subject of sonnets, the vision of his wet dreams.

'Do you, Phyllis, take this man, Peter . . .' the minister intoned while variegated color shone down on them from the sunlight filtering through the flowers over their heads.

Even Belson was moved as they said their vows.

And then it was over, the bride and groom walked down the aisle full of smiles and good spirits, followed by the wedding party, and Belson fell into step behind the others. One of the bridesmaids, a short young woman with curls pasted and piled on top of her head, stared at him as though he was supposed to know her, and then a slight blush rose to her cheeks and she turned away. But that was not unusual, people always stared at him; yet there was something familiar about her he couldn't recall, something negatively familiar. Well, no matter, he'd remember sooner or later.

Belson was what was known in Beverly Hills as a legend. 'And there aren't many of us left,' he always said. Now with Gary Cooper, Errol Flynn, and Clark Gable gone, the pickings of living legends were slim indeed. Being a legend took too much of his time, really—time he would have preferred to spend in more pleasurable ways. But it had its compensations. He probably shouldn't have bothered to do commercials for Merchants Bank of Southern California, but they'd made him a nice offer; and it felt good to be in front of a camera again, to be dressed in a tux, with a beautiful young woman gazing at him. The slogan said: 'Save at Merchants for the Good Things in Life.' And then the camera pulled back to a medium shot of the McKintridge estate, with the stables and the golf course, and the English, Grecian, and formal French gardens, not to mention the house itself.

Belson's father, Angus, had actually built the home for Belson and his bride, Sherryn, more to compete with his friend and business associate, Ed Doheny, than to bestow a family heirloom on his son. But from the very first, Belson had been fired by plans for the mansion, inspired by its design and magnificence. He'd involved himself in its concept wholeheartedly, and with every important stone and shingle the house took on more of his personality.

They began construction in 1922 and it took four more years to complete at a cost of more than six million dollars. The imposing edifice dominated an entire hilltop overlooking Los Angeles, Beverly Hills, Santa Monica, and the Pacific Ocean beyond; they patterned it after the castle at Fontainebleau in France. It had the same circular stone staircase sweeping up to a house whose walls were four feet thick. There were turreted rooftops covered with imported slate from Wales. There were balustrades and balconies. marble and carved interior paneling, enormous fireplaces brought from disassembled castles in Europe, furnishings from the finest antique dealers in the world; and with each magnificent addition Belson felt prouder and prouder.

The mansion boasted of sixty thousand square feet and seventy rooms. The dining room was a replica of the one at Versailles; the ballroom was large enough for 150 guests and paneled in wood designs taken from Hampstead House in England, carved by Grinling Gibbons. There was a sports center complete with bowling alley, indoor and outdoor pools, and tennis courts. The chapel on the grounds was a replica of the country church in Dumferline, Scotland, where Belson's father was born, made of stone imported from the area. The children's wing had its own kitchen and laundry and the fifty-odd staff were housed in separate servants' quarters nearly as opulent as the main house.

The home was an immense source of pride for Angus. But for Belson it was his life. It truly represented to the world his self-image, and when life offered disappointments and failings, the house never let him down.

Over the years Belson sold off parcels of his land, which had been developed into the area of Beverly Hills later known as McKintridge Summit, but he left intact the choicest fifteen acres that surrounded the main dwellings. These fifteen acres contained gardens of every type, and the gardens were Belson's pride and joy. The entry drive wound through a dense forest and traveled over streams replete with cascading waterfalls that emptied into a private lake. Beside the lake was a summer cottage covered with treillage whose windows were leaded and beveled in a fantasy of glass. This pavilion was suitable for twelve dinner guests. A few years ago an estimate of the property's worth would have been a conservative eighteen million, but in today's inflated market Belson figured the house and grounds were worth nearly twice that.

Belson couldn't bear to think about what might happen to McKintridge after he was gone. With today's inheritance-tax structure it was nearly impossible for a family to hang on to their inheritance, and so he had earnestly been trying not only to preserve the family fortune, but to make it grow, so there would be enough left over after taxes to withstand any economic pressure his heirs might encounter. In the process and with his zeal for preservation he had made a few rash investments, and lately he'd been inordinately unlucky. But the economy was going to get better, he was sure of it. If only there were someone in the family with whom he could share this burden, but some awful twist of fate had dwindled his heirs down to only Peter. Of Belson's four sisters only one remained alive today and she was childless. His own two daughters were dead, one from illness, the other, Peter's mother, in the plane crash that also killed Peter's father and sister. Belson prayed that Phyllis Anhalt McKintridge would prove to be fruitful and that his current portfolio of investments would result in the substantial return he expected of them. But of course they would. It was inconceivable that McKintridge would ever belong to anyone but its rightful heir.

Belson moved about the guests, overhearing snatches of cocktail party chitchat, engaging in brief conversations, accepting accolades about the estate and how well he looked and feeling rather chipper. Until he spotted Hugh Perkins heading his way. Hugh was his chief financial adviser and a permanent scowl always graced that bushy-eyebrowed face, especially lately.

'Lovely wedding,' Hugh said as they shook hands. 'But you should have let the bride's family give it.'

'You know how I feel about the Anhalts,' Belson snapped.

'Even so. This kind of extravagance has got to stop. You cannot do it anymore. Have you received notice of your board of directors meeting? I have called it for Tuesday, my office at ten o'clock,' Perkins said. 'And I don't care what you say about your damnable need for secrecy or the inadvisability of having all your people in one room at the same time. I want you there. The express purpose of this meeting is to deal with the deterioration of your financial empire. It's the only way I know how to handle it.'

'You're such an alarmist, Hugh,' Belson said, feeling his tension increasing by the minute. 'And your lack of tact is monumental. This is my grandson's wedding day, not a time to talk of financial doom.'

'You ignore my calls, Belson. You ignore my advice. You attack my integrity. If I hadn't known you for so many years, I'd have stopped dealing with you long ago. I wouldn't take this from any other client.'

'That's because nobody else provides you with the same retainer as I do,' Belson retorted.

Perkins drew himself up to his full height, which was still six inches shorter than Belson. 'You have dissipated your wealth to such an extent that it is no longer true that you are my highest-paying client. Yet you insist on living in some dreamworld, Belson, in which you believe there are no consequences for financial irresponsibility. Well, I assure you that there are. Your funds are not as bottomless as you seem to think. On Tuesday you are going to be shocked to see exactly how much bottom you have reached.'

'Goddamn it, Hugh,' Belson nearly shouted. 'I know what my problems are. If mental midgets like you insist on forecasting disaster, I'll step on you—or have you and your other little midgets been dipping into my money on your own? Is that what I'm going to discover?'

Hugh Perkins's face was flushed and mottled, crimson-

47

bright under the thick white eyebrows and the white mustache. 'I've always known you were a bastard, McKintridge. But you're also an asshole,' he said, and turned and walked away.

Belson tried to smile at several guests regarding him curiously, but it wasn't easy. At least Perkins hadn't taken his guff. They'd sparred like this for years, and still Perkins came back for more. *He doesn't want to lose my business*, Belson thought, rationalizing Perkins's warnings. Regardless of unwise investments and near disasters, he had been careful not to invade the main capital sources. Perkins and his firm often thought like old ladies twittering behind lace fans, while his tastes in business—and women, too—ran to the less conservative, the unexplored. He chuckled to himself at that assessment and continued to circulate through the crowd.

That same bridesmaid again, the short one with the silly curls on her head, turned away when she saw him—as though she didn't want him to recognize her; and then it hit him who she was. Vicky Feinstein, that low-life little tramp Peter had dallied with in college. What was she doing here? And in the wedding party. She couldn't be a close friend of Phyllis's—probably an obligation, a token Jew. If he had noticed her name on the list, he'd have sharply disapproved to Phyllis about her.

She was ducking her head, trying to ignore him. Well, he didn't want to talk to her either. But he'd damned well keep an eye on her.

The thirty-one-string orchestra was playing one of his favorite waltzes and for a moment he wished Sherryn were alive to see this day and dance a waltz with him. But most of all he wished his father were here. How Angus would have loved Phyllis.

Angus McKintridge was born the third son of a gentleman farmer near the small village of Dumferline, Scotland, where his Scottish ancestors had lived for generations. When Angus was only eighteen and newly married to the

48

minister's daughter, Mary, he announced to his family that he and his bride were going to make their home in America.

The year Benjamin Harrison was elected President was the year the young McKintridges settled in Los Angeles and the newly developing oil industry caught Angus's eye.

While Mary started a family, Angus, along with an Irishman, Edward L. Doheny, and an Englishman, Charlie Canfield, began drilling the first oil well in the city. Miraculously, they discovered oil at that site three months later.

The year Angus's second daughter was born, the team of Doheny, Canfield, and McKintridge started an oil boom in the city. And by the time the fourth McKintridge daughter was born (Angus was despairing of ever having a son to carry on his new prosperity), Los Angeles was producing 1.3 million barrels of oil a year and California was the third largest oil-producing state in the United States.

In their continuing speculation for oil Burton E. Green, Charles A. Canfield, Max Whittier, E.G. Kerckhoff, and Angus McKintridge—through the Amalgamated Oil Company—purchased the Hammel and Denker holdings: a large, beautiful ranch, situated between the city of Los Angeles and the ocean resort of Santa Monica. But water, not oil, proved to be the substance they found. And they formed the Rodeo Land & Water Company. Under the leadership of Burton Green, the new corporation dedicated itself to founding a magnificent residential community. The year Mary finally presented Angus with a son, whom they named Belson, was the year Beverly Hills was created.

A family dominated by women doted on young Belson McKintridge. His sisters and his mother believed him to be the most beautiful child they'd ever seen. And he was beautiful. He inherited his mother's azure blue eyes and carbon black hair, and his father's square jaw and cleft chin. He'd also inherited his Scottish ancestor's stubborn determination: in Belson the combination was exotic.

His family and the servants fed him stories about the land of his ancestors, and while they instilled in him a belief in the Calvinist doctrine, he also acquired their prejudices. His nanny, Nurse McGregor, would finish every childhood tale with the line: 'And so the enemy was vanquished, the *disgusting* German, the *arrogant* Pole, the *stupid* Russian, the *foolish* Swede, or the American equivalent, the *filthy* Negro.' As a result Belson nurtured a virulent hatred of people different from himself. But in spite of his spoiled social attitudes, a propensity for cruelty, and a belief in his own superiority, he proved to be an adept student.

In 1918 when Belson was the same age as the new century, he traveled east to Harvard University, where he excelled in business and dramatics. And though he had many attractive offers to remain in the East, he was a Californian at heart and longed to return home. Part of his desire to return to California was a longing to recapture the pure, provincial morality he'd left behind when he moved east. For once away from the watchful, straitlaced eye of his father, and the oppressive narrow-mindedness of his mother and sisters, Belson became an eager pupil in the adult world of debauchery. There was nothing he would not try, nothing that was beneath him, and in the brothels of Boston and New York he found plenty of opportunity to broaden the education he had gained at Harvard. His newly acquired tastes would have shocked and scandalized his mother and caused his father to disown him and he was not proud of them, but once his lust were awakened, they could not be quelled. He became the most daring of his friends, taking the lead and actually planning most of their unusual sexual forays. His reputation as a 'wild man' grew with each debacle. At first he tried to moderate his behavior, but after a while he abandoned moderation and allowed his after-hours activities to consume him. His only saving grace during the four years of his corruption when he'd awaken in his rooms with a head the size of a balloon from drinking too much, and the shameful memories of the night before haunting him, was a promise he made to himself that when he returned home his newly acquired tastes would remain in the East; he vowed to himself he would bury all his nefarious activities along with his memories of college.

But not long after he returned home, he found that promise to be one he could not keep.

Fired with ideas for increasing his father's fortune and a yen to try his own hand at the business of movies, Belson returned to California right after graduation. But something distracted him from his immediate goal. A second cousin on his father's side of the family was visiting from Scotland and she caught his eye. She was a breath of innocence after his four years of descent into hell and he fancied himself in love. But it wasn't actually love Belson felt for the beautiful redheaded Sherryn McConnell, it was more like approval. And approval was a more engrossing emotion for Belson than love, though he would have fought furiously had anyone questioned the basis of his passion. Belson felt love when he looked at the wide California sky, or heard his mother's lilting Scottish brogue, or nuzzled the new colt his filly dropped in the late spring, or caught a glimpse of the brilliant bougainvillaea cascading over the tile roofs of the haciendas. And that was far different from the overwhelming sensation Sherryn aroused in his breast and to which he responded as a man in a daze. For he'd never felt approval for anyone before, least of all himself, and now he did.

Sherryn had thick auburn hair that curled softly about her face and pale delicate skin slightly dusted with freckles; her dark green eyes gave off sparks of warmth, and the carriage of her body was erect. She spoke with assurance, demanding deference yet not obsequiousness, and he enjoyed being with her. She was like his mother in many ways, but able to quicken his blood and race his pulse when she kissed him gently on the cheek, a cousinly kiss promising much more. Ah, but she was so pure, and so chaste compared with the women he'd known. Her moral and religious beliefs were at the center of her being; her philosophy of life was based on honesty and straight-forwardness, and she was completely devoted to him. After only a few weeks he proposed, certain that an alliance with her was the best thing he could do. Marriage to Sherryn would negate all the reprehensible behavior of his past. Her laughter would be the breath of Scottish air to cool his uncontrollable fires, and she would be the peaceful waters in which he could baptize his tainted soul.

Their wedding was held at the ballroom of the newly built Beverly Hills Hotel, since Angus was trying to promote his new residential development. It was the social event of the decade. The couple honeymooned in San Francisco and that was where Belson discovered that Sherryn was the wrong person in whom to trust his wavering soul.

At first he thought her forward advances to him were because of her innocence and naiveté. She was a country girl from a foreign land; she did not know the proprieties of wifely behavior. And when she smiled and welcomed him, never hiding in embarrassment from his nudity or his thrusting pelvis, he dismissed it as unusual, for she had bled as a virgin. He did not know what to make of her somewhat wanton behavior and then he began to panic, for she was awakening something in him that caused all his buried desires to resurface.

And then on the evening of their sixth day of marriage she had a special supper prepared for them in their room. She came to dinner in a negligee, the handmade lace fabric of the bodice barely covering her considerable endowments. She poured them champagne; she fed him morsels of food as she gazed into his eyes. And then before he realized what she was doing, she knelt at his feet, slowly parted his dressing gown, and kissed him *there*, just like some eastern whore, brushing her soft lips against the tender skin. He was so shocked he struck out at her, hitting her again and again, calling her every vile name he could remember, until she cried out in pain and fear.

52

And that ended the honeymoon.

They stayed on in San Francisco to attend the social events held in their honor and Belson later regretted his harsh behavior and even apologized for it. But Sherryn had changed. She never tried anything like that again. But it was too late for Belson. His belief in her had died. He never got over his profound disappointment in her, or stopped grieving for the loss of his fantasy that she was the woman who would save him. And from then on he blamed her for his return to the darker pleasures, telling himself it was her fault, damning her for wanting to be more than a wife. And he never looked for anyone to be his soulmate again.

Shortly after they returned from their honeymoon, Belson made his first film, for Jack White. His black hair and light eyes photographed extremely well, giving him a flashy satyrlike appearance, different from the more classical features of Barrymore or the sultriness of Valentino. And there was something else about Belson, a sinister aspect to him that came across on the screen and was apparent to his female audience in his first movie. Women responded to him in spite of themselves.

Sherryn recognized it the first time she saw him play a love scene. Her comment made him fear she knew more about him than he wanted her to know. 'You look as though there is something threatening about you, Belson. When you make love to a woman, hold her and kiss her and whisper tender words, you seem to be holding something in check, your true nature, the animal side of you. You look as though you'd much rather be plunging a knife into her breast than caressing it, or ravaging her with more fury than she could physically stand, rather than being tender. There—She pointed to the screen, which held a close-up of Belson's pale blue eyes. 'That's the expression that makes me go all cold inside, that makes me afraid for my immortal soul, and yours. Yet it's so exciting even though I'm your wife, your screen image tempts me to toy with danger beyond all reason. And then in the next instant you throw back your head and laugh, and it's gone.'

Belson knew she was right. The part of him he wanted to keep hidden was up there on the screen and though it terrified him to see it, he was relieved to let it out. There was nothing to hide anymore, to keep buried. The dark desires he'd allow to well up in him that were the core of his being, now had a safe place to be expressed. He would let his screen characters be his true self, and his other self would keep up a facade of pretense. All in all, he thought it would work rather well.

And so it had . . . for a while. And then he decided that he deserved to be fulfilled in his private life as well, as long as Sherryn didn't find out. And as far as he knew, she never had.

Chapter 5

FELIX TOOK a glass of champagne from the waiter and sauntered over to the edge of the Grecian garden where a low box hedge, trimmed to perfection, was the only obstruction between him and the magnificent view spread out before him. The city was steel gray and golden in the waning light; a myriad of streets stretched out at all angles; the sun flamed over the ocean beyond the shore. This was exactly the right moment for a private toast.

He filled his lungs with the cool evening air and let it out slowly, then raised his glass and swept it from right to left, encompassing the view. 'I've done it,' he whispered to the gods before he drank. 'Just as I vowed.'

It was an excellent wine. Leave it to Belson to serve Schramsberg at eleven or twelve dollars a bottle to 450 people, and pay top dollar for a California brand rather than a French one. Belson was a loyal Californian, the one thing about him Felix admired.

A smile played around the corner of Felix's lips, indicating his elation. This was a wonderfully triumphant moment, and a glowing warmth suffused his entire body, a warmth greater than any glass of Schramsberg champagne could provide or even the last rays of the setting sun could offer. His very bones cried out with a joyous shout. *At last!*

With today's ceremony he had finally proven that the name of Anhalt was worthy of being entwined with the illustrious name of McKintridge. *He* may not have been acceptable to Belson, but his daughter was. And how he had fought to make it happen. What infinite patience he had maintained. The achievement was something only he could appreciate. There was no one in the world who would understand what this union meant to him. No one he could tell that he'd waited twenty-nine years for this day.

It had all begun right here in this garden. The day he had asked Belson's permission to marry his daughter, Margie, and had been cruelly refused. The memory was still so bitter that even the delicious dry taste of champagne couldn't sweeten it.

Margie had begged him to elope with her, but he'd said no. How many years had he regretted that decision? At the time he had wanted to be honorable. He had wanted to prove Margie's fears unfounded and insisted on approaching her father as an equal. What a fool he'd been at twenty-six, so cocksure of himself. He thought he'd experienced all of life's hardships because he'd had to give up his college scholarship to care for his widowed mother and brothers and sisters; because he'd been wounded in the war, and even begun a new housing development, suffering all the business difficulties that it entailed. But mostly he thought he knew about life because he was in love. So in love with Margie that the sight of her, the touch of her, made his heart throb with joy. But none of his previous hardships or any of his life's experiences prepared him for the devastation of his confrontation with Belson. And he had spent more than a quarter of a century since then trying to prove how wrong Belson had been about him: that the Anhalts were good enough for the McKintridges.

Ironically, Phyllis turned out to be the instrument of his revenge. It was she who provided him with the means to crack the McKintridge citadel. How beautiful she was, and how greatly she pleased him by falling in love with Peter. But she'd always pleased him, never given him cause for discontent (so unlike Audrey—her mother). Phyllis would most likely have married Peter even if she didn't love him had Felix insisted on it, but that hadn't been necessary. Phyllis took it all out of his hands the moment he'd introduced the two of them, and she'd set her cap for Peter with a single-mindedness worthy of the Anhalt name.

Of course Felix's years of planning for just such an eventuality helped: his careful comments to her about the McKintridge family; hiding his true animosity toward Belson; the careful grooming of Phyllis to be acceptable in a world where he hadn't been; and the close friendship he'd nurtured with Peter for years, serving as a surrogate father for the boy, encouraging his life choices, delicately maneuvering events as much as he could until they brought him to this day, no matter how strenuously Belson objected.

And finally he had come to the satisfaction of knowing that Anhalt blood would flow in the veins of the McKintridge heirs.

What would his father have thought about all of this? he wondered. How could Heinrich Einhaltz, the immigrant boy from a rural village in Germany, who worked his way across the Atlantic on a freighter in 1918, ever imagine that his great-grandchild would someday be heir to all this?

California was a sweet-smelling paradise in the early part of the century; the air was fragrant with the blossoms of the citrus trees, and the acrid scent of oil cut through the perfume, enticing the senses even more than the flowering blossoms. The automobile *ah-ooga*'d its way along dusty, empty roads, scattering children and chicks alike, and young Heinrich longed to own a piece of this black, rich earth, especially a ranch that grew those shiny green-leafed trees with their bright, round fruit.

But from the earliest moment of his recollection Felix hated oranges. He hated the bees that flourished among the orchards and stung him whenever his child's hands happened upon them, he hated the thick, sweet smell of the orange blossoms that hung on the air from early spring to late fall, and he hated the stain of the orange oil that permeated everything—his clothing and the house they occupied and even his dreams at night—not to mention the foul-smelling smudge pots whose odor made him want to gag.

And he hated being smothered by the relatives who lived on his grandfather's property. His mother, father, two sisters, and a baby brother all lived in a small house close by the main house where they took their evening meals. But all the aunts and uncles lived in the main house and there was always someone to tell Felix what to do, or to report his every infraction to his grandfather, J.L., or to his father. And both men found every excuse they could to wallop him. But they could never break his spirit.

He was a defiant and surly child, attracted to mischief and absolutely gorgeous. His white blond hair and clear, innocent blue eyes made him unfairly appealing and he used his looks to get exactly what he wanted. His mischievousness and his strong will he inherited from his father; his good looks he got from his mother; but his charm and innate sense of calculation were all his own.

His mother was a victim of a male-dominated family, a pretty girl who grew less pretty as a woman and took to wheedling and manipulating to get what she wanted. And Dora wanted Felix to follow in her father's and her husband's footsteps and run the ranch.

But Felix had other ideas. He was a natural athlete, strong at swimming, great at track—he ran the 440 in 50 seconds and the 100-yard dash in 10.5. But his real love was football. Ever since childhood it had been his dream to play for USC, to wear the crimson and gold and be one of the Thundering Herd.

The fall and winter of '38 were bittersweet seasons for Felix. His dream came true and he was awarded a scholarship to USC. Coach Jones started him as first string on the junior varsity team, training him the way he'd always wanted to be trained, with a firm hand, high expectations, and hard work. Felix pledged Sigma Chi, he went to beer busts and bonfires, he avoided the news from Europe, and he avoided studying anything to do with agriculture or the profession of orange-growing as though it were pestilence.

And then on January 14, 1939, just as the spring semester was getting under way, Felix's father died of the pneumonia he'd contracted the week before while nursing his threatened crops.

Henry Anhalt was buried at Rosedale Cemetery in Los Angeles, and his coffin was covered with orange blossoms and white roses. The afternoon of the funeral Dora Anhalt let her son know exactly what she expected of him now that he was the man of the family. She said it softly and without an overt demand, but it was abhorrent to him just the same: 'You'll come home now and run the ranch.'

Felix sat next to his mother on the sofa in the living room while friends and neighbors passed through the farmhouse offering their sympathies. Her eyes were tight and swollen, red from crying; her dry, wrinkled skin was shiny and pinched; there was more gray in her straw-colored hair than there had been last week; and her trembling body felt thin and weak to Felix whenever she leaned against him. There was a wild look in her eyes, like the expression of a horse when it's just seen a coiled rattlesnake and knows it can't escape those open fangs. He didn't know how he could refuse her and it made him feel as though he were dying too.

A choking sensation gripped his throat as his mother whispered to him between the nods, the handshakes, and the thank-yous. 'It's what your father would have wanted,

Felix. This ranch is all we have. There's no one else to run it. We'll starve out here unless you come back and take over. Uncle Ivar and Uncle Luke and certainly Uncle John can't handle it. They're not as smart as you, or as young. You're your father's son and he loved the ranch. I know you can do it. You will do it, won't you?'

Felix turned to stare at her. She was only a frail woman, but her needs leapt out at him, smothering his own dreams as though she were an evil spirit, a specter of living death. He hated her with all his heart and he loved her too. It was the only time he felt like crying for the loss of his father. The man whose heavy accent embarrassed him, whose temper enraged and terrified him, and whose domination of his mother caused him envy and pain was gone forever and in death drove a harder bargain than he had in life. And while Felix cried for his father, he was really crying for his own lost dreams.

Felix lasted one year as an orange-grower. At age nineteen and a half, the day after New Year's 1940, he packed a bag, left a note for his mother, bought a train ticket to New York and a steamer ticket to London. And when he arrived in England twelve days later, he went to the nearest recruitment office and joined the RAF.

Felix became a gunner because it was the most dangerous position on the plane; he was testing the gods the way he had tested his father's love. Only this time he was purging himself of the guilt of deserting his family. Ironically, he was destroying an enemy who was German, and perhaps his own flesh and blood.

Felix flew on fourteen missions until one bombing raid over Belgium when his squadron was hit and Felix was shot six times on the left side of his body. Four of the wounds pierced his arm, one was in his abdomen, and the other lodged in his left thigh. The medical prognosis was that he'd never have full use of his left arm again because of the extent of the damage.

But Felix never let up. He worked his muscles until they caused him to scream with the pain; he drove himself and the hospital staff to the edge of endurance and still he pushed even more. And then one morning he picked up a football. His legs were strong again, his body fully recovered, and as he tucked the football under his left arm, cradling it, protecting it from attack, and zigzagged across the hospital lawn to the goal line, he knew he'd won the struggle.

Four years had gone by when Felix returned to California, and things were not the same as when he'd left. His uncles had only brought in two good crops since he'd left; they'd had to sell off forty acres to keep the family going. His sisters and brothers were nearly grown and Dora was dying of kidney disease.

Felix sat at the hospital by her side horrified by the pathetic condition of her body, then he drove aimlessly around the city, looking at the changes that had happened during the war.

The USC campus was an oasis in the midst of his misery. He'd come home to escape from unhappiness and strife and found only more. But the atmosphere on campus was tranquil and serene, the green grass was invitingly soft, studded with groups of lounging students. The brick buildings and pretty coeds made him long for lost time, for a youth he would never have. He was out of touch with this world, with the sweet-faced students on bicycles who carried their books in straps on the back of their fenders instead of strapping rifles over their shoulders.

A young coed with auburn hair and startling green eyes came hurrying toward him, her arms filled with books, her expression tense and anxious; she was obviously late and didn't see him as he stepped aside. The corner of her notebook jabbed him in his newly healed arm.

'Ouch!' he yelled, the pain sudden and sharp.

'Oh, I'm sorry,' she said, realizing her sorority lavalier pendant was caught on his alpaca sweater.

She gave a yank and the chain broke. 'Oh, dear,' she said, 'keep it for me, will you?' And then she ran off to her class. Felix called after her: 'I'll attach it to the bulletin board in your sorority.' But he didn't know if she heard him.

He decided to wait for her.

She was even prettier than he remembered. And quite surprised to find him waiting when she returned to the Tri-delt house an hour later. She laughed when he told her she reminded him of Cinderella and the famous glass slipper. He had fixed the chain for her and she gratefully accepted his offer to place it around her neck again.

Her name was Margie McKintridge. She was a sophomore, studying to be a teacher. He found her warm and very lovely. She listened to all his tales of the war, to his grandiose plans about his future, to the scheme of how he was going to make millions, and she understood when he described his conflict over the family business.

'Parents can be demanding,' she said with great sympathy.

They had dinner at Julie's near the campus, he took her to the natural history museum to see the stuffed animals in their native habitats, and by the time a week had gone by he was in love.

Margie was like no woman he'd ever known. She was wise beyond her years: she knew when to listen and when to scold, when to hold him and when to laugh, when to tease him and when to cry, which she did when he came to the sorority house late one night and told her his mother had died.

It was spring of 1946 by the time Felix was free of his family obligations and could look to his own life. He had brought in two successful crops of oranges so that his uncles had enough money to buy him out. He took a course at Southern California Business College and got his real-estate license, and with an American buddy he'd met in the hospital who was trained as an architect, they pooled their resources and optioned two hundred acres in the San Fernando Valley.

It was Felix's and Charlie Bernstein's plan to build two thousand bungalows, low-priced housing for the hordes of returning GIs who would want to live in California. And they mortgaged their very souls to get enough postwar material to build these small two- and three-bedroom houses.

Construction began, and when the houses were nearly completed, Felix asked Margie to marry him. If the profit he projected came anywhere near what he expected, he and Charlie would split $250,000.

Felix knew Margie's family had money; he could tell from the clothes she wore, and her lack of concern about her possessions, and from the places in the world she spoke of with familiarity. But she had always veered away from conversation about her family and nothing prepared him for the truth of her parentage, which she had kept a secret from him.

Felix had never seen her so agitated.

'What's wrong, baby?' he asked. 'You do want to get married, don't you?'

She nodded, her lovely eyes filling with tears.

'More than anything in the world,' she replied. 'But when you hear what I have to tell you, you might not want to marry me.'

Felix experienced a sudden grip of fear, as though she were going to say her father was a criminal, or she was suffering from some rare ailment and wouldn't live past twenty-one. But when she told him who her father was, he was delighted.

'He's one of my favorite actors,' Felix exclaimed. 'Why didn't you tell me before?'

She hung her head despairingly. 'Because Father is very difficult. He sets terribly high standards and expectations for me and my sister. He thinks of us as fairy princesses and the only worthy suitors for our hands would be a crown prince, or a member of some aristocracy.'

'And not some orange rancher from Altadena,' Felix finished for her.

Again she nodded.

'But he doesn't even know me,' Felix insisted. 'How can

62

he possibly object?'

'He knows you, all right. He has a file on you that covers an entire drawer in his file cabinet. He knows everything you've ever done, from the time you dug up Mrs Caponi's vegetable garden to the Sanchez girl's false pregnancy to the missions you flew over Germany. He's very thorough.'

For a moment Felix couldn't speak. And finally he said, 'If he knows everything about me, then he knows how much I love you, and how happy I intend to make you.'

She looked away, twisting her hands in her lap. And then she sighed. 'Have you ever seen our home?'

'I've seen pictures of it,' Felix told her. 'It seems unbelievable.'

She looked back at him, despair clouding her face. 'When my father and grandfather built our house, four different workmen were killed during the construction. Two when a slab of marble broke loose and crushed them to death. One by an earthmover when the site was being cleared, and the last when he fell from a scaffold while goldleafing part of a ceiling. My father refused to pay their families any compensation because he said it was the workers' carelessness that caused their deaths. My father is ruthless. If he decides against something, nothing will move him. And he has decided against you.'

'What did you tell him about me? That I was some ogre? Some undesirable?' he asked, feeling drained, as though his own father were standing over him with a belt, raised in anger.

'I told him nothing!' she insisted, grabbing his hand in hers. 'I never told him I was seeing anyone. And whenever you and I had a date, I carefully made up fictitious names. I never brought you to our home to meet him. But none of that subterfuge did any good. He still found out.' She put her face in her hands and wept. 'It's so horrible. I feel so invaded.'

He took her hands away from her face and handed her his handkerchief, waiting until she dried her eyes. 'What shall we do?' he asked.

'We have no choice. We must elope.'

'But he would disinherit you.'

'I don't care,' she replied. 'We'll make a life of our own.'

Felix shook his head. 'I can't let you do that. All my life our family has struggled to make a living. It's been terribly difficult. You know nothing of that kind of life. I can't take you away from what you've always known. You'd end up hating me for it. I'll meet your father face to face and ask his permission. I'll tell him how important your family is to you, and how I intend to make you happy. He'll listen. I know he'll listen.'

But Margie just shook her head. 'Please don't, Felix. Please don't!'

He put his arms around her. 'It'll be all right, baby. You'll see.'

Felix's throat was dry from tension, his voice unsteady, his body perspiring the day he came to McKintridge for the first time. It was so over-whelmingly huge, so opulent, he nearly turned around and left. But he was determined to go ahead with his speech.

Belson was in the rose garden, his eyes never straying from the roses he was pruning. As Felix introduced himself, Belson only grunted.

'I suppose you know, sir,' he began, 'I've been seeing your daughter, Margie, for some time now.'

No comment, only the click of the pruning shears as they sliced through the thorny stems.

'She's a wonderful girl, sir. Beautiful and intelligent and compassionate. She embodies more qualities than I'd ever hoped to find in any young woman. I'm honored that she returns my affections.' He waited: still no reaction. 'Margie has agreed to marry me, but I felt it only fair to request your permission.'

Belson's eyes stayed on his roses but his voice was as cutting as the shears in his hand. 'And how are those "crackerboxes" of your selling?'

Felix ignored the animosity: this was his beloved Margie's father, and therefore incapable of meanness.

'You mean the tract of two hundred homes my partner Charlie Bernstein and I just finished in Van Nuys? They're not selling as rapidly as we hoped. But they will.' Felix grew earnest as he discussed his dream. 'To the rest of the country, sir, California is the promised land. Every ex-GI who is still able to walk wants to live here. And they're all going to need low-cost housing.'

'Don't tell me you're actually proud to be expanding the city's slums, boy?'

'Oh, no, sir. My tracts won't be slums. And GIs are good men. They fought in the war and they'll work hard to build productive lives for themselves and their families.'

'Such a loyal veteran,' Belson commented. 'Tell me,' he asked. 'Did it give you pleasure to kill your German relatives in the war?'

'I was fighting for my country, sir,' Felix replied, increasingly bewildered by Belson's attacks.

'Indeed,' Belson said, and finally he looked up, but still not directly at Felix. 'How noble.'

Felix didn't know how to combat this sarcasm. And then he noticed the expression on Belson's face. Such blatant fury flashed at him that the flowers Belson was tending might have wilted if they'd been more delicate than these hearty roses.

Belson's gray sideburns caught the light, glowing like the fur of a predatory wolf against the snow, and then he turned his eyes on Felix. It was blindingly apparent that Belson held total scorn for him. 'Not a sou, *Mr* Anhalt.' Belson spoke precisely as though Felix were too simple to understand him. 'Not a penny, not a franc, not a mark, not a yen, not a ruble will my daughter get if she marries the likes of you!'

Felix was amazed. 'But I'm not marrying Margie for her money. I'll make enough for us to live on.'

'*Live on? Live on?*' Belson mocked. Was this the hero's face of the silver screen? Felix wondered. The man who had shot so many villains, kissed so many leading ladies, and won so many battles for the underdog? There was no compassion behind the artist; there was no fatherly concern for a daughter's feelings.

And then Belson swept his arm to indicate the opulent surroundings, the golf course, the mansion, the guest quarters, the servants' quarters.

'*This* is the manner to which my daughter was born, you ignoramus. Do you think for one moment you could ever provide her with one tenth of it? You're nothing but a filthy German peasant from bastardized stock. My daughter laughed at your proposal when she told me about it. "Can you imagine, Father? That dolt dining at McKintridge, telling his stupid ethnic stories at our table, thinking he could mix with our friends." *She laughed,* you idiot. We both laughed because you're not good enough to kiss her feet.'

Felix trembled, mortified by his words. He had never seen such hatred. He stood there telling himself over and over that it wasn't true. It was a lie, a cruel lie. But the bayonet of words had pierced him fatally. He could feel himself bleeding inside, his self-respect oozing away to be supplanted by insidious fear and insecurity. He was a child again, when the orange crops failed, when his father's heavy accent embarrassed him, when his uncles were nothing but dumb farmers, when everyone but he could afford to go to college. How had he ever supposed he could marry a girl who had come from all this? Even if she did love him.

It took every ounce of courage to say, 'Your daughter and I love each other, sir, in spite of what you think of me.'

'She'll get over it,' Belson shot at him. 'Now get out!' And he turned his attention back to the roses.

Felix ran with acid panic in his guts. He was so demeaned that he didn't even know at the time how badly he'd been beaten. He felt an awful shame that kept him from speaking to Margie for days. And then when he tried, she wouldn't see him. At first he couldn't believe it. He wrote letters, telegrams, sent flowers. Everything was returned. And he was never able to gain admittance to the estate again. It was a fortress after all, impossible to penetrate. He was sick at heart, and frightened, enraged, and miserable. What had happened? Why had she stopped loving him? He told himself her father was keeping them apart, telling her lies. But a small part of him didn't believe that. He turned to one of Margie's sorority sisters, Audrey, to intervene for him, but Audrey couldn't get through to Margie either.

And then he read that Belson McKintridge had taken his wife and two daughters on an African safari. They might as well have gone to the moon.

He told himself that any girl who could be so controlled by that monster of a father would not have been a suitable wife for him, but the pain of her loss tore at him. Three months later Margie was dead. She died in Africa after contracting a virulent jungle disease. And all Felix had left was an equally virulent hatred for Belson.

He vowed to get even.

Someday he would prove how wrong Belson was about him. Someday Belson would say, 'I shouldn't have taken her away from you. She might still be alive today if I hadn't. How can I make it up to you?'

Felix reached down and brushed his hand along the top of the box hedge, feeling a vicarious pride of ownership as its tight bristled edges responded to his touch. Almost without thinking he snapped off one of the leaves and put it in his pocket as a memento of this day.

'It's only an ordinary wax leaf plant,' a voice behind him exclaimed. 'Hasn't it been properly trimmed?'

Felix started at the sound of that voice and felt his stomach tighten. Even now, at the age of fifty-five, that voice could make him squirm—childlike. But he wouldn't let old Belson get the best of him on his day of triumph.

He turned to face the old man.

'The wedding was beautiful, Bel,' Felix said, deliberately using the nickname because he knew the man preferred to be called Belson.

'It's not over yet.' Belson's expression was lemon sour.

'Audrey and I only agreed to let you give the wedding so we could buy the kids their house, you know. That two-hundred-fifty-thousand dollar condominium is going to appreciate like crazy. It's a good investment. But I must say, in deference to you, we couldn't have given a better party ourselves.'

'I enjoy using my home for important events such as this, Felix. Your daughter is one of a kind, though I was reticent about her at first.'

Felix saw the look in Belson's eyes. *You think she's too good to be mine, don't you?* he thought. 'Audrey and I are quite fond of Peter,' he said.

'Yes.' Belson seemed genuinely surprised and studied Felix a moment, discovering truth in his statement. 'I believe you are fond of him; you tried hard enough to worm your way into his life. He's been bringing home stories from the club about the great Felix Anhalt for years, forced me to listen. Told me how you two discussed his career plans, how you helped him improve his tennis game, and how you two play golf once a month. Let's see, it's been at least three years of golf by now, hasn't it? Peter's friendship with you is the only matter in which he's ever defied me. As you can guess, I've never approved. I always wondered why you were doing it. Peter is not the most scintillating companion. But the role of father must be comfortable for you, judging from the way you've raised Phyllis. Though I never would have believed it.'

A waiter approached them with an array of elaborate delicacies on a silver tray. Felix took one, a tasty cheese-and-pastry morsel; Belson declined the buttery tidbit. 'I've grown to love that girl as if she were my own and that surprises me. She has a quality about her very much like . . .' Felix saw a film of moisture cloud Belson's eyes as Belson turned away for a moment. Felix was almost moved, but not quite. Belson was a brilliant actor and bringing up the ghost of Margie now, especially today, infuriated him. It was such an obvious play for sympathy.

But why did Belson want his sympathy?

Belson looked back again, his eyes dry now; the last rays of the sun gave them a leonine glint. 'We're going to be seeing one another more often in the years to come, what with Phyllis and Peter forming their own family unit.' He paused a moment, his eyes boring into Felix. 'And I believe there is some unfinished business between us.'

Here it comes, Felix thought, *the moment I've been waiting for all these years, the confession of past mistakes, the contrition of errors, the asking for forgiveness.* 'Yes?' he prompted.

Belson spoke easily and without hesitation, as though he were reading lines from a prewritten script. 'I want you to know where I stand, Anhalt. I want you to know I still detest you as much as I did nearly thirty years ago. I've waited a long time to tell you.' He shrugged. 'I thought perhaps it would change, lessen with time. But it hasn't. And now I know it never will.' He paused again for emphasis while Felix fought to control himself. He couldn't believe what he was hearing. 'If you hadn't hounded my daughter the way you did, driven her to such desperation, I would not have had to resort to such drastic measures to get her away from you; I would not have had to take her to a part of the world that was dangerous for her, merely to get her as far away from you as possible. If you hadn't forced me into an untenable position, she'd still be alive today. It is because of you that she died. I'll never forgive you for her death as long as I live! It's never ceased to rankle me that I blamed you and you didn't even know it. You went about your life blithely seeking your fortune, marrying Margie's friend, siring offspring, free from guilt. Yet you killed my daughter as surely as if you'd poisoned her.'

In an instant Felix was back in time, staring at the same monster of a man, a man incapable of humanity. He was so enraged he was nearly choking on the bile that gripped his throat. But this time he had something of his own to say.

Audrey Anhalt floated through her daughter's wedding

party in a dream. This was one of the most joyous days of her life too. Not only were Peter and Phyllis radiantly happy, but it was also a day of triumph for Felix. For the twenty-seven years of their marriage, Felix had been obsessed with the memory of his first love, Margie, and the rejection he had suffered at the hands of her father. Perhaps now he would finally be able to put his ghosts to rest. Audrey's fondest hope was about to be realized, that she could live her life without the constant pain that she was second best to the memory of a dead girl. God forgive her, that was the main reason she drank, to forget the sad truth. Not that Felix ever said it was true. He told her he loved her; he was reasonably devoted. But she knew, *she knew*.

She glanced around, looking for Felix. He was deep in conversation with Belson. Perhaps they were talking about it now; perhaps Belson was admitting how wrong he had been to interfere in two young lives and Felix would be vindicated for his guilt about Margie. They were so engrossed in conversation neither of them noticed her move in closer to hear what they were saying.

Felix had never wanted to kill anyone in his life before, but he did right now. It took all his will to keep from grabbing Belson's scrawny, hateful neck and squeezing until the man's eyeballs popped out of his head. 'You disgusting hypocrite,' he snarled. 'You blame *me* for Margie's death, when it was *you* who caused it? You kept her from seeing me; you threw away my letters; you sent back my pleas; you kept her from knowing how much I loved her.' Tears of rage filled his eyes with the memories, from the injustice. 'You told her lies about me and then dragged her off to Africa before she could learn the truth. The poor girl was too heartsick to fight off that virus. She died of a broken heart, Belson. You know it, *you know it!* And you were the one who broke her heart.

'And I loved her. My God, I still do. I've never loved anyone else in my life and you took her from me. I thought we were going to settle this thing once and for all. But you're not capable of a human thought or feeling.'

Just then Belson noticed Audrey standing behind Felix, listening to their conversation.

'Madame,' he said mockingly, 'I offer you my deepest sympathies, which you undoubtedly deserve for being married to such a man as this.'

And he walked away.

Audrey's face was the color of the ecru of her lace dress as she drained the last drops of wine from her glass and reached for another. But Felix didn't notice. He never noticed Audrey's distress. He'd gotten used to it, as he'd gotten used to the corn on his left foot. It was a petty annoyance, one he endured while pursuing his own determined goals. And he was still in shock from Belson's accusations. A knife in his back couldn't have stunned him more. His fists were clenched and his face was flushed red as he stared after the retreating figure. He watched the perfectly groomed white head nodding and dipping into conversations with other guests, smiling and talking and pretending to be human. But Felix knew otherwise. Belson was an insect to be squashed. He had wrested victory from Felix's grasp. And Felix now realized that this so-called victory of a social alliance between Peter and Phyllis paled by comparison with the desire for revenge that had just swept over him. With his entire being he wanted Belson to suffer as he had suffered. Belson must lose what was dearest to him. That was the only justice. And somehow, some way, Felix was going to bring that about. I'm going to ruin you, old man, he vowed. *Ruin you!*

He was concentrating so completely on his thoughts that he didn't even feel Audrey remove her hand from his arm and move away. Nor did he see her grab a full bottle of champagne from a nearby cooler and pour herself an overflowing glass.

Chapter 6

PETER FELT as though he'd conquered the world. If he'd known how wonderful it was to be married, he'd have done it long ago even though this morning he thought he was making the biggest mistake of his life. Right now he couldn't imagine anything as incredible as being married to Phyllis. She was dancing with her father at the moment, Princess Aurora come to life, and he was filled with love just looking at her.

He felt a hand on his back, interrupting his thought. It was Vicky.

'How about a dance with an old flame?' she asked.

He smiled and put his arm around her. 'Sure,' he said. 'But let's sit this one out. I can use a break and there's something I've been meaning to say to you.'

'You looking for girl friends already?' she teased, and they both laughed.

Waiters were clearing away the main course in preparation for dessert. Soon it would be time to cut the cake. They sat at one of the tables.

'This has been a fairy-tale party,' Vicky exclaimed. 'And I wouldn't wish you and Phyllis anything less.'

'Thank you, Vicky,' he said. 'And that's what I wanted to talk about. It means a great deal to me to have you here today, especially as a member of the wedding party.'

'Really?' she said. 'I've been apprehensive about it.'

'You shouldn't be,' Peter insisted. 'You were an important part of my youth and I hope you'll always be involved in my life, even though I'm not proud of the way I treated you when we went together. You deserved better and we both knew it. But I was so scared of my grandfather then. When he barked, I jumped.'

Vicky closed her hand over Peter's. 'We both had a lot to learn. If my mother hadn't pushed me so hard to find a rich boy, I might not have gotten involved with you in the first place.'

Peter pretended to be offended. 'You mean I wasn't the man of your dreams? Just because I let my grandfather insult you and break us up, and made you keep our relationship a secret for fear he would find out. How could you not love me?'

But Vicky didn't laugh. Instead she turned away in embarrassment. 'Don't be so hard on yourself, Peter. Your grandfather was a tough adversary.'

He reached over and took her chin in his hand, turning her face toward him. 'Hey, it's okay. I finally grew up. At least enough to tell you I think you're a wonderful person. I admired the way you handled yourself back then. It was a hell of a place to be. But you never let it get you down.'

'That's what you think,' Vicky scoffed.

'Even so. I'm very glad you and Phyllis are such close friends and I hope you and I will be good friends again too.'

'That means a lot to me,' Vicky said, her lower lip quivering with emotion. 'Because I love Phyllis and I think you two are perfectly suited for one another.'

Peter reached over and hugged her. 'You'll find the right guy, Vicky. He's out there somewhere and when he gets you he'll be one lucky man.' And then he got up, gave her a kiss on the cheek, and went to find his bride.

Belson could feel the sourness in his stomach erupting beyond control. Soon the pain would be radiating in his chest. *Damn that Felix Anhalt.*

He's an asshole. The gall of that man saying I broke Margie's heart. I loved her. I was right to take her away from him. She's better off dead than with him.

And if Felix Anhalt's idiot accusations and Hugh

Perkins's predictions of financial gloom and doom weren't enough aggravation for one day, some scandal sheet had managed to slip one of their photographers into the wedding and the man had already taken some pictures. Belson had given instructions to throw the man out, but now the staff couldn't find him. He had obviously slipped into the center of the overwhelming crowd.

And then Belson spied Peter sitting with his arm draped around a woman. *That's not Phyllis,* he thought. *What's Peter doing, for Christ's sake? You can't leave the boy alone for a minute. Shit! It's that damned Vicky Feinstein. Is that little troublemaker still trying to get her claws into Peter? Well, I'll put a stop to that.*

He waited until Peter left her alone and then followed her as she headed toward the bar. She was sipping from her cocktail when he came up behind her and jostled her arm, spilling some of the liquid on her dress.

'Miss Feinstein,' he said rudely.

She turned in surprise.

'Phyllis is certainly democratic to have one of *your* kind in her wedding. Someone should set her straight about you.'

She stared at him with those cow eyes he recalled unpleasantly, but he could see that she wasn't the mealy-mouthed little girl he'd once known. 'Must I remind you that my grandson is a married man now. He doesn't need your sexual services anymore.'

She gazed at him with intense loathing, an expression he recognized easily. 'You haven't mellowed very much in your old age, have you,' Vicky commented. 'Still the same nasty anti-Semite I used to know.'

'You little cunt,' he snarled. 'It was your fault Peter didn't get into Harvard Law School. You had him so pussy-whipped, he couldn't study. Well, I want you out of my house right now and away from my grandson and his wife. Go on, get out! I'll make some excuse to Phyllis that you soiled your dress and went home to change.'

Her eyes glinted with such hatred that it caused him a

moment's hesitation. 'You don't frighten me anymore, Mr McKintridge,' she said. 'I know what you are, and I'm not leaving.' She sounded tough but her voice was quavering.

'Then I'll have you thrown out. Would you like that? Huh? Huh?' He thrust his face into hers. God, he hated her. All his animosity toward her kind came pouring out of him. He really wished he could throw Anhalt out of here, but she would do as a substitute.

He looked around for one of the servants to come and do his bidding. There was Thomas. He waved and beckoned.

'All right,' Vicky whispered, aware that people around them were staring. 'I'll go. I don't want to cause Phyllis and Peter any problems on their wedding day. But before I go, I have something for you, sir,' she said, and with that she threw her drink into his face.

At the instant the liquid hit him, Belson saw a flashbulb explode on his right. He was so startled that he couldn't react except to growl and sputter and wipe at the liquid dripping down the front of him. The alcohol stung his eyes and he couldn't see who it was, but some photographer at this awful moment was getting shot after shot.

Thomas approached on the run. 'Get her out of here,' Belson said to Thomas. But Vicky had walked away. 'And stop that photographer.' But the photographer had disappeared again into the crowd.

Chapter 7

IT WAS anything but an ordinary Tuesday in June. The twittering, comments, and questions from the students had been coming at Vicky all day. And when she received a summons in her box to report to the headmaster's office immediately following the last class of the day, she knew there was real trouble.

'Come in, Vicky,' Mr Beckwirth said. 'I suppose you know why I wanted to see you.'

She came forward across the carpeted room; outside she could hear the sounds of after-school activities, lockers slamming, someone playing piano for a rehearsal in the multipurpose room, the thwack of tennis balls echoing faintly from the courts off behind the new library wing. Her throat constricted painfully. She loved those sounds; she loved this school and her job. *Please, God, let me keep it,* she prayed.

Mr Beckwirth sat with his back to a row of square-paned French doors that looked out on a forest of tall eucalyptus trees, rolling lawns, and part of the faculty parking lot. His desk was an old mahogany relic of mediocre quality, heavily chipped and marred by years of use, something she'd always regarded with fondness. From this desk the education of countless privileged young girls was planned. But today, spread across its wide, nicked surface, was a copy of the infamous *National Chronicler* with Vicky's picture on the cover throwing a drink into Belson McKintridge's face.

Mr Beckwirth's kind eyes studied hers. His elbows were on the desk, his fingers pressed together lightly bending and pressing against themselves; the light bounced off his bald head, and the gray fringe of hair that ringed his head looked like the stubble from a row of worn-out paint-brushes.

'This scurrilous publicity is most unfortunate for you. And for us at Southwick, I might add. I've had countless phone calls all day from parents inquiring whether or not this was "our" Miss Feinstein on the cover of the *Chronicler.* I most reluctantly had to admit that it was.'

'I can explain, sir,' she began, wishing to God she could.

'I'm sure you have a viable excuse,' he commented. 'But that's beside the point. The point is that you, who represent

76

the reputation of Southwick as an ambassador-at-large, who must stand as an example to your pupils, allowed yourself to be carried away by whatever emotion prompted this display—and from the expression in the photo I would assume that emotion to be fury—and you behaved in a manner unbecoming to a member of our faculty.'

'But Mr Beckwirth—'

'Please let me finish, Vicky,' he insisted. 'I'm certain you're aware of the gravity of what I've just said; but I don't think you realize how serious an infraction this is. We at Southwick cannot allow, nor can we afford, to employ educators with controversial reputations. It undermines our goals and casts aspersions on our own merit as a sanctuary where high moral behavior and standards of excellence are revered.'

Vicky sank back in the high-backed chair whose polished wooden arms were smooth from countless encounters such as this. But she derived no comfort from the chair, nor from the serene expression on Beckwirth's face. He was known as a fair man, even a gentle man, but he was retiring this year and his outgoing reputation was crucial to him. The faculty had noticed that in the last six months he had been running the school 'by the book,' disallowing any deviation whatsoever from the charter rules, rules that during previous years had often been bent and occasionally broken.

'And to make matters worse, I received by messenger early this morning a letter from a distinguished member of our board of directors, demanding your resignation. Some serious accusations were made against you and I've had to give this request extreme consideration.'

Vicky held her breath and her expression showed her misery. Was it all going down the drain for one moment's madness? That's all it had been—a moment of fury, well deserved perhaps, but Beckwirth hadn't been there; he hadn't heard Belson McKintridge's words, hadn't seen his face, hadn't felt her pain.

'You're an excellent teacher, my dear. One of the best and most dedicated we have. Your classes are innovative;

your students rely on you and identify with you not only because you're young but because you understand them in a unique way. You've grown up here, you weren't a graduate of Southwick, but you went to Beverly High. You know the special pressures and unusual circumstances impacting on the lives of privileged children. Our students turn to you for special counseling and I've heard nothing but the highest praise from them about you.

'That is why I'm not going to bring up this matter before the board, but will deal with it myself.'

She wanted to ask him in what way, but the words stuck in her throat. Her hands squeezed the arms of the chair; her lungs felt as though they were being pressed by an iron weight.

'Although the board member who has demanded your resignation is an upstanding member of the community, there might be mitigating circumstances for the request. In lieu of no other such demands, I have decided to table this problem for the present. I expect I shall have to answer to this person as to my decision but since I'm retiring there will be scant leverage to influence me. However . . .'

Vicky moved forward to the edge of her chair.

'I shall assure this member of the board—who shall remain nameless—that I have placed you on probation, that I have stressed to you the importance of decorous behavior, and that should your name ever be linked with any future controversy you will be dismissed immediately. Is that clear?'

Vicky nodded. It was all she had the strength to do.

'I don't think you've heard the last of this,' he added. 'And as for the article in the paper, it is certain to foment inquiries. "No comment" is the best reply. Explaining and justifying one's mistakes only puts one deeper into the pudding.'

Tears of gratitude filled her eyes and she blinked them away. 'Thank you, Mr Beckwirth,' she said. 'I won't betray your trust in me, I promise.'

He smiled warmly, revealing white dentures. 'See that

you don't, my dear. See that you don't.'

As Vicky stepped out into the hall, she realized how close she'd come to losing the one thing in her life she was really proud of. Her job meant so much to her, not only as a source of satisfaction but as a means to independence. She didn't want to teach for the rest of her life. She wanted to write. But for now, at age twenty-six, only four years out of college, she needed this job, she wasn't ready yet to let go. If she chose to give it up someday, that was one thing. But to be thrown out for defending herself against Belson McKintridge, that she couldn't have stood. From now on she'd have to be very careful. Beckwirth was a sweet old guy. The new headmaster might not be.

BOOK II

Vanities

Chapter 1

JONATHAN ANHALT McKintridge had a lusty cry, louder than any of the other babies in the hospital nursery and Belson was terribly gratified to hear it. At last there was an heir to McKintridge. It was the only good news he'd had in months. He had been standing in front of the viewing window for at least ten minutes and the baby hadn't let up once. *That boy is going to get everything he wants,* Belson thought. *Only two days old and already as demanding as hell, just like his great-grandfather. Well, he'll have to be tough to hang on in this world, the way things are today,* Belson thought. The Mideast was close to exploding, South America was brewing trouble. There was just no stability one could rely on anymore. He never thought he'd live to see the economy go so out of control. It was worse than the twenties. Look at what gold had done in the past year. It was lunacy! Gold was the one area he hadn't invested in that had gone sky high, though he'd managed to find every other losing proposition in the country. The world was all a fucking mess and he was right in the middle of it.

Now don't let your blood pressure rise, he thought. *You know what Dr Larkin said.* But the thought of his cardiologist only made his heart pound even more.

Hot tears of frustration leaped to his eyes and he turned his face away from the nursery window, fighting for control. *Little Jonathan,* he thought. *Your great-grandfather is in trouble, real trouble.*

He could hear Hugh Perkins's voice repeating its litany of doom. 'I warned you three and a half years ago that you were headed for disaster and that's exactly where you are today. You've made decisions against our advice that have cost you dearly.' Belson had just come from Perkins's office and those words were etched in his brain. 'That last dip in the stock market caught you badly. You took a profit on good listed stocks but you borrowed heavily against unlisted ones with unlimited marketability. You shouldn't have switched emphasis, especially when you're on margin. Your stock portfolio will never recover from that loss.

'You invested six million in a supposedly guaranteed oil deal, but you came into that deal after others had taken their profit. You know the ratio of successful wells is eight dry ones to every one producing and the operator went broke paying off his early commitments. I told you at the time,' Hugh said, 'that if an oil deal is offered to investors on either coast it's because the smart Texas money has seen the problems and passed it up.'

Belson had just sat there paralyzed, listening to the horrendous accumulation of mistakes, realizing what a shambles he'd made of everything.

Hugh continued. 'The government would not allow your loss in that WAY-CON underwriting deal to be taken against ordinary income but only allowed it as a short-term capital loss, the kind you don't need. And your land investments have had the worst history of all. That time you acquired forty thousand acres of grazing land and four thousand head of cattle on a ten-to-one ratio, you bought in at the high and sold at the low, showing a loss of thirty percent on your investment. Your two thousand acres in Cherry Valley haven't appreciated, nor have your six thousand acres in Hinkley Valley. More capital losses. Ten million lost in mineral and oil rights, only one in four paid a slight profit. And your living expenses are astronomical. It costs you four hundred and fifty thousand a year in staff salaries at the McKintridge estate, two hundred thousand for maintenance and utilities, and another hundred and seventy-five thousand in living expenses.

'The only asset you have left is the McKintridge estate

and the surrounding fifteen acres of land.'

Belson felt the shock of that statement reverberate through him. Everything, gone? His father's entire estate—pissed away? *Jesus!* But he still had the house and grounds and they were the only things that really mattered. 'What do you estimate my assets are worth?' Belson had asked.

Hugh had given him a long, disappointed stare from under those eyebrows of his and then looked down at the balance sheets in front of him. 'The fifteen acres of land surrounding McKintridge are worth about one point two million an acre in today's market—that's eighteen million. At last appraisal the structure was worth about eighteen million too, if you could ever find a buyer, giving you a total of about thirty-six million. Everything else is gone. It might even be difficult for you to find enough operating capital to live on unless you sell off one or two acres of land.'

'Never,' Belson had stated flatly. 'The estate is too precious, it must remain intact.'

'Well, not for long,' Hugh insisted. 'After you die your heirs will have to liquidate the estate to pay their taxes. They'll owe close to twenty-five million dollars, combining both state and federal, deducting state credits.'

'Liquidate?' Belson had shouted. 'No! I won't hear of it. I won't let it happen! Peter's got to keep the house and grounds in the family. It's his heritage!'

But Hugh Perkins only shrugged. 'I know how much it means to you, Belson, how much it meant to your father. But I'm afraid the dynasty has ended. You're an old man now. You have no liquid capital to invest, and even if you did, there is no way you can make a hundred million dollars in the next few years, which is what you would need to ensure the estate for Peter's children. After all, inheritance taxes have to be paid to the government.'

'Fuck the government!' Belson had shouted. 'I'll find a way. There's got to be a way. I'm not so old. There's still time.'

And Hugh had smiled his supercilious smile and nodded.

'Of course, Belson. You'll find a way. Only calm down, you know, it's not good for you to become overwrought.'

Belson forced himself out of his reverie. His body was covered in a cold, clammy sweat and his heart beat painfully in his chest. *I've got to stay calm,* he thought. Hugh was right. Getting overwrought wouldn't help at all. There's plenty of time left. There's *plenty of time*.

But the dull pain radiating down his arms, pulsating in his chest and abdomen, filled him with apprehension. *What if there isn't enough time?*

It was midmorning on the second day of Jonathan's life when Phyllis heard a commotion in the hallway outside the hospital room and one of the student nurses came bursting into the room.

'Your father-in-law is here, Mrs McKintridge,' she said, all aquiver with the news. 'My goodness, he's still so handsome.' And she held the door wide open, stopping it with her body, so Belson could make an unimpeded entrance.

All the nurses and orderlies on the floor followed him as he entered the room carrying a basket of five dozen long-stemmed roses in one hand and a shopping bag of gifts in the other.

'My dear!' he said, setting the flowers on the dresser and leaning over to kiss her. 'How proud and happy you've made me.' He pulled over a chair, dropped the bag of gifts into her lap, and waved away the crowd in the hall, including the candy striper at the door. Then he sat down heavily in the chair next to the bed, allowing himself a sigh of relief.

'Are you all right, Belson?' Phyllis asked, concerned by the tiredness in his eyes.

But he perked up immediately and brushed away her concern. 'Of course I'm all right,' he insisted. 'Never better.'

She smiled at him. 'You caused quite a stir making your entrance. Don't you believe in modesty?'

'Not in my nature. Neither modest, nor humble, nor fool give a tumble.'

'What's that from?' she asked.

'One of those damned costume epics I was in once.' He chuckled. 'So tell me, how are you? You're looking as lovely as ever.'

'Oh, that's not true,' she said. 'But I'm feeling wonderful. The baby is a dream and I had an easy time of it.'

'I've brought you some trinkets in honor of the baby,' he said, handing her a box from Van Cleef & Arpels.

For Jonathan, whom they'd named after Peter's mother, Jo Ann, there was a golden replica charm of the McKintridge estate with the baby's name and birthdate engraved on the back. 'Just so he'll always know where he belongs,' Belson said. And for her a delicate diamond necklace to go with the bracelet he'd given her on her last birthday.

'They're lovely,' she exclaimed, more thrilled by his thoughtfulness than by the gifts themselves.

'I've put some bonds in the baby's name and some in yours too. But we'll let your lawyer husband explain all that to you. I'd like you to believe it's generosity, but in honesty setting up trusts saves me taxes in the long run.' He looked away just then and she could see a touch of sadness in his eyes. Talk of trusts had upset him, she thought, reminded him of his age.

He turned back to her and for a moment she thought he was going to cry, but instead he straightened up in his chair and took her hand. 'You know, my dear, you are a woman of substance, valuable and capable in your own right. You're carrying on the family tradition brilliantly. I know I can count on you. Sherryn would have approved of you greatly, and approval was something important to both of us.'

His words brought tears to her eyes. It was exactly what she had always wanted to hear from her own father, but never had. She was never sure where she stood with Felix, always trying to second-guess him, to figure out what it was that would please him and then do it. Her father patronized her in the same way he patronized her mother, as though her ideas were unimportant, her needs secondary, and so she tried twice as hard to succeed, to prove to him that she did have valid ideas, that her self-worth was an important concern. But even when she graduated with a master's degree in business and was able to communicate on his level, she'd been unable to convince her father that she was a valuable human being. As far as he was concerned, she was still his little girl and would always be only someone through whom he could extend his ego. But though she knew that about him deep in her heart, it wasn't important enough to confront him with or try to change. After all, she liked being his little girl; she was so good at it. But now here was this antiquated man, sitting before her—a man she'd only known for four years and he was saying the words she'd longed to hear from her father for her whole life and knew she never would.

'They'll never convince me you're so tough, Belson,' she said, her lip trembling with emotion. 'With all your posturing, you know, you're a dear, affectionate man and I love you.'

Belson looked at her for a moment with an odd expression, as though he'd been caught doing something dishonest and was embarrassed about it. 'I believe you mean that,' he said with surprise.

'Is it so hard to believe?' she asked. 'You're the only relative Peter has, and if you had three sets of horns I'd still love you.'

'Unconditionally?' he asked in disbelief.

She nodded. Now it was he who was overcome. 'Young lady, you are the one person in all the world I have wished for to carry on my name. Your son is a legacy no one can dispute. McKintridge was built with you in mind. You are the perfect mistress to grace its halls and you have a very special heritage. Don't ever let it go. Teach it to your sons and your daughters, when you have them, that they have been born to succeed.'

Phyllis had never seen him so serious. His expression was lofty and proud, yet he seemed sentimental and vulnerable. His eyes gazed into hers with rapt sincerity; his eyebrows were drawn together in a look of pleading; even his facial muscles trembled. 'That brings me to my last and final gift.' He reached into his pocket and brought out a solid gold key, pressing it into her hand.

She looked at him questioningly.

'This is the key to the guesthouse on the estate. I want you and Peter and the baby to come and live there. The estate is yours anyway; you'll both inherit it when I'm gone. And though it saddens me to say that, it will be truly momentous when the fourth generation of McKintridges assume their birthright.' He cleared his throat to hide his emotion. 'But for now come and live nearby. Let your family absorb what is theirs. The guesthouse is fully staffed, though no one's stayed there in years. You'll have your own separate driveway and entrance to the property. We won't even see one another—there's so much acreage between the two houses—but I'll have the comfort of knowing my family is nearby where they belong. And you needn't worry about my dropping in on you, or injecting myself into your lives. I'm a very private person, wouldn't want you under my feet either.'

Again she was overwhelmed at his generosity, not knowing what to say.

'Don't give me your answer now, talk it over with Peter. He'll see that it makes sense. It's yours whether or not you use it. Might as well use it. Twelve rooms, you know, lovely nursery, newly redone, not like the main house, which cries for a woman's touch. But no matter, you'll do it proud when you live there one day, I'm sure.'

He heaved a sigh and pulled himself wearily to his feet. Another sign of his age, Phyllis thought. 'It's time I'm off,' he said. 'I've got an appointment in a few minutes. Don't want to be late. My best to Peter.' And he kissed her on the forehead. Then he grinned with glee and merriment. 'I take it you never saw one of my films, entitled *The Viking Prince*, in which I played King Torgen. That speech I just gave was the one I made before I rode off into battle, with a few pertinent changes, of course.'

A bubble of mirth burst forth and Phyllis cried out in delight. 'You old fox, you!'

He threw back his head and laughed. 'You're one in a million, my dear, one in a million. I know you're going to love McKintridge as much as I do.'

But Phyllis wasn't so sure of that. She had always thought that huge museum seemed like a monument to greed and excess. She loved her own small home, the coziness of it, the security of having the baby close by in the next room. But if Peter wanted to live in the guesthouse on the estate and raise his son in the shadow of that edifice, she would never say no.

Belson had only been gone a few minutes when Peter stuck his head in the door. 'May I come in?' he asked. He too was carrying flowers.

'Darling,' she exclaimed, holding out her arms. 'I'm so glad to see you. Your grandfather was just here.'

Peter's expression exuded pleasure as he came over and hugged her tightly, then he pulled back and ran his fingers through his thick, reddish hair, trying to cover his delight.

'What did he say?'

She giggled. 'If you can imagine Belson so excited he was gushing, that's what he was like.'

Peter fairly beamed with pride.

'Have you see the baby today?'

He nodded. 'He's wonderful, Phyl. I can't believe how tiny and wonderful he is.'

'He's got your cleft in his chin,' she said, reaching up to rub the place on Peter's face she adored.

'Do you think he looks like me?' he asked. His expression of joy was so intense it made her heart rise to her throat. God, she loved him so.

'He's exactly like you,' she assured him, watching him smile. 'Oh, Peter, are you as happy as I am?' she asked.

And he nodded. 'I used to dream that life could be like this, but I never thought it would.'

'Wait until I tell you what your grandfather has given us,'

she said, watching his reaction for any signs of reticence. But when she finished telling him about Belson's offer of the guesthouse and handed him the gold key, she saw a look of wonder on his face as incredulous as the wonder he displayed over their new child.

'You don't know what this means to me,' he said, his voice breaking with emotion. 'You just don't know. There has been such a distance between me and my grandfather all my life that ever since I could remember I've been trying to bridge that gap. I've tried in every way I knew how to reach him, to find a closeness with him I needed so badly, but I could never do it. I suppose it was my fault. I felt terribly alone after the . . . accident. I clung to him and was moody. I was never the kind of kid Grandfather wanted me to be—you know, jolly and sports-minded. I was frightened of everything, and much too serious, withdrawn and lacking in adventure.' He gave an apologetic little laugh and she took hold of his hand. Peter sighed. 'It was the best thing for him to send me to boarding school. I guess my being around all the time and crying reminded him of the crash, I know it upset Grandmother. But I missed him terribly when I was away at school. When weekends and vacations arrived, I was so eager to see him, I'd actually run a mild fever in anticipation of going home. Of course, I caught a lot of colds so that might have explained the fevers. But still I felt this tremendous euphoria that lifted me out of my usual state of depression each time I knew I was going home. But my need to be close to my grandfather was so great that the euphoria was short-lived. Something always ruined my homecoming, sometimes in the first five minutes of my arrival. I'd greet Grandfather with a flurry of chatter and my overly stuffed duffel bags. I always packed nearly everything I owned, hoping against hope that I wouldn't have to be sent back again; and then I'd do something clumsy or I'd say something thoughtless, or I'd be so overeager I'd bowl him over. And then there were the times I'd be careless with some priceless object in the house, and you know how many of those there are.'

She nodded, encouraging him to go on.

'Well, he'd end up yelling at me, and pointing out what a disappointment I was to him, and of course I didn't blame him. And then I'd apologize—God how I apologized. But it would set us apart for the duration of my stay. And it never got easier. The older I got, the more mistakes I'd make—different ones, culminating in that disastrous romance with Vicky.'

Phyllis smiled to show him she wasn't threatened by that past affair.

'You know, it's funny. There was always a new set of disasters for me to find at each new age. Just when I thought I'd learned never to do "that" again, something else would happen.'

Peter got up and crossed to the window, fingering the slats of the blinds. He spoke as he gazed west out at the city of Beverly Hills. 'I came to believe that this distance between my grandfather and me would always exist, though I've never grown used to it, and longed for it to end. But since I married you, my grandfather has behaved differently toward me. It's as if I've finally done something to make him proud.' He turned to look at her. 'I'm very grateful for that,' he said.

She held out her hand and he came back to sit beside her. 'Is that why you're so happy about the gift of the guest-house?' she asked. 'Because Belson wants us near him, bridging the distance, so to speak?'

'That's only part of it,' Peter said. 'The real reason I'm so touched is because I love McKintridge itself as much as I love anything else in my life. Now don't laugh, but that house and those grounds mean to me what Tara meant to Scarlett O'Hara. That house was my only comfort when everything else deserted me. It was the only constant in my turbulent world. When everyone else who was flesh and blood either died or rejected me, the house was always there to welcome me. The house never expected anything of me. It never disappointed me either; it just was. And it wove a kind of magic spell around me, making me feel the world was all right, even when it wasn't. It offered me corners where I could dream, private places to calm my troubled soul, trees to climb and daydream in, a lake to row across and save a maiden in distress, miles of grass to roam, and corridors that were both friendly and forbidding, depending on what I needed at the moment.

'Not I don't want to sound like a poor little rich boy, though in a way I guess I was, but that house became the family I lost. It was a substitute for the happiness I craved, and it was a symbol of the future I promised myself I'd have someday when life seemed blackest.

'Until you,' he said.

The afternoon sun had moved past the window while Peter spoke and the room had grown darker. But the only light Phyllis needed was shining in her husband's eyes.

'I'm so glad you told me all this,' she said. 'It explains something I've always wondered about you. I know now why I've always seen an almost physical change come over you when we go to the estate. Your face looks serene, the tight lines of worry that are usually there seem to dissipate, and you become carefree.'

He smiled at her, surprised that she had noticed.

'It also makes me proud to have given you a son who will grow to love your family's home the way you do. Although he won't ever have to suffer as you did from loneliness or the loss of his parents. Not if I can help it.'

Peter nodded. 'We're very lucky, aren't we?'

She smiled. 'Yes, my darling,' she replied. 'Very lucky.'

Icy hands. Belson's hands were blocks of ice. They'd never thaw out. He held them together painfully between his thighs and tried to concentrate on the scenery going by as he sat in the back of the limo, but it was a blur. Was the sun shining? He didn't know. Ache, ache, ache, his guts ached. His shoulders steeled themselves for another twinge in his chest—those twinges were the devil's finger, prodding him with every pain, telling him *soon, soon.* Oh, God, he was scared. His rational mind tried to fight back. *What does that*

93

quack know? I'll go to Houston, Bethseda, Mayo's, Hart-ford. To hell. Churning inside. Everything was churning. He couldn't forget, imprisoned by the knowledge in his brain. *Soon.* And every time he thought it, anger and rage were overshadowed by this bone-gripping, icy, sickening fear. *Don't race, heart. Don't hurt. Don't fail me. Don't stop! I don't want to die!*

The car pulled up the drive, carrying its precious cargo, lord and master of so much. *All of it.* He would give all of it to make his condition go away. Make a bargain with any-body. But worldly goods didn't count this time. For the first time in his life he knew how much they didn't count. *They're all I have and I'm going to lose them,* he thought. *I've got to hold on. But there's no time left. Pull yourself together, Belson. You are made of iron. This is only another chapter, you'll write the ending the way you want it.* But he was shaking, trembling, quaking—out of control, he felt ashamed of himself.

Don't you dare! It was the voice of his father, ordering him to shape up. So loud in the confines of the car he almost jumped. Was that what happened when one approached death? The voices of those beyond grew closer; you heard them as though they were real? He clenched his teeth together, fighting the jellied sickness that churned inside and threatened to spill over.

'You wanted to be an *actor!*' His father said it with such disgust, such disdain. (He recognized that tone; he'd used it often himself, never realizing where it had come from. It was Angus-bred.) 'Then be an actor! A great one!' His father's voice boomed. 'Give the performance of your life.'

Williams came around and opened the car door for him, reaching out to help him. He felt like an infant, an ancient infant, and it was the most infuriating feeling of all. But he drew himself up to his full height, declined the offer, and walked slowly to the front door.

First there were the doctors, summoned to McKintridge. They brain-stormed with one another, including him, excluding him, talking to him and around him, being brutally frank.

'If Cedars has turned you down for a bypass, I'd advise against going elsewhere.'

'Their team does these surgeries by the dozen. The success rate is phenomenal. If they say you're not a candidate, then you're not. You'll just have to accept your fate.'

'Have any of their rejects had successful bypass operations elsewhere?' Belson asked.

They all stared at him, collective owls of wisdom, until someone ventured a reply.

'Some patients go on to other surgical centers and have successful results, others live a long time past the gloomy predictions without surgery, and so might you, Belson. But statistically the odds are against you.'

'Every case must be considered on its own merit.'

'Or lack of merit.'

He listened to them discuss the statistics of his deteriorating health, his very life's blood, the moments of his precious existence, like so many market quotations. And he endured it, praying for a spark, a hope, a word of encouragement. He didn't hear any. *I need time!* he wanted to scream.

They mentioned Texas, Buffalo, Washington. They conferred, they examined, they argued. And finally decided the best mode of treatment was to do nothing but a strict diet regimen, the most conservative approach, even though he could hardly adjust his intake of lean foods any lower than it already was. They prescribed medications and constant monitoring. But no matter what the jargon it still boiled down to the unalterable fact that at seventy-nine years of age he hadn't long to live.

Nobody said it outright, but they were all thinking: 'What more do you want, Mr Rich Movie Star?'

And finally they dismissed his case.

He felt unfinished, unresolved. There was no solace in his heart. When he looked back and saw his life, he did not feel content. Too much more to do. Too many bodies still

95

excited him, too many deals awaited him, too many adversaries surrounded him.

He had to have a plan, pace himself, utilize his remaining strength to the fullest. And what pastime would give him the greatest return? He knew without even thinking.

Preserve the estate. He would find a way. He had to.

Chapter 2

THE PINECREST Day School bus had not even pulled away from the curb before Marla was back up the stairs of the duplex and into the kitchen. It took her eight minutes to do the breakfast dishes, twelve to do the bedrooms, baths, and throw a load of wash into the washer. Twenty-two minutes later she was dressed and ready to go job hunting. What an exciting task. She'd showered, shampooed, prepared lunches and dinner the night before, hoarded names of reliable sitters in case the children were sick, and had fallen asleep, praying for the flu goblin to pass over her house. Mornings she dispensed vitamins like seeds to the pigeons. A sitter could cost twenty dollars a day, but she would find a job and hire a sitter if she had to.

Larry hated the idea of her working, her mother clucked her tongue with disapproval, and her mother-in-law wouldn't discuss it. Only the children didn't mind. Lori, age six, was a mature young lady who understood. Mommy wanted to fulfil herself—whatever that meant—and Mark, age four, went along with anything his sister said, unless it was to play dolls or dress-up. They loved the idea that Marla would earn extra money for bicycles and skates, or other amusements such as a swing set for the new house they were planning to buy.

'What a joke!' Larry had said. 'You feed them fairy tales to boost your ego. You'll earn peanuts! Aren't I a good enough provider? Aren't I working hard enough for you?'

'It has nothing to do with that,' she insisted. The truth was that Larry was doing extremely well financially. In the three and a half years he'd been in private practice, their income had soared. They'd even saved enough money for a down payment on a house and still managed to live quite comfortably. But his tight-lipped expression made her abandon the attempt to make him understand that his personal success wasn't hers. She wanted something for herself. He thought she was attacking his manhood by wanting to get a job when all she was doing was expressing a creative need. Her friend, Vicky, said Larry's attitude was Cro-Magnon, and she agreed, but nevertheless it made her doubt her motives. He was so adamant that she began to wonder if she was merely rebelling against the role model of her own mother, who was a statistic in the files of Germaine Greer and Gloria Steinem. And then she realized that of course she was rebelling, but with a mother like hers why wouldn't she have a fierce desire to succeed? Babs Raskind was a Marilyn French heroine before enlightenment, a Marabel Morgan follower who didn't want to be. And Marla had decided long ago not to give up on her own dreams the way her mother had. Her mother married a dentist who was sweet and loving but not as bright as she, and yet she praised his intelligence and denied her own. Marla would never do that. Her mother deferred to her husband's decisions because that's what wives did. And she'd spent a lifetime pretending she didn't have sparks of genius flaring in her heart. Instead she doused them with devotion to the Sisterhood and found other ways to protest that Marla thought were even more tragic than divorce or extramarital sex. She had psychosomatic illnesses. Yet she was a woman who did everything: cooked, sewed, polished her silver with ashes from the hearth, baked, baby-sat for her beloved grandchildren, and made them lamb chops for lunch and liver for dinner. Taught herself to type eighty words a minute, ran five miles four times a week, observed the Sabbath, crocheted, knitted, painted china, and did Sol's monthly billing because the girl at the office worked so hard. Never had there been a woman so driven who refused to do anything about it. And the more Marla watched her suffer, the more it underscored her own determination not to fall into that trap.

For after all, Marla's mother quoted, 'Marriage is what it's all about.'

And Marla's father always smiled and said, 'That's right, honey. Marriage is a holy institution.'

Maybe it is, Marla thought, *but I'm not going to live my life devoted to it. I'm going to have my own identity if it kills me.* And that's exactly what she felt it was doing, killing her. She felt as though, inside, she were dying bit by bit. She couldn't reach Larry. It had gotten more difficult the longer they were married, as though their communication occurred in some clouded abyss they called a relationship. Her children knew her as Mommy the carpooler, Mommy the lunch-maker, Mommy who fights with Daddy. But not just as Mommy-Mommy. And no one knew her as *her*. Least of all herself.

The showroom of LPW Inc. was located on the short fashionable block of Melrose Place, only one mile outside of Beverly Hills. It was on the south side of the street, a few doors from Paul Ferrante and across the street from Barbara Lockhard. Leslie Paxton Winokur was the top designer in the city and Marla wanted this job so badly she was afraid to hope.

She pushed open the ornate wrought-iron gate and stepped into a Vicorian courtyard, complete with ferns, sculpted flowers beds, a Japanese umbrella tree, and stone benches. Moss-mortared bricks covered the floor of the courtyard, and the sparkling paned windows of the show-room reflected Marla's awed face as she approached the enormous brass knocker in the middle of the ebony lacquered door. An empty receptionist desk sat inside, adjacent to the entry door, and Marla waited there, not knowing whether to enter the showroom or turn and run. She'd never seen such opulence.

The main room was two stories high with an enormous fireplace at one end. A second-story loft ran the length of the main floor separated by wooden turned railings and a circular staircase. All the floors were highly polished and intricately parqueted. The antique tabletops glowed with a hand-polished luster, while the scent of rich wax, woodsy perfumed candles, and freshly brewed coffee filled the room. Soft classical music played in the background and Marla felt as though she'd walked into a permanent state of Christmas. The treasures were worthy of a museum: horned legged tables and chairs, gold-encrusted grandfather clocks, tapestries of richly woven silk threads, all mixed perfectly with polished steel and lacquered pieces that appeared all the more modern by their contrast to the traditional. Objects of every size and description graced the tables and chests around the room. At the sound of someone approaching she looked up guiltily, as if her glance might insult the precious objects surrounding her.

A man in his early forties glided toward her from across the room and stood behind the desk with a haughty expression. He had light sandy hair, thin on top; a perfectly trimmed goatee graced his chin; his white chambray shirt was collarless, unbuttoned nearly halfway, revealing gold chains on a thin, tanned chest. His beige garbardine pants hung perfectly around his slim hips and a gold Gucci belt threaded through the waistband.

'I'm Billy D.,' he announced, giving her a bitchy, competitive look that showed his distaste. '*She's* too busy at the moment, so have a seat.' Marla sat on the antique bench opposite the desk. 'Here for an interview?'

She nodded.

'Tell me a bit about yourself, dear. Saves Leslie the time.'

Their conversation was interrupted by three women who swept in with a flutter of capes and coats.

'You know we're not open yet, Annette!' Billy insisted, hands on hips.

'Ohh, don't be a toughie,' Annette replied. 'Just a teensy peek. Mrs Haddad is in from Palm Springs for the day.'

Billy raised his eyes to the heavens, waited while they signed the register, and then he ushered them into the showroom.

Marla realized she was staring, when a woman in her late forties, plump and gray-haired, came out of a side door hidden in the paneling near where Marla waited.

The woman called Billy's name and beckoned furiously to him. 'We need you in the back immediately,' she hissed. 'The builder on the Bensinger job says the beams have been designed improperly and if he cuts them according to your measurements they'll be six inches too short. We can't afford to wait for another six months for a shipment of African ebony!' She turned to Marla. 'Are you the new receptionist?'

Marla stood up quickly. 'I'm here to see about it.'

'Well, sit right here,' the woman said. 'I'm Ruth.' And she pulled Marla around and sat her in the leather chair behind the desk. 'Just answer the phone by saying: "LPW Incorporated, may I be of service." Write every message down word for word no matter how nonsensical it sounds. *Do not,* I repeat, *do not* buzz Leslie's office under any circumstance. This is my extension.' She pointed to number 39. 'I'll decide whether it's an emergency or not. Otherwise punt. And ask every single person who steps through that door to sign the register or fill out a resale card.' And she disappeared back into the paneling.

Mara was dumbfounded, but that only lasted a moment, for after that pandemonium reigned. The shop opened at 10:00 A.M. and there wasn't a minute to breath all day. At one o'clock Ruth came out and took over the desk so Marla could go to lunch, warning her to be back in half an hour.

At five o'clock, when they closed, Marla felt she really

belonged here. It was the most fun she'd had in years. The customers were friendly and high-powered, the sales staff was polite and courteous, the phone never stopped ringing—every call was an emergency for Leslie—and now and then some member of the staff would come over to give her a word of encouragement or instruct her in some aspect of her job.

At five fifteen she stood at the door in the paneling, waiting for someone to tell her whether she was hired or not, when the phone on the receptionist's desk buzzed. She waited and watched, but she was the only one there. Finally she picked it up.

A husky female voice demanded, 'Who is this?'

'This is Marla Gilbert at LPW Incorporated. May I be of assistance?'

There was a pause and then, 'This *is* LPW. Take the back staircase to the second landing. I'm the last door at the end of the hall.'

Leslie Paxton Winokur looked like the Queen of Hearts sitting behind a magnificent copper-trimmed steel desk, which made Marla feel like Alice. Slender ankles were crossed above plum snakeskin sandals, while blue-blood lacquered nails tapped out a rhythm on the dull surface of the desk. Intense violet-blue eyes stared out from under thick black lashes; sharp elbows, sharply arched eyebrows, and the painted bows of her lips all formed punctuations of power at various positions on her body, proclaiming her the boss. Marla was impressed.

'Sit down, dear.' Leslie spoke with a slight Southern accent and took in everything about Marla at a glance. 'Billy D. and Ruth tell me you've pitched in beautifully. That's what I like to see in my people—enthusiasm, loyalty, and initiative.'

'It's been a wonderful day, Mrs Winokur,' Marla began. 'But no one has told me if I'm hired, and what my duties would be, or anything about my salary.' The last word she swallowed.

'*No* one told you? *How* distressing. But it *has* been an

incredible day.'

Leslie Paxton Winokur emphasized key words in every sentence, giving her speech pattern the sound of a quasi-Philadelphian-American accent.

Marla suspected that every day with Leslie was an incredible day.

'Now tell me all about your background and your work experience.'

Marla handed her a copy of a résumé, listing all of her art projects and awards, her job experience in the field of interior design, and her aspirations for the future. Leslie glanced over the page and nodded.

'You are a find. In this organization anyone with talent like yours could make a place for herself. Of course you'll have to start at the bottom, learn the sources, observe how I run my business. I pride myself on efficiency and cohesiveness.'

From what Marla had seen today, it was more like wild abandon.

'Now don't take this as an insult, dear, but I do have a certain image to maintain. I would prefer it if you'd consider losing some weight. The interior-design business is actually the process of selling dreams. We're trying to translate our clients' vision of heaven on earth into the reality of limited space, limited budgets, and availability of material. Not to mention the overabundance of their impossible personality flaws. I find it a great advantage to look as good if not better than my customers. I look the way they wish to look. It's easier for them to imagine that you can design a room to suit their tastes if you look as though you're the one who should live in it. They get the message that it's your ideas that matter, not theirs. Of course that's a long way off for you. In the meantime I suggest you take yourself off to Jôna's and buy some suitable clothes. They'll help you choose the image I like.' She paused, glancing down at the résumé again. 'I see that you're married?'

Marla nodded.

'And two children. That will be a problem.'

'Oh, no, it won't,' Marla assured her.

'Oh, yes, it will,' Leslie insisted, and Marla's heart sank. She wanted this job.

'But I'm a compassionate person, and a mother after all. But I'll say this only once, dear. I demand your first loyalty to be to LPW Inc. Your husband and children will have to come second to your job. If you give me that loyalty, it will be rewarded. Working with me is an advantage you cannot begin to assess. There is no one in this town as highly regarded in the design field as I am, and I intend to stay here.' She softened her tone a bit. 'But I need people like you to support me.

'Now, as to your duties. You'll work the showroom for a short while, handle the desk until I hire a receptionist, and then you'll be a gofer, pick up fabrics, accessories, wall coverings, so forth, and work as Billy D.'s and my assistant. He's just become a full-fledged designer and he's quite good, but don't tell him I said so.

'And as for salary. You'll start at four dollars an hour, ten to five, five days a week, and on Saturdays and Sundays we catch up, do inventory, buy at auctions, and speak to clients.'

Marla stared at her. 'Saturday and Sunday?'

'Well, what do you want? A job or a career? How do you think I got where I am today?'

Marla shook her head silently, more in shock than negativity. Larry would never agree to this.

'Oh, all right,' Leslie said with a magnanimous sigh. 'Half day on Saturday. I guess I can't ask everyone to be as dedicated as I.'

Marla wouldn't dare mention that she'd been hoping to find a part-time job. This opportunity was too good to pass up. LPW was the finest and highest-paid designer in the city. It had become de rigueur to have your home done by Leslie. Her taste was impeccable, her designs individual for each client, yet every job had that unmistakable LPW stamp. To work under her aegis was a dream come true. And if Marla was being asked to sacrifice her time, and

103

starve her body, then Marla would do both.

She rose and reached out for Leslie's hand. They shook firmly. 'I'm thrilled with this opportunity, Mrs Winokur,' Marla said.

'Call me Leslie,' the woman replied. And then, 'Well, maybe you'd better not. At least not at first.'

But Marla didn't care. She'd call Leslie Madame Queen as long as she got this job.

'Welcome to LPW Inc.,' Leslie said, withdrawing her hand. 'I'll see you at nine thirty in the morning.'

'I thought you said ten?' Marla turned at the doorway.

'Oh, you get paid starting at ten.' Leslie smiled. 'But we'll need you at nine thirty.'

Chapter 3

LESLIE PAUSED for a moment after Marla left to consider her new employee. Pretty face, awkward taste in clothes, a bit overweight, hadn't yet come into her own creative opinions. All well and good—she was malleable. Could she ever be a threat? Seeing her today, one would say definitely not. But Leslie had to be positive. Her people had to have enough backbone to be of assistance to her, enough initiative to carry on when she couldn't be there, but never, absolutely never, could they have enough potential to pose a serious competitive threat. It was a delicate balance she had to maintain, staying supremely LPW. And only because she knew human nature as well as she did, knew that at the core of each adoring employee and fellow worker there beat a heart as avaricious and competitive as her own, could she keep her throne from any and all pretenders. The person hadn't been created who could unseat LPW and she'd be damned if she'd give any of the drones tools to mastermind her own downfall. She'd do with Marla what she'd always done, teach her just enough to be useful, nothing more. And then if Leslie saw any hint of independence, any sign of threatened individuality, she'd unsheath her stinger and halt the predator in her tracks. They didn't call her the Black Widow of Beverly Hills for nothing.

Why the pep talk, Leslie? she asked herself. *Are you more concerned about this little twit than you are about anyone else? No,* she thought, *certainly not. But the girl is fresh off the farm and so were you back then. So were you . . .*

But there was another bit of important business to concern herself with at the moment. Debra, her fifteen-year-old-daughter. *Why me?* Leslie wondered. *Why did I end up with a juvenile delinquent when other children are well mannered and well behaved. Wasn't it bad enough that I was widowed at thirty-six?* She'd never had a problem with Terrence, who was eleven, but Debra had gone to many of the best therapists in town and none of them had been able to do anything with her. She had an impossibly fresh mouth, she was completely irreverent with authority figures, and usually it took only two sessions before she decided her latest therapist was a quack and refused to go back. Of course the therapists always insisted that Debra was merely resisting their help and they weren't quacks at all. But Leslie could see Debra's point. If they weren't quacks, why weren't they able to interest a fifteen-year-old girl in her own well-being enough to get her to stay in therapy?

Leslie had to admire her daughter's spunk, even though she was as exasperating as hell; the kid was a chip off the old block—a skeptic until shown otherwise. And at least Debra wouldn't start out in life a naive little bunny the way Leslie had been. But Debra had to realize that the path she had chosen for herself could ruin her future chances for happiness. Yet she wouldn't listen to anyone, especially her mother. The only person Debra responded to in any way was one of her teachers at Southwick School, the one who taught English, Ms Feinstein. Since Debra had been assigned to Ms Feinstein's class, there had been a small improvement in the girl—at least her fresh answers were grammatically correct. And she'd slowed down with the wild boyfriends and the shoplifting, but drugs were still a problem. Where did she get the stuff? Leslie wondered, thinking if she ever ran into one of those suppliers, she'd kill them with her bare hands. And Debra's precious Ms Feinstein was very little help as far as the drugs were concerned. She suggested Debra go away and join some drug-addict program. But Leslie would never agree to that. In the first place Debra wasn't an addict; she was an occasional user. In the second place she'd eventually have to come back to Beverly Hills and face the community and the situation that sent her away. And in the third place Leslie knew what went on in those places where boys and girls lived together under the same roof. But that damn Ms Feinstein had put a bug in Debra's ear about it, and whatever Ms Feinstein said, Debra thought was gospel. Leslie was sure Debra only wanted to go so she could get out of the house and run wild. But her Ms Feinstein didn't agree. Well, if Debra did go away for a while, at least Leslie wouldn't have to hear about Ms Feinstein all the time, Ms Feinstein this, and Ms Feinstein that; it was enough to drive anyone crazy. Debra ate, slept, and drank that woman's praises. There was something unnatural about it, about the attachment Debra had formed with a mere teacher. Leslie didn't like it one bit. In fact Leslie had finally forbidden Debra to see Ms Feinstein except during class time. She'd even spoken to the teacher about staying away from Debra, but it hadn't done any good. Ms Feinstein was downright rude, and Leslie knew rudeness when she heard it.

'Your daughter is going through a difficult time right now, Mrs Winokur,' as if Leslie didn't know. 'And I don't think it would be wise to insist that she stop seeing me. She would feel more abandoned than she already does.'

The nerve! Implying that Leslie had abandoned her daughter. She'd done no such thing. Yes, she was devoted to her career and worked long, hard hours that kept her away from home, but she'd never sent her children away to school as some parents did, and they were given everything their hearts desired, a damn lot more than she'd been given. But what did a spinster schoolteacher with no children know about such things, even though she set herself up as an expert? Child Guidance, big deal. According to Catherine Weeks, the art teacher at Southwick who wanted to become a designer and work for Leslie, Vicky Feinstein had a controversial reputation. Leslie knew the type, one of those too-vocal quasi-ethnic liberals who marched for every conceivable feminist or minority cause. Well, good influence or not—and that was debatable—Ms Feinstein wasn't going to brainwash Debra. If Debra didn't stop hanging around with Vicky Feinstein, then Leslie would do something about it. And when Leslie decided to do something, it got done. She was an extremely determined woman who seized every opportunity and made the most of it. If she hadn't seized every opportunity, she'd still be stuck in Tyler, Texas, raising kids and milking cows instead of living in Beverly Hills as the most important designer in California.

Tessie Mae Paxton was born beautiful, and beauty was a quality that even those in the small town of Tyler, Texas, recognized. Tessie Mae was voted the prettiest girl in her sixth-grade class at Sam Houston Elementary; best-looking, best legs, and most popular, from Lincoln Junior High; and most beautiful, most artistic, and most likely to marry a rich man, from Tyler High School. But even though she won the Miss East Texas beauty title, and was a cinch to represent Texas in the Miss America Beauty Pageant, Tessie Mae dropped out of the running for a very important reason. The summer of her nineteenth birthday something was happening right in her hometown of Tyler, something stupendous. A movie company from Hollywood was going to be shooting a film right in her own backyard, starring Belson McKintridge and Linda Darnell. She'd heard stories about local residents being used as extras in movies, sometimes even being discovered and given a part. And if anyone in Tyler deserved to be discovered, it was Tessie Mae.

Once the filming started, crowds of locals hung around the location out by the oil fields and Tessie Mae couldn't get close enough to be noticed by a horsefly. But it was tantalizing to be so near. She watched and waited for her opportunity, filing away bits and pieces of information in her crackerjack memory along with other accumulated knowledge such as the stock figures of cattle-price increases over the last ten years, the batting averages of every one of the New York Yankees, and the color of every Revlon product since Dorian Leigh modeled 'Fire and Ice.' She didn't know why she accumulated information except that she hoped someday it would help her to get out of Tyler, Texas.

When Belson McKintridge's wife arrived in town, everyone's attention shifted to her. Tessie Mae had never seen anyone like Sherryn McKintridge except on the screen. She was cool and tall and regal, a cross between Katharine Hepburn and Joan Crawford. And all the young girls in Tyler, most of whom Tessie had known all her life and who had been traipsing in and out of Belson McKintridge's trailer on the set or in and out of his hotel room at the Tyler Pavilion all hours of the day and night, suddenly ceased to be required.

The details Tessie Mae heard about Belson McKintridge's sexual exploits absolutely curled her toes with a kind of fascinated curiosity. The stories went round and round how Belson liked 'em young—the younger the better—and he wouldn't bed a girl unless she was a virgin, or unless she brought a friend with her. But in spite of Belson's distasteful reputation as a womanizer, Tessie Mae's admiration for his wife knew no bounds. Whatever

108

else Tessie Mae decided to do with her life, she wanted to be as much of a lady as Sherryn McKintridge.

One afternoon Tessie Mae was sitting at the counter at Jimmy's Five and Ten having an ice-cream soda when Mrs McKintridge came through the swinging screen doors. While Tessie Mae watched with open curiosity, Sherryn took a deep breath, fanned her face, and sat on one of the counter stools; then she glanced at Tessie Mae, noting the thick black lazy curls, the long tanned legs wrapped around the stem of the stool, the violet-colored eyes that glanced sidelong and then back to her soda. Tessia Mae's pulse was racing as she smiled shyly and then went back to sipping.

'It's not as warm today as yesterday,' Mrs McKintridge commented to Jimmy behind the counter. He nodded to her. 'I'll have an iced tea with lemon, please,' she told him, and turned to smile at Tessie Mae. 'You young people are so fortunate to be able to drink delicious concoctions like that without worrying about your figures.' She seemed so friendly, Tessie Mae's heart skipped a beat. Maybe this was her chance.

Before long they were chattering away as close as could be, and Tessie Mae confided that she was thinking about changing her name, being careful to keep out of earshot of Jimmy, who was chopping onions for his famous potato salad. If Jimmy ever told her mother that he heard her say she thought Tessie Mae sounded like the name of a cow, she might as well never go home again; Tessie Mae was her grandmother's name.

But Mrs McKintridge agreed with her. The name lacked a lyrical quality essential for a girl of Tessie Mae's looks and stature. Mrs McKintridge was intrigued with the idea of choosing a new name for Tessie Mae. But she thought that Tessie's favourite choices—Stardette, Babette, and Claudette—were too much like names for hookers. Tessie Mae was surprised to hear Mrs McKintridge use a word like that, but suddenly those glamorous-sounding names lost their glitter for her too and seemed to tarnish like a brass-plated prize at a carnival.

For the duration of the time that the crew of *The Battle of Brawny Creek* stayed in Tyler, Texas, Tessie Mae and Mrs McKintridge spent hours trying to decide on a fitting name that would carry Tessie Mae through the rest of her life. And all the while they were choosing and rejecting names, they were getting to know one another. Mrs McKintridge grew more and more attached to Tessie Mae, who knew exactly how to foster this interest. She was demure and polite, complimentary and witty. She peppered her obsequiousness with just enough self-confidence, her devotion with just a touch of down-home witticism, and leaned on Sherryn for all kinds of motherly advice. Mrs McKintridge had lost both her daughters, the first one from an illness, the other, more recently in a plane crash, and the poor lady was starved for this kind of a relationship. Tessie Mae knew just how to play on Sherryn's needs and become her surrogate daughter. Besides, coming from a family of six, it was fun to have the undivided attention of such a grand lady. She never had so much attention in her life, although her cleverness and ingenuity got her more notice than anyone else in the family. And even though Tessie Mae was nothing like Sherryn McKintridge's daughters, she found out as much as she could about them and pretended to be like them so as to endear herself even more to Sherryn.

By the time shooting was over and the crew returned to Hollywood, Sherryn couldn't bear to be parted from her newly 'adopted' daughter. It was decided that Tessie Mae would move to California and, with Mrs McKintridge's guidance, study interior design. From Sherryn's description of the business it was exactly what Tessie wanted, and of course she never discounted the importance of having a patron with the social prominence of Sherryn McKintridge, who regarded her as a member of the family.

Tessie knew she had some rough areas in her background and her personality to be smoothed out, and a great deal to learn. But didn't she have a crackerjack mind? Just before leaving Tyler, Sherryn and Tessie settled on the name Leslie as perfect for an interior designer; combined with

Tessie Mae's surname, Paxton, it had a glamorous sound. The fact that Tessie, or Leslie, had never been exposed to interior furnishings or design in her life, other than the lumpy sofa in the front room and the divan on the screen porch, next to Grandma's rocker, made no difference to the newly named Leslie Paxton. She would learn. And Sherryn was thrilled to teach her.

What Sherryn did not know was that shortly after Leslie's arrival in California, Belson too became Leslie's benefactor. As hard as she tried not to, as much as she hated herself for it, and as much as she admired Sherryn, Leslie found Belson irresistible. He was so famous and so sophisticated, and so handsome. And he wanted her. He wooed her and teased her and courted her until she fell in love with him. And she fell very hard. It was the first time she'd ever been in love and she was overcome with the excitement of who he was as much as how he made her feel. She was still young enough and naive enough to believe that he loved her too, that only their mutual respect for Sherryn was keeping them from a permanent relationship. But it was a strange affair. Belson refused to consummate it. He would touch her and kiss her all over her body until she was mad with desire. He would show her what to do with her hands to assuage her own needs while he observed. But never, never would he do it himself.

After a while she finally began to realize he was toying with her. That was when she started to wheedle gifts from him. It was Belson who gave her the most important pieces of her fabulous art collection, a collection that included one work by each of the major impressionists, one by each of the Fauvists, something by every old master she could get her hands on, including an etching by Rembrandt. She even had a small oil by Goya, her pride and joy. But what she had to do to get these treasures grew increasingly difficult. For not only did she have to agree to keep her virginity intact, Belson started asking other things of her as well. He wanted her to watch him perform the sex act with any number and combination of partners. At first she was

111

disgusted and terribly hurt at the suggestion, but after a while her curiosity got the better of her and she decided to try it. It turned her stomach, but even more than that she was consumed with jealousy to watch him give to some boy or two young girls what he so madly withheld from her. After one of his group sessions she would beg him to make love to her. And when he wouldn't, she'd cry for hours. After a while she taunted him with her virginity, threatening to deflower herself merely to defy him. But he had the last word. As long as she remained a virgin, he would be good to her. Once her hymen was gone, he would be too.

Their never-consummated affair lasted for nearly four years until Leslie was established as the up-and-coming arbiter of taste in Beverly Hills and she no longer had to endure the monthly physicals to prove her hymen was still unbroken. The affair ended when Sherryn died after a lingering illness. *Now*, she thought, *he is free to marry me*. And she waited for his proposal. But he informed her he would never marry a cracker off the Texas plains. She screamed at him and beat at his chest with her fists; he was a hypocrite of the worst kind. Here he was rutting with animals and yet he had the nerve to tell her she wasn't good enough for him. The problem was that she suspected he was right.

She went out and slept with the first man she could find rather than let Belson have what he'd paid so dearly over the years to get. She hated him with such an intensity that she never laundered the sheets on which she lost her virginity, keeping them wrapped in plastic, yellowed with age and brown spotted, as a reminder that she'd never have anything to do with him again.

For five long years she'd wanted to be mistress of Mc-Kintridge and he'd let her believe it was possible. He'd dangled it before her like a carrot to a donkey, letting her make an ass of herself, making her a party to his unspeakable behavior. How she wanted to let the world know what he was, the things he had done. But there would be a better way than mere gossip to get her own back. Someday she would have the last laugh. Someday she would own that house and live in it on her own!

But as long as Belson was alive, he was a finger of accusation pointing at her, saying that she had sunk very low because of him. He was living proof that she had come from nothing and, deep down inside, knew she would always be nothing.

Chapter 4

IT RAINED the night of orientation and Vicky cursed the gods of moisture. The classroom felt like a greenhouse, steamy and dank, while all the flowers raised their heads toward her for sustenance of her praise and approval. Parents fussed over rainwear and boots, sprucing up the blooms otherwise known as offspring.

And every garden has its weeds, Vicky thought as Amanda Hatch approached.

'Vicky! How are you? God, it's been years, and now you're my daughter's teacher.'

'How are you, Mandy,' Vicky said.

Amanda Hatch gave her a withering look. *A-manda* was the name she preferred. 'I see you're still *Miss* Feinstein? Never married?'

'No,' Vicky acknowledged, embarrassed at the reminder. But it was better than marrying someone like Roy Hatch, whose family owned one of the largest plumbing-supply companies in the city, but who was such a bore that he was stuck for an answer to good morning.

'Are you still friends with Phyllis?' Amanda asked, as though Vicky couldn't possibly be.

'Of course,' Vicky said. 'I was bridesmaid at her wedding.'

'I thought by now you two would have drifted apart.' Her meaning was, *What does Phyllis see in you*? 'Phyllis is a lovely person. She just had a baby, didn't she?'

Vicky felt those old stirrings of inadequacy. 'Yes, two weeks ago—a boy.' She tried to change the subject. 'About your daughter Janet, Amanda.'

'What does she need English for when she's going to have a modeling career?' Amanda asked. 'You know she's already done three commercials.'

Vicky held on to her beleaguered goodwill. 'I strongly suggest that we have that parent's conference, A-manda. I requested it last spring, but you never made an appointment. So far this semester Janet's comprehension has not improved. We should talk.'

'If you insist,' Amanda agreed. 'But it will have to wait until after Thanksgiving. The Helpers November Gala is only seven weeks away and that's my priority right now. I'm chairing the auction committee and it's my job to collect all those fabulous items we auction off at the ball. You have no idea how time-consuming that is; but our work is so worthwhile. I've been thinking about speaking to Phyllis about joining Helpers. She'd be such an asset, don't you think?'

'Yes,' Vicky agreed, feeling her face begin to burn. Naturally Amanda belonged to Helpers, the most prestigious charity organization in Beverly Hills. The membership consisted of ninety-five attractive women who were either successful or famous in their own right, or married to successful or famous men. They raised money for a center in Beverly Hills that treated emotionally disturbed children. Most of the members were dedicated to their cause, but others were only in it for the contacts. Their yearly gala was the most exciting and exclusive social event of the season. And Vicky had always wanted to belong to Helpers, to count among her friends the most glamorous

114

women in the city. It would mean she was finally accepted by the people who had always rejected her. But only ladies like Amanda or Phyllis were invited, not spinster teachers who had been born, brought up, and still lived on the wrong side of Wilshire.

'I'm surprised to find you still teaching, after all this time,' Amanda was saying. 'When we were in college, you were going to be a writer. Where is that great American novel? We're still waiting to hear from little Vicky Feinstein.'

A thousand poisonous darts shot directly at the silk scarf peeking through the throat of Amanda's cashmere sweater would not have assuaged Vicky's anger. She would have used a chain saw at the moment to shut her up! But there was nothing cruel left for Amanda to say. In five minutes she'd dredged up every one of Vicky's bêtes noires tonight and laid them out like an autopsy of an infected corpse. But of all of them the most painful was Vicky's desire to be a writer. That glorious, unattainable goal. That thorn in her side, the villain in her nightmares, both golden and hated. Golden because it was noble and desirable, and hated because in spite of her promise, her talent, and her efforts, she still hadn't finished her first novel. There were a million reasons why. None of them rang true, except that she was scared to death to fail.

'I do have to make a living,' Vicky replied, finding that excuse empty and hollow. 'You have no idea how time-consuming supporting oneself can be, not to mention trying to ram English facts into the dense heads of children like Janet who don't want to learn.'

'Oh, well.' Amanda smiled, taking no visible offense at Vicky's jibe. 'I guess it's literature's loss and all that. What is it they say? Those who can, do; and those who can't, teach.

'Oh, look who's here.' Amanda spotted friends among the other parents and waved excitedly. 'I'll call you soon and make that appointment,' and she moved away through the crowded classroom to chat with Wendy Glass, Lorraine Erlich, and Mimi Cooke, leaving Vicky holding her incompleted dreams.

It was ironic that the children of those four women were in Vicky's class. They represented everything in life Vicky had never had and desired above all else. Yet she detested what they stood for. She had gone all through school with them, but they were worlds apart. Vicky had gotten A's while they got sports cars on their sixteenth birthdays. They had formed a club in high school, but she hadn't been invited to join. They had joined sororities in college, but she couldn't afford to rush. And only once in all the years she had known them had they befriended her. It was in the third grade and she had invited Amanda and Wendy home with her after school. 'Is this where you live?' they'd asked in amazement, carefully not touching anything as they followed her up the stairs to the second-floor apartment she shared with her mother. She was suddenly aware of the dinginess of the place as the two girls did the rounds of the three small rooms, looking with curiosity at the one television set in the living room and at Vicky's meager toy collection in a box in the closet and at the twin beds in the single bedroom. Vicky was fully aware of their distaste, not that they were intentionally cruel; it was beyond their experience to know what poor was like. But later as they grew older and their wardrobes reflected the money they took for granted, their cliquishness became blatant.

Not that Vicky didn't have friends. Marla was her friend from religious school, and Phyllis, who was really rich, was her friend in spite of their disapproval. But when Phyllis and Vicky walked up to their group at lunch, their circle opened only wide enough to let Phyllis in, even though she was two years younger.

I ought to fail every one of their little darlings to get even, Vicky thought nastily, pausing to shake hands with other parents against whom she bore no grudge. Not that all their daughters were as bad as Janet. But she detected the same cliquey disregard for others apparent in their offspring as she had seen in the parents growing up.

Why did she care, a grown woman? What the hell difference did it make who accepted her and who didn't? But as she watched them standing in her classroom where she ruled, in their three-hundred-dollar Burberry raincoats, with their forty-dollar haircuts that never drooped even in weather like this, so absorbed in one another's trivia that the building could have blown to bits and they wouldn't have noticed, she made a vow. Someday, no matter what it took, she'd be accepted by them. She'd show them she was as good as they were because of who she was and what she accomplished, and not because of what she had. They would want to include her in their lives, they would invite her into their organizations, they would fix her up with their eligible male friends and ask her advice on party lists and vacation plans. And once and for all she would be free from this constantly cloying feeling, this ever-present ache inside that without their acceptance she could never be happy.

That night she lay stretched out on the sofa, arms behind her head, staring at the ceiling. Finally she lit a joint to help her forget seeing Amanda Hatch's face and the memories.

It was a warm summer evening in July and Vicky had just turned five. It had been the best birthday of her life. She'd had a party with cake and ice cream for several of the children on the block. They'd played pin the tail on the donkey and musical chairs, and she'd received a new jump rope and a large box of crayons, and an Alexander Doll from her mother. The day before had been the Fourth of July and she'd gone to the beach with her parents to watch the fireworks. It had been foggy in the morning and they'd sat huddled under their blanket. But by one o'clock the sun had come out and her father had taken her into the ocean and taught her how to jump over the tiny foamed edges of the breakers. Vicky had squealed with delight as the chilly water splashed up her legs, hysterical with the joy of having her father's undivided attention and his miraculous presence with her for a whole day. For Jack Feinstein was a traveling salesman who sold raincoats in different cities all over the country and was seldom home. While he was on the road, Vicky waited for his return in an emotional state of constant longing. But his homecomings were never as good as her fantasies. Reena would no sooner get her husband in the door and cover his face with kisses, than she'd begin to pick at him about what she called his 'sport' line.

'Such a sport,' Reena would say. 'I'll bet that isn't all you service, is it, Jack? The sport line? Isn't it? You leave me here with your child while you go off scot-free, as easy as the breeze, giving away all those free samples. Well, I want some samples of my own. I want you to stay home, do you hear? I want you to get a steady job in a store right here in town. Travelman's wants you, Haggerty's wants you, even Yvel's. And Vicky needs a steady father in her life. Someone to be here when she scrapes her knee, or gets the measles. Do you realize that I nursed her through a strep throat last winter? That's nothing to scoff about, a strep throat. And where were you?'

Vicky would huddle in the hall outside their bedroom listening to them, the hardwood floors pressing against the bones of her behind as she squatted there, her ear glued to the wall, her knees jammed up against her chest, so that she would be ready to take flight the moment the bed creaked, which meant one of them was getting up to go to the toilet or get a drink of water.

'I'd go crazy in a nine-to-five job, Reena,' her father would say. 'I'd go bananas. You knew that about me when you married me.'

'A sorry day that was,' Reena would comment, and Vicky would press her fist into her mouth to keep from crying out: 'No, it wasn't a sorry day, Mommy, no it wasn't.'

And then Vicky's magic wish had come true. Reena finally convinced Jack to take a full-time job managing one of the men's haberdashery stores in Beverly Hills. The

London Shop on Rodeo Drive snapped him up, for it was true that Jack Feinstein was in demand. His good looks, charming, ready smile, and his knowledge of the business were an asset to any establishment.

Vicky loved the London Shop. It was a wonderful mixture of dark wood and red, white, and blue colors with royal gold seals on all the hangers. There was a picture of the Queen of England on the wall and Vicky thought she was quite lovely in her diamond tiara and blue robe trimmed with ermine. She looked exactly like the principal of Vicky's school, Mrs Maloney. And even though Mrs Maloney bristled at the idea, and heightened her Irish brogue when denying that there was any possible resemblance between her and Her Majesty, Vicky was convinced that they were long-lost cousins.

Jack took the job at the London Shop in February, and for the following five months life at home was better than Vicky had ever dreamed. Her parents didn't fight like they used to—of course they didn't talk much either, but that was all right. Only when her father skipped work and went to the track and came home smelling of whiskey did Reena resume the nagging, accusatory tone that brought Vicky such a miserable feeling in her heart. It felt as though she were an ice skater, skating along on a beautiful glassy surface of the lake, admiring the snow-covered hillsides and pine forests in the distance, and as she glided, the strains of beautiful music filled the air (like the music they played on the merry-go-round at Griffith Park). But all the time she was skating, inches away under the surface, bubbling hot liquid was melting the ice on which she skated. If she ever broke through that thin layer of ice, she would be burned all over in a pain so terrible that she'd feel it all the rest of her life.

The day of her fifth birthday it happened. She broke through the ice.

She was playing kick the can with some of the kids on the block whose parents hadn't taken a beach house for the summer or sent their kids to sleep-away camp.

Vicky had pleaded with her father to play the game with her and her friends, and because it was her birthday, he'd agreed. He was told to hide his eyes and count to one hundred, while Vicky and her friends hid behind the bushes, the trees, and the parked cars. Then when Jack went to look for the children in their hiding places, the ones who were the most daring ran home to base and tried to kick the can before Jack could tag them. If anyone was tagged before kicking the can, then that child would be 'it' next time.

As soon as her father started to count, Vicky scrambled behind a nearby bush, keeping her eyes glued to her father's back. This was an easy hiding place, but Jack was new at the game and wouldn't know that.

Jack had counted as far as twenty-five when a long, white car with a convertible top folded down across the back came gliding slowly down the street and stopped at the curb in front of where Jack stood hiding his eyes.

Peeking through the bushes of her hiding place, Vicky could see it very clearly. She had never seen a car so big, and so white, or a lady so beautiful as the one driving it. 'Twenty-nine, thirty,' Jack called out and walked toward the car. Vicky noticed that the lady's golden hair fell in waves down her back, just like a waterfall Vicky had once drawn in a picture at school. For some reason Vicky held her breath.

'Thirty-two, thirty-three,' Jack called. He was smiling and laughing at something the woman was saying, and though he didn't have his eyes shut any longer, Vicky could tell that he wasn't peeking either; he had lost interest in the game. The woman said something to him, and he answered, 'I can't. I'm playing a game with the kids.' Vicky heard his words with great relief and let out a huge swallow of air. But her heart was beginning to beat very fast.

'Thirty-eight, thirty-nine, forty!' Jack called again.

Then the lady reached across the large white leather front seat and opened the door of the car on the side where Jack was standing. The car was so big that she almost disappeared when she leaned over to open the door. Vicky couldn't hear the words, but it was clear the lady wanted Jack to get into the car.

'Martha, Martha, what am I going to do with you?' he said. And then, 'Forty-one, forty-two.'

Vicky's heart skipped a beat as he climbed into the car and closed the door. And then he gave one backward glance and waved at the bush where Vicky was standing.

By the time Vicky had counted to fifty, the car was out of sight.

She never saw her father again.

The ringing of her buzzer interrupted Vicky's reverie. Her joint was dead in the ashtray on the coffee table next to her; only a few puffs had been taken from it. Who was buzzing her at twelve thirty at night? she wondered.

'It's me, Ms Feinstein—Debra,' the young voice answered when she inquired who was there. 'May I come up?'

Even over the intercom Vicky could tell that Debra was crying.

She buzzed open the front door and then quickly sprayed the room with freshener, putting her half-smoked joint back into the box on the bookshelf where she kept her stash; there were never any more joints in the box than three or four at a time. She kept it in the house more to be sociable than for herself.

From the looks of Debra Winokur, she'd been crying all evening. Her makeup was streaked, her eyes red and puffy, her hair disheveled. She stepped into the foyer of the condominium, put her arms around Vicky, and hung on tightly.

Vicky was moved by the gesture and held the girl until she calmed down. Debra gave the appearance of being so sophisticated and worldly, but she was only a child in a woman's body. And it was obvious to Vicky that the girl was needy for more than just affection and comfort. She was begging for someone to set limits for her; she wanted to be protected from herself.

'What's wrong, Debra?' Vicky asked. She led the girl into the living room. 'What are you doing out at this hour?'

Debra turned her huge tragic eyes on Vicky, her lower lip trembling. 'I've run away from home.'

'I see,' Vicky replied, keeping her expression impassive as she always did with Debra's histrionics. The girl needed a calm, unperturbed facade against which to batter her emotions. Eventually she'd lead Vicky to the heart of her problem if Vicky only listened nonjudgmentally and lent a sympathetic ear.

Vicky had an innate ability to reach her more troubled students. She knew exactly what they were feeling when they hid their pain and acted out in ways that relieved them for the moment but that caused them no end of controversy, especially with their parents and other authority figures. Vicky knew how they felt because she'd done the same things herself.

'Do you want to tell me about it?' Vicky asked, indicating for her guest to be seated.

Debra shook her head no, and glanced around the apartment, appraising it with a mature disdain. 'This place is ok-ay,' she said. 'A bit unimaginative and commercial, but then you're not the custom-decorator type, are you?'

The competitive comparison with Debra's mother was not lost on Vicky. 'I'm glad you like the apartment, Debra.' Vicky waited for the girl's lead.

But Debra wasn't in the mood for confiding. It was enough that she'd shown her vulnerability. Now she had to regroup for a while and save face. She got up and walked around the room, studying Vicky's collection of lithographs—a Miró, a Diebenkorn, several original drawings by artists who hadn't yet made it. She took in the well-tended plants, the natural oak furniture, the view of the city from the front window.

'Got another joint?' she asked abruptly, glancing at the aerosol can that Vicky had left on the side table.

Vicky winced and admonished herself silently for being careless. She supposed the scent of pot still lingered in the air in spite of her precautions.

'Where do you keep it?' Debra asked. Like a blood-hound she had honed in on the one thing that truly interested her at the moment. 'In that box over there?'

Vicky tried not to smile. It was a pretty obvious hiding place, she realized. A carved teak Indian box from Pier 1 Imports was where everybody had kept their stash when she was in college. It never occurred to her to change it.

She ignored Debra's question and countered with one of her own. 'Why are you here?'

Debra's expression turned more sober and she came back to where Vicky was sitting on the sofa. 'I wanted to ask you if I might stay with you a while.'

Vicky just looked at her. 'Did something happen?'

'Nothing blatant,' Debra insisted. 'I just finally got fed up with *her* attitude. Her values suck, you know that?'

A litany against Debra's mother, Leslie Paxton Winokur, was nothing new, but Vicky sensed an underlying current on Debra's complaints tonight. 'How's Morgan?' she asked. Morgan Coombs was Debra's boyfriend, a senior at Howard Academy, an exclusive boys' school in Pasadena, and as troubled as Debra. Vicky thought of the two of them as mischievous monkeys egging each other on.

'Don't ever mention his name to me again, all right?' Debra snapped. 'As far as he and my mother are concerned, I might as well be dead. He doesn't understand me, all right? But then, how could he? He's got problems that make mine look like kiddie games.'

Vicky nodded. 'And it takes one to know one? Right?'

'Very funny.'

'Debra. Your mother will be worried about you. Don't you think you should call her?'

'Let her worry, let them all worry,' Debra replied. 'Besides, she doesn't care anyway. I waited all evening for her to come home so I could talk to her about something very important. And when she came home she stayed on the phone for the entire time. I told her I needed to talk to her but it was "not now, Debby," or "when I'm through with this call, Debby." So I waited some more while she bathed and dressed and made up her face with the receiver glued to her ear, and then she left without talking to me, damn her. Gone with the wind and the exhaust from her Rolls.'

Vicky could see how hurt Debra was. She hadn't been this agitated in a long time; in fact Debra'd been behaving more calmly lately, had been less volatile. She'd toned down her use of makeup and profanity, and Vicky had thought she was getting through to the girl. But tonight her hostility was full blown again and so Vicky waited for it all to come out, knowing that sooner or later it would. If not tonight then some other time.

Debra sighed and flopped down on the sofa opposite Vicky, crossing her legs Indian style. Vicky noted the expensive lizard sandals, the skin-tight jeans, the wild printed Kenzai sweater, the Fendi clutch bag. Debra was wearing one of the most expensive sportswear wardrobes in town.

'What did you want to talk to your mother about?' Vicky asked.

Debra replied in a small voice, 'It's not what you think.'

Vicky waited.

'You won't tell anyone, will you?'

'You know I won't, Debra.' She pulled her chenille bathrobe more tightly around her waist.

'It's about my brother.' She paused as though to gather courage; took a deep breath, and began her story. 'This afternoon I went into Terry's room looking for a pen—mine had run out of ink. I opened his drawer—I wasn't snooping, I really needed a pen.' She waited for Vicky's nod.

'And you know what I found? A whole bunch of camping knives. You know the kind, where the fork and the corkscrew and the nail file are all inside, but if you try to get the different gadgets to come out, you break your fingernails?' Vicky nodded, smiling. 'Every kid loves to have a knife like that, but my brother Terry had at least ten in his drawer.

124

Nobody could love them that much, unless they were really weird. And then I realized he had probably swiped them.' Her eyes held a pained expression as she talked.

'I was so furious with him,' Debra said. 'I thought, *not you too, Terry!* He's only a kid, eleven years old, you know? So I waited till he came home from school and asked him into my room.' She smiled at the memory. 'He's never allowed in my room and this really amazed him. He came in with his arms folded across his chest, real tough, kinda like me.' She stood up and demonstrated how her brother had looked with his arms folded across his chest and his head cocked in a defiant manner; Vicky saw what a natural mime she was, how talented. If only that talent could be channeled.

'Go on,' Vicky encouraged.

'So he shuffles in.' Debra walked just like her brother, back toward the sofa. 'And I patted the bed next to me for him to sit down.' She laughed in spite of her seriousness as she sat back on the sofa with the same motion her brother must have used. 'He was trying to be cool, but he was blown away. Never, I mean *never* is Terrence allowed on my satin quilt. So he sits down, and I put my arm around him, and . . .' Her voice quavered as a look of sadness swept over her. 'And I go . . . "I know all about the knives, Terry," ' She looked at Vicky with misery on her face. 'He started making a bunch of excuses, but I wouldn't let him. "I don't want you to say anything right now," I told him, "not a word. Just listen to me." ' Tears were glistening in Debra's eyes, but she controlled herself and wiped them away. 'I told him, "If you don't understand what I'm saying, then stop me and I'll say it again, okay?" And he nodded.' Debra's face was glazed with the pain of the memory but Vicky was gratified that her ability to relate to her brother honestly and openly was a result of what she had learned from the process of conversations with Vicky.

'I had to make him understand he shouldn't interrupt me, Ms Feinstein. He's got as smart a mouth as I do and I was afraid he'd make some crack and I'd get mad and not be able to tell him what I had to tell him.'

'You showed great patience and wisdom with him, Debra,' Vicky told her.

The girl gave her a shy smile of gratitude.

'So I said, "Terry, I know you took those knives, but you can't keep them. You have to give them back." He looked very scared, but he didn't say anything, just nodded. "I'm going to go with you when you take them back so you don't have to be scared," I told him. "We'll go to all the stores where you've stolen things and we'll tell them that you and I came by these things accidentally and they don't belong to us and that's why we're bringing them back." I was very firm about it so that there was no way for him to get out of it. And then . . .and then . . .' Her eyes filled with tears once more, her lips shook, and her voice grew tight as she tried to talk through the emotion. 'I said, "Honey . . ." ' The tears were spilling over now, and this time she couldn't control them; she cried openly. Vicky had never seen her cry like this with such a deep inner pain.

'And I said, "Honey, you don't have to take things from the store ever again. Because you're only doing that to get someone to notice you and love you . . .I know that because that's why I do it." ' She was crying harder now. 'And I said, "I love you, Terry. I love you very much. You don't have to steal to get someone to love you." ' A sob punctuated each word and she wiped at her nose with her arm. Vicky reached into her robe pocket and handed a package of tissues to Debra, overwhelmed by the courage the girl was showing.

'And he hugged me back, Ms Feinstein. He hugged me so hard. That same brother who hasn't come near me in years. And I kept saying over and over, "I love you, Terry. It doesn't matter what Mom does; I'm here. It's gonna be all right." '

And with that Debra put her head down on her knees and sobbed as if her heart were breaking. Finally the sadness passed, but still she stayed there for a while, her head on her arms, her body shaking from the aftermath.

Vicky came around and sat next to Debra, putting her arm around the girl and hugging her tightly. 'You've done a wonderful thing for your brother, Debra,' she said. 'You really reached him. You got through all his defenses and reassured his most basic fear. I'm very proud of you.' She waited until Debra's body had stopped trembling. 'But why does it make you so sad?' Vicky asked.

Debra raised her tear-stained face and leaned her head against Vicky. 'Because,' she said, 'I kept thinking over and over, why didn't somebody ever do that for me?'

Vicky felt a stab of sorrow pierce her heart as she hugged the girl. 'I don't know, Debra,' she replied. 'I just don't know why some of us don't get what we need. But we can learn to do that for ourselves.'

She was so absorbed in Debra's pain that she was startled by the chiming of the clock on the mantel. It was one thirty already. 'I had no idea it was so late,' she said gently. 'Would you like to stay here with me tonight? We could talk some more.'

Debra nodded with a grateful smile.

'Then why don't you call your mom, tell her where you are while I go and get you some clean sheets for the sofa bed.'

It was as if Vicky had slapped her. 'No!' Debra shouted. 'I will not call her. Haven't you been listening to me? Don't you see what she's done to me and now to my brother? She doesn't deserve anyone's consideration—least of all mine.'

Vicky took hold of her hand to calm her again, but she yanked it away.

'Debra,' Vicky pleaded, 'I'm your teacher, not your school chum. And I'm an adult. I'm responsible for your safety while you're in my home. I cannot let you stay here without notifying your mother where you are and that you are safe. It wouldn't be right of me.'

Debra stopped her protest but glared at Vicky with obvious fury. Vicky's heart felt bruised as though all the progress and all the closeness had just been destroyed. But she had to do what was right. Good or bad, a parent had a right to know where her child was.

'I'll make the call for you, if you like,' she offered.

Debra nodded, stiffly. 'First can I have a Coke or a diet drink?'

Vicky was only too glad to oblige.

But when she returned from the kitchen, Coke and ice in hand, Debra was gone, and so were the four joints Vicky had saved in her carved Indian box.

Oh, Debra, Vicky thought, *you foolish child.* She went right to the phone and dialed Mrs Winokur's home.

No one answered.

On the twentieth ring she hung up. Where was Mrs Winokur? Where were the servants and Debra's brother? Didn't they answer the phone if Mrs Winokur wasn't home? And then she realized that it was a good thing Terry hadn't been awakened by the phone. There was no reason to bring to the attention of an eleven-year-old boy that his sister had run away and his mother was unavailable. *This is criminal,* she thought. She had an impulse to drive across town and ring that bell, pound on the door until someone inside acknowledged that Debra was missing. If they didn't care, at least they'd know about it. Her frustration was maddening and she had a slight inkling of what Debra must have gone through for her entire life.

It wasn't until the next morning that Vicky reached Debra's mother.

'Mrs Winokur, it's Ms Feinstein,' she said with a rush. 'I've been so worried about Debra. Is she all right?'

There was a long silence at the other end and then the bitter invective of Leslie Paxton Winokur came blasting through. 'You have some nerve to call here after what you've done.'

Vicky's heart leaped to her throat. 'What is it? What's wrong, Mrs Winokur? Is Debra all right?'

'She is now, no thanks to you. She was arrested last night and taken to Juvenile Hall for having the drugs she got from you. I hold you fully responsible for this!'

'Oh, no!' Vicky cried. 'They must have picked her up

128

after she left my house.'

'Then she was with you. You admit it?'

'Yes, but—'

Leslie didn't let her finish. 'Why in God's name didn't you call me?'

'I did,' Vicky insisted. 'I called you several times. No one answered.'

'That's a lie. I have a twenty-four-hour answering service on my phone and they are extremely reliable. If you had called me, I would know about it. I certainly got the message from the police that they were holding my daughter.'

Vicky felt her anger rising. She'd be damned if this obnoxious woman was going to get the best of her. 'I don't care what you say about your reliable answering service. I called last night, several times, to inform you of Debra's actions and her state of mind and no one answered.'

'Well, that's beside the point, considering what you've done. I'm going to see that criminal charges are pressed against you,' Leslie said, foaming with rage.

'Why?' Vicky asked, dumbfounded. 'What have I done?'

'As if you didn't know! Debra was arrested for possession of marijuana that you gave to her, Ms Feinstein. The girl is in a great deal of trouble thanks to you. And even if she only receives probation because it's her first offense, she still has to appear at a hearing, and so do I. Do you know what that means to me? And then she has to face possible expulsion from Southwick. My daughter! Well, let me tell you, she is not going to be the one to suffer for this crime. You are!'

The next two days were a nightmare for Vicky. The students all gossiped, the faculty speculated, and Vicky wrestled with her conscience. Debra had lied. She'd taken the marijuana without permission and didn't want to be accused of stealing. But her lie had really put Vicky in a terrible bind. Now Vicky might have to lie too. There was no proof that the drugs found on Debra had come from Vicky. Debra could have gotten them anywhere. But

Vicky's consciense tormented her. If she hadn't had the marijuana on her premises, Debra couldn't have taken it.

If only she could talk to Debra, get her to admit the truth. But Debra wasn't in school and Vicky couldn't go to her house. All she could do was hold her head high and go on with her work.

When the summons came at the end of the second day to report to the headmaster's office, Vicky thought she was prepared. She had run the gamut from despair to depression and back to despair again, feeling certain she could get them to understand her side of the story without making it look too bad for Debra. After all, she was the teacher and should have more credibility than a troubled student. But the former headmaster's words haunted her. 'If there is even a touch of controversy in your life or the slightest blemish on your record, you will be dismissed.' And she was filled with dread. What would she do without her job? If they fired her, she'd never get another teaching position. Who would hire a private-school teacher with a tainted reputation? And it was so unfair! She was innocent.

Mr Sonnegaard, who had taken over the headmaster's job following Mr Beckwirth's retirement, was thirty-eight years old; he had a pink complexion, white-blond thinning hair, and an oily film ever present on his forehead in spite of constant wiping. On the surface he was a sincere and soft-spoken man, but he had an inner core as unyielding as a rod of steel.

'You know, of course, that I must ask for your resignation,' he began without preliminary.

Suddenly all of Vicky's explanations died in her throat. She hadn't expected this to come so quickly and be so hurtful. All the fear, tension, and feelings of injustice broke through and she lost control, bursting into tears, sobbing in misery. 'I haven't done anything,' she managed to say.

'Ms Feinstein.' He spoke with a touch of sympathy. 'It is not my place to judge the way you have chosen to live your personal life, or how you wish to abuse your physical health, but you are a teacher, responsible for setting a moral standard for your pupils. You have beeen sadly remiss in setting that example. After this unfortunate incident your reputation has been ruined. I'm afraid that it can never be regained.'

'But it is my word against hers,' she insisted, refusing to accept his verdict that she was now 'damaged goods.' 'I am not admitting that Debra got the marijuana from me, but if she did, she stole it. I also happen to have some codeine in my medicine cabinet from when I sprained my wrist last year. Suppose she had taken that? Would you still think I was such a moral leper?'

'The fact remains'—he pursed his lips together in a line of distaste—'that we are discussing an illegal substance the child says she got from you, not a prescription drug.' She could see he wanted to say, 'Tsk, tsk, tsk,' but was restraining himself.

'Most of the teachers in this faculty use some form of drug in a social context,' she countered.

He seemed to bristle with indignation. 'Don't try to shift the blame from your shoulders to others' because you do not wish to accept the consequences of your own choices. What you say about your fellow faculty members may or may not be true. I know it isn't true for me, and even if it were, it is distasteful to hear you stoop so low as to accuse others just to mitigate your own guilty conscience. Now, even if Mrs Winokur was not pressing for your dismissal. I would not keep you. I have the reputation of our school to consider.'

'But this is my life we're discussing,' she pleaded. 'My career. What about the grave consequences I'm suffering being accused of something I haven't done?'

He softened his tone again but Vicky could see she was fighting a losing battle. 'It's not merely the narcotics issue,' he stated. 'Mrs Winokur is most insistent that there were other, even more serious complaints. She has accused you of fomenting a rebelliousness in her daughter against her own authority as a parent. It is true, isn't it, that you have befriended the Winokur girl far beyond the customary pupil-teacher relationship? That she did come to your home the other evening, seeking support for her cause in a disagreement with her mother?'

'The child was suffering, Mr Sonnegaard. What would you have me do, ignore her pain the way her mother does?'

'There, you see!' he said, almost pointing a finger at her. 'That's exactly the kind of attitude a teacher must guard against; we must be ultra-cautious to avoid the specter of such misconceptions and not interfere among family members.'

Vicky was nearly in tears again from frustration, and he looked down at his hands, uncomfortable with her suffering. 'I am aware of your zeal and enthusiasm as a teacher, Ms Feinstein,' he said. 'And there have been times when you have overstepped certain bounds without adverse consequences—I guess we all do. But this incident is different. It's become too public, and it's messy; it can't be ignored. This time there is a parent of the highest standing who wishes you dismissed. Ordinarily I would never allow a parent to dictate to me who remains on my staff, but the extenuating circumstances have changed all that. The board, too, is very sympathetic to Mrs Winokur's complaints—after all, she's made valuable donations to this school. We are greatly in her debt here at Southwick.'

'So you'll take her daughter's word over mine because she's a wealthy contributor when you know my work is of the highest standard?' Some of her devastation was giving way to anger. 'I'm an excellent, dedicated teacher. Even Mr Beckwirth said so.'

'I know you are,' he agreed with a degree of sympathy. 'But your record will not hold up under scrutiny. Do you know about this?' He picked up a letter from his desk.

She didn't want to ask about it, but she couldn't help herself. 'What is it?'

'It was in your file. It's a letter from a member of our board of directors. I never would have seen it myself if Mrs Winokur hadn't lodged her complaint against you. But now

I have seen it and it's very damaging to you. In light of both these complaints I have no choice but to ask you to leave.'

Vicky took the letter from him; the paper rattled in her trembling hand. It wasn't from Leslie Paxton Winokur; it was from Belson McKintridge and it had been written following Vicky's altercation with him at Phyllis's wedding. *I should have known.* Vicky thought.

It was a scathing diatribe. He called her morally corrupt, accused her of seductive and reprehensible behavior, stated that she had been guilty of aborting her baby when it was illegal to do so, and threatened to withdraw his support from the board of directors if they didn't fire her. *Bless Mr Beckwirth,* she thought, *for suppressing this explosive information for so long.* Beckwirth must have been tougher than anyone imagined to stand up to Belson McKintridge and not fire her three years ago. How could she fight this? she wondered. With two powerful enemies against her she didn't have a chance. The irony was the Belson believed she'd had an abortion when she was in high school.

If she wasn't so angry with Debra, she would have felt sympathy for her, to be cursed with a mother like Leslie Paxton Winokur. But Vicky was the one who needed sympathy right now. She was the victim of jealous, self-righteous snobs, of vicious, cruel behavior. What had she ever done to deserve such treatment?

And what could she do about it? Dear God, what could she do? How was she going to live with all this consuming hatred she felt for Belson McKintridge and Leslie Paxton Winokur? A hatred so strong it made her think of murder, a hatred so hot it rivaled the flames of hell.

Under Mr Sonnegaard's watchful eye she summoned the last ounce of her courage, gathered up her battered self-respect, and left his office. 'We'll get a substitute for you immediately,' he said as she closed the door.

She stepped blindly into the hall; utter despair clouded her mind and shaking terror filled her insides with jelly. It seemed as though the students passing her knew everything she'd done, knew all her secrets. They could see the ugly scales on her body, the horns protruding from her scalp. And as their eyes met hers with knowing looks, she felt cheap and poor and undesirable. Even her brain felt dead though she was grateful for the numbness of shock; when it wore off, she didn't think she could stand the pain of this cruel rejection, the shame of this loss.

She didn't realize she was holding her breath until she reached her car and unlocked the door. And then as the pent-up heat inside the car enveloped her and she exhaled, all the built-up agony slashed through her reserve and the pain nearly blinded her. *Oh, God, oh, God,* she screamed, but the scream was silent, and more intense because it was inside her head. *Don't let go of it here,* she thought, *wait until you get home. Don't let them know what they've done to you.*

And so, with deliberate calm, as careful as a novice ascetic on his first bed of nails, she drove home to the safety of her modest four walls amidst the golden palaces around her, where she could cry, and exhort the gods, and think about dying while she tried to salvage what was left of Vicky Feinstein.

Chapter 5

LARRY GILBERT'S feet were up high on his country French desk and he leaned way back in the matching upholstered desk chair, gazing at the view of Beverly Hills from his luxurious office, while he listened to his wife's friend, Vicky, tell her tale of woe. When she finally finished, he brought his gaze back to her and clucked his tongue in sympathy. 'It's a real tough break, baby. You've been shafted royally and by my wife's boss and my partner's grandfather. Small world. But as far as I can see, there's no legal recourse open to you.'

She was annihilating a piece of Kleenex as she listened to him, her large brown eyes were filled with pain and underscored by dark circles.

'Of course, it's not my specialty. If your problem related to acquisitions, or escrow instructions, or revisions of wills or property law, I'd be your man. Maybe you ought to see an Equal Employment Opportunity counselor, or the state agency of Fair Employment, or the ACLU.'

'I've been there,' she said. 'They don't think I have a case.'

'Because it's a private school?' he asked.

'Yes.'

He took his feet down from the desk and leaned on it with his elbows. 'Let me explain about private schools. They come under the rules of private-enterprise laws. If the school hasn't discriminated against you for race, country of national origin, sex, age, or disability, then they have the right to fire you. Is that what they told you, the agency lawyers?'

She nodded sadly.

'You might have a case if you sued them for inflicting emotional distress. Then you'd be able to collect punitive damages, but those cases are difficult to win. Or if you sued for your job back and won, you'd be reinstated in a school that didn't want you and you'd be trying to teach students who gossiped about you.'

Vicky cringed at the idea.

'It really is a rotten break,' he said with sympathy. 'Suppose I have a talk with Leslie Paxton Winokur? See if I can get her to back off?'

'I've been to see her already,' Vicky admitted. 'It was one of the hardest things I've ever done and one of the most horrible experiences. She screamed at me, called me names I've never even heard of. She's a real witch, that woman. There's no chance there.'

'How are you handling it?' he asked.

She looked at him and he could see what these past weeks had done to her. She seemed lost and frightened. Gone was the confident, spunky young woman he knew. 'It's taken its toll on my self-esteem, which was never my strongest asset. I've been furious and sick, and very sorry for myself. Oh, yes, a lot sorry for myself. Right now I'm kind of numb, as though this can't possibly have happened to me.'

'Ever thought about changing your profession?' he joked. 'Maybe you'd enjoy a career in law?'

But her sense of humor had been lost along with her job and her eyes filled with tears. 'I'm already educated, thank you. I have a profession I like. I only wish I could work at it.'

'What about switching to the public-school system?'

'The public system is in mess right now, with busing and all. If I'm assigned to inner city, I'd have unruly students and violence to contend with. Not a pleasant prospect after the insular world of Southwick.'

'That situation won't last forever.'

'Well, right now Judge Egly is in charge and he keeps ruling in favor of busing. It will be a long time before the State Supreme Court hears the case.' She looked off into space. 'Maybe this was meant to be. Maybe I should be philosophical about it and try to find something positive out of all this mess. I could end up feeling grateful to Mr McKintridge and Mrs Winokur for getting me fired. And someday when I'm successful and Barbara Walters interviews me, I can say I owe it all to them. If it hadn't been for their cruel viciousness, I wouldn't be where I am today.' She gave him a rueful smile and stood up to go. He came around the desk and gave her a kiss while she clung to him gratefully. 'Speaking of favors. Do me one, will you? Don't tell Marla about this right away. I'd like to tell her myself when I'm ready.'

'Don't worry,' he said. 'I hardly ever see her; she's so busy lately with her *job*.'

'Well, she'd better be careful of her boss, Larry. The lady's a baracuda.'

He smiled.

'And thank you,' she said as she left.

What a tough break, he thought. *A nice kid like Vicky.* But she'd probably land on her feet, she was sharp and attractive. As he watched her tight little ass swing out the door, he could feel the stirrings of desire in his groin. *Not now, Gilbert,* he thought. *Down boy.* But there was something about the stress of her situation, the helplessness and the need to protect her, that really turned him on. He wished Marla needed him like that.

Larry pushed open the oak door to the Saloon and entered the crowded foyer; he waved to Mike, the maître d', and headed for the bar. It was overflowing as usual at this hour with medium-top executives and fairly attractive women quenching their thirsts, vying for position, checking each other out. The great singles rat race; he loved it.

He tried not to think of Marla as he edged his way in, saying hello to the regulars he knew, avoiding some greetings, accepting kisses and handshakes. Marla had been disappointed when he told her he wasn't coming home for dinner. She said she had champagne on ice and scampi for dinner, and when he questioned her on her sudden domesticity, she'd gotten angry.

'The children want to see their father, Larry, and I have a surprise for you.'

Well, surprises would have to wait, this was business. *Sort of.*

Sheila was sitting at the end of the bar, wearing a low-cut blouse; her long blond hair flowed around her shoulders, and she gave him that delectable smile. No wonder she was the top-selling newcomer in the Goldman office. He had a wild fantasy that he'd like to remove her clothes, one by one, in a striptease, and then screw her right on the bar at the Saloon, while the other guys drooled over his technique and her desirability. Or maybe she'd go down on him while he sat at the bar on a stool, sipping his Beefeater's martini, with that yellow hair all silky and loose, like a wheatfield blowing in the wind.

She had a drink waiting for him, and as he moved over her to reach it, she rubbed her hip against him and smiled into his eyes.

'Drink up so we can blow this joint,' she said. 'I've only got two hours. We'll have to eat and screw before eight thirty so I can pick up a deposit receipt from a client who's making an offer on a house.'

'Another sale? Jesus, you're phenomenal.' He took a generous swallow of his drink and patted her knee. 'Forget about the dinner, baby. Because I plan to do you real good tonight. I'm going to start at your toes and work my way up, down, and sideways. And when you've had your third come, you're going to forget every other man you ever met.'

Her lips were moist as she smiled at him. 'What you do to me, lover.'

He reached his hand under her long hair and fondled the side of her neck.

'And what do *you* want?' she asked.

'Nothing, baby, it's your turn tonight.'

'You must want something, or it would be in-and-out as usual.'

'Am I that callous?' he said, pretending to be offended. She didn't get where she was by being stupid.

'Yes. Now tell me what you want so I can really enjoy my reward.'

'I want to try and acquire the property on Wilshire from the southwest corner of Hickory, west to the middle of the block. I only want to pay five dollars a foot and I want it yesterday. I understand from Peter that Felix Anhalt is interested in it, and if I can deliver it I know he'll be in my pocket for good. I want his business and this is the way to get it, not through nepotism. So far in the past three years he's only given me and Peter handouts.'

'Forget it,' Sheila said. 'I'd like to help you, but that

property is not for sale. Those stores are newly remodeled, which means the tenants have new leases. It's owned by the Carmichael Corporation and they have plans of their own three years down the line.'

'But, Sheila baby, give it a try. I know you can work miracles.'

She laughed, acknowledging his flattery. 'You're right, Larry, I do work miracles. And I know Flynn Carmichael very well. I'll see what I can do.'

He breathed a sigh of relief and felt the fire for her go out of his loins. She was on his side. She'd get him the options on that property if it was at all possible and that's all he wanted from her. Now he had to deliver on his promise of a monumental fuck. He shouldn't have told her what he wanted from her until after the sex, then he could have remained hot for her all evening, keeping himself hard with the promise of what she might do, stroking himself with the conquest. But now that he had what he wanted, it was all downhill. Damn, it was always like that, except with Marla.

He took a sip from his drink and tried not to feel guilty about Marla waiting at home for him with champagne, scampi, and a surprise. She probably wanted to tell him about some new work assignment. Damn! When was she going to see that two careers under one roof were impossible? She was so damned stubborn, it drove him wild. And another thing that drove him wild was imagining what she did all day when she was away from him. Whom was she with? The thought of her with another man sickened him. When *he* screwed around, it was a different thing altogether. His women meant nothing to him, but he didn't want Marla doing it. She was his wife; they belonged to one another. What if she found someone else and left him? He couldn't bear the idea. Couldn't she see how much he needed her at home, to be his wife, to show him she really loved him? She didn't used to be so independent. When they were first married, she was sweet and loving. If only that had been enough for him. Why did he have to make love to everything in skirts? The question perplexed him, yet he couldn't leave the ladies alone. Just like his old man.

When Larry was sixteen and a half he fell in love with Ardis McCoy. Ardis was eighteen and graduating from Uni High that June, but Larry looked much older than his age, and his early experiences with women had given him an air of sophistication beyond his years. He had been initiated into the delights of sex by ladies in their twenties. He had made love to wives of his father's friends and female tennis partners sometimes ten years older than himself. 'My son's a natural born lover,' his father would say, 'just like his old man.'

But Dave Gilbert was clearly the expert and he never let Larry forget it. Any woman who had a soft place between her legs was fair game and he rattled off the statistics of his latest conquests to his wide-eyed son as soon as Larry reached puberty. It killed Larry to know what he had to compete with. His father still had bed privileges with almost every one of his former lovers, a real test of a cocksman, including Larry's mother, for as long as ten years after their divorce, whenever he came around, which wasn't often, considering the frantic nature of his father's sex life. 'Hey, Flo. How ya doin', baby?' Dave would say as he'd sidle into the kitchen where they were just about to eat Larry's mother's famous brisket of beef. Dave would grin that rakish lopsided grin of his, and that's all he'd have to do. 'Want some brisket, Dave?' his mother would say. And Dave would reply, 'And that's not all I want, gorgeous.' It made Larry sick, but he had to admire the technique. And except for the way Dave treated Larry's mother, Larry wanted to be exactly like him. At least he did at sixteen. But at that age he knew he had a long way to go.

The day Larry got Ardie's parents to agree to let her spend the weekend at his father's condo at La Costa was the happiest day in Larry's sixteen and a half years. Of course Larry told the McCoys that his father would chaperon them and be their constant companion, and Ardie would have her own room. Larry typed a letter full of these promises, worded it like an invitation from an adult, signed it with the exact replica of his father's signature he had perfected over the years, and then presented it to Mr and Mrs McCoy. They were pleased to say yes.

Larry spent days describing to Ardie the sensual delights of the La Costa Spa, the fun of riding horseback along the beach at Del Mar, the great tennis matches they would have—Larry was nearly pro status, and Ardie wasn't bad either—and of course the wonderful restaurants in the La Costa complex where they would dine courtesy of Dave Gilbert's charge account.

When Larry and Ardis arrived at La Costa late Friday night, timed so that they were both hungry and tired, and discovered that Dave was on the road for two weeks and wouldn't be there to chaperon them, no one acted as surprised as Larry. How he cursed his father's poor memory and unreliability; how he berated himself for not calling earlier in the day to check things out. 'Only two days ago, when I talked to him, he promised to be here,' Larry said, in his most convincingly concerned voice. 'I'm so embarrassed.' He insisted that they drive home that very night, even though, he told her, 'I am feeling kind of dizzy and nauseated from the long drive.' He was banking on Ardie's sympathy. She wouldn't let him turn around and drive back. She was too considerate, too understanding, too tired, and too disappointed to go right back home.

And so they stayed. The scenario went exactly as planned.

Almost.

Either the excitement and anticipation of what would follow this evening's meal was making him slightly dizzy and nauseated, or it was something he ate. *He couldn't be getting sick.*

So Larry ignored his stomach and toasted Ardis with a bottle of wine, and then insisted that they drink some before, during, and after the sumptuous dinner they consumed at La Costa's Steak House where Larry easily passed for twenty-one. Ardis was charmed and compliant, demonstrative and captivated. After dinner they went back to the condo, walking along the darkened golf course under a canopy of brilliant stars. And when they began to neck on the sofa in front of the fireplace, Ardis was more passionate than she'd ever been. Gone were the restraints of 'no hands, please,' or 'no bare skin,' or 'no fondling, please either here, or there, and especially there!' She was his for the taking. And how delicately and tenderly he intended to take her. Even Dave Gilbert couldn't do it better.

He'd actually gotten one hand up her skirt as far as her thigh, and the other had just unhooked her bra, when the touch of dizziness and nausea he'd felt earlier began to work on him in earnest. It was all he could do to bolt for the bathroom, leaving his panting and clearly excited Ardis rather bewildered on the sofa.

When he returned twenty minutes later, weak and shaking from his ordeal, smelling of Lavoris, and devastated to recognize the clear symptoms of the stomach flu in full swing, Ardis was sitting on the sofa exactly where he'd left her, deep in conversation with his father, who must have arrived unexpectedly while he was barfing his guts out in the bathroom. There were his father's suitcases dropped at the still open doorway, his coat flung over a nearby chair, and old Dad had already made a beeline for the honey pot his son had so kindly provided and was in no condition to protect. Nooo, Larry groaned, as King Bee moved in for the nectar.

Approval? Was that the expression on Dave's face as he gazed at Ardis, who was hanging on his every word? Larry had to laugh at that idea, sick as he was. *Large lech* was more like it. *But why my girl?* he thought. *Why mine?*

And Larry's heart sank into his traumatized stomach as he saw his girl looking at his father with the same expression his mother got every time Dave breezed in the kitchen door. And in that moment Larry changed his mind about the kind of woman he wanted to marry. She would have two important requirements. Not only would she have to

142

make him cream at first glance, but she would be the only woman in captivity who would not—repeat, not—succumb to the charms of Dave Gilbert.

And that was Marla.

He knew it the first moment he saw her refuse to dance with his father at his Cousin Tony's bar mitzvah. Everyone was there that night at Temple Emanuel social hall in Beverly Hills; his Aunt Laurel and his Uncle Henry the dentist (the proud parents of the bar mitzvah boy), his mother, wearing a new fuchsia dress and nervous because his father was there, and of course his father (the dapper son of a bitch) wearing a navy blazer with a white open-collared shirt to show off his fabulous tan and new gabardine bell bottoms that made his tush look great. Larry felt awkward and unattractive by comparison in his old tweed blazer; he'd had it since his freshman year at UCLA and now he was a senior.

Larry spotted Marla during the service, sitting a few rows in front of him across the aisle. He studied her now and then and caught her looking at him a couple of times, but he was afraid to seem too interested or his father, who could also see her, would notice and hone right in.

Larry thought she was very beautiful. She had dark hair and a full face, incredibly long eyelashes, and gorgeous blue eyes like Elizabeth Taylor's. She wasn't as pretty as Elizabeth Taylor, but when she smiled, big dimples appeared in her cheeks. Later at the reception he noticed that she had a voluptuous figure and great knockers.

Larry watched her help herself to dessert and take a seat at a table with her parents. He helped his mother do the same and sat down, waiting for a chance to approach her.

They were making great eye contact and he was about to make his move when suddenly from out of nowhere his father approached her table. Larry's heart twisted in his chest as he watched his father give the girl and her family a winning smile. He shook hands with her parents, told them a joke, and made them all laugh. And then he leaned in to her, gazing down at her, right into her cleavage.

Larry didn't want to watch, but he couldn't tear his eyes away.

And then as though he could hear the words from across the room, his father asked her to dance.

She said no. Dimples and all, she said no!

Handsome Dave shrugged his well-tailored shoulders and walked away. And then the girl did the best thing of all. She looked over at Larry and smiled.

In that moment Larry knew he could love her.

'Hey, Larry, let's go,' Sheila said, bringing Larry back to the present.

'Yeah, sure,' he said, placing money down on the bar to pay for their drinks.

He waited for Sheila to put on her sweater and even though she gave him an impatient look, he didn't help her with it. He was impatient too. He didn't belong here. He belonged at home with his wife and kids. If only Marla wouldn't keep pulling away from him all the time, making him crazy, making him angry, making him want to get her, just get her.

'Shit,' he whispered under his breath. How was he ever going to get through this next hour? Oh, well, the old Gilbert technique had never let him down. And if it did, he could always use his old standby and fantasize about Marla.

Chapter 6

PETER TRIED to suppress his annoyance at being summoned to McKintridge today. For as much as he enjoyed going there, this was his Saturday, his one free day at home, and he wanted to spend it with Phyllis and the baby. He couldn't get enough of that baby; he didn't want to miss one magical moment in his son's brand-new life. How he loved to watch him nurse, observing the way his little mouth worked so earnestly as he sucked the milk from Phyllis's breast, or the way his eyelashes lay closed in contentment on his tiny cheeks; sometimes they would even flutter a bit from some infant fantasy. He loved the newborn scent of him; the way he looked when he was nude or swathed in baby clothes after his bath, and the feel of the baby in his arms was irresistible. And when Peter contemplated the blank slate of Jonathan's brain at six weeks old, just waiting for life to write its incredible lessons there, he was filled with such wonder he could hardly contain it. He wanted with all his heart for those lessons to be only beautiful ones. Of course, having Phyllis at home again in their bed made everything complete. While she was in the hospital with Jonathan, he missed her terribly.

More and more lately he had the feeling that life was just beginning for him now that he had entered the realm of fatherhood. At last he had a family of his own. He found himself thinking a great deal about his new role that had added tremendously to his sense of responsibility, sometimes to the point of being a burden, and yet it made him feel so important. He was quite humbled by the miracle of creation and wanted to be an active father, to take the kind of interest in Jonathan that no one had ever taken in him. But above all he wanted to stand as an example for the boy, teach him the right values, principles.

This is the first time I've ever been to McKintridge as a father, Peter thought with pride as he climbed the front steps.

The beautiful November day added an extra sense of poignancy to his mood of elation and suddenly he was glad he had come; it would be good to share his feelings of joy with his grandfather. The thought made him walk a bit taller.

Mr Albert, his grandfather's majordomo, escorted him to Belson's study, and Peter beamed as the kind black man offered effusive congratulations on the birth of his son.

'You'll be able to see him very soon,' Peter promised. 'We'll bring him over next week.' They both grinned at one another happily.

But the moment Peter stepped through the door of Belson's study into the large paneled room, his delight evaporated.

Something was wrong.

Belson's appearance shocked him. His eyes were sunken in his head and he was slumped so low in his bottle-green leather chair that the oily spot on the back of the seat where his head usually rested loomed a good six inches above him. Belson's hands lay on the fruitwood desk in front of him. They were clawlike and bony; the skin was stretched taut and looked waxen over the gnarled fingers. He looked so old, Peter wanted to cry.

'What is it, Grandfather?' he asked with alarm. 'Are you ill?'

'Sit down, Peter,' Belson directed.

Peter sat in a chair in front of the desk and gazed at his only living relative, while he tried not to imagine what had reduced his formidable grandfather into such a state of dejection. His fantasies were all morbid and he felt his formerly buoyant heart diving into his stomach. The fact of

146

Belson's advanced age had suddenly become a terrible reality to him, one he had deliberately been overlooking for some time. Seeing his grandfather like this, he could not do that any longer.

Belson sighed. 'This is very difficult for me to say, Peter, but I might as well say it straight out.' He paused as though to gather strength and another terrible clutching grabbed Peter's guts: this was going to be bad, very bad.

'The doctors have given me some terrible news, my boy. It's my heart. I have an inoperable blockage of the artery.' Belson's gaze moved slowly from Peter's face to the handsome photoportrait of himself above the mantel taken by George Hurrell when Belson was thirty-eight. The youthful, unlined face mocked him. 'Maybe I should have been a vegetarian, taken more vitamins when I was young, gotten into jogging. Well, no matter. There it is.'

Peter felt a sudden hot rush of fear course through his body, and he broke out into a cold, clammy sweat, *No!* he thought. *No, it can't be true. I don't want to lose him.*

Belson turned back to him. 'I know what you're going to say. Believe me, I've said it all to myself. I've consulted the best. They've poked and prodded me and dyed my arteries.' He shook his head slowly, hopelessly. 'There's nothing they can do. It's terminal.'

Peter didn't know what to say. He was fighting not to cry. Belson abhorred any display of sentiment. But Peter felt the depth of his hurt welling up in him as the sharp knife of loss ripped at him. Belson's eyes were boring into him, daring him to break down, and Peter dug his nails into his palms so he wouldn't, waiting for some indication that an embrace would be welcome, that there was even the smallest desire in Belson to share his grief and fear. But moments passed in silence and the only indication of need was two bright spots on Belson's cheeks showing his anxiety. The tension was almost palpable; Peter had no idea how to alleviate it. Finally Belson spoke.

'There's more bad news,' he stated flatly, and Peter further steeled himself. What more could there be?

'My financial empire is in a shambles.' Belson's voice was hoarse as he forced out the words. 'And in some ways this is even harder for me to face than my failing health because I've always prided myself on my brilliant business acumen.' He sighed with discouragement. 'But even brilliance when it is surrounded by incompetence can disintegrate. Don't ever make that mistake, Peter. Be certain, absolutely certain, that the people you choose to advise you are successful in their own right and have nothing to gain by your failure.'

'What are you saying, Grandfather?' Peter asked. 'What kind of a shambles?'

'All of it,' Belson said. 'I've lost everything. The only thing left intact and unencumbered is the house and acreage, and there's not enough money to run it for even another month.'

A moment ago Peter wouldn't have believed he could feel any more pain for his grandfather than he already had, but now he felt a deep, hot, agonizing rush of pain bolt through him, leaving him breathless, making his heart pound wildly. He could not bear to see what this was doing to Belson, a man who had always been impervious, a man who defied the gods. But Peter could see behind Belson's strong facade; this abject, miserable soul in front of him was hardly the same person and Peter shared his misery.

'Well, why don't you say something!' Belson burst forth suddenly. His exasperation banished the brief moment of pity he'd allowed himself, and annihilated any possibility of their moving closer. 'Why are you just sitting there staring at me like that? Didn't you hear what I said? I'm nearly broke! I have no liquid assets left. I shall have to mortgage the estate just to keep it afloat. And I'm dying! Every single beat of my heart brings me closer to death. Oh, what did I expect? What could I ever expect from you.'

Peter jumped out of his chair as if pulled by the pain of remorse, yanked by his inability to ever do the right thing. 'I'm sorry, Grandfather,' he stammered. 'What can I say to you, except that I'm sorry, and I love you,' he cried. 'I don't want to lose you.' He could feel his eyes welling up. *Oh, God, don't let me cry, not now,* he prayed.

Belson looked away, struggling with his emotions; Peter's outburst had touched him but he refused to allow himself to soften. He pulled his mantle of gruffness around him, and then he sighed. 'I wish instead of being sorry, you'd be helpful.' He paused to study Peter. 'Tell me, what would you do if you were in my predicament?'

Peter stared at him, dumbfounded. He hadn't the first inkling of what he would do if someone pronounced such sentences on him.

'Oh, stop pacing and sit down,' Belson said, losing his small amount of patience. 'I want you to listen to me.' Peter sat, gladly. His legs were barely holding him up.

'If I waited for your advice, I would atrophy and die a pauper sitting right here in this chair. Well, not I! I'm going to do something about it!'

Peter was caught up by awe and admiration; he'd always felt that for his grandfather and it returned in full force. The man had not been defeated after all, even in the face of everything that had happened. 'Are you going to tell me what you're going to do?'

'Why else do you think I asked you here, to listen to myself complain?' Belson said testily. And then seeing the hurt look on Peter's face, he turned away and cleared his throat before speaking again.

'I'm certain we both agree that the McKintridge estate must be preserved at all costs for you and your children and their children. It is your heritage, a symbol of our family's pride, much the same way the European castles are to their nobility; am I correct?'

'Of course,' Peter agreed readily. 'That goes without saying.' Ever since he could remember, his grandfather had fostered a love in him for this house and all it stood for, which only enhanced the way he felt about it himself. In loving the house he was loving his grandfather, and that, his

149

grandfather could understand. Every rock and stone, every pane of glass, every slate shingle on the roof, was precious to him.

'Well, I'll be damned if I'm going to lose it and leave my heirs with nothing but a memory. This house is the only thing that has ever meant anything to me. I refuse to let it go!'

It was painful for Peter to learn that the house was so much more important to his grandfather than he was, and yet he understood. He too could not bear to lose everything he held dear, namely this house and his grandfather, all at once. He'd always comforted himself in his darkest moments with the thought that the estate was the one place in all the world where he felt safe, and it would always be there for him, steadfast, even after his grandfather was gone. Now the thought that it wouldn't filled him with an icy terror, completely overwhelming him. Suddenly he longed for Phyllis to be here with him, to hold him and comfort him. He felt lost and alone and unable to be strong for his grandfather. His voice was barely audible as he asked, 'What can I do to help you, Grandfather?'

'I don't know if you're up to it, Peter,' Belson said sadly. 'I don't know if you have the guts to do what I have planned. Oh, if only I were ten years younger; if only my health weren't so bad. Damn!' he exclaimed. 'What's the use of saying "if only". Things are the way they are.

'Now hear me out. I'm going to go through everything with you step by step.' Peter leaned forward, indicating his rapt attention, and Belson continued. 'In order to preserve the estate I'll need a great deal of money; enough so that when I die the house and grounds will be free and clear, and you and Phyllis will be able to pay your enormous inheritance tax and have enough left to maintain the estate during your lifetime. I don't delude myself into thinking that you could earn four hundred thousand a year, after taxes, from your law practice, just to maintain this place with a minimal staff.'

150

'How much money would you need to make?' Peter asked.

Belson poured himself a glass of water from a cut crystal decanter on the desk and took several deep swallows before he replied. 'I figure close to a hundred million.'

'What?' Peter was absolutely stunned. The amount was so staggering, he almost laughed. 'But that's impossible! There's no way in the world you could ever make that kind of money, and besides, you're too ill to even be thinking about such things. You'll push yourself to the breaking point; you'll diminish whatever time you have left. Please, you've got to listen to me. There's not enough time in most lifetimes to make that kind of money. Let it go, Grandfather,' he pleaded. 'Don't be crazy. Live out the rest of your life in peace and don't worry about what's going to happen later. That's my problem, not yours. Why don't you go to Hawaii for a rest?' Belson had always loved the island paradise. 'Phyllis and I will join you there as soon as the baby can travel.'

Belson slammed his water glass down on the desk in exasperation. 'No!' he said with violent determination, scorning Peter's suggestion. 'I have an eternity to rest. Haven't you been listening? I want to go out with a warrior's cry, not a whimper of defeat the way you would. I want to do something to save my legacy and I'll die in the attempt! And If I'm right, if I succeed, what I do will go down in financial history.'

'What are you talking about?' Peter asked.

'There's only one way in the world I could earn the kind of money I need in the short amount of time I have left: by speculating in the commodity market.' He paused to emphasize his next statement, ever the dramatist. 'And that's what I'm going to do. Not only am I going to speculate, I'm going to try to squeeze a commodity.' He noticed Peter starting to object, and he raised his hand. 'Now, it won't be easy, but nothing worth doing is ever easy.' He ventured a wry smile at Peter's dubious expression. 'I'm going to need your help,' he continued, 'though ordinarily, I wouldn't ask for it—you know how I feel about self-sufficiency. But circumstances being what they are, I require someone I can trust who can get around better than I, and that is you. It's a delicate situation and I wouldn't say you're the ideal one for the job, but you're all I've got, so I guess we're stuck with one another.'

Peter ignored the left-handed compliment; it was the only kind he ever got from his grandfather. 'It's impossible,' he stated emphatically. 'Not to mention the problem of legality.' He waved his hand in exasperation. 'Here I am, terrified that you might drop dead at any moment from over-exerting yourself in your delicate condition and you're talking about becoming a robber baron.'

'Never mind about my delicate condition. I'll take care of myself and my concerns. As for it being impossible, that too is a matter of opinion. Now hear me out, and don't be such an old maid,' he insisted. 'I contacted my old friend, Henry Cronyn, in New York and explained my predicament to him. It just so happens that he is extremely knowledgeable about this sort of thing and has agreed to advise me.' Belson chuckled. 'Actually, "leaped at the chance" is more like it. He called what I'm doing the geriatric attack. Remember, Henry is seventy-eight. He considers it a rallying point for us senior citizens.'

'But it's crazy,' Peter said. 'There are safeguards against such schemes—regulations, checks and balances. And consequences,' he said ominously.

'We have ways to get around the safeguards,' Belson said slyly. 'People do it all the time. Some of them succeed beyond your wildest dreams. And I say, damn the consequences!'

Peter had the awful feeling that he had just entered a dangerous place from which there was no escape. Everything his grandfather was saying to him went against his beliefs. He wanted no part of it; he wanted to turn and run and never look back. But there was no way he could do that. No way at all. And he realized that this beautiful, carefree autumn day had just become one of the most terrible days of his life.

'We've decided on the perfect commodity to squeeze,' Belson said happily.

'I'm almost afraid to ask what it is,' Peter replied.

'Well, it's platinum,' Belson told him. 'Platinum is undervalued right now, and traditionally it's tied to the rise in gold prices. You know what gold is doing, and the price is likely to keep on climbing too. If I can control enough platinum, I can make a hundred million dollars in nine months and all I'll need is about two million to start.'

'You're really serious?' Peter asked in amazement. 'And where are you going to get your stake of two million? Borrow it against McKintridge?' He was hoping that it wasn't true, but Belson was nodding in agreement.

'That's right. See? I knew you could be smart when you wanted to be. I've had feelers out to friends in the mortgage business and just received my loan commitments. The savings and loans will only loan a maximum of eight hundred thousand, even on a multimillion-dollar property such as this one, especially since we're refinancing and not selling. So I'm using private sources. The interest and points will be steep, but beggars can't be choosers. I'm getting a first, for five years of two million, and a second for three years for one and a half. The two million I'll invest in the market, and the million five hundred thousand I'll use for payments on the loan and for living expenses.'

Belson actually looked cheerful as he wrestled with the details of what lay ahead for him; he was excited by the potential of his scheme. This attempt to earn back his losses and make up for his mistakes had involved him more in the process of living than any doctor's prescription could provide, and whether or not it was legal was beside the point. Peter had to admit grudgingly that there was a residual benefit to what his grandfather was doing if it bolstered his mental state instead of leaving him with nothing to do but give up and die. He only wished he didn't have to be involved in it himself.

'What are the risks?' Peter asked.

'Risks? What do I care about risks?' Belson said. 'I'm in a desperate situation.' He caught Peter's skeptical look. 'All right, all right, I suppose I could lose more than my investment. I could be forced to declare bankruptcy. The mortgage brokers could foreclose on the estate. But that's highly unlikely. You think I'd jeopardize the estate? Henry has never been wrong in his life. He's worth three or four hundred million. He and his associates are the ones who make the market. Besides, the commodity market is a manipulated business anyway.'

'But what about federal regulations? You can't just ignore them.'

'The Commodity Exchange has had more presidents than Italy. They don't know what they're doing, and besides, platinum is traded on the New York Merc. They won't catch us, and if they do, they'll only slap our wrists or levy some fines.'

Peter doubted that, but he kept his doubts to himself. In his experience government regulatory agencies often worked with great dispatch and efficiency. And his grandfather's denial of the potential for disaster made him sink even lower into the mire of despair. 'How would you go about actually accomplishing your goal?' Peter asked. Part of him was curious, but mostly he did not want to know at all. My God, he was a lawyer, sworn to uphold the law. How could he justify or condone criminal behavior before the fact? And then he looked at his grandfather's aged and excited face, realized how soon it would be that he would never see that face again, and knew he could not say no.

'What I'm about to tell you is absolutely confidential,' Belson said. 'Do I have your solemn promise?'

Peter nodded and then stopped. 'I'll have to tell Phyllis, of course.'

'No!' Belson nearly shouted. 'I don't want anyone to know, especially Phyllis.' He glanced away, trying to hide the sudden look of embarrassment that sprang to his eyes. 'I don't want Phyllis to think of me any differently than she did before. It's important to me. I don't want her to pity me, or feel disappointed in me. And I don't want Felix to know any of this. If Phyllis finds out, she'll tell him.'

'No, she wouldn't, Grandfather,' Peter said, thinking how terrible it would be for him if he couldn't confide in his wife.

'She will, I tell you,' Belson said, the color of his cheeks flushed with excitement, alarming Peter greatly. 'Now, I want your word. Not a detail of this to anyone, especially Phyllis, is that clear?'

Peter nodded miserably, and Belson began to outline his strategy.

'We're going to buy platinum futures contracts on margin. Right now twenty-five hundred dollars will secure fifty ounces of platinum at the current price of approximately four hundred an ounce. That means for twenty-five hundred I can control twenty thousand dollars' worth of platinum.'

Peter did some quick calculations in his head, but he was skeptical. 'Even if the price doubled, you'd need to control one hundred million dollars' worth to make any money. You'd have to put in ten million right now and pray that platinum goes to a thousand.'

'I don't have ten million, and I'm not going to wait until platinum doubles. We're going to pyramid.'

'What does that mean?'

'Start out controlling sixteen million dollars' worth with my two million, and as the price goes up, we'll take the equity we're building and buy more contracts on margin. Eventually we will achieve the equivalent of controlling one hundred million dollars' worth of platinum and doubling our money. In the trade they call it a Chinese Pyramid, heavy on the topside. Now, of course, since the price will be increasing, we can't expect it to double from any price we buy it. So to achieve our goal, we may have to control a hundred and fifty million dollars' worth if some of it only increases fifty percent from our purchase price. Henry will tell me when the market has peaked and we'll sell out.'

'What if he doesn't know?'

'He'll know,' Belson said confidentially, insistently.

'But why platinum?' Peter asked.

'There's a short world supply right now, and a high demand, plus the world economic conditions make investing in it a smart move. Platinum is being used in catalytic converters and in other high-technology uses. It's perfect for our purposes. Besides, while everyone else is playing with gold and silver, they won't be interested in what's happening to platinum. Platinum rises higher and faster than gold as gold rises because it's a thinner, smaller market, therefore the movements are more exaggerated.'

'But isn't there less liquidity and doesn't it fall further than gold when gold sinks?'

'Yes, but that won't happen,' Belson insisted. 'I know this will work. Henry has told me that the Hunts are doing a similar thing in silver.'

'The Hunts?' Peter said. 'You're not in their league.'

'Don't be so sure,' Belson replied.

Peter felt numb from the incredible seesaw effects of this conversation. Belson had come back to life, but it was the euphoria before the fall. His burst of energy was only a facade hiding a rotting hull, and he expected Peter to use himself as a plug for all those holes. He didn't know if there was enough of him to go around.

'Is what you want me to do illegal?'

Belson's eyes brightened at Peter's distress. 'Not exactly illegal,' he said. 'Only a little bit unethical. But nothing much ever happens to the guys who do this stuff. Now, here's what I want you to do.' And he reached into a manila folder on his desk and handed Peter two pieces of paper.

'Here are two lists. The first one is a list of commodity brokers in various brokerage firms in Los Angeles, San Francisco, San Diego, and Phoenix. They're all close to home and ones that Henry has recommended as easy to work with. In other words, they won't ask too many questions.

'And the second list is a set of names you may use on the

different accounts. They are all names that mean something to me and I'll be able to recognize them.'

'Why do you need different names on the accounts?'

'So it won't come to the attention of the Commodity Futures Trading Commission, or the New York Merc computer, that one person is buying up one specific commodity. I don't want them to limit me.'

'What are the limits of platinum contracts?'

'There are none,' Belson said excitedly. 'That's the beauty of this thing. I could buy as much as I wanted, but this way I have more freedom from scrutiny. It's merely a precaution in case they decide to limit it in the near future.'

Peter nodded thoughtfully, thinking he'd check out those facts himself. 'Isn't it illegal to have accounts with several different brokerage houses?'

'Not exactly illegal,' Belson hedged. 'Merely unethical. The principle being that the brokerage house is extending me credit and they want to be sure I can pay back my debts if they are incurred.'

'But none will be, right?' Peter asked sarcastically. 'You're not going to overextend yourself and get caught?'

'No!' Belson insisted. 'After all, I am worth close to thirty million with this house and grounds and furnishings. If I had to liquidate my assets, these creditors could recover their supposed losses.'

'And how are you going to estabish credit for all these "relatives" and corporations?' Peter asked. 'They have no assets.'

'We'll make sizable deposits of cash in each account and I'll be the guarantor of their debts in a separate and private agreement. My bank will verify it.'

'How in God's name are you going to get a bank to do such a thing?' Peter exploded. 'They won't allow you to open twenty different accounts in fictitious names all funneling into one name.'

'You just let me worry about that,' Belson said slyly. 'The less you know about it the better off you are.'

'Grandfather,' Peter said with alarm. 'I cannot be a party

to graft. I won't!'

'You won't have to be, Peter. Your lily-white lawyer's hands will stay clean. Don't worry.'

Peter shook his head. He couldn't do it, he just couldn't.

Belson was staring at him, waiting. 'What is it, Peter? Are you going to chicken out now, after leading me on? I thought you were with me. I need you, for Christ's sake. And you owe me. By God, you owe me!'

Peter felt a grinding of two opposing forces pulling inside of him while his mind raced with possibilities. Technically he would not be guilty of bribery if he was not personally involved in any payoffs. But he knew about it now. Christ, this was not going to be easy.

Belson waited.

Peter sighed. 'I'll have to know the name of a bank official to whom I can refer all credit checks. There will have to be a bank name on credit applications and accounts.'

'George Benning,' Belson said.

Peter nodded. He felt as if he were stepping into a bottomless chasm. 'When do we get started?'

'Right away. We're going to buy platinum futures for next October. It will take that long because we have a great deal to do. We have to consider the market's natural fluctuations—there will, after all, be some ups and downs. It takes some time to grow enough profit on margin. There's the world situation, inflation is rising into two figures, we don't know who's going to win next year's election—all those things.' He seemed almost cheerful.

'All right,' Peter said dejectedly. 'I was just hoping it wouldn't take that long. That's all.'

'There's another thing,' Belson said, and Peter thought, *Oh, please, no more*. 'You're going to be very busy with my plan. Your practice will have to be curtailed. Think your partner will cover you without knowing why?'

It was getting worse and worse. Now Larry was involved. 'He'll cover me,' he assured his grandfather.

'Good, good,' Belson said. 'Well, that's all for now. Why

158

don't you go on back to your family. We'll talk more about this later, as soon as my loans are transferred to the bank.'

So Peter left, but he was filled with despair. He wanted nothing to do with this scheme, but he felt an obligation to support his grandfather in this. Not only was it Belson's legacy, it meant the future of his family—oh, God, he was so frightened. With his entire being he dreaded what lay ahead.

Chapter 7

VICKY PROMISED herself she wouldn't cry, but the moment she saw Phyllis's sympathetic expression, the tears wouldn't stop. Phyllis held out her arms and Vicky came into them, sitting on the edge of the bed next to her.

Even through her tears Vicky could see that Phyliis looked like an angel, relaxing after an afternoon nap in a handmade peignoir from Juel Park. Her blond hair was tied to the top of her head with pink ribbons that matched the dusty-rose Porthault linens on the bed; next to her on the nightstand was a cut crystal water pitcher with matching glass and a bouquet of fresh flowers, while cards and gifts for the baby were piled on the dresser next to a stack of thank-you notes. No princess could have looked more composed, more regal, or more contentedly maternal than this new mother. And that only served as a blatant contrast to how Vicky saw herself, as a miserable failure.

'I'm so sorry for you,' Phyllis said when Vicky had composed herself. 'What an injustice. And to you of all people. You're so devoted to those students, you always fight for the underdog, and you're a brilliant educator. It isn't fair!

The school has lost the best teacher they'll ever have.'

Vicky felt a bit cheered. Phyllis was the most loyal person she knew, always there to bolster her when she was down, and lord knew she was down now.

'Do you know why they fired you?' Phyllis asked.

Vicky told her the details of the incident, and as Vicky talked, Phyllis's mouth drew into a tight line of disapproval. 'How could Leslie do such a thing?' she bristled with indignation. 'The woman's motives are beyond my understanding. I've never liked her. I remember when she decorated my parents' house, she wouldn't leave my father alone and treated my mother horribly—put her down—made her feel as though her decisions were worthless. I can't imagine what it's like for Marla to work with her.'

'I've thought about bringing a lawsuit,' Vicky said. 'I talked it over with Larry.'

'Yes,' Phyllis agreed. 'You must force them to reinstate you.'

'But they're within their rights as a private institution to fire me. And any action I might bring would be painful and expensive and public. Even if I succeeded against them, afterwards I wouldn't be comfortable working there.'

'But, Vicky,' Phyllis said, 'wouldn't the board of directors be sympathetic to you if you presented your case to them?' Suddenly her face lit up with a smile. 'I just remembered, Peter's grandfather is on that board. I could ask him to take your side.'

It was so ironic that Vicky almost laughed. She had vowed not to tell Phyllis and Peter about Belson's vendetta against her, knowing how it would hurt them, and besides there was nothing they could do about it. But at the moment Vicky had an uncontrollable urge to tell Phyllis everything. If Phyllis knew what kind of person Belson was, she would detest him as much as Vicky did. A perverse side of Vicky also wanted to hurt Phyllis because she was envious of all that Phyllis had—a rich, handsome husband who adored her, beauty and intelligence, and a new, healthy baby in the next room. But the main reason Vicky wanted to bare her soul to Phyllis was that Phyllis was so understanding. Somehow, because of her capacity to love, or her loyalty to her friends, she was the only one who could take some of the sting out of Vicky's pain; and right now Vicky needed that more than anything.

Phyllis was watching her expectantly, observing the changing expressions on her face while she struggled with her conscience. Finally, Vicky took a deep breath and just blurted it out. 'You cannot ask Peter's grandfather to intercede with the board on my behalf because it was even more his fault than Leslie's that I was fired.'

'What do you mean?' Phyllis asked.

'The day of your wedding when I had that argument with him and threw champagne in his face, he wrote to the headmaster demanding my resignation and telling Mr Beckwirth all about my affair with Peter when I was sixteen. He said that I was unfit to serve as an example to my students.'

Phyllis's expression was thoughtful as she listened. 'But that's ancient history.'

'To you and me and Peter it is, but to Belson I'm Hester Prynne. At the time, Beckwirth put me on probation, and now with Leslie's complaints added to Belson's the board has exercised their right to fire me. They're a private school, after all, and Belson's voice carries weight with them.'

'I can't believe he'd do such a thing.'

'Believe it! I read the letter, it was vicious.'

Phyllis was visibly uncomfortable, torn between what she'd just heard and her desire to deny it. 'But perhaps he wasn't aware of what would happen to you, maybe he just wanted you reprimanded. After all, he was extremely embarrassed by that photo in the *Chronicler*.'

Vicky's eyes flared with indignation. 'The man is a flagrant anti-Semite, he's lecherous, untrustworthy, despicable, and capable of great evil. Even your purity cannot excuse him or combat the damage he can cause. Stay as clear of him as you can, Phyllis, or he'll destroy you and everything you love.'

Now it was Phyllis who felt the thrust of a painful injury. Her eyes filled with tears from Vicky's invective; she could not believe ill of anyone she loved. 'I know you're speaking out of pain and I don't blame you. I admit it was a low, unkind act. But Belson is Peter's only relative and Peter is very devoted to him. Because of that devotion I've come to see a softer side of Belson, one he does not usually reveal. I know he truly loves us, Vicky. And if he did something wrong, what can I say but I'm sorry?'

Vicky sighed and looked away. The only softer side to Belson was his rotten core.

'What are you going to do?' Phyllis asked.

'That's the real question, isn't it?' She took a deep breath, and when she exhaled, it became a sigh. 'I've had some time to think about all of this. It's quite sobering to find yourself cut loose from your job, your self-respect, and your identity, though it wouldn't be easy to face at any age. But perhaps it's to my advantage to be young and in trouble. Hopefully, I still have time to find a way out. I've had to ask myself some important questions of late. Such as what are my goals? What do I want to do? And amazingly the answer was there just waiting for me to ask.'

'And what is it?' Phyllis asked with genuine interest.

'I'm going to finish my novel. I've been wanting to do it for a long time and if I tighten my belt financially and live off my savings for a while, I can give myself a good six months before I have to get a job.'

A delighted smile lit up Phyllis's face and now Vicky felt the true comfort she'd sought. 'What a wonderful idea,' Phyllis said. 'Turn the negative into a positive. Are you starting right away?'

Vicky smiled at Phyllis's optimism. 'There's a small hitch. Just my luck, my apartment building is going condo and I'll have to move. That will take some diligent hunting; you know what rents are these days. So after I settle into a new dump. I'll begin working.'

Phyllis nodded thoughtfully, and then her eyes crinkled

with excitement. 'I have the perfect solution. You can move in here. Peter and Jonathan and I are moving into the guesthouse on the estate and you can have this place.'

'What do you mean "have this place"?' Vicky answered. 'I can't afford to live here.'

'Sure you can,' Phyllis insisted. 'What were you planning to pay for rent?'

Vicky shrugged. 'Somewhere between four and six hundred.'

Phyllis didn't flinch. Lies were sometimes important between friends. 'That's *exactly* what our mortgage payments are, five hundred a month. You'd pay utilities anyplace you lived. And you could find a housemate and rent out the two other bedrooms. Now I know what you're going to say, so don't bother. "It's much too generous and all that stuff." Well, it is generous, but I want to do this for you. So please let me. And besides, it's the least we can do under the circumstances.'

'Under what circumstances?' Peter asked from the doorway, startling them both.

'Oh, darling, I didn't hear you come in,' Phyllis said.

He came over to the bed and kissed her and then kissed Vicky on the cheek. 'What shouldn't she bother saying?' Peter asked and sank tiredly into the club chair in the corner. Vicky could see fatigue seeping off of his muscles; his head nearly dropped to his chest.

'That she won't let us rent her our condominium for the price of our mortgage payments of *five* hundred dollars a month,' Phyllis emphasized, alerting him to what she had already told Vicky, 'since she's been fired from her job and is going to live on her savings for a while until she completes writing a novel.' She finished her sentence with an excited upswing of her voice.

In spite of his fatigue Peter smiled in agreement with his wife. 'She's right, Vick, don't bother to say no. We move out of here in two weeks. Think you can handle the time delay?'

Vicky was so overwhelmed with gratitude she could

hardly speak. 'I'll handle it!' And then her eyes filled with tears as she hugged Phyllis and then Peter. 'You two are wonderful,' she said. 'And just so we understand one another, whatever the subsidy is between what I'm paying you and what this place actually costs per month, I'm going to consider a loan, okay? When I'm a well-known author and Merv Griffin interviews me, I'll pay you back. Deal?'

'Deal,' Phyllis said with a grin, and Peter nodded.

Vicky could see that they wanted to be alone so she thanked them again and said good-bye. But when she reached the street and got into her car, she had a terrible pang of conscience and had to force herself not to be sentimental. Peter and Phyllis were her best friends, but their friendship could have no bearing on her plans, except that she would disguise the characters in her novel as much as possible so as not to hurt them. But no matter how good they were to her, or even if she accepted their generous hospitality, she would be deterred from writing the story that was burning inside to be told.

She was going to take the semi-autobiographical novel of three young women growing up in Beverly Hills which she'd started years ago, and turn it into the spiciest best seller of the year. And the two main characters were now going to be Leslie Paxton Winokur and Belson McKintridge. Leslie, with her vicious vendettas, who destroyed anyone who competed with her, anyone who didn't conform to her ideas, including her own children. And Belson, the cruel tyrant, incapable of love, a despicable racist who managed to hide his foul soul from the world and instead of being vilified was revered and beloved. How she would expose them, how she would get even with them for doing to her what they had done.

It was a great idea. She was going to find out everything she could about them, how they dirtied the lives of those around them, how they abused their privileges, and she'd make sure they received retribution in the end. She would uncover all the skeletons in their closets and disguise the incidents just enough so she wouldn't be sued. After all,

164

truth was a defense. And that's what people wanted to read about. It would be a resounding success. Just as Phyllis said, she'd turn her misfortune into a fortune. Even if it killed her.

After Vicky had gone, Phyllis came and sat on the ottoman in front of Peter's chair. He put his arm around her waist, but he was staring across the room at the refracted rainbow glancing off a cut crystal decanter by the bed.

'Hard day?' she asked. He'd been like this for more than a week—tired and depressed and uncommunicative. She couldn't get him to tell her what was bothering him, yet she could see that something was; ever since he returned from his grandfather's last week, he'd been upset.

'My day was about the same,' he responded, and told her about some of his business dealings. But his voice had none of its usual excitement.

She reached to brush the hair from his forehead in a tender caress but he stopped her. 'Don't do that,' he said.

'Honey, what's wrong? You haven't been yourself for over a week. What is it?'

His face darkened as though he wanted to snap at her, but he didn't; instead he looked away. 'Nothing's the matter,' he insisted. 'I've been working hard, that's all. Larry gets us involved in too many get-rich-quick real-estate investments and it's up to me to be levelheaded enough to protect us. I have to do the research and find out that his harebrained ideas are impractical and won't work, while he's galloping off to the next deal.'

'It seems to me he's made a few good finds in the past years.'

'I didn't say he hadn't,' he snapped. 'I'm just tired of it sometimes, that's all. For every deal that works there are ten that don't. That's a lot of wasted effort, you know.'

He was wound up tightly. She could see the lines of tension around his eyes and mouth indicating the capped volcano inside, bubbling with eruptive emotion. She felt helpless about easing the pressure on him.

'Have you spoken to your grandfather today?' she asked. 'Is everything all right with him?'

Peter looked at her sharply, almost suspiciously. 'Of course, he's all right. And no, I haven't talked to him since a week ago Saturday. What are you doing, checking up on me?'

'Peter!' she was surprised. 'What is it? Did you have a fight with Belson? Was it about Vicky?'

'Of course not! And what the hell has Vicky got to do with anything? My God, you're getting dense, aren't you?'

Phyllis just stared at him until he looked away.

'I'm sorry I said that,' he said a moment later.

'You know,' Phyllis offered, 'sometimes husbands experience a kind of postpartum reaction when there's a new baby in the house. They feel jealous of the new intruder, especially if it's a boy. They're afraid the baby will come between them and their wife and they'll lose their wife's affection.' She wanted to put her arms around him and hug him, but at the moment he was unreachable. 'I just want you to know that no one will ever come between us.'

He seemed embarrassed by her reassurances. 'I'm not jealous of Jonathan, for God's sake.' But he moved aside and got up from the chair. 'I'm going to have a drink. Do you want one?'

'I'm not supposed to drink while I'm nursing,' she reminded him. 'You know that.'

'I can't be expected to remember every little detail of your life,' he nearly shouted, and left the room.

Phyllis was stunned. This wasn't her Peter at all. Something was terribly wrong. And it had to be the baby. What else could it be? It was a difficult time for both of them, getting used to the responsibility of another life. She hadn't regained her physical strength as quickly as she would have liked and they hadn't had much social life. But it would straighten out soon, she was sure. In a few weeks they'd be able to make love again and Peter wouldn't feel so alienated. In the meantime maybe she could get him to talk to her about what was on his mind. And if she couldn't get him to tell her, maybe he'd confide in someone else.

Perhaps her father might be able to get Peter to unburden himself. Peter was so fond of Felix.

Chapter 8

FELIX SAT at the head of his table, sipping B & B, enjoying the incomparable flavor of his Cuban cigar, and surveying his guests. Audrey's dinner had been adequate for young people on the rise though he would have preferred something more exotic than beef Wellington for the main course. He'd heard that lately Phyllis had become an expert at making chili. But such was the palate of the younger generation. At least Audrey had better taste than that. But on the other hand Phyllis was not a lush. In fact Peter and Phyllis had turned into the ideal young couple; they'd given him a beautiful grandson on whom he doted, the heir for whom he'd prayed. And even though Phyllis still looked a bit peaked nine weeks after giving birth, none the less she was lovely tonight in a moss green wool dress, sitting on his right, next to her husband.

Marla Gilbert, who was on Felix's left, next to her husband Larry, had become a stunner too, and Felix had been anxious to engage her in a private little flirtation all evening, but there hadn't been any opportunity under Audrey's watchful eye.

Just as he was about to give Marla another try, Phyllis leaned over to speak to him. 'Have you had a chance to talk to Peter since I asked you to, Dad?'

He nodded, shifting so that only she was privy to his reply. 'You were correct. Peter is concerned about some-

167

thing, he's not himself, though he assured me everything was all right. But he sloughed off my questions as though they were an annoyance to him. It was most unlike him to be short-tempered.'

She pulled away and studied Felix's face, a worry line drawn between her brows.

'I did what I could,' he said.

'Don't stop trying,' she pleaded, leaning in again. 'He needs someone to confide in.'

Felix nodded and patted her hand reassuringly. He had no intention of stopping his inquiry into Peter's mental unease; he was intensely curious about it and in fact had asked Larry Gilbert to pick up where he left off, to try and find out exactly what was going on with Peter, using their mutual concern for Peter as a reason. Felix figured Larry's innate deviousness and his close friendship with Peter were enough to get the truth. Felix prided himself on his ability to judge character and Peter was acting as though he were guilty about something. He acted like a man with a secret who is unused to deception. If Felix didn't know Peter better, he'd suspect him of cheating on Phyllis, but he was certain that wasn't the case.

In Felix's opinion Larry was brighter than Peter, more ambitious, and definitely on his way to success. It was Peter's lucky day when he hooked up with a smart operator like Larry. And even though Peter had some advantages of his own to offer a partnership, such as the right social contacts and an orthodox approach to law, Larry had the guts they needed to take chances and make deals happen. Felix had seen evidence of that already with the Wilshire Boulevard property. How Larry had gotten that one for him was still a mystery. Yes, he was impressed with Gilbert, who was obviously trying to get more of the business Felix could throw his way. But he wanted to go slowly with Gilbert even though he liked him, because any success Gilbert enjoyed, Peter would share. And Felix preferred to let Peter struggle a bit more. He didn't want to make it too easy for the boy.

The one thing he would have to be careful of was allowing Larry Gilbert to become too strong an influence on Peter. It was all right for them to be partners and even for Peter to rely on Larry's strength as an adviser. But when it came down to a choice, it must be Felix to whom Peter would turn, to whom he would owe his first allegiance and devotion. That's what Felix had endeavored to achieve by befriending Peter. So that when the time came, and Felix found a way to destroy Belson, Peter would still remain loyal to him and there would be no rift in the family. Peter might even be the one who would show Felix the way to get to Belson.

Felix turned back into the conversation.

'Was your offer on the new house accepted?' Peter was asking Larry.

'Yes.' Larry grinned. 'We're in escrow. It's in the six hundred block on Bedford Drive. I always say you can't go wrong with a house in the flats of Beverly Hills, even if it is a fixer-upper and way overpriced.'

'That's great news,' Phyllis exclaimed. 'I'm so thrilled for you; I know a great decorator.' She looked meaningfully at Marla.

They all laughed.

'It sounds like you two young people are off to a fine start,' Audrey Anhalt said.

'Yes,' Felix agreed. 'A go-getter like you, Larry, with such an attractive, talented wife.' He turned to Marla. 'When is Leslie going to give you more responsibility, my dear? From what I've seen in your preliminary meetings on the decoration of my yacht, you're ready for it.'

'Oh, you know Leslie,' Marla said. 'She believes in a long apprenticeship. But in these past two months, I have learned a great deal from her. The practical examples of on-the-job training are far different from the hypotheticals of the classroom.'

Felix noticed a subtle change in Larry's expression when attention focused on Marla's work. *So he's possessive, is he?* Felix thought. *Well, that won't stop me from admiring*

169

his wife. She's damned attractive.

Marla saw him studying her and returned his suggestive glance with one of her own. He couldn't keep his eyes from her cleavage; two creamy smooth young breasts framed by a ruby-red velvet dress, cut into a deep V. The skin on her bare shoulders and throat was unblemished, her hair was long and full and she was thinner than he remembered; it brought a hollowness to her cheeks, a sophistication to her demeanor.

He reached over and covered her hand with his, speaking quietly. 'You've become a real beauty, Marla. And right under my nose. How long have we known one another?'

'Since Phyllis and I took ballet class together when we were in grammar school. I was twelve and she was ten.'

'And she used to bring you home for weekends. The two of you would eat pizza and watch television and then, in no time at all, you were calling boys on the phone. I remember you had a touch of acne, and new breasts. What a wonder it's been to watch you two young women develop from pretty little girls into even more appealing young women, and now you've turned into a devastating beauty.' He gazed at her seductively.

'I'm not beautiful,' Marla protested, but she was responding to him. 'Phyllis is the beautiful one, with her blond, regal elegance.'

'You have spunk, independence. You're a woman to admire. You're holding down a full-time job with someone as exacting as Leslie Paxton Winokur and succeeding too.'

Marla discreetly moved her hand from his, placing it in her lap. 'It's nice to hear that someone approves of what I'm doing. Larry doesn't like my working.'

'I can understand that. He wants you home where he can keep an eye on you. I would too. But I admire your determination.' There was a bright flush on her cheeks, a slight quivering of her nostrils, and suddenly she shivered and goosebumps appeared on her smooth skin. Her nipples tightened beneath the fabric of her dress and he felt a rush of excitement surge through him. She was interested. And

170

so young. What a fascinating idea. His mistresses were usually older, but he could make an exception in her case. And what about her friendship with Phyllis? That gave him a momentary twinge of conscience but he dismissed it.

He leaned forward to speak more intimately to her, breathing warm air into her ear, smelling the fresh scent of her hair. 'I think I shall insist that Leslie use you exclusively as her assistant when she gets more involved in the job of redecorating my yacht.'

Marla didn't pull away though his face was very near her own. 'Would you really do that?'

'I never joke when it comes to spending my money, or getting what I want.' He smiled. 'I think you're wonderful and I look forward to spending more time with you.'

She was flustered now. 'Leslie will be difficult to convince.'

'We'll see,' he said.

She smiled at him as Audrey stood up from the table, ushering the guests into the living room. He could tell the girl wasn't certain whether or not to be pleased by his advances. Good. He liked a woman who was uncertain. It made the seduction all the more interesting. But would she be difficult to pry away from her husband? In time, probably not. He noticed Larry eyeing them hostilely, so he left Marla's side and approached her husband. No need to make an enemy of someone he needed.

'We haven't had a chance to speak privately all evening. Come on, take a walk to the john with me,' Felix said, putting his arm around Larry and leading him down the hall toward the bedroom. 'How's everything going?'

'Fine,' Larry acknowledged, his hostility lessening.

'And did you have a chance to talk to Peter as I suggested? I'm really worried about that boy.'

They reached the bedroom and Felix went into his bathroom, a large room with silk upholstered walls, marble accoutrements, and antique accessories.

Felix stepped into the toilet cubicle and raised the seat while Larry stood in the doorway waiting his turn. 'I've spoken to Peter more than once,' Larry said. 'But he's very hard to crack. I've taken to outright prying and questioning him whenever I catch him looking somber and quiet. I've even tried to cajole it out of him, but it hasn't been easy.'

Felix shook himself dry and zipped up his pants, vacating his spot for Larry to have his turn. 'You mean you haven't gotten anywhere with him either?' Felix asked. 'This is a mystery.'

Larry took his turn. 'No, I did find out that he's worried about something! He admitted that much. It's very serious and it has to do with his grandfather.'

Larry finished, zipped himself, and flushed the toilet.

But his statement had brought a rush of excitement pounding to Felix's brain. He forced his voice to remain calm. 'Peter is worried about Belson? But why, for heaven's sake? Is the old man sick?'

'When I asked him that, he said no, everything was fine with Belson's health. But after I got that out of him I couldn't get anything else. It was as if he'd said too much already and was not only sorry but wanted to deny the whole thing.'

'Really?' Felix said happily. Larry was staring at him curiously and he didn't want to seem too inquisitive. 'Well, I guess when Peter wants us to know what his problems are, he'll tell us. In the meantime see what you can find out, and if there's anything I can do to help, you let me know. You know how much that boy means to me.'

Larry nodded and they headed back to rejoin the others. But just as they reached the living room, Larry turned to Felix. 'You've seen my wife at work, haven't you?'

'Yes,' Felix replied.

'Do you think she plays straight with me?' He stared into Felix's eyes, trying to determine the truth.

'Absolutely!' Felix insisted, staring right back at him.

'Would you tell me if you noticed anything, anything at all?'

'Of course,' Felix assured him.

Larry nodded curtly and they both returned to the living room.

He's warning me. Felix thought. *But he's too late. In the end it will be the lady's choice after all.*

'Well, you certainly had a good time tonight,' Larry commented, his voice tinged with sarcasm.

Marla nodded, trying to seem noncommittal. 'It was a lovely evening.'

'How would you know? The only person you talked to was Felix.' He was edging closer to anger.

'That's not true. I talked to everyone.'

'You may not be aware of how absorbed you were with Felix. But Audrey Anhalt was aware of it. I saw her looking at you.'

Marla clutched the armrest so as not to lose her control. Did it show how much Felix affected her? she wondered. If Mrs Anhalt could tell, she would die. 'I wasn't absorbed in him,' she said to Larry. 'We only spoke briefly while you were dominating the conversation, as usual.'

'I wasn't dominating, I was contributing, which is more than you did.'

She was immediately sorry she'd baited him. Now he would want to know why she thought he dominated conversations when all she wanted to do was to be left alone with her own thoughts. Thoughts about Felix. Her mind was full of him: the way he looked at her, the way he listened to her and made her feel desirable. She'd never had this feeling before. There was an indefinable yearning in her to possess him, to be possessed by him.

Stop it! she told herself. *Stop thinking about him right now!* She turned and looked at Larry, at his boyish, familiar face with the prominent jaw and the mole high up on his cheek and the easy, wonderful smile that made her heart turn over, even when he exasperated her. She sighed, and felt guilt rush through her like a molten river.

'I think you'd better stay clear of Felix Anhalt,' Larry

said. 'He's got the hots for you.'

'Oh, he does not!' she countered too quickly, feeling caught while her heart pounded with excitement. 'And what about you? Who do you have the hots for these days?'

'Only you, baby. Only you,' he said easily, sliding his hand up her thigh and into the V of her crotch. 'You really looked gorgeous tonight. Who could blame old Anhalt.' He rubbed his fingers over her crotch. 'God you turn me on.' His hand was on her breast now, and for a moment, only a brief moment, she let his hand be Felix's. But then the guilt absorbed her again and she moved him away.

'There she goes, folks.' He yanked his hand back and gripped the steering wheel. 'The ice water expert. How does it feel, Gilbert, to be doused again? Tell the radio audience.'

She reached over and touched his arm. 'I'm sorry, honey. It's just that I get nervous when you take your hands off the wheel.'

'Bullshit!' he said. 'You're a cold, frigid bitch. And that's behind everything you do, including this half-assed job of yours.'

Here we go again, she thought, feeling caught in the same devastating web. They both spun it and occupied it together, spider and fly, victim and inflictor, each adept at both roles. How she wanted to break free from this painful place and fly away. And, she imagined, so did Larry sometimes. She knew exactly how he had felt tonight; why he'd lashed out at her, and she didn't blame him. She hated it when he flirted with other women in her presence. It made her feel ashamed and embarrassed, as though she weren't interesting enough to hold his attention. But tonight, that's exactly what she had done to him and she'd felt heady with power. It was no way to conduct a marriage, making one another jealous, preying on each other's weaknesses. Then why do it? Because she couldn't help herself. Felix made her feel so desirable, something she longed to feel.

Do I want a divorce? she wondered. But her own voice told her no, that wasn't the answer. And yet she didn't know what it was she wanted. Damn, she just didn't know.

Chapter 9

JAMES CLARENCE did not look like a classic private eye; there was no rumpled raincoat or slouch-brimmed hat, though he was one of the best in the business. He wore a well-tailored business suit, carried a Mark Cross briefcase, and earned a handsome living by supplying information to irate spouses, banks, and attorneys on errant mates, plaintiffs, and borrowers. He had brown, thinning hair, wore a Stanford alumni tie and Ralph Lauren cologne. Felix recognized it because he wore the same one himself. Felix had hired the well-reputed Los Angeles firm of Clarence and Kotlier at a considerable fee to obtain for him all the information one could on Belson McKintridge's financial and personal involvements, ostensibly because Felix was contemplating entering into a deal with McKintridge and wanted the man checked out from every aspect.

Clarence and Kotlier were given that sort of explanation all the time, and accepted it as true. But so far, explanation or not, this high-priced detective had come up with nothing.

'What do you have for me today?' Felix asked after the usual formalities of greeting.

James Clarence leafed through his file and brought out his report on Belson McKintridge. There were pages filled to capacity with hours, dates, and time spent—it was more documentation for fees earned than information. Felix glanced down the sheets, his practiced eye searching for anything of substance with which he could hang his long-time opponent. Anything that would tell him what was going on between Peter and Belson.

'I see you've substantiated Belson's ownership in Albany Oil,' Felix read. 'But it's widely known that he lost money there.'

'Yes,' Clarence pointed out. 'At least two million, maybe three.'

'Over what period of time?'

'Several years, I'm afraid.'

'Then it could have been absorbed by other gains. Did he have the capital gains against which to write it off?'

Clarence seemed embarrassed. 'I haven't established that yet.'

Felix gave him a look of impatience. 'Good lord, what are you waiting for?'

'The man is a mole, Mr Anhalt. I don't mean to apologize for our work, but Belson McKintridge makes Howard Hughes look like a blabbermouth. I've never had so much difficulty determining anyone's net worth before. We know his holdings are substantial and we know he's involved in diverse financial enterprises from land to oil to investment banking, but every trail we follow leads to a dead end for lack of substantiation. It's as if the man has lived his financial life in anticipation of just this kind of scrutiny and has guarded against it extremely well. The sources of his income are as private as can be. We don't even know the names of his closest advisers and only by searching through the social columns in the newspapers have we been able to associate him with anyone at all. We're working on obtaining his medical records, but we haven't had any luck. Hopefully, we'll have something on that soon.'

Felix nodded. At least James Clarence was honest about his failures and Felix appreciated it.

Clarence continued. 'The court records of his inheritance from his father are public knowledge. The elder McKintridge, Angus was his name, left Belson about thirty-five million plus the McKintridge estate. Belson's increased that original inheritance several times over, though not by selling off that acreage in McKintridge Summit. He only got about twenty thousand an acre for it in the sixties. No great killing there.'

Felix felt the gears of anxiety pulling at his guts, grinding against one another in an eager desire to chug ahead. *I have to know what's going on with Belson and why Peter is upset,* Felix thought. *This is my chance to get the bastard.* 'You've got to get me more, and right away!' Felix insisted. 'I don't care if the man is a "mole," as you say, his affairs can't be totally impenetrable!'

Clarence nodded in agreement. 'Well, we have had some indication that there's a recent activity going on in his financial life. Either he's trying to cover a major diminishment of his assets or he's about to make the biggest score of his life.'

'How do you know that?' Felix asked, feeling his excitement rising.

'Because he's borrowed three million five hundred thousand against the McKintridge estate.'

'What?' Felix exclaimed. Why didn't you say so?'

Clarence looked at him as though the questions were superfluous. 'It's all in the report, sir.'

Felix began leafing through the pages again.

'McKintridge's liabilities may indicate many things,' Clarence commented. 'We do not yet know to what use he is going to put his money.'

Felix's curiosity was fever pitched. *Why would Belson borrow against the estate?* 'How did you find out about this recent development?'

Clarence looked rather smug. 'All trust-deeds against a piece of property have to be recorded with the city. We check with the title companies as a matter of routine.'

'Do you know who holds the paper?' Felix asked.

Clarence nodded and pointed to two names; a mortgage company in Texas held the first trust-deed for $2,000,000, and a mortgage company in New York held the second for $1,500,000. 'This is excellent,' Felix said. 'Excellent work. But is there any way you can hurry the process along and find out more for me?'

Again Clarence nodded. 'It may be possible to infiltrate

his domestic staff.'

'How will that help?' Felix asked. 'It's his business affairs I want to know about.'

'I understand that,' Clarence said patiently. 'But men like Belson McKintridge often confide in trusted personal employees, or perhaps our man may be in a position to overhear certain information. He's sharp and good at what he does. He's been working on just such an eventuality for the past three weeks, since we received your retainer, and he's gotten friendly with Belson McKintridge's major-domo. It wasn't easy, let me tell you. Belson's staff have been with him for years. They're so well paid they never quit and can't be bribed, at least not the ones who'd know anything important. But our man is well trained and posing as a masseur. It's possible he'll be able to get close to Belson. In the meantime, we'll keep chipping away at all other sources of public information. More will open up as time goes by, you'll see.'

'It better,' Felix insisted. 'And soon.'

Chapter 10

VICKY WOKE up again at 5:00 A.M., instantly alert and fully conscious, her mind already hyperactive. She didn't want to be awake this early and thought longingly of her past life when she'd slept like a rock till the alarm rang. Now she slept fitfully, if at all, and woke up with cramped bowels, shoulders in knots, and a clenched jaw that made her molars ache up into her skull.

Another dreaded day ahead, time to sit down and work again, time to fend off the enormous self-doubt and self-criticism that she heaped on herself. She had used up every excuse she could find not to pick up that blank yellow pad again, to try and make this novel come alive. Whatever made her think she'd had a good idea in the first place? Was revenge enough of a motive to go through this painful process? Sometimes, like now, she doubted it.

Write about what you know, was the advice. And that's what she was doing. She knew about Leslie and Belson and Marla and Phyllis firsthand. But that didn't give her well-rounded characters. She needed more.

She'd outlined her plot, she'd outlined her chapters, she'd researched her time period, and then scrapped the first attempt and started over. Because *they* were there, the gods of her existence, the great writers, looking down at her, smirking at her attempts. How dare she attempt to do what 'they' had done so well, so brilliantly, so effortlessly, when she was so limited, when she felt so short of the ideal.

And time was running out—money too. Yesterday she'd sat down to type out her notes and found she wasn't able to breathe, started gasping for air, hyperventilating like some fish out of water. *Ye gods, Vicky, get hold of yourself,* she'd said; and hold she had. But now in the wee hours of yet another dawn she wasn't holding on very well. What was wrong with her book? she wondered. But she knew what was wrong: it wasn't gripping enough. It didn't pull her along as a reader needed to be pulled by a fascinating story.

She switched on the light and reached for her pages by the side of the bed. They were never very far from her. She'd have slept with them under her pillow, except that they crinkled noisily and she was afraid she'd forget during the night and blow her nose in one of her more brilliant paragraphs, mistaking it for a Kleenex.

Writing was so damned hard—more difficult than she had thought it would be and she'd never thought it would be easy. That's why it had taken her so long to commit to it. Occasionally she had bursts of glory, when the metaphors were original and the work ran out of her like syrup on pancakes. But mostly it came in spurts and starts like constipated turds, all cellophane-wrapped by her own efforts. *Go on Vicky, take a look,* she told herself. *What could be so bad?*

She started to read . . . .

There was an intensity about Toni Klein that almost hurt. She appeared before the world totally exposed, her raw needs presented like a piece of newly butchered meat, undressed and bleeding. Whatever was her latest quest, whether searching for a new boyfriend, an A grade from a professor, or a new job, she was unswerving in her dedication to achieve her end and she attacked each task with all the force of her 148 IQ. Toni was small and slender with a womanly shape. Her round hips and full breasts suggested a minor Italian actress and her unblemished complexion always protested any overexposure to the sun. Her eyes were large and round, capable of showing occasional flashes of bitchiness. If left to her own devices, she might have become a Marilyn French, a Germaine Greer, or, even better, a Joan Didion. But her mother (name?) . . .*Hilda.* Her mother, Hilda, interfered, placing her own values on Toni's fertile, hungry mind. If Toni had grown up in Brooklyn or The Bronx, she'd have met and married a graduate student of physics or a minor professor of philosophy. But she grew up in Beverly Hills, the only daughter of a lonely, bitter woman who had been deserted by her brilliant husband twice during their marriage—once when he went off to fight in World War II, even though he was an intellectual and in those days intellectuals often preferred the teachings of Karl Marx to hand-to-hand combat against the Nazis—and then again after the war, when he returned to California and stayed only long enough to father Toni, carry on a love-hate relationship with Harry Truman, and take off again for parts unknown, never to be heard from again. Max Klein (good name) left his pretty but vacuous social-climbing wife to fend for herself and her daughter. In defense of Hilda, she did the best she could and she did have certain admirable virtues—like honesty and a fierce devotion to her child. But it was just these qualities that ruined Toni. Hilda's loyalty, her devotion to her daughter, and her bitterness about what life had dealt her all influenced Toni adversely. Toni became a vicarious tool for her mother; she was molded into a social-climber with intelligence who had an uncompromising desire to succeed in life. The intellectual aspect of Toni's personality which she submerged and refused to pursue never gave her any peace. Ignored, pushed aside, her finely educated mind was shunted off; but it refused to die a quiet death. Instead it never allowed her mundane pursuits to give her pleasure. It served as her conscience and gnawed at her to do something worthwhile in life other than being a model.

This is too personal, Vicky thought. *I can't let my mother know what I think of her. It would break her heart. But what can I write about if I can't be honest? And how will Marla and Phyllis feel if they recognize themselves on the pages of my book? They will hate me.* She had promised herself she wouldn't reveal personal information about them. But what about her own opinions and observations, could she use those? Were they permissible? What did other writers do? Get sued? Lose their friends? She sat there frozen, her hands on the pages she'd written. She couldn't do it. How could she do it? She turned to the page she'd written about Phyllis.

Grace McFarlane [No, McFarlane is too much like McKintridge.] Grace . . . *Lawrence* was the embodiment of virtue. She lived for other people, married her husband to please her father, and then lived to please her husband. A consummate hostess, Grace did everything to perfection but never considered herself above others. She pretended to a dependency on people, but was actually quite strong. She even asked for advice just in order to flatter others, and then excused herself from taking their advice by saying she was too shy to do as they'd suggested. She earned a master's in business administration and was a true patron of the arts. Certain paintings moved her to tears, and copies of works by Tolstoy, Flaubert, Aristotle, or Shakespeare always lay on her bedside table. Her friend, Toni, thought Grace had the potential for greatness if she ever pursued a career; anyone who ran her life so effortlessly could easily run a corporation, for example. But under the cool surface of Grace Lawrence lurked gestating emotions waiting to be born. And even though Grace was governed by an invisible vise of control, and years of obeying had formed a tough outer layer around her, someday she would shatter those hard, clear layers and free herself from constraint. And Toni thought that would be something to see.

Am I the only one who knows that about Phyllis? Vicky

wondered. *And if so, how can I reveal it to the world?*

She was slightly relieved after reading her work. It wasn't so bad. Maybe a part of it was even good. But part wasn't good enough. A book had to be good all the way through.

Suddenly she couldn't stand to think about it anymore. She jumped out of bed and hurried into the bathroom, her mind racing, trying to free itself from her turmoil and not succeeding. She needed answers, real answers, and she needed information—all she could get!

Chapter 11

MARLA EDGED her way into the back of the classroom and took her place in line. The class started promptly at 8:00 A.M., and everyone was already bending and stretching. She was late because Mark had a stomachache this morning and she'd driven him to school. It was nearly impossible to find time for everything she had to do, and a morning crisis had a way of fouling up an entire day.

She bent forward and swung her head and arms through her legs while Nick Conti stood on his platform at the front of the room, demonstrating the exercises. His usual hyper-attention was focused on three new ladies, giving them his introductory dose of charm. They were clustered around his platform like sea gulls around a fishing boat waiting for the trolling of the bait. They tried to follow his expert moves, but their bodies looked like penguins on land wad-dling in outlandish outfits. Eventually they would fit in, and if they stuck to it, they'd even improve their abused, over-fed, lumpish bodies.

Nick was a tenacious, tireless worker, and the biggest flirt she'd ever seen. But she couldn't fault his explosive energy. It was damned difficult to be here every morning and face this pack of baby hippos with enthusiasm. Sometimes his cheerfulness was downright disgusting.

By the time Marla fed Lori and Mark their breakfast, got them off to school, organized her day, made lists for the maintenance of her household, called the people who were imperative to expedite her life, and gathered herself together into some semblance of order, she was so resentful and self-pitying that she didn't smile until ten o'clock. And if that wasn't enough, she now had a new house to occupy her thoughts and to decorate in the style to which her up-and-coming husband was becoming accustomed. But at least it kept her mind off Felix Anhalt.

'Tuck that butt in tightly, ladies,' Nick was saying, urging them on, showing them how. 'And release and tighten . . .'

Marla squeezed her buns with the rest of them. *Maybe I'll have hamburgers for dinner,* she thought, inspired by the association of *buns* to *buns,* as she tightened and released. But Larry didn't like hamburgers unless they were mixed with mushrooms and onions, and the kids wouldn't eat them that way.

'Are we working our tushes off?' Nick asked.

Marla decided she'd buy chicken or lamb chops. Either way someone would complain.

She did her pliés, trying to enjoy the burning sensation in her thighs. 'It's good for you when it hurts,' Nick always said.

After class Marla headed for the showers, noticing that there were fifteen women surrounding Nick. It amazed her how transparent they all were, how eager for the master's attention. They asked his advice on marital problems, discussed their broken appliances, sought encouragement on their slightly improved bodies, and all just to get him into bed. And Nick was only twenty-two. What could he possibly know? Most of these women were way over forty and he was no prize. He was brash and conceited, pushy and outspoken, and they devoured his every word. Perhaps they liked his irreverent manner disguised as honesty. 'That color looks like caca on you, Mona,' he would say, and Mona would never wear it again, at least not to class. Or, 'Why don't you do something with your scrambled-egg hairdo, Lynn?' and Lynn would make an immediate appointment with her hairdresser and then fluff the new one under Nick's nose until he noticed. 'Better!' he'd say. Marla couldn't understand it. Unless they'd transferred their usual devotion from their gay hairdresser to Nick, a legendary cocksman. With Nick every woman was fair game.

Marla was not interested in being one of his devotees and she established her sexual indifference to him early in their relationship. Nick had come over to her during one of the classes; he'd leaned in close to her reclining body, pulled up on her leg as though he were showing her the maximum stretch, while all the while he was checking out her 'possibilities.' Marla stared at him with a blank expression until his smile began to harden on his face, and then she removed his hand from the back of her thigh and continued to pull her own leg exactly as he had shown her.

'That's fine, Margaret,' he had said.

'It's Marla,' she corrected, but he was already back up in front of her class, correcting one of his more compliant ladies.

He never made another overture, which was fine with her. She admired his ambition and aggressiveness, but she wouldn't be one of his groupies.

Now, Felix Anhalt was another matter altogether. She was obsessed with the man. She thought of him constantly. On days when she and Leslie had meetings with him to show him swatches or designs for his yacht, *The Perspicacious*, she was in a fever of anticipation. She dressed with great care, made sure her makeup was perfect, found herself wearing more and more provocative clothing, leaving strategic buttons unbuttoned, crossing her legs so her skirts hiked up higher than modesty would allow. It was a strange one-sided seduction, for Felix remained businesslike, always polite with her. Still, every lingering touch of his hand or innocent kiss of greeting sent shivers through her. The scent of his cologne when he bent over her to see her sketches made her mouth yearn for passionate kisses. Yet he always seemed intent on the work at hand.

Marla waited breathlessly for him to respond to her more overtly, and some of his glances were more intimate to her than they were to Leslie—his smiles to her more full of meaning, making them co-conspirators. But she had to be cautious around Leslie, never to let her interest show. Leslie would be furiously outraged, and rightly so. Her business was far too important to allow flirtations between employee and client.

She was thinking about Felix as she drove east on Burton Way toward Robertson. The morning activities of antiquing on Santa Monica had made her hungry and she realized she wouldn't have time for lunch today because she'd taken out the time to go to exercise class.

As she approached En Brochette, a lovely French bistro with an outdoor patio at Wetherly and Burton Way, the traffic in front of her slowed down to allow a Mercedes sedan two cars ahead of her to unload its passengers. The Mercedes was the same color and model as Larry's car, and when the driver got out, she saw it was he. Her heart skipped a beat at the sight of him. How amazing to still react like that after eight and a half years of marriage. She loved the way he combed his hair; the light gray worsted suit matched the silver color of his car. She was about to honk, but she decided to wait until she was closer; she wanted to see the look of surprise on his face. She checked the left lane and then pulled around the cars in front of her, coming abreast of him, ready to call his name. But the greeting died in her throat when she saw the attendant open the passenger door to help a blond woman get out. It was Sheila Conway, their real-estate agent.

Give them the benefit of the doubt, Marla thought. But then Larry placed his hand possessively around Sheila's waist and guided her into the restaurant and Marla was stunned. She knew that gesture well. It was calculated to let every man in the place know Sheila was with him.

A hot burst of acid filled her stomach as she stared at them. Sheila's blond, silky hair moved like a shampoo commercial as she turned her head, pretending an innocence she did not possess; and Larry's expensively tailored three-piece suit covered well his cloven hooves. The sun dappled the pink-linen-covered table through the lace of nearby trees, the crystal glasses of ice water sparkled in the sun, the waiters scurried around in black pants and white shirts, and Sheila smiled up at Larry provocatively. Definitely not a business-lunch smile.

As if in slow motion Marla watched them. She wanted to reach out with a giant arm and sweep them both into the gutter, knocking them like chessmen violently to the floor in a loser's rage. But instead she somehow found the strength to step on the gas and the car lurched forward. But she could barely breathe. Her face and hands alternated between extreme temperatures of hot and cold while her heart beat in wild, sore thumps against her ribs.

Don't be an idiot, she told herself, *it's only business. It has to be.* But she was gripping the wheel so hard that pains were shooting up her arms, and she clenched her jaw so hard that her teeth ached. None of the reasonable arguments could erase the feeling of seeing Larry, her Larry, with another woman. Even though she told herself that if they had anything to hide, they would never be seen in such a public place, the hurt was almost unbearable. She felt that someone very dear to her had died, but she didn't know whom. She had a terrible longing to hug her children, to bury her head in the crooks of their sweet necks and breathe the fragrances of their young bodies, feel their arms around her neck, hear them say, 'We love you, Mommy, Daddy's a bad man.'

When she arrived at Leslie's building, she had no recollection of how she'd gotten there. She couldn't bring herself to go in. She couldn't face Leslie now, that assessing glance, that scrutinizing look, the checking out of her demeanor from top to toe. How she trembled until she saw the slight raise of Leslie's left eyebrow that meant she'd passed inspection for that day, how she held her breath waiting for Leslie's list of her latest mistakes, her shortcomings, sparingly laced with brief compliments like 'adequate,' or 'inoffensive, Marla dear.' And even though she knew her work was exemplary—after she checked and rechecked every detail, pored over her choices, swept every corner of her mind for innovative ideas, wrote pages of justification for her choices—Leslie always found something not quite right. After the shock she'd just received, she didn't trust herself to smile and take it today. She might say something she'd regret so it would be better to take an hour off for herself. Have a manicure, have a haircut, have a sandwich, have an affair. *I'll go see Felix*, she thought. *I'll call him,* and she almost smiled; but first she headed for Ed's Coffee Shop, a watering hole for those in the trade, wondering if homemade vegetable soup would mix well with the knives in her stomach.

Chapter 12

FELIX HAD to admit that he got a kick out of the cloak-and-dagger arrangement of meeting Bob Delman for lunch at Barney's Beanery. Sleazy though it was, the place had atmosphere. Delman had refused to meet him at first, but Felix insisted. When Clarence and Kotlier said they had something for him, he wanted to get the information directly from the man who discovered it. Besides, his excitement was so high, he was willing to go anywhere, to meet clandestinely, even fly to San Francisco if necessary to meet with Delman. But they'd settled on this local restaurant. Certainly no one in Felix's world would see him here. His only minor regret about this meeting was that he'd had to forgo a possible interlude with Marla Gilbert. Her phone call had caught him just as he was going out the door. But Marla Gilbert would wait for another time. She was almost ready for the big move, tremblingly ripe for picking. But getting information on Belson took precedence over everything else.

Delman turned out to be young, in his early thirties, with a muscular build, cropped curly hair, wearing a white T-shirt, gray sweat-suit jogging pants, and sneakers. Instead of a private investigator he could have been any muscle-worshiping macho type the way he blended in with the bikers and out-of-work actors who frequented this place. Felix felt as conspicuous as a cherry tomato in a green salad in his three-piece business suit.

They eyed one another over menus until they'd ordered and the waitress had left; Felix fought to keep his eagerness in check. 'What have you got for me?' he asked, leaning forward on his elbows.

But Delman was a man who did things in his own time and wouldn't be rushed. First he described his bi-weekly visits working as a masseur for Belson and their budding relationship.

'Yes, yes,' Felix said impatiently, 'but what have you got?'

They were interrupted by the waitress bringing them their drinks and had to wait again until she left.

Delman was quite pleased with himself as he leaned forward and spoke quietly, his words meant only for Felix. 'I've been able to document that Belson is in deep financial trouble, and he is gravely ill besides. He's borrowed heavily against his assets and looks as if he's about to go under. Everything he has left is balanced by threads. If one of those threads snaps, it all goes. The man is nearly broke.'

Felix fell back against the booth as if struck by a javelin

bolt. 'What?' he exclaimed. 'That's impossible. The man's as flush as they come. Worth millions. *Millions!* All in blue-chip securities.'

Delman shook his head and leaned back, confidence gazing out from half-closed lids. 'Not anymore,' he insisted. 'You don't know what we went through to get this information. The man's affairs are like a computer terminal box after being dismantled by a chimpanzee. Every lead led to another lead and back to itself again. But by god we untangled it. Enough to know that I'm right. And the medical information is unshakable. I've even got a copy of his angiogram report if you want to see it. He has very little time left.'

Felix shook his head in wonderment. *So that's why Peter's been so upset lately.* But Felix couldn't assess everything so quickly; and he was grateful when the waitress brought them their order, giving him a moment to think while the immense possibilities bombarded him. He watched Delman dig into his burger cheerfully, the dispatcher who'd delivered his burden and now deserved his reward. Damn right, Felix thought, he deserves the Medal of Honor for this job. *The kid's a genius.* But what would Belson's losses mean to him? Though he was overjoyed to hear about them, it meant that he was cheated out of causing them. How he had longed to engineer Belson's ruin himself. Still, there had been no opportunity for him to affect the man, though he had tried. Lord knows he had tried. But now the fates had smiled on him, handing him the man's ruination on a silver platter. No, not on a silver platter, on a chipped dimestore dish and an enamel embalming table.

So you're on your way out, old man, Felix thought, a smile tickling the corners of his mouth. *I won't miss you. I'll only be sorry to lose someone to hate. Hating has a way of spicing up life.*

'We'll send you the written reports in a few days,' Delman said, wiping drips of tomato and mayonnaise from his mouth. 'We still need to solidify a few details.'

189

Felix felt so euphoric that his appetite became suddenly ravenous and his delight was so expansive he wanted to embrace the world.

'You look pleased,' Delman said. It was rather obvious as Felix chomped a huge happy bite out of his burger. But *pleased* was an understatement. *Ecstatic* was more like it. He shrugged, trying to hide his happiness from Delman.

Delman went down the list of financial disasters Belson had encountered, and Felix marveled at their diversity and stupidity. 'The man has developed a knack for screwing up,' Delman said.

'Maybe I too would be desperately grabbing at straws if I saw my estate dwindling like this at that age,' Felix said, keeping up the pretense of why he had hired Delman in the first place. 'Even though he's in trouble, his experience and advice are still valuable.'

Delman nodded, stirring his coffee and taking a sip. 'That's true and he's not out yet. That could be why he's making some sort of last-ditch effort to catch up.'

'What effort?' Felix asked, feeling the edge of his delight diminish slightly.

Delman shrugged. 'Dunno yet. Something his grandson is involved in helping him with. All we know is he's scraped the bottom of the barrel for his last remaining cash source.'

'What is he doing with it?' Felix demanded sharply, and then forced himself to remain calm. 'Is there a chance he could recover his fortune or his health?'

The corners of Delman's mouth lowered as he shook his head from side to side. 'No chance. The man's in a hole so deep they're expecting him in China any day now, and he's only got a few months to live, according to our independent medical examiner.'

'Then what's Peter involved in?' Felix asked.

'He's your son-in-law. Won't he tell you?'

'I can't question him anymore. I've tried too many times as it is. And I don't want him to know what I know, or how I found out. Don't forget my daughter is involved in this; whatever affects Peter, affects her.' *And Belson would know that I know too,* Felix thought. *It's too soon for that.* 'Just keep digging, Bob,' Felix said. 'Anything else you come up with, anything at all, is vital to me. I want to know every detail you uncover. Nothing is unimportant. I want to know the regularity of his bowel movements.'

Delman gave him a long, thoughtful stare. 'That's not the way I work,' he replied. 'When I'm hired to locate financial holdings or determine the physical condition of a subject, that's what I stick to. I don't do character assassination, and I don't relish the idea of discovering fruit from the rotten tree.'

Felix bristled at Delman's tone. Ultimatums from underlings were intolerable. But Delman was the first person ever to penetrate Belson's strict security. That was worth a great deal. *My luck,* Felix thought. *He turns out to have scruples.*

Felix smiled pleasantly. 'Clarence and Kotlier never said anything about limiting their information before.' He was trying to call Delman's bluff.

'Maybe so, but not with me on the case. I won't be a party to blackmail, sir.' Delman flagged the waitress for the check.

Felix was certain he was making a gesture about paying the check; he was probably on an expense account.

'This isn't a divorce case, or fraud, or nonpayment of a debt. I know because I always insist on knowing what I'm doing beforehand, or I won't take the job. I'm not on salary with C and K. I'm an independent contractor and I'm very strict about my terms of employment.'

'Here, let me take that,' Felix said, reaching for the check. But Delman got it first.

'We'll split it,' Delman said, opening his wallet and handing Felix the cash to cover his own lunch.

'Don't be so proud,' Felix said.

Delman smiled. 'I was born that way.'

The sun was bright as they came out of the restaurant; there was a slight chill in the air. Delman winked at an attractive young woman walking by and looked around as though surveying his domain. His young face was unlined, his dark eyes clear of guile, and his manner cocky and self-confident. He was right: he was born proud, and Felix envied the lack of complications in his life. 'Gorgeous day, isn't it?' Delman asked, not waiting for a reply.

How could Felix make him understand that he had to know *everything* about Belson McKintridge?

'I won't meet you in person again,' Delman said. 'And if you ever see me anywhere, you look right through me.' He gave a wave and walked over to a Harley-Davidson in the parking lot, donned a helmet, and straddled the seat.

Felix followed him anxiously, hoping to get in a last word before he took off. 'Bob,' he said, 'I didn't mean to imply that I wanted you to go against your own ethics. It's just that there's still so much I don't know about McKintridge yet. Especially about this recovery plan of his.'

'I'll tell you what,' Delman said with an exasperating grin. 'There *is* something else about Belson McKintridge that intrigues me and it hasn't anything to do with finances. I was going to let it go by, but it's a piece of the puzzle that doesn't fit. Once or twice in the time I've been working with him, I've seen a character hanging around the estate who has criminal connections. I know because I had him checked out. He doesn't work for Belson, though maybe he once did, and maybe he's visiting a friend or relative on the staff. But everyone else surrounding Belson is so whistle clean this guy stands out. His name is Raphael and he's been a pimp, a drug dealer, and a fence. If anything turns up to connect him to Belson himself, I'll let you know. But I'll have to let the police know too. Fair enough?'

Felix nodded gratefully, feeling he'd just won a difficult round with young Delman. He stuck out his hand and Delman took it.

'Thank you,' Felix said, but Delman didn't turn around as he took off up the street.

So, Felix thought. *There's more waiting in store for me. But this time the prize is within my sights. God, I hope Belson lasts long enough for me to stick it to him, somehow, some way. I've got to have that satisfaction. I've just got to.*

And then he thought of something wonderful. *The estate. Who's going to get the estate if Belson loses it before he dies and Peter can't hang on to it anyway?*

Wouldn't it gall Belson to think that I owned it? Felix thought. *Wouldn't it just!*

Chapter 13

A SILVER stretched limousine was parked at the curb and two huge bodyguards stood outside the door of her shop when Leslie arrived in her office after lunch. Billy D. greeted her with a raised eyebrow and an exasperated nod toward her upstairs office.

'It's three forty-five P.M. *Les-lie*. He's been in there for hours.'

'Who is it?' she asked. 'Joseph Bonnano?'

'Only the best-looking man I've seen all week.' He gave her the knowing smile of a homosexual authority.

'And I bet you've seen plenty,' she said, starting up the stairs, her adrenaline pumping. This heightened anticipation was what she did it all for, the long hours, the dedication, the obsessive involvement in work, just to provide herself with this sense of treasure about to be unearthed, of a challenge about to be conquered. Whoever was in her office was wealthy, important, mysterious, and piqued her curiosity no end. She shook her head and fluffed her hair, licked her lips, and then made her entrance.

Sheikh Ammani and an exquisite young woman were seated in front of Leslie's copper and steel desk. Leslie would have recognized him even if *The Beverly Hills*

Courier and *Beverly Hills People* hadn't had his picture dominating their front pages for weeks. Ammani was as talked about a social addition to the Beverly Hills scene as Hugh Hefner had been when he moved into Holmby Hills, and Sheikh Ali Fassi was when he painted the Whittier mansion pistachio green and detailed the plaster statues surrounding the mansion in living color, including their genitalia.

Sheikh Ammani was gorgeous; he wore a custom tailored suit from Bijan and appeared to be in his early forties. His jet black hair, shot through with gray, framed a dominating stare. His skin was darkly tanned but not swarthy, though there was a touch of purple to his lips, which were full and sensual, accented by a trimmed black mustache. He broke into a charming smile as she entered and advanced, hand outstretched.

Leslie was poised and controlled. 'Sheikh Ammani, what a delight to meet you.' But her heart was pumping wildly in her chest. If Ammani had come here for the reason she suspected, she was about to be offered the most exciting and lucrative job of the decade.

'Ah, you know who I am,' the sheikh said, showing his pleasure. 'May I present Princess Saarit. She is visiting Beverly Hills with her parents. Her father is an associate of mine.'

The princess rose and took Leslie's hand, appraising her with a rather frank stare. Leslie had already noted the excellently tailored French dress; she'd seen one like it at Giorgio's for a small fortune. The girl was no more than twenty-two, with translucent skin stretched thinly over high olive-toned cheekbones that accentuated high black eyes and softly waving black hair.

'*Votre boutique, c'est merveilleuse,*' the young Arab woman said. Her voice was low and well cultured.

'The princess speaks only French and Arabic,' Sheikh Ammani said. 'She loves your shop. We both do.'

Leslie glanced down. The girl had the calves and ankles of an aristocrat. Legs were something Leslie always noticed first; she judged their quality on a rating scale she had devised, beginning with perfection, like her own, to acceptable, like the average woman's, to embarrassingly thick or plump, like the heavier women of her acquaintance. Princess Saarit's hands were beautiful too, unadorned and slender, like her legs.

'Merci, mademoiselle,' Leslie said, wishing she remembered more of her high school French. She turned to the sheikh, indicating for him to take his seat while she stepped behind her desk. 'I have been keeping abreast of your exciting foray into our city's business life. I must say, I have the highest admiration for what you're doing. Dealing with city bureaucrats must be terribly frustrating.'

'Not for me, dear lady. If one has dealt with my countrymen as successfully as I, one would find the Americans far easier to do business with. The American bureaucrat means what he says, though he is sometimes tied by the red tape of his department. In Saudi Arabia a man seldom means what he says. You have to learn to listen for the subtleties.'

Sheikh Ammani's smile was truly dazzling, halfway between evil and innocence; she was absolutely smitten. 'I shall remember that bit of information, Sheikh, even though I'm aware that you pursue your goals with tenacity and perseverance.'

Just then the princess leaned forward and whispered something in his ear. He nodded, and said to Leslie, 'Saarit would like to go downstairs and browse in your shop while you and I discuss business. Would that be all right with you?'

'Of course,' Leslie said, smiling at the girl. There was nothing she'd like better than being alone with this incredible man. And he seemed to feel the same way, for as the young woman left, he never turned to watch her go but kept his eyes glued to Leslie. She could feel the color in her cheeks heighten. *Good,* she thought. *Nothing like a bit of feminine blushing to make a girl more attractive.*

Leslie and her closest friend, Dianna Cunningham, had

195

been discussing Sheikh Ammani and his latest project this very morning during their daily phone call. They decided Leslie had to have him as a client and they'd gone down their list of acquaintances, searching for anyone who knew the sheikh and could recommend Leslie to him. And now here he was, no strategy needed. *Wait until Dianna hears about this!*

It was amazing how far Ammani had gotten with the city fathers, even though he'd had his difficulties. He was pushing through an ordinance to rezone the last remaining industrial property in Beverly Hills and turn it into a mini-complex, with lakeside villas, town houses, and individual specialized shops catering to the residents. There would be several private screening rooms and a recording complex available for residents, most of whom would be in the entertainment business. It was such a clever yet difficult plan that no one had ever conceived of it, mostly because it was nearly impossible to get zoning laws changed.

'How do you estimate your chances of approval with the city council on your new venture?' Leslie asked, leaning forward on her desk with studied concentration. She was glad she'd worn green today. It was her most flattering color. She always added a touch of it to every job; nothing ostentatious—never that, a soft Boston fern or maidenhair would do.

'Oh, I've had approval for weeks,' the sheikh admitted slyly. 'The controversy one reads in the papers is a ploy to sway public opinion in my favor. I'm afraid the overabundant wealth of some of my countrymen has made it difficult to operate as openly as we would like. We are careful to keep—how do you say—a low profile, so that when others are denied their permits and ours are granted, there is no outcry against us. Actually my plans are nearly complete. Mr Charles Luckman is our architect.'

Leslie was amazed. What power he must wield. She'd seen the influence of Arab money before, but this was frightening. If only she could land this job.

196

All her phone lines were ringing at once but she pressed her DO NOT DISTURB button. Clients like the sheikh were far too precious to interrupt. Whenever there was a choice, she turned over the ordinary Beverly Hills matrons to her other staff members and concentrated on the industrialists with megadollars. They could spend millions in the same time it took others to spend thousands, and she was the one who could coax it out of them. She leaned back in her chair and smiled, assuming an attitude of calm and repose. Mustn't seem too anxious; one's attitude of self-confidence was essential when dealing with people who had the kind of money to spend that Sheikh Ammani did. Arabs especially appreciated the appearance of control. They were masters of the bluff, of the hard deal, of the convoluted arrangement that ended up benefitting them. But Leslie could outmaneuver anyone. 'And how may I be of service to you?' she asked, adding a touch of subservience to her voice. The sheikh would respond instinctively to the female inferior tone.

'You may not be aware that I have had you investigated, Mrs Winokur, along with several other designers. I intend to invite one of you to assist me in my new project.'

Leslie nodded. 'I presume that you have made up your mind or you would not be in my office right now.' She behaved as though what he had just said were perfectly natural, yet she was seething. Nobody checked her out anymore! She had a world-famous reputation. She was the biggest name in this town, head and shoulders above Barbara Lockhard or Sally Sirkin. She made Stephen Chase look like small potatoes, and only Cecil Beaton or Tony Duquette or Valerian Rybar could come close to her in talent for design. 'A man of your taste level has the superior judgment to choose exactly the right person to fulfill his needs,' she said.

'You are quite right, madame,' he said, standing to his full height of six feet. 'I have made my choice.'

Leslie's heart gave an authorized jump. This Persian

peach could be falling right into her lap, all ripe and juicy, ready to be devoured. Now that was a pleasant idea, she thought.

'When I have more details, you will be hearing from me, Mrs Winokur. I believe in notifying my associates of my exact intentions. Then they may anticipate my needs, a most useful quality.' His eyes raked her body and she felt herself suddenly exposed and vulnerable. A delicious shiver ran through her. She knew exactly what he meant. What an antithesis this man was to her late husband, Craige, who had fought the city council so many times and never won! Craige always went through channels, greased palms, played golf, kissed asses, and even bedded a few well-placed wives to make his deals. But he'd never succeeded like this. That's why he'd gone out of state to build condominiums in Idaho and Hawaii. Dear, sweet, unobtrusive Craige, he'd been gone five years now.

The sheikh was watching her with an enigmatic smile. If she said no to his offer, he would turn to others. But she wouldn't say no.

'What is your schedule for the next six months, may I inquire?'

'Extremely busy, as usual,' she replied, keeping the arrogance out of her voice, willing her posture to remain calm. It was against her better judgment to indulge her libido with a client. It could ruin a business relationship and give the client an unfair advantage when neither was sure who was using whom. But this man would be a tough one to ignore.

'Hire another assistant,' he said. 'Perhaps even two or three. I shall need you very soon.' And he turned to go, but as he reached the door, he turned back.

'Was there anything else?'

He looked slightly perturbed by her question but covered it up. 'Yes,' he replied. 'There is. I've been given to understand you were once a close special friend of Mr Belson McKintridge?'

Leslie's blood ran cold and she stared at the man in her

doorway. 'I knew him quite well,' she said. 'Why do you ask?'

'I should like to meet him one day,' the sheikh told her. 'Perhaps you could arrange it?'

'Possibly,' Leslie agreed—anything to land this job, she'd worry about Belson later. 'But I haven't spoken to the man in years.'

'Are you still on good terms with him?' He was watching her closely.

'Oh, the best,' she lied, holding up two crossed fingers. 'We're like that,' she said.

'Excellent,' he declared. 'Excellent. But I shall approach him first through my regular sources and if that doesn't prove satisfactory, perhaps you will help me out?' He had the most suggestive way of asking for a favor that Leslie had ever seen.

'My pleasure, Sheikh Ammani,' she said.

'Call me Banir,' he insisted, taking her hand and kissing it. 'If I may call you Leslie?'

She nodded, her heart in her throat. And then he left, leaving her with the feeling she'd just been struck by a blazing comet. *Meet Belson McKintridge, indeed. Not if I can help it,* she thought. Those two should be kept as far apart as possible, otherwise she'd have to protect herself from Belson's particular poison.

She waited until the sheikh and the young princess had left the building and then pressed every buzzer on her panel, summoning her staff. In a moment they were all assembled: two draftsmen, three full-time designers, two secretaries, a receptionist, Billy D., and Marla Gilbert, who did a bit of everything and who'd become more useful than Leslie had expected in a shorter amount of time. Marla had lost weight, but her clothes still looked like the junior department at Bullock's.

'For those of you who are not aware, we've had a "visitation." It is possible that I shall be offered the opportunity of a lifetime,' she stated. 'And I must have the freedom to pursue it. I want a plan on my desk in two hours detailing how we can reorganize our situation here so I will have a free schedule for the next six months.'

A collective groan rose from her assembled troops. They were all working twelve hours a day as it was, and Leslie handled a full load of clients too. She was indispensible to certain 'special clients' who required her unique services and deserved them. The staff could only service these 'special clients' so far and then Leslie had to take over. She knew this as well as they did.

'Now, now,' she soothed, 'I'm not dying. I'll be here to hold hands and troubleshoot where necessary. And we can hire, hire, hire all the extra help we need, pets. But you've got to help me. This could be the biggest one we've ever gotten, with millions of Saudi dollars to spend and a proposed plan for eighty luxury condominiums, all to be individually furnished by us for different owners. Each unit starts at eight hundred thousand, basic price. My ideas would be included in the planning stages, my opinions contributed to the architects, and of course I design all the interiors.' Her eyes were glinting with excitement; she wanted to charge them all with the fierceness of her desire. 'Two hours, darlings,' she said waving them away. 'Be creative, use each other's talents. If you weren't all miracle workers you wouldn't be here!'

'Leslie,' Marla interrupted timidly. 'What about Felix Anhalt's yacht? He's not going to accept a substitute for you.'

Leslie was caught for a moment and studied Marla with a knowing look. 'I'll give him to you,' she said with a wicked smile, watching the color spread to Marla's cheeks. 'Felix won't mind. You know the job. It's about time you earned your salary around here. Finish that price workup you've been dawdling over,' she commanded, 'and show it to Billy D. He'll assist you.' She turned to Billy. 'Marla knows what I want, love. We'll have to trust her sometime. And Marla,' she added, 'will you please go out to Jôna's and buy some more clothes?'

Billy's expression of exasperation showed his agreement.

Marla gave Leslie a shocked nod of amazement as Leslie shooed them all out of her office. Let Marla have Felix Anhalt, Miss Moony Eyes. Felix was chicken feed compared to the sheikh. That little sparrow Marla hadn't had a chance with Felix while Leslie was around, but now maybe she would.

Chapter 14

'THE UPSHOT of it all,' Marla told Larry at dinner, between 'eat your green beans, Lori, and take your feet off the chair, Mark,' 'is that I've been made an assistant designer, but I'll have full responsibility for Felix Anhalt's yacht and Billy D. will assist me only if I need it.'

'Felix's yacht?' he commented sharply.

'It's a wonderful opportunity,' she said, rushing ahead, praying that he wouldn't start an argument over this. 'A major career move. There's no limit to how far I can go.' All day she had dreaded this evening, planned her attack, but all her preparation couldn't calm the wild beating of her heart or erase the memory of her chance encounter with him and Sheila earlier today.

'How far *do* you want to go?' Larry asked, stressing the double-entendre. There was a tightness around his mouth, a narrowing of his eyes: all the signs that rage was brewing just under the surface.

'As far as I can, *in business,*' she said, being careful to make that distinction. She wanted him to realize she was ambitious too. 'I have an exciting career ahead of me, Larry. Someday I'll have the kind of prestigious jobs offered to me that Leslie gets, like the McKintridge estate; I might even be able to convince Belson to let me do the estate someday. Just think of that!'

His smile was tight and sarcastic. 'I don't want to think of that, or of you working intimately with Felix. The man's a lech. He's only out for one thing! And you're so gullible you won't even know it until he's got his hands in your pants.'

'Larry!' she exclaimed, indicating the children, who were listening to every word.

'Well, I don't like it!' he repeated. 'I don't like the way it looks.' His eyes were round, adding a touch of wildness to his expression.

'And how do you think you looked today at En Brochette? Like the example of a trustworthy husband?'

For a fleeting instant he looked caught, but then anger flashed across his face, deepening the line between his eyebrows. 'That was business!' he snapped. 'And what were you doing? Spying on me? Or were you off in a corner behind some screen with one of your "special clients"?'

'Is that what she is to you, Larry, a "special client"?'

'Yes! As a matter of fact.' He stuck his chin out at her and she wanted to punch it, let loose with a Muhammad Ali right cross. 'What *were* you doing there?'

'I was driving by. Minding my own business, feeling hungry, and wishing I could go to lunch with my husband. And then I saw my husband with his goddamned arm around another woman.'

'Don't swear in front of the children,' he said through clenched teeth. 'I didn't have my arm around her. And if you were home where you were supposed to be, maybe I would have invited you to lunch because I would have known where to reach you. But are you at home? Not you!' His voice was stronger and full of antagonism as he fed on his own anger. 'You were out God knows where. When I was a kid, my mother was home every day after school. If there was an emergency during the day, we knew where to find her. But not you! You're out in the field when Mark sprains his wrist, or Lori vomits in painting class.'

Marla hadn't noticed before that the skin around his mouth turned white when he was angry. 'Your mother never left the house, Larry, because she was afraid she'd run into your father with one of his tootsies, and now I know exactly how she felt. And that time when Mark sprained his wrist and the other time when Lori got sick, the school reached you, didn't they? Daddies are parents too, you know. That's why they put two phone numbers on the emergency card.'

'It's really clever of you to pick on my mother to make a point. What did she ever do to you except set an example of what a mother should be like!'

Damn it, she thought. *He's the one who was out with another woman today, and he's got me on the defensive again.* She tried a new tack. 'Why can't you be happy for me, Larry? I'm happy for you when you succeed, when Peter brings new clients into the office, or you make a brilliant maneuver, or even when Sheila helps you out. But I can't just drive car pool or play tennis my whole life. I'm young and alive and vital and a woman as wonderful as Leslie recognizes that in me. Why can't you?' Her expression pleaded with him to understand, but he was glaring at her, unmoved. 'We'd better discuss this later,' she said, noticing that the children had stopped eating and were watching them with seeming curiosity, the hunch of their shoulders telling Marla how miserable they were with this argument.

'Goddamn it!' Larry shouted, his anger suddenly erupting. 'I will not discuss this later. I don't want you working with Felix. He can't be trusted.' And he threw down his fork, which clattered loudly on the plate, bounced off the table, and slid to the floor. Snuffy came over immediately to scavenge the bits of roast beef that were scattered about.

Lori flinched and pulled away as if Larry might strike out at her next. 'Please don't swear, Daddy,' she pleaded.

'Like you told Mommy not to.'

Mark began to cry.

'I'll swear if I want to, Lori,' he yelled. 'I'm your father and don't tell me what to do. This is none of your concern.' He couldn't see how frightened Lori was.

'Please, Larry,' Marla begged. But he was on his way, a rampage about to begin. Her stomach tightened in knots.

'No wife of mine is going to be jiggling her fanny in front of a man like Anhalt. A full-time career, my eye, when there are children to raise. You can have a career when they're in junior high, but not now! *I'm* building *my* career, Marla. You don't seem to understand that. The competition is cut-throat out there! I need all the help I can get to stay alive. I need a wife who'll entertain in my home, for my clients. It's extremely important. And I'm not wealthy enough yet to take them to the Bistro or hire Milton Williams, like Felix does. I need a wife who'll join organizations where I can meet new people, who'll join the Lawyer's Wives Council because I don't have the god-damned time to do it. Do you understand?' His fists were clenched and he was pounding them on the table.

'I understand perfectly,' she shouted back, knowing with sudden clarity that they weren't arguing about whose career should take precedence, they were arguing about Felix. 'And there's something else I understand,' she said with a degree less of anger. 'I'm the one who saw *you* today, not the other way around. And if that's what you want, maybe you're married to the wrong person. Because I don't like it any more than you do. And as for my career, I'm entitled to one too.'

'Oh, sure.' His voice rang with sarcasm. 'Some career, at a hundred a week.'

'And what did you make when you started practicing?'

'Oh, so now you're going to bring that up, are you? Well, if I recall, you weren't supportive of me then. But I did all right, didn't I? And besides, that was different.'

'Why was that different?' she yelled back. 'Except that at the time we had no security and now we do.' She calmed down a bit. 'Larry, do you have any idea what Leslie makes a year? At least five hundred thousand. We're not talking about peanuts here. I could make money like that if I had my own firm someday.'

'Your own firm? Don't make me laugh,' he scoffed.

'Do you think I have so little talent? Do you think it's impossible? Well, what about this new house you're living in. Who decorated it? Who got all the raves and compliments for turning this ancient dump into a beautiful place? I did, Larry, because of my talent and my knowledge!' Again fury gripped her entire body. How could she get through to him? 'I have just as much right to succeed as you do!' *And to flirt too!* she thought.

'And who do you think's paying for all this? Certainly not Felix,' Larry yelled.

'You and I both are paying for it,' she insisted.

Mark was still crying and his volume increased with their shouting. 'Stop crying, Mark,' Larry insisted, 'or leave the table.'

Mark swallowed hard, and tried to stop, but he was in the hiccoughing stage where it was beyond control. He bowed his head and Marla saw his tears falling onto his plate while his small body shook convulsively. At this moment she could have killed Larry. Her heart twisted for Mark and she glared at her husband, the boy she'd married, this male tyrant, who cried in sad movies and always remembered the flavor of her favorite ice cream, whose greatest pleasure in life was buying her special gifts and who never forgot their anniversary or their first date, or 'their' song, or her shoe size, was the most unreasonable, mixed up man she'd ever known. She had the distinct feeling Larry was not only jealous of her attraction for Felix, but because Felix was giving business to her and not to him. Yet she loved him so much, that when he gave her ultimatums, like he was doing now, the 'no wife of mine will ever do that' routine, she almost wanted to say, 'Okay, I'll stay home and make terrific dinners for your clients; I'll put aside my career for yours if it will give you the security you desperately need, and keep our son from crying himself to sleep again.' But most of all she was tempted to say it because it would keep her away from Felix Anhalt. God only knew how she was going to avoid that now.

Mark was still crying.

'I said shut up, Mark,' Larry shouted at him again.

'That's enough, Larry,' she said, reaching over to gather Mark into her lap to cuddle him. Then she grabbed Lori's hand too and squeezed it tightly as if to say, 'Just hold on, kids, Mommy understands, she'll make it better.'

But Lori reached out with her other hand and took hold of Larry's. Marla was touched by her daughter's gesture. As angry as she was at him, she realized she was trying to divide the children's loyalty against him by her action. Lori's gesture had made them all a unit again.

'Sweetheart,' she said to Mark, trying to calm him, to bring some semblance of understanding to this craziness. 'When you and Lori fight over your Fisher-Price toy, or the talking telephone, and sometimes even hit each other, do I sit and cry about it?'

Mark looked up at her with Larry's brown eyes and Larry's reddish freckles across a button nose made redder from his tears, and she saw a hint of a smile through the hiccoughs. He shook his head no.

'So if Daddy and I yell at each other, I know you don't like it, but that doesn't mean we don't love each other. But sometimes people have to fight and stand up for what they want, even if it's hard. Just like you have to fight for your turn on the trampoline, or the rocking horse.'

'But Daddy sweared, and he said shut up, and he's so mad all the time.' He turned to Larry. 'Why are you so mad all the time?'

Larry looked as though he'd been punched and had all the wind knocked out of him. He sat there for a minute, trying to regain his composure, trying to explain himself to his son.

'I'm sorry, Mark,' he said finally. His voice was trembling. 'I guess I got scared, so I yelled. My dad used to yell a

206

lot at me and maybe I thought that's the way fathers are supposed to be.'

'Why were you scared, Daddy?' Lori asked.

Larry stopped a minute and looked at Marla. 'Because I don't want to lose Mommy,' he said quietly.

'But you're not going to lose her,' Lori said with the same logical tone in her voice that Larry used when he explained things to her. 'Mommy's only going to work, not to Alaska.'

Marla smiled, and then Larry smiled and Mark laughed, until everyone including Lori was laughing at her comment and the tension eased somewhat.

'It's not so funny,' Lori said. 'I saw this movie on television where this lady went to Alaska and she was never heard from again. She musta got lost.'

Larry leaned over and kissed her on the forehead. 'You're right, pumpkin. Mommy's not going to Alaska, only to work for Felix Anhalt.' It had an ominous sound the way he said it.

Marla put Mark back in his chair, realizing that the crisis had passed, but the problem certainly hadn't been solved.

'Mommy,' Mark said, 'if you're too busy to *in*tertain, we can help you to have an "outertain".'

'What's an *outertain?*'

'You know,' Mark said. 'With hot dogs and hamburgers and everybody does it hisself. Then nobody'll be *in* the house and you don't have to set the ta-ble, and do the cook-ing, and I can be in charge of the mustard!'

Larry looked at Mark for a moment in surprise and then Marla realized what Mark was saying. She felt laughter bubbling up from inside and incredible joy that life had granted her such a blessing as her children.

'What a wonderful idea, Markie. We'll have an "outertain".'

'With hot dogs?' Mark asked.

'Yes,' she and Larry answered together.

'And hamburgers and corn on the cob?' Lori asked.

Marla nodded.

'Yeaaa!' the children yelled.

Larry smiled at her from across the table. 'I'm sorry,' he mouthed.

'Me too,' she worded back, wondering how an outdoor barbecue in December could possibly satisfy Larry's needs or assuage his fears. It couldn't assuage hers. And suddenly she felt afraid. Her entitlement to life, to the pursuit of her own goals, was thoroughly confused with her attraction to Felix Anhalt. How could she ever reconcile it? She certainly wasn't going to give up her goals simply because temptation had been placed right in her path. She realized how fortunate it was that Felix had not been in today when she called him. How did other people come to terms with the pulling of divergent ideals, the drawing and quartering of a marriage? And which one of them, she or Larry, was capable of pulling up on the reins before the galloping steeds of their lives ripped them both apart? She felt as though she were struggling all alone, with no one in her corner. And the only bright spot in the darkened arena of her life was her excitement about working with the one man who could ruin it all. Most of the time lately, except where the children were concerned, she felt deadened and over-burdened. But Felix made her feel frivolous and childlike, although the potential of their relationship was anything but adolescent. Was that what Larry felt like when he was with Sheila? The thought twisted another knife inside of her. She looked at him guiltily across the table and saw him looking guiltily at her. Where was this all going to end? She wondered. Where?

Chapter 15

PETER HATED Palm Springs. If it had been his choice, he would have gone to San Francisco. But it was Phyllis's birthday and she wanted Palm Springs—at Felix's suggestion and Felix's treat. Peter felt that same rising sense of panic in his throat when he thought of the desert city where his parents had died, but he couldn't argue with everyone, so he fought to contain his reluctance. That city was a jinx for him, but it was thoughtful of Felix to include Belson in his invitation. Peter was amazed when Belson accepted. But then Belson never passed up a challenge. He wanted to show Felix how well he was doing and that he could still keep up with the best of them. Peter thought it was courting disaster for him to go with them for the weekend and tried to dissuade him, to no avail. Having Belson along was going to add even further strain to the never-ending tensions he lived with daily. And Felix's watchfulness only added to his stress. Felix seemed to know something was going on, though he wasn't pressing to find out anymore what it was. Peter longed to confide in him, in anyone, but he didn't dare. His situation was terribly difficult for him and he desperately wished to put an end to this deceitful way of life. Yet he would never do anything to cause his grandfather further stress. The slightest upset could prove fatal. He had to follow his grandfather's wishes to the letter.

It seemed to him as though Belson was courting suicide with this commodity scheme. Peter thought the man had aged terribly in the last few months, but no one else seemed to notice. In front of the others Belson kept up the pretense that he was in excellent health, so much so that Peter was afraid his bravado would necessitate him to accept one of Felix's frequent invitations to play a set of tennis. Peter wished Felix would stop taunting Belson with that offer.

The pressure of the platinum scheme had caused his grandfather's blood pressure to rise alarmingly, something he could ill afford, and no matter how Peter tried to calm him, or protect him from the daily events, or anticipate and fulfill his unspoken needs, Belson would not be calmed or removed from day-to-day events. He had to know every detail of what was going on; he barked orders like a carny boss, 'fly to San Diego'; 'we need two new accounts,' 'hop over to Houston,' 'tomorrow you must be in Phoenix.'

To make matters worse Peter was a white-knuckle flyer. Plus he had to do it all in one day so no one would know he'd been out of town. If Larry found out that he was flying all over the place, he'd be very suspicious about what was going on. Larry knew they didn't have clients in all those other cities. If only Peter could alleviate this feeling of impending doom, but it had hung around him, suffocating him, ever since the day his grandfather had told him about his deteriorating health. The terrible sadness of that news had opened up old wounds; God, how they festered. He realized he was the world's biggest fool for thinking they would ever fully heal. *Stupid idiot!* he berated himself. *You'll never forget. Never!*

Sometimes he marveled at how raw his old wounds still were, so raw that the pinprick of learning about his grandfather's condition had rent the thin scars of time into jagged edges again and let all the noxious poisons come pouring out. He had lost weight, he wore the expression of the permanently hunted, and yet forced himself to appear up, to laugh and joke and make love as if he hadn't a care in the world. He wasn't always successful at the pretense either. Phyllis and Larry, the two people who knew him best, saw through his subterfuge, and then he had to try even harder to cover it up. Especially for Phyllis's sake. She deserved the person she had married, that naive, kind young man who worshiped her. Of course he still worshiped her, but he'd lost his naïvité; he no longer believed life could have a happily-ever-after ending for him, though he had dedicated himself to keeping this disillusionment from his wife.

And he supposed if pressed he'd have to admit the commodity investments were under control. The funds for the first and second mortgages had been deposited in Belson's account at Union Commerce Bank early in October and Peter had spent the last three months opening their initial commodity accounts and purchasing a total of two million dollars' worth of platinum futures contracts for a total of eight hundred contracts at fifty ounces each. During the time that Peter made his purchases, over a period of several weeks, platinum was selling for an average of four hundred dollars an ounce; the margin requirement was twenty-five hundred dollars a contract. So by the time he had spent all two million of their dollars, they controlled sixteen million dollars' worth of platinum. And that's when the waiting began. *Would it go up?* It was nerve-wracking! And not only was the waiting intensely difficult, but Peter was afraid that each day would be his grandfather's last.

The only solace Peter could find at the moment in his unstable life was Jonathan, his four-month-old, sweet-faced cherub son. Those little fat hands that patted his mouth when he made popping noises, those little smiles of delight when he blew tickles of air on that incredibly soft belly, gave him much satisfaction. And when the baby was curled up in his arms asleep or on his shoulder with his head lolling in perfect contentment, it was the only time Peter felt at peace.

Sunday-night dinner was a disaster. They ate the Racquet Club buffet, all of them slightly pink with mild January sunburns, but the tension among the group was thick and heavy.

Felix began table-hopping at the cocktail hour and Audrey Anhalt grew quieter and drunker as the evening

211

wore on. Even though she only had two drinks, she made frequent trips to the ladies' room and Peter suspected that she had a flask in her purse. The more Felix strayed to other tables and danced with other men's wives, the more morose Audrey became. Phyllis tried to brighten the conversation and rescue the evening, but it was lost among the roast beef and snow peas.

And then Audrey Anhalt, who Peter had never seen behave any way but exemplary, even when completely inebriated, began flirting with his grandfather.

'I always thought you were the most romantic one of all the screen lovers. And you were such a terrific dancer. Do you still dance?' she asked, coquettishly forming her words carefully so as to appear sober.

'Of course I still dance,' he replied, standing up and extending his arm to Audrey.

'Grandfather,' Peter cautioned, frightened that dancing would be far too strenuous for him. 'It's getting late, why don't you and Mrs Anhalt dance another time?'

But they ignored his protest and he watched helplessly as Belson led Audrey onto the dance floor. It was obvious they were both trying to irritate Felix, who had been inconsiderate. But when Peter saw the look on Felix's face as Audrey and Belson danced by, Peter felt sorry for him. And then much to Peter's alarm, Felix left his current partner and started toward the dancing couple.

As usual Belson's timing was impeccable. He saw Felix approaching, whirled Audrey in a quick pivot and out the door of the ranch-style room, while the other dancers closed in the gap they had vacated.

Felix looked like a bull who had just received his second stab from the picador; as though the first one had been bad enough, but this second one was just too cruel. He couldn't chase after them and look like a fool and he was painfully aware of all the eyes on him. Peter could see from the set of Felix's shoulders how mortified he was; Peter looked away in embarrassment. At this moment he could have killed his grandfather for behaving so badly.

He turned to Phyllis. 'I'm awfully tired. Would you mind if I went to bed?' The thought of another scene when Belson brought Audrey back was more than he could take.

'Of course, darling,' she said, kissing him. 'I'll join you as soon as I have a dance with my dad.'

'Goddamn her!' Felix said to Phyllis as the two of them watched Peter go. 'How could she do that to me?'

Phyllis put her right hand in her father's left and her left around his shoulder. 'Come on, Dad. Let's dance.'

He moved her around the floor as though he were a boxer and she his punching bag, hook and jab. Even his shoulders were hunched as if to ward off blows.

'Your mother is impossible, Phyllis,' he snarled, moving less to the music than to his own angry beats, one-two-three, jab-two-three.

'But, Dad,' she said. 'You were the one who left her alone all evening. Why didn't you stay with her? You know how much it means to her.'

'What did I do?' He was all innocence. 'Dance with a few wives of some of my friends? I have to be nice to those women. I do business with their husbands. They don't mean a thing to me, Phyl. Audrey knows that. But does she understand? Not her. The injured queen.' He was squeezing her painfully and she wiggled her fingers to ease the pressure.

'I know it's not easy,' Phyllis said, 'but you've got to be more understanding of her. She's not a well woman; she needs help.'

'My God, she's had help. What about the therapies and the treatments and the spas and the drying-out farms?' His voice caught in his throat and Phyllis's heart went out to him. She hugged him closely, feeling the same helpless feeling she always had when she was caught between her parents like this; divided loyalties tore at her. Her father was a vital, attractive man; how much must he be asked to endure? But her mother was a woman of delicate sensibilities and her father's ambitions and his gregariousness played havoc with Audrey's exquisite sensitivity. It was a

213

vicious cycle, and one Phyllis had been caught in most of her life. She was the center of their world, the apex of their triangle; and sometimes, like now, she felt as though her heart were pierced by the sharp points of their warring psyches.

I'll never make that mistake with Peter, Phyllis thought, leaving her father to join Peter in their room. *We will never accuse one another of untruths, or make each other ill by keeping secrets or being inconsiderate.*

She had a sudden, overwhelming desire to be next to Peter, to hold his hand and stroke his hair while he slept. She would be careful not to disturb him; he hadn't been sleeping well lately, not at all.

Audrey Anhalt's hands were shaking badly. She desperately needed another drink but was afraid to ask. She wasn't a public drinker and arrived at most public events already in the state of inebriation that allowed her to exist in her painful world. Of course no one knew how much she drank because she only had one or two cocktails with dinner. But now she was sober, much too sober, and the tall, thin man holding her arm and guiding her purposefully toward his suite of rooms was the cause of her sudden soberness and her extreme agitation.

It was true that she'd told Belson she had loved him in her youth, felt her heart pound with desire from his passionate screen kisses; but he was an old man now, not the heart-throb of her youth. However he was a sharply honed weapon to use against Felix. The trouble was, she was a pacifist.

And yet Belson McKintridge was the one man in the world who could cause Felix the most pain. So she had grabbed on to him like a tentacle around a pole and hung on for dear life.

She walked with Belson along the outdoor path, not speaking; the warmth of his hand in hers said enough. The night was sharply cold from the clear desert air; a canopy of brilliant stars shone above, much too numerous to be real.

Her head pounded sharply and she shivered even in her lynx jacket.

'Invigorating, isn't it?' Belson said, glancing up at the sky, taking a deep breath of the cold January night air.

She murmured her agreement, and then he was inserting his key in his lock and opening the door to his room.

This is it, she thought.

There was a fire in the fireplace that threw a happy glow on the casually furnished room, Palm Springs modern. Audrey followed him in and watched him as he crossed to the bedroom and began taking off his clothes, not looking at her: first the sheepskin jacket, then the cashmere sweater, followed by the silk shirt and flannel slacks. His underwear was silk knit.

She was standing there in her fur jacket, her heart pounding and her toes nearly frozen from cold and fright.

'Well, take off your coat,' he said impatiently.

He was very thin in his underwear, thin and bony. She was shocked at how he looked and she suddenly felt quite young and attractive at fifty-five compared with him.

He had a slight erection pushing against the fly of his shorts. He lay down on the bed and stared at her. 'I'd like you to remove my shorts slowly,' he said. 'And when you suck me, be very careful of your teeth. And remove all of your lipstick!'

'What?' she asked, but the word was strangled in her throat.

'Remove all your lipstick!' he repeated. 'It sickens me.'

Automatically she reached in her pocket for a handkerchief and started wiping her mouth. Part of her wanted to laugh hysterically and part of her wanted to die. But she was frozen to the spot, unable to move except to wipe at her lips again and again.

'Well, get on with it,' he said. 'I don't have all night. I don't want to catch a chill lying here like this.' His voice was harsh and she realized how hateful he was.

Still she just stared at him.

He pulled himself up on his elbow and looked down at

himself. 'I'm losing my erection. Will you hurry up?'

'I don't understand,' she said.

'What do you mean, you don't understand?' he mimicked her. 'Are you as dumb as your husband?' His eyes glinted cruelly. 'Don't tell me you expected me to make love to you?' He gave a short, gruff laugh. 'Lord, woman, I would never fuck an old lady like you. Sucking me is all you get. Either do it, or don't. But don't just stand there gaping.'

Slowly she backed out of the room. She could hear his cackling laughter as she closed the door and it echoed in her head all the way back to her room. She would have to drink a great deal of liquor to blot it out, a great deal. But somehow, she realized, in spite of her humiliation and Belson McKintridge's devastating rejection, Felix didn't have to know what had happened. Certainly Belson wouldn't tell him, and she could let Felix think the worst. The idea made her smile. For in spite of the way Belson had made her feel, for the first time in all the years of her marriage she knew she had won. She had finally fought back and it felt wonderful.

Instantly awake, Phyllis's eyes flew open at the sound of Peter's agonized cry. She reached out for him, thinking, *Not again!* He was thrashing in his sleep, crying, moaning, whimpering. He'd slept badly since she'd known him, but these awful nightmares terrified her.

'Peter, Peter,' she called, grabbing his shoulders with one hand and holding his head to the pillow with the other.

His arms lost their tenseness and relaxed; his loud moans subsided to a whimper and then he cried—shallow, miserable sobs. 'Phyllis, Phyllis.'

She pulled his trembling body toward her and cradled him in her arms. 'I'm here, darling, I'm here. It's all right.'

'It was so horrible,' he cried.

'The plane crash again?'

His acknowledgment was a choking sound in his throat. 'It's being in this damned place again.'

216

'It's over, darling. It happened a long time ago. You're safe.'

'But they all died,' he said, his voice muffled by her breasts. She could feel his words vibrate through her.

'So long ago, darling, a long time ago. Shhh, darling,' she said. 'Oh, Peter, I love you so much.' She held him for a while longer until his shaking had subsided and he could pull away from her.

He reached for a tissue at the bedside table and wiped his eyes and nose. Then he gave a deep sigh. 'I'm sorry to do this to you.'

'You're not doing anything to me. I love you. I only want to help.' She waited a moment and then asked, 'Are you feeling better?'

'I guess so.'

'Did being here bring on this terrible reaction?'

He nodded. 'I guess so. I haven't had such a bad one in a long time. I thought they were gone, that I'd licked them. I guess I was wrong.' His voice held despair. 'I can still see everything as though it had just happened. The dream always starts out the same way. We're in the plane. Dad is in a good mood, smiling and teasing me like he used to. And Mom looks so pretty. She's wearing a flowered print dress.'

'Yes,' Phyllis said, recalling the details from so many of these episodes.

'And Carole and I are playing near the pilot's compartment. Carole has a toy plane in her hand and she lets it fly through the air towards me. I catch it. It seems light and weightless, you know, like a balsa-wood glider. But as I catch it in my hands, it gets very heavy. I put my arm back and try to sail it to Carole again, but I can't lift it. It's so goddamned heavy. Carole starts to look frightened. Her eyes are wide with fear. "Do something, Peter," she says. And I try so hard, but the plane tips sideways as I let go of it and we both fall to the side and there's tightness all around me as though the air was thick and heavy and I'm so scared I can't breathe. The sound in my ears is like the roar of a tidal

217

wave. I see the huge wave gathering on the surface of the ocean. Its hugeness is so immense that I am helpless against it, like a matchstick against a ton of steel. It bears down on me and pours over me, but it isn't water, it's hot deadly fumes. And then there's a terrible noise and the plane stops and I know we've crashed. I hear screaming. I'm on the ground outside the plane, looking back. I see my mom and Carole trying to get out. I have to help them. I see Dad. He's not moving. Jack, the pilot, is cut in half, lying through the windshield, and there's so much blood, it terrifies me. I'm pinned down; I can't move. I can't reach them though. I try and try to crawl; but my body won't move. Everything hurts so badly, the pain is unbearable. The plane is on fire, flames begin to engulf my mother and Carole. They are screaming, crying. So am I. Smoke is choking me. I feel the heat of the flames that consume them. They're still crying and struggling and I'm still trying to reach them, and then as I watch, all the flesh on their bodies melts off their bones. They disappear in a red hot fire that disintegrates their skeletons.'

No matter how many times she'd heard it, the horror never ceased to overwhelm her with each retelling. Her cheeks were wet with tears and she reached out to hold him again. He was purged of the horror of his dream now, but never the sadness.

'It will go away, Peter. I promise. Someday it won't haunt you anymore.'

'How do you know?' His voice had a desperate edge to it. How much he wanted to believe her.

'Because we love each other so much. Because that love will heal you.'

He shook his head. 'I'm not worthy of your love.'

'Yes, you are!' she insisted. 'You've got to believe in yourself.' She hesitated, reluctant to bring it up again. 'I do wish you'd talk to someone about it. Someone who could help you.'

'Who? A shrink? And relive these nightmares over and over again while I'm awake? No thank you. The dreams are bad enough. And besides, what could a therapist do? They couldn't bring back my parents or my sister and that's the only thing that would help me.'

'Maybe a therapist could help you understand that you aren't guilty for being spared, for not dying in that crash.'

'I don't feel guilty,' he snapped.

But that's exactly what she thought he did feel. He couldn't live with the knowledge that he had survived that terrible crash while the rest of his family had been killed. But no matter how many times she asked him to seek some kind of help, he always had the same negative response. No way, forget it! And so she struggled along with him, fearing his outbursts of pain, fearing the night time as if he were her child who was guaranteed to have the same highly intense fever every night. A fever could be treated with aspirin; Peter's tortured soul couldn't.

She soothed his forehead lightly with her fingers until his even breathing told her he was asleep again. And then she turned over on her side and pulled her knees up to her chest, wondering what new responsibility in his life, what new intrusion, could have unsettled his delicate equilibrium again. She would have to watch him carefully from now on to find some clue, some sign of what had caused this. Whatever he was doing at work, it was not worth the kind of tension and inner turmoil he displayed. And as soon as she discovered what it was that was upsetting him so, she would make a move to eliminate it for him.

Chapter 16

SHEIKH BANIR Ammani of Saudi Arabia was more than just a challenge, Leslie thought, as she stepped into the elevator at the Beverly Wilshire Hotel. He was the brass ring on the merry-go-round, the pot of gold at the end of the rainbow, and the title of the Miss America contest for a girl from East Texas who had passed up the chance more than twenty years ago. And he was possibly the lover of her dreams.

For the first time in her life she had met her match. The man flustered her, he unnerved her, he set her aglow with emotions she had never felt before. He reduced her to near kittenish behavior. What charm he had, what poise, what command of self, what *riches;* how he fascinated her. She wanted to be dominated by him (to a point), to be ravished by him (nicely of course), to be adored by him (wildly). But most of all she wanted to be loved by him. Yet she resisted these feelings with her entire being.

Leslie lived by certain iron rules. Never give the other person an inch. Hold fast to what lessons you learn out of bitter experience. Do not mix business with pleasure, or allow a client to see you unsure or unnerved. And never, absolutely never, tell your clients you care about their problems, their tragedies, or their budget worries.

Her sole function was to design, which she did brilliantly, to expedite, which she did expertly. And of course to get paid. And that was all. As far as becoming social friends with clients, that might occur after a job was completed, definitely not during.

Her black Krizia outfit, trimmed in loden green with its slender skirt and full-sleeved top, was a perfect choice for today's appointment. A green silk jabot finished the ensemble, which hugged her well-formed body and outlined her model's figure, with its small breasts, long legs and arms, and no hips. Her soft leather pumps and bag were Bottega Veneta, her jewelry from Fred, her perfume Mitsouko. Leslie always wore Mitsouko.

She had studied the declining elasticity of her skin critically in the mirror that morning while annointing herself with 'her' fragrance, examined her nude body, which was still in great shape at forty-two thanks to workouts with Joel Nall (but how did I ever get to be forty-two?), noted the puffiness under her eyes, which was more or less permanent these days (next year she'd have that removed), looked at the slight rippling of flesh on her thighs and behind, and the small amount of loosening skin between her legs. All in all it wasn't bad. She liked the plentiful gray in her dark hair; it softened the lines around her eyes and the few around her mouth. After all, a woman couldn't reach forty-two without some indication of having lived.

And she was proud of her age, of being so accomplished. She had decided long ago to adopt the European attitude about women. Youth was sweet and lovely, but only experience could bring true elegance. There were still a lot of good years left in the old girl, she thought, as she strode briskly down the dimly lit hallway of the hotel. If only Sheikh Banir Ammani thought so. But she knew he did. He'd hinted many times at the possibility that there could be more between them than merely business.

Grudgingly she admired the decor of this new wing. It had a modern, slick quality one found only in certain Hyatt hotels in America and possibly the Ciga chain in Europe. She raised her hand to knock, realizing that her mouth was very dry and her knees were trembling. *Damn it, Tessie Mae,* she told herself, *cut the crap!*

Clutching the portfolio of designs and the price estimates of the magnificent renderings her staff had labored so long to complete, she rang the bell. Both Marla and Billy D. had offered to accompany her today and were surprised when she declined: Leslie seldom made presentations on her own, nor would she scramble to unroll drawings or hover with nervous expectancy while waiting for the client's approval. But today she had left the staff at the office. She wanted to be alone with Banir to see where his appreciation of her work, and his attraction to her, might lead. If he were dazzled by her designs, he might be doubly dazzled by her.

A servant dressed in a dark suit and tie opened the door for her and escorted her into the enormous suite. The main room was done in purple and grape tones with walls of light gray flannel, the furniture was imitation Italian modern, but Leslie found it effective, considering the hotel designer had been limited by budget considerations. The best thing in the room was a Lucite-and-chrome-trimmed staircase ascending to the second floor.

A large private terrace overlooked the pool of the hotel twenty floors below, which from up here looked like a small blue lake surrounded by guests. Banir was seated on his terrace in slacks and a chambray shirt open just enough to show a sexy tuft of hair. Five other Arab men were with him. The men were all older than Banir. They seemed swarthy and, to a man, paunchier, with the exception of his young son. Avrim, a boy of seventeen from a former marriage. Avrim was dressed like his father, and he had the same dark eyes, carefully cut hair, and sardonic expression. Leslie hadn't expected a greeting committee.

Banir made the introductions. 'Gentlemen.' She nodded as each of them looked her up and down. They were either his associates, his money-men, or his lackeys, none of which was clear, all of which was possible.

But it was clear he was the leader.

'Mrs Winokur has brought us her presentation this morning.' He offered Leslie some thick, dark-looking coffee, or tea, which she declined, and a glass of water, which she accepted.

The five men continued their conversation in Arabic,

ignoring her. She didn't know whether to leave or stay; she'd come here with the highest expectations and was now nonplussed. But no matter how crude or ill-mannered these men were, she would have to outwait them. If the designs and the figures she planned to present today were acceptable, she could retire on the profit she'd be making.

She perched herself on the edge of the only available chair; it was not in the shade. The hot California sun beat down on her silk-knit outfit and she cursed the eighty-five-degree weather, in the middle of February no less. It wasn't civilized. But then neither were the men sitting here in their dark suits, with their skin glistening and oily from the heat, sipping cups of tea they poured from a constantly refilled pot and to which they each added five spoonfuls of sugar or honey.

She kept her patience for twenty minutes, during which she ran the gamut between fear and fury, insecurity and outrage. Then she lost her temper. 'Sheikh Ammani.' She stood up and six pairs of eyes swung her way. 'I can see that you're busy this morning. I shall be happy to arrange another meeting for us at *my* office anytime you like.'

'Oh, no,' he insisted. 'We shall be finished here in a short while. Why don't you go inside and set up your drawings. Then we will be able to study them all together.'

Leslie raised an eyebrow and nodded, turned on her Bottega Veneta heels, and left, feeling six pairs of black eyes on her back.

She didn't know whether to scream, to plead, to insist, to cajole, or to grin and bear it. She chose the latter. After all, these people did not respect the American compulsion for keeping appointments. Their business clocks ran on a different time schedule.

A servant, female this time, cleared the dining-room table of the remains of the breakfast meal. Slowly, lovingly, carefully, Leslie set out her renderings one by one, eighty versions of paradise, costing more than any paradise had a right to. The ingenuity it had taken to design interiors for all these different dwellings and not repeat herself had

223

taken months out of her life. Never before had she stretched her talents to such a limit. Hardly a color scheme was repeated, certainly not a fabric or a wallpaper unless it was in a closet or bathroom. 'After all,' she said to her staff time and time again, 'if you were paying three hundred thousand dollars plus commission to furnish your home, wouldn't you want it to be special?' And when the eightieth unit had been designed, and the choices by then had dwindled to only a few remaining acceptable fabrics and color schemes, there had been such a cause for celebration that Leslie had actually gotten drunk on Dom Perignon and nauseated from eating too much caviar.

And now the reward was on its way. And the proximity of such a huge profit made dollar signs dance in her eyes.

Thirty-three and one third percent of three hundred thousand dollars, times eighty houses, came to eight million dollars gross. It was rare in the design field to make a profit like that from one job or even eighty jobs, if you wanted to be picky.

Leslie stepped back to admire her artwork, making certain that the placements of the drawings complemented one another. There were so many that they overlapped one another around the room. Then she checked the time. It was twelve fifteen. She had been here more than an hour and the men were still sitting on the terrace sipping endless cups of tea, talking amongst themselves. She'd have given half her profit at the moment to be able to speak Arabic, or was it Farsi, and know what they were saying. They were so goddamned relaxed out there, while she was in here tied in knots. What kind of business could they be discussing that didn't need any papers or briefcases or secretaries to take notes?

She studied them through the shutters of the dining room, watching the way they related to one another and suddenly she realized that they weren't conducting any goddamned business at all. They were having what she would call a bachelor party, a leisurely get-together with the boys while she was kept cooling her heels.

Damn!

She ought to go out there and tell them she was ready, interrupt their little party. Or should she wait another fifteen minutes?

She waited.

A half hour later she appeared at the door to the terrace and told Banir she was ready for him.

'Very good,' he told her. 'We will be with you in a moment.'

Dismissed and dismayed again.

She couldn't understand it. He'd never treated her like this before, with such indifference. If she were a man, he wouldn't be doing this. What now? she wondered. Demand that they come inside immediately and give her an answer or she'd leave? No one was forcing her to stay. She could easily leave and tell them to study the drawings on their own. But that was a bad business choice. Her presence here was crucial to closing the sale. She couldn't turn her back on the merchandise and hope it would sell itself, not when there were profits like this to be made.

Then she got an idea of how she could hurry things up. She went to the phone and called the office, instructing them to call her right back. And while she waited for the call she stood, visible in the doorway, so when a servant came to tell her she was wanted on the phone it seemed legitimate. After the call she went back to the terrace.

'I'm afraid I must leave, Sheikh Ammani,' she said. 'My office needs me.'

'I understand,' he said. 'But could you ask them to be patient? We are most anxious to see your designs. Or you could go now, take care of your business, and then come back; we could wait for you.'

The five men nodded.

'No,' she said, cursing her weakness with this man. 'I'd prefer to stay and show you everything right now. It is all in the other room awaiting your attention.'

'Yes, yes.' He nodded, sipping another cup of tea and beckoning her to join him again.

Maddened, infuriated, humbled, she came outside and perched on the edge of the same chair while five pairs of eyes studied her.

At two o'clock they were all still sitting and luncheon was being served, wheeled in on a cart by members of the hotel staff.

But at least Banir was holding her hand. At one point, about one o'clock, he reached for her and started making lazy circles on her palm with his fingers, turning her hand over and over, playing with her fingers, the sensitive flesh on her inner wrist. At first it startled her, and then it excited her, but at the same time she was unnerved. What was he doing?

Nine sumptuous courses were served; curries and Arabic dishes, lamb and vegetables, breads and sweet wines, with sesame on everything but the wine. To decline was an insult and so Leslie ate and ate and ate. The heaviness of the meal in the middle of the day left her feeling heady, sluggish, and out of sorts.

By four o'clock her hand had been caressed raw, but each time she mentioned leaving, Banir convinced her to stay until her will felt as manipulated as her hand and she had given up all hope of showing her designs today or any other day. She couldn't imagine what had gone wrong, but something had. She would have to chalk it up to a sad expensive lesson and write the job off; leave while she still had some pride left. But every time she tried, she just couldn't do it. How could she walk away from eight million dollars? *Do it, Leslie! Don't do it, Leslie. No, do it!* The debate went on.

What could she tell the world when she was asked how the job was going? Say we stopped working together because he insulted me? What could she tell her staff? I lost patience with him? That was inexcusable when one did business with Arabs. They never lost their patience, they prided themselves on it, viewed life in terms of its greater scope and not in terms of immediate gratification. And besides, nobody got the better of her. And so she waited all day.

At four thirty, when she returned from a trip to the bathroom, she was amazed to see all five men, including Banir's son, were gone and only he remained. Banir was standing in the midst of her drawings, studying them.

She felt the slightest edge of concern. 'Where are your associates?' she asked. 'I thought you needed them to hear my presentation.' *Damn my bladder,* she thought. They'd all gotten away in the three minutes she was in the john. She couldn't believe those lethargic, tea-soaked men could move so fast.

'Their presence isn't really necessary,' Banir said, turning to her. 'I make the final decision. Of course, I consult with them. But there is something else I wanted to discuss with you. Do you recall my asking you if you knew Belson McKintridge and your offer to intervene with him on my behalf?'

She looked at him in utter amazement. *Not this again, and especially not now.* 'Yes, I recall,' she said, feeling her nerves fraying to the breaking point. Here she had waited all day for the man's attention and this was what he had on his mind.

'I told you when we first met I would approach Mr McKintridge through regular channels and if that proved difficult I might call on you for assistance?'

She nodded impatiently. 'But he's not that difficult to meet. Surely you know one of his current acquaintances, someone who's been with him more recently than I, to introduce you.' It was almost impossible not to get testy with him, especially when she was feeling so frustrated.

'Oh, it's not exactly an introduction I need. I have reason to believe he may be considering the sale of his house and I would like to buy it. I hesitate to approach him directly. If you could persuade Mr McKintridge to contact me . . .' His eyes left hers and traveled the length of her body and back again. 'I should be very grateful. Can you do that?' he

227

asked. And this time he glanced at her designs and back to her again, as if he was saying, 'If you want this job, you'd better deliver on your other promise.'

Belson selling his estate? Leslie's mind reeled, but her face showed no expression. 'If anyone can persuade Belson to sell you his estate, it is I,' she said with all the bravado she could muster, but she was thinking, *Belson will not even talk to me, let alone sell his house to anyone I'd recommend. And certainly not to an Arab.*

And then Banir dismissed the subject of Belson, content that she would do as she promised, and turned his attention back to her designs. His tone became a command. 'May I see the complete price list on the costs of your work?'

'Certainly,' she said, startled by his abrupt change, and hurried to her briefcase. She handed him the breakdowns for eighty units, the cost projections a team of accountants and assistants had slaved over. It was a volume in itself.

He weighed it in his hand and smiled. 'Expensive, eh?'

'Not if you consider the labor involved and the quality of the merchandise.'

He held up his hand to silence her. 'Your people have cataloged the prices, verified everything?'

She nodded.

'And you have added the percentage of profit you quoted me.'

She nodded again. 'Thirty-three and a third.'

His eyes gazed into hers. 'I will only pay you twenty percent.'

She tried to hide her shock. 'I never work for less than my usual percent, Sheikh Ammani.'

He walked slowly toward her. 'But you will this time. Won't you, dear Leslie?'

Her mind was racing as she calculated the difference between the original percentage she'd quoted him and the cut. It would mean she'd receive nearly $5,000,000, but that was far less than she'd expected. Dazed, she shook her head. 'I don't understand. We had an agreement.'

'I can always go elsewhere.' He smiled, stepping up very

228

close to her and tracing her cheek with his finger.

She was absolutely livid. Nobody ever got the best of Leslie Paxton Winokur, especially when they expected a favor. Intercede with Belson on his behalf indeed. She wanted to slap his face, to knee him in the groin, to claw him with her nails. But she did none of those things. She just stared into his eyes, trying to keep her voice from quivering as she replied, 'I couldn't possibly do this job for less than twenty-five percent.'

'Eighteen,' he said.

'But you just said twenty!' she exclaimed.

'That was before you tried to bargain. I never bargain.'

'What do you call this?' she asked, watching his slow easy smile and his infuriating shrug. *I don't need him,* she thought. *Forget the five million dollars. Forget it? Forget it?* How could she forget it? It was an incredible amount of money. If only she hadn't been led to believe she'd get the full thirty-three and one-third percent. And now she was even afraid to agree to the eighteen percent he had just offered when she still might be able to get twenty. But if she said twenty, and he was firm at eighteen, he could lower it to sixteen. 'What *do* you intend to pay me?' she asked, avoiding a commitment, 'especially since you want me to help you acquire the McKintridge estate,' she added.

'As little as possible,' he said with a cool smile, studying her. 'Why don't we go upstairs where we can discuss this matter with more privacy?' He turned to go.

She summoned whatever strength she had left to fight the urge to follow him. But so many variables tugged at her. Her pride had been exhausted from being battered throughout this terribly frustrating day, her belief in the excellence of her work had been diminished by the way he tossed it aside without so much as a compliment, and she was terribly afraid of losing this job; her business reputation would go along with it. And as for talking Belson into selling McKintridge to an Arab, a man with his prejudices—that was nearly impossible, especially coming from her. But besides that she had done the best design work of her career. If she didn't get this job now, everyone in the trade would believe the worst of her, that her designs hadn't been adequate. No one would sympathize with her for being cut down from eight million to five. 'Only five million? Poor Leslie.' She could just hear them.

But more than anything else racing through her mind at the moment was the realization that she wanted this man more than she'd ever wanted anything in her life.

What fantasies she'd had about making love with him. She, who was seldom interested in sex except as a way to relax after a hard day, had thought of nothing else since the day she'd met him. She'd always thought sex was an over-rated pastime; why it made the world go around was something she couldn't comprehend. And besides, she disliked intercourse. Her vagina was always too tight or too dry, and she only reached a climax by oral or hand stimulation. But from the moment she'd seen Banir, she knew that with him it would be different.

What the hell, if she lost the job at least she'd get something out of it; the chance to find out what a five-million-dollar fuck was really like.

She followed him up the stairs.

He led her through the bedroom, which housed an Italian lacquered platform-style bed complete with floating end tables. She'd planned to use one like it in one of the condominium designs. They continued through the dressing area and into the bathroom, which was large and square and mirror-lined, designed in keeping with the rest of the suite.

What had she hoped to find here? she wondered. Silken couches with spiced incense burning in braziers? Candied dates and sweetmeats to feed one another, the sound of Tanbūr music wafting on honeyed breezes? Well, if not that, at least turbans and chiffon curtains blowing in the air and winds of love softly whispering as each caress moved him closer and closer to *there*.

His mouth would graze her inner thigh; she'd feel his breath hot against her belly, and his mustache would move delicately over her trembling aperture, which would be throbbing before the sensitive foray of his tongue. She would reach down and stop his head from continuing, lift his face and gaze into his expression of desire. Then she would place her hand over his mouth and gently say, 'No, my darling, that's not necessary. Come here.' And she would guide him up the length of her body, raise him above her with a smile of joy, and open herself completely to be filled by him as he dipped into enough wetness to take them both to ecstasy. His motions would be slow and steady, filling her just right again and again, until she could actually feel it happen, just the way it did when Craige used to use his tongue or she used her own fingers; only this time it would be a real vaginal climax, with a real man. Not just some form of clitoral stimulation as it had been with Craige, who had depended on her and deferred to her in all their joint and conjoint decisions.

But that's not exactly what happened.

Banir led her through the large bathroom and stood her in front of one of the mirrors. If she wanted to look, she could have seen herself from every angle. But she didn't. Then he stood behind her and looked over her shoulder at her face in the mirror. And before she had a chance to anticipate him, he lifted up her skirt, pulled down her hose with one swift motion, and indicated for her to step out of her stockings and shoes.

She stared at him curiously, but he just smiled. She couldn't bring herself to look down and see the lower half of her body, exposed and vulnerable. It was decidedly unerotic.

Nevertheless she was excited.

She wondered what he was going to do next and a thrill of anticipation and apprehension coursed through her. But she didn't have long to wait, for he unzipped his fly and dropped his pants to his knees. Still smiling at her in the mirror, he took his own hand, rubbed himself four or five times, then pushed her head forward, placing her hands on the mirror, palm to palm, hiked up her skirt again, and tried to enter her vagina from behind.

She was so stunned, so shocked, it was all she could do to keep from shouting, Stop! His fingers were opening her up; he must have used saliva on himself because he somehow got into her usually dry orifice.

Sweet Jesus, she thought, raising her eyes to see him standing behind her with that handsome face, that dark mustache, that intense expression. So this was a five-million-dollar fuck?

And as he pushed her forward and spread her cheeks with his hands to thrust his penetration deeper, she felt her insides suddenly fill with liquid to cushion his way. It was such an exquisite sensation that she gasped out loud and stared at him in amazement, watching his smile widen across his face.

The bastard! she thought. He knew, he knew! But it felt so good. And though she didn't come, she was closer to it than she'd ever been in her life from intercourse. If only he'd taken a little longer, she might have actually done it. If only he hadn't grunted, 'You fucking whore, you god-damned fucking whore,' just before he came, and then pulled out to spurt his semen on the mirror in front of her, she might have actually climaxed. He was completely unconcerned with her pleasure. But that didn't matter to her. What mattered was the power she felt from seeing him this way. By receiving him in what must have been as needful a release for him as it was for her, she suddenly lost all fear of him, along with any awe she had felt about him before. She understood him. He had been testing her. If he could screw her by lowering her commission, then screwing her from behind was only a symbolic gesture. The fact that she enjoyed the hell out of it was beside the point. He had an Arab's view of women as inferior beings. But in business she could force him to respect her. If she let him cut her fee, their relationship would be a disaster. She had to be willing to gamble. It was all or nothing. And now she knew the money and this job were unimportant to him. What he really wanted from her was the McKintridge estate. And it just might be possible for her to get it for him.

As she replaced her stockings and shoes and smoothed down her skirt, she was the one who smiled. Turning to face him, she reached up and kissed him lightly on the mouth, running her tongue over his lips to see if she could actually taste his disdain. But there was only the lingering hint of the curry he'd eaten for lunch.

'I hope we will do that again, Sheikh Ammani,' she said, slyly. 'And since you brought me here so that we could discuss finances with greater understanding, I want you to know that my price has just gone back to thirty-three and a third percent. Take it or leave it. But if you leave it, you won't find anyone who can service you the way that I can.' She kept her face expressionless, but there was a twinkle in her eyes.

When he saw that she meant it, he offered no further obstacles. 'That will be fine, Mrs Winokur. I'll have the papers drawn up immediately.'

She gave an inward sigh of relief. 'And as for the other matter, I will be glad to see what I can do about Belson McKintridge.' Her expression held just a touch of triumph.

'Very good,' he said, matching her expression with one of his own.

But before she could enjoy her moment of success, Sheikh Ammani reached down and unbuttoned his slacks again. 'Now get down on your knees, whore, and suck me off. I want to ram my cock into your face.'

And Leslie did exactly as she was told.

Chapter 17

VICKY STOPPED her red Dodge Omni in the brick parking area in front of Phyllis's house, rolled her shorts up higher on her thighs, and fluffed her hair. Then she reached in the backseat and gathered the feisty German shepherd puppy in her arms that she'd borrowed from the neighbors next door to her condominium. He wiggled against her chest, kissing her face and threatening to break out of her grasp as she got out of the car with him.

'Not yet, Buster,' she warned. 'Not yet.'

The driveway that led from Schuyler Road, behind Phyllis's house, continued on past the house and intersected farther up with the servants' entrance to the McKintridge estate. Vicky headed in that direction. She had been spending a great deal of time at the servants' entrance lately, because she wanted to get to know the McKintridge servants. It surprised her to find that Belson had a relatively small turnover of help considering how many people were employed on his staff. And the ones that were more transient were only gardeners and caretakers. The servants who took care of him personally were well paid and loyal, and also difficult to approach. Vicky used binoculars and stationed herself on Phyllis's bedroom balcony when Phyllis was away and by now she could identify most of Belson's servants by sight, had learned their days off and their habits, and had managed to meet a few of them in their lives away from the estate. Several of the household maids spoke only Spanish, but fortunately

Vicky was fluent in the language and she often rode the bus with them downtown, striking up conversations, trying to learn whatever she could. They didn't know much, except what a grand house they worked in; that there wasn't much work caring for one lonely old man, that he changed his sheets every day, slept on the finest linen, ate a bland diet, and never entertained anymore. *Quelle bore*, Vicky thought, wishing she could meet Belson's majordomo, Mr Albert; he would be a wealth of information, but he was a loner, drove his own car, lived on the premises, and only went to the movies on his time off.

Carrying the dog, who was getting heavier by the minute, Vicky padded up the drive in her espadrilles to the intersection of the two roads, being careful not to step in the puddles left over from the February rain they'd had last night. The sun was shining, and it was warm enough to get away with shorts even though she had goosebumps all over. She waited until she heard the sound of a car approaching and went into her act, praying that the masseur was on schedule today and she wasn't going to all this trouble for the vegetable vendor. She let go of Buster, tossed a dog biscuit across the drive into the bushes, and crouched down by the side of the road. But Buster ate his biscuit in a flash and came bounding back for more.

'Go 'way,' she motioned. 'Go on!' Luckily she had brought several biscuits just in case and she tossed three more out into the bushes. Buster disappeared after them just as an old Volkswagen convertible rounded the bend.

The driver screeched on his brakes when he saw her waving frantically and she gave an obvious sigh of relief. He was cute up close, with curly brown hair and brown eyes, tanned and muscular. She was going to enjoy this.

'Are you all right?' he asked.

'What do you think?' she asked, rubbing her ankle. 'My dog ran off into the bushes and I tripped and fell, chasing him. Buster!' she called for emphasis. 'Come back here.' (Thank God the dog didn't obey.) 'I was afraid you were going to hit him,' she said. They could hear the dog scuf-

235

fling around in the heavy forestlike undergrowth, probably chasing a squirrel.

The masseur left his car in the middle of the road and got out to help her up. She stood too quickly and fell against him, on purpose. There was a line of perspiration on his upper lip and forehead, his clothes smelled as though they were freshly laundered, and she recognized the scent of Downy fabric softener. Then she looked up into amused eyes, which didn't mean he was tall, because Vicky was so short she always looked up at everyone. She thanked him. 'I'm a friend of Phyllis McKintridge. Do you know her?'

He shook his head. 'How's your ankle?'

She made a show of testing it; it was fine. 'Are you a dog fancier?'

'Why?' he asked.

'Because if I go into those bushes after Buster, I'll scratch my legs.'

'But I'll get my clean white ducks dirty,' he teased. 'They're tough to iron.' She laughed and he laughed too, infected by her amusement. Then he turned, put his fingers between his front teeth, and gave one of those whistles Vicky would have traded both her braids when she was ten years old to be able to do. The silly pup came running and jumped all over their legs, sniffing for more biscuits. Vicky scooped him up, trying to avoid muddy paws, and ruffled his head.

'Good dog,' he said, reaching over to fondle the pointed silky ears. 'What's his name?'

'Buster,' she replied.

'And yours?' he asked.

'Vicky Feinstein,' she answered, about to offer her hand, but the dog wiggled in her arms and reached out for the man. Vicky grabbed at the dog, to re-establish her hold, but when she looked up, the masseur was getting back into his car.

This wasn't working, she thought, flustered and unsure of how to approach him. He wasn't some maid on a bus

236

with sore feet and his eyes on Saturday night. True, he was only an employee of Belson's, but he was so damned attractive. She was having trouble keeping her mind trained on her goal.

'Hey wait!' she called. 'I haven't thanked you properly.' She crossed in front of his car and stood there smiling at him. 'I don't even know who I'm thanking.'

'Bob Delman,' he said, starting his motor. 'Nice to meet you and take care of Buster.' He ruffled the dog's tummy, exposed by Vicky's grip, waved, and drove off.

Damn. She'd blown that one, and it was one of her cleverest maneuvers. She ran back to her car, tossed the dog in the back seat, and started the motor. Maybe she could catch up with him and see where he was going. She backed the car out of the driveway on the run and headed out toward Sunset, but when she got to the corner of Sunset and Hillcrest, he had already turned left and she was caught at the light. Cursing and fuming, slamming her fist against the steering wheel, she had to wait and watch him drive away.

As if on cue, Buster came up behind and nuzzled her neck. 'Sweet doggie,' she said, pushing him gently back into the seat. 'Now sit down. Aunt Vicky's on the move.'

The light changed and she tore through the intersection before the uncoming traffic shot forward, praying there were no police around or she'd never catch Bob Delman.

She lost him at Doheny going east and drove the rest of Sunset disconsolately muttering to herself. And then at Ben Franks Coffee Shop, miracle of miracles, she saw his beat-up car in the parking lot. So Mr Delman eats.

She parked her car in the shade close to the restaurant where she could watch Buster while she ate, left the car windows ajar, and prayed nobody would dognap him. He was the prize possession of Cory and Jordanna Hughes and she didn't want anything to happen to him.

Nobody ever feigned as much surprise as Vicky when she walked into Ben Franks and ran into Bob Delman sitting alone at a table.

'I don't believe it! Twice in one day. Do you come here often?'

He looked up from a notebook he was writing in and smiled. He did have the damnedest grin. White even teeth flashed against tanned skin, and there was something else about him she'd noticed at first and which now registered with more accuracy. He seemed tranquil, at ease with himself and his life, and that sense of calm made her heart flutter.

'I come here for lunch every Monday, Wednesday, and Friday after Mr McKintridge's massage.'

'Imagine,' she said, standing and eyeing the empty place opposite him. 'And I've never been in here before. I just thought I'd stop in today.'

'Great pea soup,' he said.

'I'd *love* to try it. I'm *really* in the mood for pea soup. But I never order soup when I'm *alone*. It's such a *lonely* dish.'

He looked at her as though she were crazy.

'I mean,' she stammered, determined to get him to invite her to join him. 'When one is *alone*, one should eat salad, or french fries. They're both such friendly foods. They invite *sharing*. But soup just can't be shared, certainly not as easily as splitting a hamburger or a club sandwich. Now that's the ideal food to share, a club sandwich. Do you like to *share* your food? Or are you a *lone* eater?'

He finally got the hint. 'Would you like to join me?' he asked, closing the black notebook and slipping it to the seat beside him. It looked like a journal of some kind. And the way his eyes flicked when he passed it out of sight made her realize it was private. And that of course made her curious.

'Is that your payment account book, or something more personal?' she asked.

His eyes darted to her face with a question. She noticed green flecks among the brown and she smiled. He answered easily, 'I make notes after each workout with my customers on their physical condition. If they're responding to my work, I want to know it, then I'll remember what

238

their specific complaints are, what they want to work on, and how their conditions differ physically from time to time. My work isn't only to relax someone, it's physical therapy as well.'

She was staring at his hands as he talked, imagining what those hands could do to her own body, and not just therapeutically either. His hands were medium-sized with well-trimmed nails, not much hair on his arms, which were well developed. Forewarned is forearmed, she thought. She'd never been so turned on by a man's looks before; his mere physical presence was enough to excite her.

'Do you have that many clients that you can't keep their bodies straight?'

Again he studied her.

'Maybe I should hire you. What do you charge?' She was surprised that her heart skipped a beat as she asked him, as if he could read her thoughts.

'Oh, the first session is always free. After that it's forty-five an hour.'

'Ye gods!' she exclaimed. 'That's as much as a psychologist makes, and you don't have to pay for any office overhead.' She nodded her head. 'I'm impressed.'

He seemed embarrassed by her calculations.

A redheaded waitress brought him his soup. Vicky ordered the same.

'That all you want, honey?'

Vicky nodded.

'Is this another one of your cheap friends, Bob, who eats nothing? Jeeze, I won't even make a buck tip,' she teased him with a raspy voice. Obviously the waitress knew him well. Vicky wished she did too.

'How about hustling for your fifty cents, Rita?' he said. 'You think I came in here to talk to you when I've got this pretty lady at my table?'

Rita winked at her. 'Watch out for him, sweetheart. He's a killer.' She hooted as she walked away.

Bob was actually flustered. 'I'm sorry about her. We're very close. Have lunch together every other day, except she always stands by my table and never sits down. And I'm always alone so she's miffed that she can't tell me her problems today. She's got five sons and each one is more trouble than the last. I commiserate with her.'

'You don't owe me an explanation, you know,' she said, pleased that he'd offered one.

Rita returned with a bowl of soup on a plate brimming over onto the saltines tucked in at the side of the bowl. Vicky rescued them from sogginess and tasted the soup.

He waited for her appraisal with feigned anxiety.

She gave it a smile and a nod, and he relaxed. 'Have you ever had Marie Callender's pea soup?' she asked. 'Puts this to shame.'

'How about if we have it for dinner?' he asked.

'Pea soup twice in a row?' she was amazed. 'You're a fast worker.'

'I figure if I meet a girl—excuse me, woman— who knows about Marie Callender pea soup, which they only serve on Tuesdays, I'd better grab her.'

Vicky was suddenly stopped by his invitation. Here she'd been sitting mooning over this muscleman with the cute earlobes and cute pointed nose and clean-smelling clothes and he was taking her seriously. She couldn't actually date a masseur. Make love to one, maybe, but date one? Uh-uh.

She was slightly embarrassed and looked down at the carrot chunk in her spoon. 'I can't tonight. Besides, today is Wednesday. How about next Tuesday? I'll buy two tureens to go . . .'

'With corn bread and honey butter,' he added.

' . . . and we'll meet at my place.' He really had the nicest eyes. They twinkled with a new idea as he asked her, 'What do you think is the best hamburger in the city?'

'Hampton's,' she stated, 'without question. Though Marie Callender's Frisco burger runs a close second, and my choice for third is the Malibu Pharmacy Executive Burger with grilled onions.' She stopped and laughed. 'What is this, a survey for *L.A. Magazine?*'

He ignored her question. 'Okay. We'll go to Hampton's

on Thursday, Marie Callender's on Friday, and Malibu on Saturday. That gives you Sunday and Monday for your other boyfriends or your husband . . .?' He stopped and waited for her reply.

She shook her head and he gave a huge sigh, raising his shoulders up and then collapsing down into his bowl. 'I didn't see a ring, but you can never tell. And that brings us to Tuesday,' he said, straightening up. 'Tuesday's so-up, just like the song. Monday's bread and butter, everybody happy? Well, I should say.'

Vicky laughed delightedly, forgetting her reluctance with him. 'You know that song? I don't believe you know that song! My mother taught it to me.'

'So did mine?' he said. 'Maybe we've got the same mother.'

'Victor.' She squinted at him. 'Is it really you? My Siamese twin after all these years.'

'Ah, VickyVickyVicky.' He took her hand across the table. 'How I've searched for you—Tibetan monasteries, the New York subway, the pleasure palaces of Saigon.'

'Thanks a lot.' She was extremely conscious of his hand on hers.

He raised his eyebrows in rapid succession and did a passable imitation of Groucho. 'I got waylaid in those pleasure palaces for a time.'

'I'll bet.' She laughed. And suddenly all the color drained out of her face. 'Ohmigod. I forgot about Buster.'

'Where is he?' Bob looked up, expecting to see the dog bounding down the aisle.

'He's in the car and I'm scared to death to think of what he's been doing. He thinks he invented pee-pee.' She fumbled in her purse for some money, put three dollars on the table, and slid out of the booth. 'Leave Rita whatever's left,' she insisted. 'I'm sorry!' And she grabbed her purse and ran.

The carpet of her beloved Omni was soggy in front of the passenger's seat, and there were dog hairs all over the black vinyl and a foul, yellow mess on the floor in the back.

'Oh, God,' she wailed. 'I didn't deserve this.' Nearly gagging, she rolled down the windows and tried to think of what to do. She couldn't go back into the restaurant and get paper napkins to clean up Buster's mess; Bob would know what happened. She had to try not to breathe, force herself to get in her car, and go to the nearest gas station. There was one nearby, but every moment alone in that car was torture.

'Oh, Buster,' she cried while he wagged his tail and grinned at her from the passenger seat. 'I might have to sell my car if I don't get the smell out. Oh, God.' It was all she could say.

It wasn't until she cleaned up the mess, got Buster back to Cory and Jordanna, went through the car wash twice and bought every car deodorant they sold that she remembered she hadn't given Bob Delman her number. And damn it, he hadn't asked for it either.

Chapter 18

AS THE winter weeks progressed, Peter could see a steady decline in his grandfather's health. Belson's hands trembled constantly, even when he was in repose; his voice had lost its commanding timbre and he had to spend nearly two weeks in bed to recuperate from his weekend in Palm Springs. But still he was consumed by the platinum scheme.

And Peter had to admit, he too was finally getting excited by it. The price of their futures contracts had risen, just as Henry Cronyn predicted, to an unbelievable price of six hundred an ounce. So far they had cleared a 50 percent profit on their original investment.

'I think we should quit while we're ahead,' Peter said as he studied the latest figures Henry Cronyn had had computed for them on one of his master computers. When they first bought in to the futures market, they entered their buy-in price on the computer and that determined the running average of their profit/loss statement to date, taking into consideration the daily price fluctuations and a predictable trend of a steady increase. Without Henry's master computer they would not have been able to predict or compute anything about their daily position, and that was essential to their scheme.

'There's no way I'm going to quit now,' Belson insisted. 'Eight million dollars' profit is not nearly enough. I would only have four and a half million left after I pay back the encumbrances on the estate and three fourths of that would go to taxes. I need so much more to keep the estate going. No!' he stated emphatically. 'We're going all the way. I say it's time to take our eight million profit and reinvest the entire amount in more contracts.'

'Even with the price as high as it is?' Peter asked.

'Yes,' Belson said. 'Because it will keep rising and if we're even more leveraged, our profit potential is tremendously increased.'

Reluctantly Peter agreed.

And again he bought platinum futures contracts gradually over several weeks, opening more accounts so that each of their original accounts never contained more than a hundred contracts per account, so as not to exceed the reportable limit as required by the CFTC.

Some of the new platinum contracts he purchased he was able to get for as low as $575 an ounce, but others cost him as much as $625. Still the principle of the pyramid was holding true. They had their original eight hundred contracts, and now had added it to thirty-two hundred new ones, which meant they now controlled $120 million worth of platinum futures contracts spread out over a three-quarter period. However at this great a leverage the price fluctuation was terribly crucial and Peter's tension was multiplied in equally increasing increments. Any upward movement in the price of platinum futures of only one point above their average purchase price meant they had earned $200,000. But every time the combined market price of their holdings dropped even one point, that meant they were down $200,000.

Peter's life was not his own. He had gone back to smoking a pack of cigarettes a day and his hands, like Belson's, never stopped shaking, though for a different reason from his grandfather's. Further, Larry was always annoyed with him for not being available for their clients. He felt terrible about shirking his responsibilities to his law practice and his partnership with Larry, but he couldn't help it. The market speculation took up most of his time and consumed all of his thoughts. In fact he could never really get it out of his mind because of the stakes involved. And not merely the incredible profit potential. For Peter, underlying the daily activities of keeping on top of the accounts, watching the ebb and flow of conditions, and keeping his grandfather content, was the knowledge that he was holding in his inept and trembling hands the very fabric of his life. Only by continuing to serve as his grandfather's messenger, only by continuing with this scheme no matter how difficult, could he provide himself with some semblance of stability, could he believe he was actually preserving that which he held so dear.

And now his dreams were even more tortured, only instead of dreaming of the plane crash that had haunted him for most of his life, he dreamed of the daily market prices of commodities, and they were always out of his control. His nightmares were clouded with repeated nightly efforts of the scaling of actual pyramids. Only the pyramids in his dreams were as slick and treacherous as marble and took all the effort of his being to make any progress. Each night he would climb in frustration and fear and dig his nails into the alabaster surface only to slip two feet backward for every foot gained. The more he tried, the more impossible it became. Yet he knew in every dream that if he fell off, he would die.

Chapter 19

THERE WAS something churning inside of Marla that was close to fury, a kind of despair she thought was never-ending whenever she was caught in it, as now. She couldn't remember ever feeling anything else but this all-consuming anger caused by watching Larry on the dance floor of Pips with Sheila Conway while the music blared in her ears, and the heat of bouncing, gyrating bodies pressed and ebbed around her. She almost didn't care what Larry was doing she was so angry, almost, but not quite. This was supposed to be their evening, hers and Larry's, one they needed very badly. First they'd had dinner at Jimmy's and then they were going home to make love. Dinner had been excellent, she felt relaxed and even affectionate for a change and she'd managed to put her fantasies of Felix out of her mind. Larry had been so attentive and interested in her work, questioning her about details; he even seemed proud of her. In fact everything had been wonderful until they'd gotten in the car and Larry said, 'I feel like having a drink at Pips, baby.'

'Not tonight, please,' she'd said. 'Let's stick to our plan and go on home. You know what happens at Pips. You'll get waylaid by some client or another attorney and I'll be left alone.'

'If there's anybody there we know, I won't talk to them, I promise. But I'm too keyed up to go right home. Come on, babe,' he'd said, and he'd given her such a sweet smile, she'd agreed. One drink wouldn't hurt.

And then they'd seen Sheila in the disco with the same

boring gray-haired real-estate broker who had talked Marla's ear off the last time they'd met. It had been at Pips then too.

Marla spotted Sheila the moment they entered the room. She stood out from the others like a fluorescent mask on a black stage. Her dress was cut to the waist, her siliconed breasts were planted on a narrow chest, her hips were bumping to the music, and Larry waved to her before Marla could stop him.

'She's with that same guy again?' he said. 'God, we have to rescue her,' and he grabbed Marla's hand and headed toward them.

Marla knew she was prettier than Sheila; her body— thanks to her constant workouts—was better too than Sheila's. But she couldn't match Sheila's display of blatant sexual hunger.

Until Sheila saw them, she had seemed almost bored, moving in a lackadaisical manner, biding her time. But when she caught Larry's eye, Marla could feel the electrification of heightened competition; suddenly Sheila was dancing as though her life depended on it. She moved as if she were participating in some ancient tribal rite that would decide her fate: execution of life, ruler or ruled. And for some reason Marla felt that she had acquired the role of co-contestant. Larry, not looking back, made straight for the dance floor while Marla took a seat next to the broker, hemmed in by sweating, shouting bodies. She pretended not to be able to hear when he told her how beautiful she was and walled herself off in pain.

Larry's and Sheila's hips were glued together as they swung in a circle, moving, bumping; they leaned their backs and chests away from one another as though from the waist up they were proper friends, but from the waist down was another matter. Marla had never seen him dance like that before. She wanted to kill Sheila. But killing was too good for her—slow torture would be much more satisfying.

She excused herself from the broker and made her way across the floor to the powder room. She felt shut off, deadened inside, and for a moment she didn't even know where she was. Seeing them together, she was sure they were lovers. How could Larry be so indiscreet in front of her? And then she thought maybe he wanted to be.

Marla stared at herself in the mirror, in front of the powder-room attendant's incredible array of cosmetics, knowing that powder and rouge could not fix her now. The wine dress, the matching makeup on her eyelids, her dark hair, her creamy upright breasts, were evidently not enough for him. *Why doesn't he want me,* she wondered, *instead of Sheila Conway?* She wanted to hit him, rake her nails across his cheek, cut off his balls, anything other than go home with him now and make love. She was ice cold inside, but soon the ice would thaw and the pain would fill her up again inch by inch, grabbing her in its awful grip.

'You all right, sweetie?' the black attendant asked, and Marla looked up at her reflection in the mirror. She was startled to see that she was crying. There was a line of wet tears running right straight down through her cheek blush, making white snail tracks across her face.

The attendant handed her a Kleenex and a compact filled with cheek color. A perfect match. She took the Kleenex and declined the blush. *Let him see me like this,* she thought. *Let him damn well see.*

But then she thought better of it, dried her eyes, and reached for the blush to repair her makeup. If Larry saw she'd been crying, then Sheila could see it too. In only a moment she had repaired the damage. She wished that she could repair her life as easily.

She stepped back into the noisy club with a renewed determination not to let Larry's behavior get the better of her. He and Sheila had left the dance floor and were seated at a banquette with Sheila's date. But Marla didn't want to rejoin them, so she waited until she could catch Larry's eye and then beckoned to him, indicating she wanted to go. When she saw him getting ready to leave, she claimed her coat from the check girl.

As she struggled into her coat, she felt someone behind

her helping her on with it.

'Thank you,' she said, turning to discover Felix smiling at her. He seemed so much like a figment of her imagination, a genie come to her rescue, that she was shocked to see him. 'What are you doing here?' she demanded almost angrily, as if he had been following her in the shadows of her own mind and suddenly manifested himself at the moment she needed him most.

'I was having a game of backgammon in the other room with my friend Harvey, when I saw you going into the ladies' room. You looked rather upset. Then I saw Larry on the dance floor. I thought you might need some support.'

'Well, I do,' she said, her lower lip quivering. His kindness had made her feel very sad and destroyed her resolve to be strong.

He put his hand under her chin and lifted it so she was looking up at him. 'You're worth ten of him,' Felix said. 'And two million of her,' and then he leaned forward and kissed her lightly on the lips.

Her response was mercurial. Instant explosions of desire rushed through her along with the fear that Larry might see her, and a fierce wish that he would.

Felix looked up and evidently saw Larry heading their way because he moved back a step. 'I'll see you tomorrow, beautiful,' he said, making reference to their appointment about the yacht, and then made his way back to his table, leaving her more vulnerable to him than she had ever been before.

And when Larry reached her side and said, 'I hope you're not too angry with me for dancing with Sheila,' she gave him a dazzling smile, tossed her head and said very convincingly, 'Not at all.'

But Larry was subdued on the way home, glancing at her often to see if she was really angry with him and not just saying she wasn't. It surprised her that he was so concerned about her anger. Yet he had humiliated her by letting Sheila flaunt herself that way. He might not be sleeping with the woman; but it looked to the world as though they were screwing their way around the block. And what if she came out and asked him if he was having an affair? He wouldn't admit it. Well, she wasn't going to ask, nor was she going to fight with him tonight. She was too excited about seeing Felix tomorrow. Something irrevocable had passed between them tonight, some invisible line had been crossed, and they both knew it. It was only a matter of time.

The first time Marla saw Felix's yacht it had surprised her: it was not what she'd expected. He should have had a sailing sloop, a sleek fifty-foot job trimmed with chocolate brown canvas over highly lacquered decks, instead of this broad-beamed, top-heavy, motor-powered boat with cut blue velvet fabrics on the sofas, gold-veined mirrors on the bar and coffee table, and white fluted shades on porcelain statued lamps. 'Double yuck,' was Billy D.'s description. But now all the offensive gaudiness had been removed and in its place she'd ordered tan and coffee leathers, oatmeal fabrics and carpets, and touches of tangerine color to heighten the polished steel lavishly used everywhere. As with every job, interim chaos ensued. Carpenter's tools, sawdust, pieces of wood, old and new cabinet fixtures, lay about, waiting for her to orchestrate their placement. But today she wanted to sweep them all aside, clear the decks so to speak, and concentrate on him.

Felix was barefooted, dressed as usual in jogging shorts and open shirt; a cigar smoldered in the ashtray, two glasses of chilled white wine sat on the counter, and classical music was on the stereo.

'Hello,' he said admiringly, looking her up and down. 'Did you bring your suit? It's a wonderful day for the sun.' She sighed in mock complaint, 'I'm working, Felix. I'm not supposed to play.'

Being alone with him in close quarters with Felix in such a provocative state of undress made her acutely aware of him and she strained to busy herself with her work, but she was unable to concentrate, and he knew it because he kept staring at her, undressing her with his eyes. She tried to maintain her control as Leslie had insisted. 'Never let a client ruffle you. They must believe that their taste and choices are foolish and inadequate compared with yours, only your opinions count. Let them give you an initial argument so they feel they have a say in the decisions, but never go beyond a moment of protest. Let them know you are setting the limits, that they can trust your expertise. It's very comforting to meet someone who really "knows."'

Well, Marla knew about design. She could see at a glance that the carpenters had done a poor job of fitting in the new cabinets in the galley and would have to be forced to redo them. But she didn't know what to do about the wild pounding of her heart and the feeling of warmth spreading throughout her lower body as Felix came close to her as he was doing now and took her hands in his.

'Does it embarrass you that I find you irresistibly attractive, Marla? Surely I'm not the first man to pay the compliment of staring at you. If you were mine, I'd ravish you the moment I walked in the door at night. Doesn't Larry?'

The irony of his question made her smile. 'Actually, no. But I often get home later than he does and I'm usually too tired for ravishing.'

'Pity,' he said, staring at her again. 'You're a woman who's been made to be ravished.' His voice grew husky. 'I want to make love to you, Marla.'

There. He'd finally said it, exactly what she wanted to hear. Her pulse was beating at the base of her throat as he reached out to touch her. He must have thought better of it and held his hand back, his finger poised above her chest, halted in mid-air, while he gazed into her eyes.

Acute disappointment flooded her when he stopped. How many times had she come here and played this game with him? Well, no more playing. She was as excited as he was. Her knees felt absolutely weak.

She raised her chin and stared back at him, acknowledging their mutual attraction, finally daring him to touch her, finally daring him to cross that invisible barrier of intimacy he'd never overstepped before. She was tired of denying

250

herself. She was tired of fighting with Larry, or trying not to fight with Larry, of being dissatisfied in bed. She was tired of turning away from the most exciting man she'd ever known. She wanted him. She wanted him to make love to her. She'd thought of nothing else for weeks. She'd imagined him making love to her without the pressure of performances, with just the glory and sensuality of light, lovely passion, and she shivered, signaling a deeper trembling from within. Only the flick of his eyes to the raised flesh on her arms indicated that he'd noticed, but his hand moved to her throat and his finger delicately traced the pulsing vein in her neck. Her whole body shook when he touched her, though his touch was so light she could barely feel it. But the anticipation of what was to come took her breath away.

Slowly he traced his finger down from her throat to her chest, making larger and larger sideways movements across her chest until his finger was inside her silk blouse and he was lightly touching the tops of her breasts. Her chest was moving up and down and she knew she was breathing, but it felt as if no air were entering her lungs. Her breasts tingled with a life of their own, aching to be crushed against his chest, but instead she stood there, staring into his eyes, while his finger caressed her lower and lower, moving into the V between her breasts, giving them tiny butterfly kisses.

Before she was aware of it, his fingertips were inside her blouse and he was running them over the tips of her breasts, alternating from one to the other. The nylon fabric of her brassiere seemed to magnify his touch, radiating the movement of his hand to the entire fullness of her. She felt suspended in time; there were no thoughts except of the next movement of his hand.

His other hand unbuttoned her blouse, pulled it out from her skirt, and unhooked the front of her bra until she was exposed to his gaze. The expression on his face was one of wonder. Then, overcome with emotion, he leaned forward to kiss her and pulled her against him. She felt as though

251

she'd fallen into a warm pool of water.

Her mouth was filled with saliva; she'd been too excited to swallow and the liquids of their mouths intermingled. She could feel the gray grizzled hair on his chest against her breasts. It seemed to act like tiny tentacles, caressing her, exciting her even more. Her knees were threatening to buckle. She'd never been this excited in her life, never wanted the feeling of a man inside of her as much as she wanted him.

She reached down and unzipped her skirt, pulling it off until it fell around her ankles. Felix broke their kiss and pulled away to look at her. She was nude to the waist, her blouse and bra were pushed back over her shoulders. She moved her arms and the clothing fell to the floor. She had on flesh-colored bikini panties and hose and for a wild moment she was glad she had worn them today.

'God, you're beautiful,' he said.

'So are you,' she replied, and he smiled.

'Are you certain?' he asked.

She nodded. 'I want you, Felix. I've wanted you for a long time. Maybe for my whole life.'

He took her hand, helping her to step out of her skirt and shoes, and then she followed him down the stairs to the master bedroom.

He was as wonderful a lover as she'd imagined. His tenderness was so exciting it made her want to cry, as though her youth and her unlined flesh was something he not only adored but revered beyond the person she was. She couldn't get enough of him and although she reached a climax early in their lovemaking, it seemed incidental to her need for touching and fondling and the languid, careless use of time. She told herself over and over that she had to make this last. This was their first and only time. She'd never do this again, so she had to hold in as much pleasure and as many memories as she possibly could.

When Felix fell asleep with his head on her chest, she stared at the top of his head, trying to memorize the color of his hair; she touched the scars on his arm from old war wounds while she relived the way he smelled and tasted and felt inside of her, even the way his weight pressed on top of her. And then the impact of her infidelity hit her full force.

Felix awoke, rolled over, and sat up to watch her.

'Having second thoughts already?'

She was startled by his perception as if he could look into her. 'A little.'

'Well, don't.'

She turned to protest. 'I don't want you to tell me what I should or shouldn't feel.'

'All right,' he said hastily. 'Have all the second thoughts you want. But they won't do any good. They're a waste of time. I only want you to know that I'm not going to make things difficult for you. I won't hound you or bother you or make innuendos when we meet outside of here. You can count on me and you can trust my discretion.'

'Been there before?' she teased. But she was grateful for his reassurance.

'Of course,' he said matter-of-factly. 'But that doesn't mean that I won't want to jump your bones every time I see you.'

'Don't speak about making love that way,' she said, turning away. 'You spoil it. Larry uses little-boy slang as a guard against intimacy. Please don't you do it too.'

'I'm sorry,' he said. 'What I meant to say is that I'll want to make love to you whenever and wherever I see you, but I won't make any overtures unless you do. You'll always know where to find me and I'll always try to be available for you on five minutes' notice.'

She smiled at him. The perfect lover. 'Thank you, Felix, but I won't ask you again. I wouldn't be good at clandestine arrangements. This was the one and only lapse in my marriage vows I shall allow myself.'

She was up the stairs and into the salon, putting on her skirt, when he caught up with her.

'You're very tough on yourself, Marla Gilbert. Don't make any promises you can't keep or burn any bridges before they're crossed. Tell yourself anything you like to get yourself through life, but never, never lie to me. You'll be back for more.' And he winked and kissed her lightly on the lips, then went back downstairs, closing the hatch behind him.

Marla finished dressing, made some notes about the carpentry, and gathered up her belongings. But Felix's words rang in her ears as she walked up the dock to her car. All the way back toward Beverly Hills, down Olympic Boulevard, she argued with him in her mind. 'I won't be back again, Felix,' she repeated over and over. 'I won't be back.'

Chapter 20

LESLIE'S DINNERS were famous in Beverly Hills. Dianna Cunningham always reported them in her column. Only 'A' list people were invited and Leslie was an excellent hostess. Milton Williams prepared dishes for Leslie's parties he'd never consider doing for anyone else, or she might use one of her secret finds, such as the young French vwife of an architect she knew. Lisette was a cordon bleu chef who prepared wonderful French dishes with the delicate touch of nouveau cuisine. The girl wanted to become a cateress, specializing in private parties in Beverly Hills, and was expecting to get referrals from Leslie, who knew everyone. But so far there had been no referrals. Leslie told the girl she still needed to prove herself before Leslie would recommend her. In truth Leslie didn't want anyone else to know about her.

Tonight's guest list included Ralph Miller and his wife,

Edith. He was the general manager of I. Magnin's southern California division. Leslie had heard they were looking for a new design firm and she wanted to be first on their list when it came time to make a choice. Dianna Cunningham was attending the party, of course, and Marla Gilbert, along with her attorney husband, Larry. Leslie couldn't put off having them any longer, and for a touch of spice to enliven the evening, as he enlivened her life, she'd invited Sheikh Ammani.

Ralph Miller was an average businessman without much spark or specialness—a pencil pusher who dealt with figures more than fashion—but nevertheless he was quite influential in the company. His wife was boring and Leslie had avoided her for years. Edith wanted Leslie to do her home; Leslie couldn't be bothered. But she'd consider allowing Marla to do the job for a return favor.

'Edith, how smart you're looking,' Leslie said, greeting them at the door. Ralph was in the same dark business suit and tie he usually wore; Edith was in red silk. For a woman her height and weight it was a disaster. Why doesn't someone tell her? Leslie wondered. Her husband worked for a chain of elegant department stores and she went out looking like a field of giant tomatoes. Leslie silently clucked her tongue. It was true what they said about the shoemaker's children.

Leslie introduced Edith to Marla. 'She has the most wonderful house, Marla. I've been trying to find the time to get to it. Perhaps it will be our next project. Why don't you let Edith tell you all about it?' Leslie winked at Edith, whose eyes were sparkling with possibilities. Then she left them and steered Ralph over to the bar, handing him a double Scotch.

'I'm so glad you could come tonight, Ralph.' She smiled. 'It's been far too long since I've seen you. But I've been unbelievably busy.' She launched into a description of exactly how busy, and how successful and how desirable a designer she was.

Banir, who was keenly astute where human relations

were concerned, watched Leslie playing with her quarry and smiled his wide, white grin. Having Banir in her home added an excitement to the evening. She felt more electric and invincible than usual. She watched the others to see if there was any sign that they suspected her relationship with Banir went beyond business, but there was none. Why should there be? Leslie was circumspect with her private life, terrified of adverse gossip. As purveyor of some of the best tales, she had a loathing of being discussed. And tonight she took special pains to be cautious that none of her inner fire showed.

It was not difficult to mask her liaison with Banir. He himself manifested none of the romantic behavior she'd always associated with an affair. In fact she could hardly call their time together anything more than fierce couplings. And, oddly enough, that's what made them so exciting, the brevity and ferocity. Gone were her fantasies of lazy afternoons of love-making, tender kisses in darkened stairwells, cheese and wine on a windy beach, followed by sandy sex. They'd been replaced by the rough reality of a man who could easily be termed the least subtle lover of them all. He was demanding and harsh, often brutal and very direct. And that excited her more than she'd ever been excited before. She had discovered a similar response within herself, an equally brutal and demanding part of herself she'd never let be expressed in sex, only in business. To blend the two parts of her was an unbelievable relief, but at the same time addicting. She had grown to need Banir, and Leslie never needed anyone. That frightened her, because she didn't want to lose him. And yet when their other work together was complete, how could she get him to continue their other relationship? He had no idea what his sexual behavior did to her. To him she was another receptable, a Western whore to be treated like a dog. He seldom faced her when he fucked her—she couldn't dignify what they did by calling it lovemaking—nor did he kiss her. That he reserved for his sexual partners in Saudi Arabia, such as they were. And yet there were times when she knew

256

she meant as much to him as he did to her.

She was grateful that she had an agenda for this evening other than flirting with Banir; his presence was so hypnotic that it exerted a stronger pull on her than she felt was comfortable. And she was surprised by Larry Gilbert. Each time Leslie had met him previously, he'd seemed bourgeois and hostile. Tonight he was neither of those things. Witty, charming, and bright, he and Banir hadn't stopped talking long enough to eat their dinners, and even Ralph had been drawn into their conversation. Leslie's opinion of Marla had altered considerably by seeing Larry tonight. If little Marla could catch someone as sharp as her husband, perhaps there was more to her than appeared on the surface.

During dinner Dianna, who was seated on Banir's right, next to Ralph watched Leslie's interplay with the sheikh and her toying with Ralph Miller. Dianna knew all about Leslie's business and private relationships. They always confided in one another.

Dinner and dessert went well; Ralph Miller was suitably impressed, and after what seemed to Leslie a great deal of time, Banir Ammani came up to her. 'I want to speak to you a moment,' he said.

She turned. 'I thought you'd never ask.' She could feel her body flush with anticipation. She led Banir into the library, but he didn't approach her as she hoped he would. Their affair wasn't what he had on his mind.

She poured him a brandy and took one for herself, positioning herself next to the fireplace. A magnificent portrait of herself painted by Claretta White graced the mantel while the flickering light from the fire cast an exciting glow on the iridescent tone of her dress. She had hoped they could be alone this evening in just such a room as this. She wanted Banir to see her in her domain, watch her in action, observe what an asset she could be to a man like him. Together they could rule the international set.

'I shall get right to the point, Leslie,' he said. 'It surprises me how American I'm becoming. I seek to avoid the

257

niceties of the Middle Eastern customs and have begun paying tributes to time instead of allowing Allah to put things in their proper span. So I'm asking you now, what progress have you made in convincing Mr Belson McKintridge to sell me his property?' He let his eyes study her body suggestively.

She was both frightened and excited by his expression. Excited because they were so attuned to one another, but frightened because of the unleashed fury inherent in his tone. Banir was a man unused to being thwarted in his desires. And she had made him a promise, she had led him to believe she would accomplish what he asked. Even boasted that she'd do it.

'Oh, Banir,' she coaxed. 'Belson is a Scotsman, don't forget. You know how loath they are to part with any of their possessions.'

'As a matter of fact, I am unfamiliar with the ethnic idiosyncrasies of the Northern European countries. I don't believe I've ever known any Scotsmen at all, nor do I know anything about the way they behave.'

Leslie's mind flashed on the brown bloodstained sheets, yellowing in folded plastic in her upstairs linen closet, and the Renoir and the Chagall on the wall opposite the fireplace.

'But I do know that you agreed to perform a function for me and you have not fulfilled your part of the bargain.' He came toward her and took the brandy glass from her hand, placing both their glasses on the mantel. Then he traced his finger down her bare chest, over her shoulder to her arm, down her arm to her hand where he stopped to play with the inch-wide diamond pavé ring she always wore. 'I thought you knew him well enough to convince him to sell me his house.' The muscles in his jaw rippled as he clenched and unclenched his teeth. He pulled at her ring, twisting it and moving it back and forth over the joint of her finger. 'If you succeed in doing what I ask, we two could be even closer than before.'

She was aware of his sadistic, teasing nature, and now he

was bending her finger back until it hurt, staring at her face, watching her expression. But she didn't flinch, nor did she remove her hand from his. 'You never told me what you would do for me if I did,' she said. There, she'd finally asked it. The question that had tormented her for so many months.

'Perhaps I shall do nothing,' he replied, giving her finger a painful push. 'Or I will do everything. You know I have been thinking of remarrying.' And then he smiled, releasing her finger and bringing her hand up to kiss it where the ring met the back of her hand. It was her wedding-ring finger and by his gesture he was making himself clear that there could be a permanent union in their future. She felt an electric thrill course through her and her knees grew weak. This was much more than she'd expected.

'I'll keep trying, Banir,' she gushed, anxious to please him. 'I'm certain I can bring Belson around.' Her head was throbbing from the nearness of him. She wished he would take her right now, in the ashes and coals of her own hearth, burning her flesh as the desire for him burned in her veins. 'I will get you that house even if Belson wants to die in it,' she vowed. 'I have ways of doing it.'

'Tell him I'll pay him anything he asks. I belong there, Leslie. And I know someone who belongs there with me.' He smiled a slow, meaningful smile and turned to go, leaving her shaking because she wanted him so, and afraid that she wouldn't have the strength to stay where she was and not run after him, promising him anything, just to get him. It took every ounce of strength in her body to wait where she was and listen to the sounds of his leaving and the front door closing before she allowed herself to come out of the library. And then she went upstairs to join Dianna and have one of their debriefing sessions in which they dissected every action, every gesture, every word anyone uttered during the entire evening and both fully understood the exact meaning, nuance, and countermeaning contained therein. Dianna was as much a genius at intrigue and social intercourse as she, and Leslie had full trust and faith that

259

together the two of them would find a way to pry Belson away from that house. But it wasn't going to be easy.

Chapter 21

WHEN VICKY'S front-door buzzer rang, it was the last straw. After days of failure to discover anything unusual about Belson McKintridge she was in a terrible mood. And the fiasco with Bob Delman and Buster hadn't helped her spirits either. She had really liked him, but he'd never called her, and her pride wouldn't let her engineer another chance encounter. Either he would follow up, or he wouldn't. And the book was still not going well. There was an emptiness inside of her when she wrote about Belson and Leslie. She could not invent things for them to do that were as bad as the things they had done in real life. If she were being honest, she'd have to admit that on her worst days the novel about her and Marla and Phyllis was better than the one she was writing now. But this book was the one she had chosen to do, and she had to infuse some life into it.

Her buzzer rang again; definitely an intrusion into her state of self-pity.

'Go away!' she yelled, without bothering to go to the intercom and see who was buzzing.

The sound continued aggressively, as though someone were certain she was here. But the way she felt, it was better to pretend she was out.

The buzzer stopped.

Three minutes later there was a knock at the door.

'Who is it?' she called out, afraid even to approach the door.

'Land shark,' came the muffled reply. 'Candygram.'

Vicky broke up, remembering her favourite skit on *Saturday Night Live*, a take off on *Jaws* where a land shark outsmarted its victims by pretending to be a delivery boy and then gobbling them up when they fell for his tricks.

Fully intrigued she approached the door and got an unmistakable whiff of cooked food as she peeked through the peephole. Bob Delman was standing there, grinning, carrying an armful of paper bags. She opened the door with surprise.

'Do you have a microwave?' he asked.

'Why?' She couldn't believe how glad she was to see him.

'Because I have to heat up one Hampton's Slam Dunk Burger, one Marie Callender's Frisco burger on sour dough, one Malibu Pharmacy Executive Burger with grilled onions, an order of french-fried carrots from D.B. Levy's, and an order of onion rings from Tony Roma's. I've been driving around this city for an hour and the first orders are cold by now.'

'I spent time in India after I dropped out of college,' he told her, scrounging for the last morsel of french-fried carrots. 'All the way to Katmandu. I was there post-Beatles and Mia Farrow, but pre-Leigh Taylor-Young. I ate macrobiotic, I meditated up to eight hours a day, and afterwards I was on such a spiritual high I joined the Peace Corps. I spent two years in Guatemala, then came back here and worked with minority juveniles in Oakland. I've done some boxing, light middleweight. I was pretty good too. But I didn't have that killer instinct that kids off the street have. When I was boxing, I learned the art of massage.'

She was impressed by his history. She'd never known anyone who'd done the things he'd done. What was it like to be a prizefighter in a ring, to hear a crowd scream for blood? She wanted to crawl under his skin and know what it felt like to be in Katmandu and eat the food. That to her was a major accomplishment.

'Where are you from originally?' she asked. They were

sitting on the floor on either side of the coffee table, stuffed from overeating, their legs and bare feet intertwined. And Vicky's mood had gone from the pits of despair to euphoria. Bob Delman not only fascinated her, he attracted the hell out of her. Vicky leaned against the sofa; he was against the chair facing her, the evidence of their hamburger orgy spread out before them. After two beers and all that food, Vicky's bladder was screaming for relief, but she didn't want to get up and break this intimate mood. It was light out when he arrived, but now it was dark and the lights from the city twinkled in between the taller buildings that partially blocked an otherwise perfect view. The only illumination in the room came from a scented Porthault candle flickering on the coffee table and his eyes, which reflected the candle glow.

'I am L.A. born and bred. Mulholland Junior High in the valley, Birmingham High—go Braves! And then a year at Valley College.'

'Your life experience is certainly more impressive than your credentials.'

'You one of those intellectual snobs?' he teased.

'Education is important,' she stated defensively. 'It's not as though you're mentally incapable of it or anything.' She paused. But damn it, his lack of education *was* the only thing wrong with him. 'So what are you going to do next?' His toes traced a line up the bottom of her left foot, while his other foot caressed her right calf. Her feet were in foot paradise.

'I don't know what I'm going to do next.' He smiled. 'But I might race you to the bathroom if you've only got one in this place.'

'No. I've got two bathrooms, but no races, please. If I bounced my body one centimeter over what they call a gingerly walk, I'll be rivaling Buster's performance.'

'Hey, where is Buster?' he asked, realizing the dog was missing.

Vicky bit her lip, avoided his eyes, and pointed to the guest bath while she headed for her own. 'I gave Buster

262

away to the two girls next door. He was too tough for me to handle.' *And so are you,* she thought, closing the bathroom door. The more she knew about him, the more he appealed to her; everything about him was terrific, his sense of humor, his uninhibited manner. She'd loved it when he burped loudly and with deep satisfaction after finishing half a bottle of beer. She'd followed suit right afterward and hadn't even excused herself.

But a masseur? Come on, Vicky. Oh well, she thought, *he'll be fun for a while until the real thing comes along.*

When she came out of the bathroom, he was waiting in the dark hallway, the candle from the living room in his left hand. She gazed up at him and her heart began to pound. 'Eurydice,' he teased, 'I came to guide you back through the labyrinth to earth.'

She giggled, aware that his nearness made her blood race. 'Orpheo—Orpheo, wherefore art thou, Orpheo.'

'Right here, Vicky.' He sighed and leaned forward to kiss her gently on the lips; tiny touches with his tongue sent shivers down the sides of her neck and she responded with her own.

He pulled away and looked into her eyes. His shadow flickered and loomed largely on the wall behind him. 'I haven't thought of anything else but kissing you since I saw you by the side of the road the other day with that scowl on your face squatting on those great legs of yours. You really got me. And then when you walked into the restaurant you made my day.'

He slipped his fingertips into her hair, playing with her ear, rubbing her cheek, touching her lips.

'How *did* you find me?' she said. 'I forgot to ask you.'

'I have a friend in Sacramento who traced your license plate.'

'A regular detective,' she said.

Her comment made him pause for a moment, and for a brief frightening instant she thought he was going to stop what he was doing, but then his hand was on her shoulder, down her arm, at her waist, underneath her sweat shirt,

263

touching her body, finding the small of her back, the sides of her breast, underneath her arm. She gasped, and trembled with desire while they gazed in each other's eyes. And when she started to feel as though she couldn't stand up any longer, she reached under her shirt and found his hand and led him to the bedroom.

'Do you use contraception?' he asked, setting the candle down on the night table. 'Or should I?'

'It's all right,' she whispered, turning to embrace him. 'I do.' And by his question she knew she could fall in love with this man.

Chapter 22

LESLIE'S HEART began to pound as soon as she drove past the gatehouse and up the winding, tree-shaded drive of the McKintridge estate. Diverse memories battled for prominence in her mind, but she fought to remain calm; remaining calm was essential for any meeting with Belson, yet she was extremely apprehensive. Seeing him today was far more difficult than landing the job with Banir; there was much more at stake.

The thickly wooded underbrush broke free now and then from its unruly tangle long enough to allow her a glimpse of the lake, accented by the beautiful gazebo and dotted with white swans floating on the still, opaque water. But as her eyes feasted on the lush greenery all she could see were images of Sherryn's smiling face. Suddenly Leslie missed her with a hot, fierce pain. She'd forgotten how dear Sherryn had been to her and how devasted when Sherryn learned about her affair with Belson. Was that betrayal

264

what really killed Sherryn or had she died from pneumonia? *Don't think about that now. It's too unpleasant.* But the memory had cast a pall on her already skittish state of mind. *Get hold of yourself, girl. You don't need to add guilt to your apprehension.* She took a deep breath and exhaled it slowly, willing herself to relax. But her mind wouldn't co-operate. Would she be able to convince Belson to do what she wanted him to? Of course she would; she had an ace she'd been saving for years against him. But to re-establish an intimacy with him again after all this time was nearly impossible. Yet she anticipated it intensely. For if she *could* accomplish it, then everything she'd ever wanted would be hers, the McKintridge estate and an incredible man to share it with her.

It was fascinating to think how Belson might behave toward her now that she was not who she was. Would he suspect her reasons for coming here? Probably not. His ego wouldn't allow him to believe she was here for anything other than nostalgia. And yet the word *shrewd* was invented the day he was born. She'd have to be extremely cautious about broaching the subject of the estate. In fact if Banir hadn't insisted she convince Belson to sell him the estate, she wouldn't be here now. But Banir kept pressing her until she couldn't put it off any longer. *Banir.* The mere thought of the man sent electricity through her veins. She wanted him more today than the first day she had met him. And she was as determined as Banir to get what she wanted.

She left the Rolls on the curved front driveway, fluffed her hair, straightened her shoulders, and ascended the magnificent curved staircase to the front door. There was nothing in the world she enjoyed as much as a challenge, but today's chill of apprehension was definitely spoiling her pleasure.

A tall black man with a cool Jamaican clip to his speech opened the door for her. 'This way please.'

He led her through the intricately inlaid marble entryway, past the great hall, the dining room, and into the morning room. In spite of her tension and rapid pulse Leslie could see how the paneling had yellowed with age and the wall coverings had faded.

'Mr Belson will be right down,' he said, and bowed his head as he left.

She watched him go and then sat in one of the six hand-painted Louis XIV chairs around an Italian renaissance table. The eclectic mixture of the room and the rare beauty of the furniture captured her admiration though the tables and chairs were worn at the edges. The sun dappled the surface of the scuffed stenciled floor and played against the thick green richness of the hanging fern in the leaded bay window. The whole house needed redoing badly, but even so, Sherryn had had an incredible eye for arranging beauty. Leslie noticed every detail as she tried to relax, but she was too tautly drawn.

Belson entered soundlessly, wearing a light blue velour jogging suit the same color as his eyes. Seeing him was almost a physical shock and she was amazed at how he still affected her. Everything he had once meant to her came flooding back as if no time had passed at all and again she was a young, untried opportunist and he was Midas, owner of everything. *I will not weaken*, she thought.

A middle-aged Latin woman in a pink uniform poured tea from Belleek china fashioned into opalescent seashells accented with twig handles, and passed an assortment of sweet delicacies on a plate surrounded by handmade lace doilies carefully mended. Leslie wondered if they had been mended out of reverence for craftsmanship, or penury. Next to the sweets was an array of tea sandwiches, caviar, smoked salmon, steak tartarè, and watercress.

When the woman left, Belson gave her a kiss. 'You're looking well,' he offered.

'And you're awfully thin, Belson,' she said, noticing how he'd aged. It only increased her nervousness, as though now he had an even greater advantage over her than ever. Why this was so she didn't know. Perhaps it was his unpredictability. At any moment she feared he was capable of slapping her, merely on general principles. She felt her heart beating wildly against her rib cage and forced herself to turn her attention away from him, to collect her bearings. Outside on the lawn a team of gardeners mowed and trimmed, planted and watered, while indoors the scent of lemon oil and brass polish hung in the air. If she listened hard enough, she could almost hear the sound of soft flannel cloth being rubbed against antique wood. *Be calm.* So much depended on this meeting today: she wanted Banir and he wanted this house.

'What are you doing here, Leslie?' he asked sharply, as though reading her mind. 'I thought we had an unspoken agreement not to intrude in one another's lives except at large functions. I came to Craige's funeral, you attended Peter's wedding. That suited me fine.'

She forced herself to be pleasant. 'It was good of you to come to Craige's funeral.'

'I did it for the children. So they would see their father had known important people. And how are they?' he asked.

'They're fine,' she said. 'They give me purpose in life, keep me from being lonely.' *If he only knew,* she thought. After that incident with the teacher at Southwick School, she'd had to send Debra to boarding school in Arizona. And now Terry was showing signs of misbehaving. 'And speaking of children, isn't it lonely for you rattling around alone in this huge mausoleum?'

He looked at her sharply, trying to probe her mind. After all, he'd always rattled around in this place. But she kept her expression light and clear of ulterior intent.

'That's a strange question,' he commented, not put off by her appearance of innocence. 'As if you could possibly be concerned about me after all this time. Now let's see,' he mused. 'You're not fishing for business—I hear you've plenty of that—and you've never worked for a charity in your life, so you're not soliciting funds.' He stopped, waiting for her to fill in the answer. When she didn't, he said hostilely, 'How can I be alone with forty-five servants in attendance?'

'That's not my idea of company, Belson. What do you do for entertainment? Watch Mr Albert remove the cork from his ass every night before you go to sleep?'

Belson's laugh was deep, a genuine, welcome relief. 'With all your success you haven't changed, have you, Leslie? Or should I call you Tessie Mae? Still the same crude cracker from East Texas you always were. You can take the girl out of the hick town . . .'

'. . .but you can't take the hick town out of the girl,' she finished for him. 'Now let's not get nasty, shall we? I came here for a nice visit with an "old" friend.' She emphasized the word *old*, and he cracked a half-smile. 'I thought we'd talk over fond memories. And I know you're wondering what I'm doing here after all this time; out of the blue I drop in for tea. But in all honesty, Belson, I just wanted to see you.' She gave him a sweet smile before taking a sip from the delicate porcelain cup and hitting him with her zinger. 'You're not getting any younger and I thought I'd better see you while I still had the chance.'

Belson's cup rattled in his dish and he glared at her. 'Don't write me off so easily, my sweet.'

The use of her old nickname cut through her steel barriers.

'I have my great-grandson to live for—to strive for.' There was such a look of pride on his face at the mention of Jonathan that she remembered in a rush how human he could be. At this moment she almost liked him. It was the perfect time for her to segue into what she'd come to discuss.

'I'm surprised Peter and his family aren't living here in the house with you.'

'They're close enough in the guesthouse,' he replied. 'Besides, they'll live here after I'm gone.'

She feigned horror. 'Don't tell me! You're not leaving this white elephant to Peter and his family, are you? Oh,

Belson, how could you do such a selfish thing?'

His eyes widened in surprise. 'Whatever do you mean?'

'That's a horrible burden to inflict on anyone, especially on a little boy raised in modern freedom, who's always been able to play with his neighborhood friends whenever he likes, or walk to school, or to the movies, take the public bus with his classmates, go to the beach, or run around outside the castle walls. You know there are simple pleasures of being a commoner that the members of royal families long to enjoy. You of all people should recognize that.'

He was perturbed by her comments. Belson never liked to be criticized. 'I never thought of it that way.'

'Why should you? All you want to do is keep a dynasty alive and damn the consequences to the little prince who has to swim across his moat in order to buy a sidewalk sundae from the ice cream man.

'And what would it mean to Phyllis and Peter to have to keep this place going? Ye Gods, Belson. Think what you're doing.'

'Sherryn and I raised our family here.'

'Those were different times. In case you haven't noticed, Belson, it takes millions to keep McKintridge going. How can you inflict that burden on Phyllis and Peter? It would cast a terrible shadow over their life.'

He clamped his mouth together in a thin line of displeasure. How well Leslie remembered that expression. 'It's been a dream of mine to pass this house on to my heirs and nothing will ever change that, *nothing!* No matter what you say, McKintridge *will* be occupied by our family.'

Leslie shrugged, took a last sip of her tea. 'Suit yourself, Belson. You always did. But if I were you I'd sell this house and get rid of the burden it would be on my family. It's been my experience in life that it is wrong to inflict our desires and needs on those we love.'

He knew her well. Suddenly he reached across the table and grabbed her upper arm between long bony fingers. Then he squeezed with all his might. 'What are you hinting about, you crow?'

She was shocked by his vehemence. 'Why, nothing,' she said. 'I only meant that you'll probably come to agree with me; your family needs to be protected from ending up in this fancy jail of a house, not forced to be incarcerated in it.' She removed her arm from his tight grip and made a wide gesture with her hand, indicating the lush surroundings as though they were shoddy and meaningless.

He harumphed loudly and stood up; the audience was over. Two shrewd operators had engaged in a contest—no one had won.

Leslie felt panic begin to grip her as she realized he was showing her out and she hadn't accomplished anything. *Do something,* she thought. But Belson was on his way to the door and she had to follow, pretend she didn't mind leaving. His long strides kept pace with hers; his body was taut and lean beneath the softness of his clothes. And damn it, he was still attractive.

As they reached the massive double doors, she realized that she had run out of excuses for wanting to stay, so she turned and kissed him on the lips, letting it be an open-mouthed exploration. Immediately his tongue darted into her mouth and she had to allow the foray. She almost wished he'd bite her and draw blood, then she could have bitten him back. She broke the embrace, smiling a fake, lazy smile. 'We should never have had that falling-out, Belson,' she said. 'What a couple we'd have made.'

But his expression was cold as he said, 'Not likely. And you can tell that filthy Arab who sent you to try and get my house away from me that I'd see you both with skewers up you asses before that will happen.'

So he knew more than he said. Leslie was filled with that familiar rush of hatred for him that she hadn't felt in years. It grabbed her so intensely she almost spat his kiss back in his face. With great control she draped her purse strap over her shoulder. It was time to play her ace.

'I didn't want to have to bring this up, Belson, didn't want to be so blunt. But that "filthy" Arab you referred to is a close personal friend of mine—'

'I'll bet!' he sneered.

'—as well as an associate of mine. And he has asked me to intervene on his behalf to get you to sell him the McKintridge estate. I've told him I would do it.'

'And how do you propose to accomplish it?' he asked, his eyes glaring knotholes through her.

'Because if you don't agree, I shall go to the papers with the details of what I know about your sexual aberrations. What a honey of a story that would make: Mr Conservative himself—the paragon of moral virtue—turns out to be a disciple of Smut and a worshiper at the shrine of Disgust. Not to mention the criminal aspects of your sordid life. Now that would be some heritage to leave to Jonathan.'

And damned if he didn't stand his ground. He hardly even flinched. 'Go ahead, Leslie. Tell it all, every detail if you like,' he said. 'I shall include your participation in my admission of guilt. At my age I couldn't care less who knows about my past. I've lived my life. But you have a lot to lose. Do you think that Muslim of yours would want you if he knew what you'd done? Not on your life. Muslims expect their women to be pure. So go ahead, tell your friend the witch Dianna Cunningham to print everything she wants. I'll call her rival columnists and bring you right down with me.'

Leslie felt her nerve disintegrating, but she wasn't ready to give up yet. 'Then I'll wait until you're gone, Belson. Before I ruin your name,' she threatened. 'What could you do then?'

He gave a little laugh, as though he were truly enjoying this, and she thought she had never seen anyone so cool, so evil, in her life. 'I shall leave a detailed account of your participation in my past acts, along with some interesting photographs of you that you weren't even aware of. And I shall send them to my attorney with instructions to release them immediately if any unpleasant publicity is printed about me after my demise.'

He was indeed unbeatable. She could feel the color

draining from her face, just as Belson shoved her out the door. And then he yelled after her, 'Go ahead, you slut. Tell it all! Go on, tell it. I dare you.' And then he slammed the door.

She was shaking with fury as she got back into her black Rolls Carmargue and sent it barreling down the driveway, demolishing the edges of newly planted tulips. She would have run over Belson if he had been there. 'Getting that house away from you is going to be a pleasure, Belson,' she said aloud. 'And I'm going to do it if it kills me. I'm going to do it!'

Chapter 23

VICKY WAS confused about Bob Delman. He was the best thing to have happened to her in a long time, but she was torn at certain elements in their relationship. She needed to get information from him about Belson and yet it was unfair to use him. That's why she waited so long before bringing up the subject uppermost in her mind. Since their first night together when Bob had appeared at her apartment with half the hamburgers in Los Angeles, they'd seen each other on a regular basis. She felt at home in his place in Laurel Canyon—a woodsy, converted cabin on Briarwood Drive—they went to neighborhood movies, and they'd taken weekend outings to Santa Barbara and Palm Springs. But still she hadn't broached the subject of Belson McKintridge. She was afraid that if Bob found out what she really wanted from him, it would ruin what they had going together. And what they had was something special. The man was definitely getting under her skin. She liked everything about him except what he did for a living. And God help her, she couldn't discuss that with him either. She was ashamed of herself for feeling this way but it embarrassed her for anyone in Beverly Hills to know she was dating a masseur. She told herself over and over that the way Bob made his living shouldn't make any difference to her, but it did. She just couldn't reconcile what she felt about him with what he was, even though there was so much about him that excited and stimulated her. She was even thinking about asking him to move in with her, but the fact that he could be satisfied with a job so mundane and lacking in potential made a statement about him that she couldn't ignore. And though she shared her deepest confidences with him, her opinion of his livelihood was one thing she hadn't shared.

In the time they'd been together, she'd told him about her background as a teacher-cum-novelist, he'd told her about his one broken engagement and another serious romance, they'd discussed her mother and her mother's influence on her, his parents, their views on marriage (he believed in it, she wasn't so sure), their politics (he was a Democrat, just right of Tom Hayden). She admitted to being a Republican and listened to his tirade about how the social services were going to suffer, the cancer of big business would metastasize even more, and the environment would deteriorate into a sewer under Reagan. It was ironic that everything he was afraid of were things Belson McKintridge probably welcomed. But she couldn't continue to speculate about Belson McKintridge or his life; it was time to ask about it or forever hold her peace. If asking for what she wanted was going to break them up, it had better be now, before they got even more involved. Before she whispered his name to herself twenty times a day instead of only eighteen. The thought of breaking up with Bob gave her a sharp jolt of pain and she grabbed on to him now tightly.

Mistaking her desperation for ardor, he responded and they ended up making love a second time; still she hadn't asked him.

Afterward he sat up in bed, pulled her next to him with his arm around her, and clicked on the TV.

But before the dark screen had warmed into an image, she took a deep breath, crossed her fingers, and said to him, 'Will you tell me something about Belson McKintridge?'

He looked at her in surprise and she was immediately certain he'd read her mind. Her body tensed, waiting for him to leap out of bed, throw on his clothes, and storm out of the apartment yelling, 'You bitch, you've only been using me for what I can do your career,' and she'd never see him again.

But that's not what he said.

'What do you want to know?' He was watching Errol Flynn battling Basil Rathbone in *Robin Hood*. *Click, click, click,* went their swords.

'Anything you can tell me,' she answered.

'Well, there's not much to tell,' Bob replied pleasantly. 'His muscles are fairly strong for a man his age. His flesh isn't too loose, he wears expensive cologne, and his bath towels are blue.'

Vicky laughed a bit nervously. 'No, that's not what I mean. I'm not interested in his muscles or his underarm deodorant. I want to know about *him*.'

Bob was unconcerned, concentrating on the film. 'I never discuss my clients with anyone beyond what I've just told you,' he said, patting her knee.

'I see,' Vicky said, feeling rebuffed. Of course a man with a social conscience wouldn't gossip. Damn, now what was she supposed to do?

'Ah-ha,' Flynn said, almost thrusting a killing blow to Rathbone, who recovered and forced Flynn back against the dungeon wall.

'This is a great scene,' Bob said. 'Now watch this. Robin forces Sir Guy of Gisbourne up the stairs, backward. Neither of these guys ever used a double.'

A close-up of Errol Flynn revealed his young, beautiful

274

face and long Robin Hood hairdo, and only a furrow of concern blemished his smooth brow, indicating his concentration.

'You know, don't you,' Bob commented wryly, 'the real genius of this duel is the choreographer. I wonder who that was?'

As Basil Rathbone fell off the edge of the balcony after being impaled by Flynn and landed on the hard stone floor, Bob clicked off the set and sighed. 'They don't make movies like that anymore.'

'Phyllis has told me quite a bit about Belson,' Vicky ventured, hoping he'd pick up the hint. 'More personal things. But Belson McKintridge is certainly not your average, everyday rich man. He's powerful and he's been known to abuse that power in nasty ways. I'll bet there is plenty of inside information people don't know about him.'

Bob looked at her sharply. 'Such as?'

'Did you know Belson was anit-Semitic?'

'Oh sure,' he scoffed. 'Just like Errol Flynn?'

'I guess you gentiles don't care about things like that,' she said testily. It was one thing for him not to tell her about Belson; it was another for him to defend the man.

'Gentiles?' he laughed. 'Vicky, I'm Jewish. Delman is short for Delmansky. My family came from Russia on my father's side.'

Again she was amazed. 'A Jewish masseur?' she hooted. 'That's even worse. My mother would call it a *shanda*.' Her derogatory comment had popped out uncensored and she instantly regretted it. But he frustrated her with his complacency, expecting her to accept him as he was when he could be so much more.

'Wait a minute,' he exclaimed, pushing himself up higher in the bed, beginning to sense a deeper meaning to her words. 'It's not a disgrace to earn a living at physical labor. I make people happy, I bring them relief and pleasure in an honorable, efficient way, and I get paid for it. There's nothing wrong with that. If I spend an hour with someone and it helps to rid them of their stress and tension, is that any different from their being entertained by a book you've written?'

'Oh, they're nothing alike,' she snapped, feeling her ire rising, not because she resented his comparing the noble profession of writing to the inanity of pressing on muscle tissue, but because she couldn't think of any logical reason with which to out-argue him. So when cornered it's best to attack. 'Methinks you've made this defensive little speech before, Robert. Perhaps to Mama and Papa Delmansky who wanted little Bobby to be a doctor or a lawyer. I'll bet they've found it nothing short of embarrassing that you earn your living by putting your hands all over naked bodies.'

The expression of fury on his face frightened her. 'You've never minded when my hands were all over your naked body,' he said, forcing the words through clenched teeth. 'And what's so great about being a doctor or a lawyer?' He nearly shouted the question. 'Take lawyers, for example. They charge outrageous fees, and many of them have no qualms at all about perverting justice. They think that by saying they're preserving the letter of the law it justifies all the reprehensible things they do in the pursuit of their profession. And they create more hostilities between adversaries than the litigants ever dreamed of.'

His vehemence overwhelmed her. 'All right, already, so don't be a lawyer, and don't be a doctor. Be anything you want.' *Except a masseur*, she thought. 'Be an investigator.' She grabbed a profession out of the air. 'You've already got that hot connection in Sacramento, the one who gave you my address.'

He flinched and moved away from her as though she'd suddenly become contagious. 'What are you, clairvoyant?' he asked.

'Me?' Vicky asked in surprise. 'No way.' The expression on his face told her she was pushing too hard. *Back off or you're going to ruin it, Feinstein*, she thought. *You'll never get what you want, him or the information.* 'I wish I were clairvoyant,' she said, altering her tactic, 'then maybe I would know how to stop arguing with you. It's not what I want to be doing right now.'

He looked sideways at her and nodded, his suspicious nature diminished a bit. 'You're right. It's foolish to argue. So why don't you tell me what's really going on?'

She searched his face, trying to find a way out, but there was none. She couldn't avoid this any longer. 'I've got a character in my novel loosely based on Belson McKintridge and I could use some details about him to lend authenticity.'

'Why don't you just ask your friends Phyllis and Peter?'

She could feel her cheeks blushing. 'I have, but I wouldn't want them to think I've presumed on our friendship.'

'But you don't mind presuming on mine?'

She looked away in embarrassment. 'Look, you don't have to tell me if you don't want to.'

'And what do you need to know?' He was watching her intensely.

She glanced down, trying to seem casual but she didn't think she was pulling it off: her heart was pumping too wildly. Her hands had a life of their own and fought her control, wanting to flail and flutter about. 'I just want to know things like what he does for excitement, what the names are of some of the people he's stepped on over the years, and what the chances are that he's done anything illegal or dishonest in his life.'

His stare made her even more nervous, as though he were seeing a side of her he'd never seen before. It made her squirm with discomfort.

'You have the strangest expression on your face,' he said. 'All tight and pinched, almost avaricious. You remind me of a predatory animal enjoying a scavenged meal, salivating over the spoils of life. It's unworthy of you, Vicky,' he added softly.

She was agonized that he had seen through her and leaped to her own defense. 'Who made you my moral conscience?' she asked harshly. But her anger was covering the fear that he would find her out. 'What do you know about being emotionally mutilated, or rejected, or ambitious?'

'Only what you tell me,' he said.

'Well, unlike you, I burn with ambition. I want my name on all the lists. "A" lists, party lists, best-seller lists, Franz Liszt's lists, if he had one.' She half smiled at her joke, but he didn't respond. 'It's difficult to do what I'm doing,' she insisted. 'Creating real characters out of my imagination, making them come alive and bring the reader to joy or to tears. I want my characters to succeed, very badly,' she added. Still she couldn't bring herself to look at him. Of course all that was true, but it wasn't her only motive for wanting what he could tell her.

He was silent and all she could hear was the pounding of her pulse in her ears. Finally he said, 'When I see what ambition does to you, it reminds me how glad I am what I am.'

'Oh, you and Popeye,' she retorted, hostility grabbing her again. 'Both of you are musclebound.'

'Come on, Vicky, why so angry again? What's going on?'

'Nothing but your superior attitude,' she said. But she was unnerved by his comments about her rampant ambitions and terrified of being transparent. He seemed to dig right into her soft spots and press on them, like a dentist's drill to a cavity.

Finally he sighed. 'Okay, enough?'

And she nodded, feeling close to tears.

He leaned back and put his arm around her, pulling her toward him, then he nuzzled her and reached his hand into her lap to rub the inside of her thigh with a practiced touch.

She was amazed that he could get over their argument so easily. She felt anything but affectionate.

'What do you say, we make love one more time,' he asked, 'and then go have Chinese food and see a movie? Or better yet, let's go skating. I do a *mean* roller-disco.'

Skating? she thought. *In public?* And her hesitation

turned into a loaded pause. 'Not tonight,' she said apologetically. 'How about some other time?'

His deflated ego showed in his most vulnerable place and she could feel him getting soft where he pressed himself against her thigh. He pulled away from her, placed his arms behind his head, and stared up at the ceiling. 'Do you realize that's the fourth time you've turned me down for a date? What is it with you? Are you agoraphobic, or don't you want me to meet your friends? Isn't your mother curious about your new beau?' He leaned over on his elbow to look at her. 'My folks know all about you. They know what you look like, and how smart you are, and that I'm crazy about you.'

Her heart skipped a beat; she felt small and embarrassed for the second time in only a few minutes. But his words were etched in her heart. *He's crazy about me,* she thought, feeling a warm flush of joy rush through her.

He took her chin in his hand, turned her face toward him, and gave a short hurt laugh. 'You're not ashamed to be seen with me, are you?'

She tried to laugh with him, but it wasn't funny. 'Of course not,' she lied. 'And as for my mother, she'd like you just fine.' She paused and forced herself to say the rest. 'She'd like you until you told her what you did for a living. And then she'd give you the famous Reena Feinstein look.' Vicky raised her eyebrows, looked down her small turned-up nose, and gave a curt, judgmental snort. 'No.' She shook her head. 'I don't want Reena to get hold of you just yet.'

He was studying her quizzically. 'You know something? That may be your mother's expression, but I've seen you do it too.'

'When?' she asked, feeling caught again.

'Whenever you ask me questions about my profession or my future plans. I think you're as upset about what I do for a living as you pretend your mother would be. Only you won't admit it, and she would. She has a good excuse. She wants something better for her daughter than she had. She was raised in a world where people succeeded and survived because of their drive, but with you those criteria are like stale bread, like leftover garbage.' He was angry with her again, and he had a right to be. She'd been carelessly transparent after all and she'd hurt him. She hated herself for feeling the way she did. Damn, she was crazy about him too.

'If you take me for Mexican food instead of Chinese,' she said softly, running her hand lightly over the hair on his chest, circling his navel, and gliding gently down to his genitals which were limp and unresponsive, 'I'll out-disco you at the skate rink anytime.'

A delighted smile lit up his face and there was an even more obvious response beneath her hand. 'Lady, you're on,' he said hoarsely, kissing her ear and her neck and her shoulder. 'And I'll see if I can think of any details about Belson McKintridge that wouldn't compromise his privacy and would still add a touch of spice to your work.'

'Oh, Bob,' she whispered, abandoning herself to his kiss as his lips found hers. 'You're wonderful, you're so wonderful.'

And what does your boyfriend do for a living, Miss Feinstein? a tiny voice in her brain asked. *Oh, shut up,* she told the voice. *He makes me happy, and that should be enough.*

Chapter 24

PETER COULD not believe the figures. As of 8:00 A.M. on May first, platinum had shot up to a selling price of nine hundred dollars an ounce, which meant they had gained another 50 percent above their last investment of six hundred an ounce. If his early calculations were correct, they were showing an additional profit in their combined accounts of nearly sixty million dollars.

His excitement was at a fever pitch as he jumped into his jeans and raced up the long winding driveway to the main house to find Belson. *At last,* his heart pounded as he jogged, at last they could sell out their holdings and take their profit. They could be done with this devilish business. All he wanted to do was go back to his normal life knowing they had succeeded in their endeavor. So what if they were a bit short of their goal? Sixty million would be enough. And it was a good thing it happened now, because he just didn't think he could go on with this tension one moment longer.

Belson was on the phone with Henry Cronyn in his study and he was beaming as though his death sentence had just been commuted. But that wasn't true and Peter knew it. Even though Belson looked better this morning than he had in months, his last cardiovascular tests had shown marked deterioration. Yet here he sat, as bright as could be, the picture of health, and again Peter was filled with admiration for his courage. The whites of his eyes were a clear bluish color this morning with none of their usual yellowy tinge, his cheeks were pink with a robust glow, and he had even put on a little weight, which made him look less cadaverous. For him to be so active nearly nine months after his doctors gave him only six months to live ought to be enough to make him glow. But Peter knew today's well-being was a result of the jump in platinum prices and not gratitude to God.

Peter listened to his grandfather's conversation and suddenly his own spirits began to flag. The more he heard, the more he realized that his grandfather was not going to sell out now. He was going to continue.

The minute Belson got off the phone, Peter rushed over to the desk and leaned on it excitedly. 'We've got to stop now, Grandfather,' he stated. 'Sixty million is enough! There's too much risk in going any further and I just can't live under the strain any longer. I don't care what you say,

I'm quitting as of right now! This goddamned platinum thing is ruining my life.'

But Belson wasn't even listening to him; he was too busy writing figures on a scratch pad and using his calculator as he chuckled and grinned over each total.

'You see!' he said, finally looking up. 'What did I tell you? Come around here and look at these figures.'

Peter came around the desk to look over his shoulder.

'We're almost there,' Belson stated. 'Just one more pyramid should do it. Now here's what I want you to do.'

But Peter interrupted him, circling back around the desk to face him again. 'You haven't been listening to me. I want out, Grandfather. I want you to sell it all!'

Belson stared at him with as much amazement as if the pastoral painting by Winslow Homer on the opposite wall had just come to life and the milkmaid in the painting had stepped out of the frame and offered him a fresh bucket of milk. 'You want out? Are you kidding? Who do you think you are? You're the one who said we should forget about doing any of this. You're the one who said it would never work, who said I should lay down and die, in Hawaii no less; slink away with my tail between my legs. And you'd be the one who would be the sorriest of all if I listened to such advice. Are you going to make me believe you won't enjoy my money and my house if I preserve them for you?'

'But, Grandfather,' he protested, stung by Belson's bitterness and at the same time feeling guilty for causing his grandfather so much upset. 'It's just that it puts us both under such a strain.'

Belson's face showed contempt and the look was enough to stop Peter's protest. The moment of confrontation passed. 'Listen, son,' he said, 'we need more—we're not there yet.'

Peter was moved by Belson's show of patience.

Belson glanced down at the sheet in front of him where he had been totaling figures before Peter arrived. 'All right. We've got sixty million profit on the appreciation of our contracts from the six hundred to nine hundred rise in price. And eight million profit currently being used as margin. The other two million of margin was our initial borrowed down payment.

'The estate tax or even income tax, if I survive to the end of the year, on sixty-eight million would be about fifty-one million, leaving only seventeen million after taxes.'

Peter shook his head. 'They make it hard, don't they?'

'Okay,' Belson continued. 'If McKintridge is worth in assessed value about thirty million, then the estate taxes would be between twenty-two and twenty-three million. And don't forget I have a debt of three-and-a-half.

'So the total owed is twenty-three million, plus three point five in loans, plus the interest and points at fifteen percent comes to twenty-seven million. Add to that a cushion of three million in liquid assets you'd need to put into municipal bonds to throw off about three hundred thousand a year tax-free to run the estate with minimal staff. That totals thirty million; we've only cleared seventeen. We're short thirteen million.'

He had stated his case perfectly and Peter could see with a sinking heart that if they quit now, all their previous effort would have been in vain. They had to go on after all.

He gave a brief, resigned nod but he felt as though he'd just given away his sanity.

'To keep your mind at ease,' Belson said, as though pulling a rabbit out of a hat, 'I'll agree to take thirty million out of the sixty and put it in the bank as a cushion. All we really need to reinvest it is the remaining thirty. Will that make you feel any better?'

Peter was so relieved that he wanted to hug Belson but he restrained himself. 'God, yes!' he exclaimed. 'At least we'd have some ready cash in case there was a margin call, something we haven't had so far.'

'All right then.' Belson chuckled, his good humor restored. 'Get to it.'

Gradually over the next several weeks well into May, Peter completed all the necessary transactions for their final pyramid. He took their profit and reinvested half again. He bought an additional six thousand contracts at nine hundred dollars an ounce at an increased margin requirement of five thousand dollars a contract. By the end of the purchase period they now controlled a staggering $450 million worth of platinum futures. And now when the price rose one dollar an ounce they earned $500,000, but if it dropped merely two points, they would lose one million.

He was making an ordinary check-in call to Frank Logan in Phoenix, one of the most accommodating brokers they worked with. Logan had a robust face, sported a handlebar mustache, and could have stepped directly out of a daguerreotype of the Old West, or been the twin brother of Lovis Corinth, the post-impressionist painter. But Frank's reply was anything but ordinary.

'Someone's been asking about you, Peter,' he said, lowering his voice two octaves to a conspiratorial whisper.

A sudden, icy dread clutched Peter in an iron grip. 'What do you mean?' he whispered back.

'Some guy from L.A. has been asking questions about you. He was hanging around the office and then made an appointment with me, ostensibly to invest in commodities, but he used your real name as a reference. That really spooked me. I'm not supposed to know from McKintridge, right? So I tell him I don't know you and he gets smart. Says he saw you here. Now, I figure he's fishing, 'cause you've only been here twice. Once when you set up the account and two days ago to pick up the cash your "client" made. Right?'

'Right,' Peter said.

'Then the guy wants to know what I'm hiding. Asks what kind of a scam we're running here. Scared the bejesus out of me.'

Peter was frightened too.

'I asked him to leave, said our transactions are confidential, and whoever he thought he saw could have been anybody. But I have a feeling we haven't seen the last of him.'

Peter's hands were shaking so badly he could barely hold the phone. 'Do you think the Commodity Exchange sent him?'

'I don't know,' Logan said. 'Those guys usually identify themselves. Maybe he's a private man. Want me to check with the Commodity Exchange or the CFTC and see if they've got anyone on your case?'

'No!' Peter almost shouted. 'I don't want you to call attention to us if they aren't involved. And if they are, we'll know soon enough.' *Jesus*, Peter thought, *they're on to us*. Suddenly, the awful enormity of what he'd been doing came crashing into his awareness, cymbals clanged in his ears, neon fingers of guilt pointed at him flashing on and off, 'Here he is, folks, the cheat and the liar, see what a truly immoral bastard really looks like.'

'Can you give me a description of the man so I'll know whom to watch out for?' Peter asked, wondering how he could have gotten so careless and not noticed if someone was following him.

'Sure,' Logan said. 'He was just over five ten, well built, in his mid-thirties with a toothy smile, curly hair, and a California tan. His clothes were strictly off the rack.'

Peter thanked him and then hung up.

His head was throbbing so hard it felt as though his brain had been replaced by a thousand-kilowatt generator. His whole life had just disintegrated around him and he was fighting not to throw himself out the window of his office. The roaring in his ears grew worse with every second and that old terror clutched his heart, that sickening metallic ache; he heard the sound of fingernails screeching across a blackboard, the howling of a murderous beast, the scream of an airplane as it plunged into a fiery inferno. His armpits dripped inside his linen jacket. *Oh, God, what have I done?* He felt caught again. Memories flooded him, topside down, vulnerable, barely alive, the flames of hell devouring his family, *his fault, his fault*. His stomach heaved and he fought for control. He'd better tell his grandfather. But then he realized he couldn't do that. News like this might be too much for him. He'd have to handle it on his own. But what could he do? Whom could he turn to? He had to talk to someone. And if he did, what good would it do?

The jig, as they say, might be up.

Larry met him downstairs in the restaurant because Peter had suddenly become paranoid that his office could possibly be bugged. He sat huddled in a dark corner of the dimly lit fake-English pub atmosphere, trying to find the courage to speak. He was torn by the desire to unburden himself and the knowledge that he was going against his grandfather's expressed wishes. But there were legal implications he had to discuss with someone. He couldn't let them go unanswered any longer.

'You look terrible, buddy,' Larry began. 'What's going on?'

Peter sighed and shook his head. 'I'm in real trouble, Larry. Real trouble. It's been going on for a long time and it's getting worse. I know you might hate me when I tell you about it, but you've got to help me. I don't know where else to turn.'

Larry's agitation increased immediately. 'So tell me, for Christ's sake.'

And Peter told him everything, about Belson's failing health, about the loss of the family fortune, and about their desperate scheme to earn back the money and preserve the McKintridge estate by speculating in platinum. He confessed about his own involvement, about their recent success, and then about his fears that he had been discovered and was being investigated by the CFTC.

By the time Peter finished talking, Larry was leaning forward on the edge of his seat, his face a mixture of disbelief, incredulity, and fury. But what Peter was desperately looking to see was compassion.

'Let me play this back,' Larry said, his voice tight with sarcasm. 'I want to be sure I've got it all. It seems your grandfather pissed away his considerable fortune because of his monumental ego and his basically greedy nature and you found him crying in his tea about what a mess he'd made of his life and what he'd done to poor old posterity. Plus, he finds out his heart is in a chokehold and he's liable to croak any minute. So he devises a scheme to make it all better. He's going to put a little squeeze on platinum, drive up the price, screw a lot of people in the process, and come out with his own hide intact. And all he wants from you is to be his errand boy.'

Peter had never seen Larry so furious.

'He's not screwing anybody,' Peter said.

'Oh, yeah? And what do you think happens to the investors who ride the commodity on the climb, believing in the false inflated price, and then are left holding the bag when your grandfather sells and the price plummets? And you've gone along with him, supporting his craziness, sacrificing your peace of mind, jeopardizing your career, your reputation, and mine!' he shouted, carried away by his own anger. 'So this is what you've been doing for the last six months while I've been carrying the dead weight of you around on my shoulders. No wonder you haven't been available for work. No wonder you aren't billing the kind of hours we need to survive. Do you know what it costs to live these days for us ordinary peons who aren't involved in a hundred-million-dollar swindle? I've been supporting your family as well as mine. And I haven't even complained. Not me! I've been worried about poor Peter. He's having a slow time of it. But he'll pull it together, I've told myself. A slow time, Jesus!'

Peter dropped his head into his hands. He'd barely given a thought to how his actions might be affecting Larry's career and Larry's income or their partnership. He had relied totally on Larry's generosity, on his enormous energy, without even considering the cost.

'You're really something,' Larry said with disgust.

Peter's eyes pleaded for mercy while his expression transmitted his deep misery. 'What can I say to you? You're right. There's no foul name you could call me I

287

haven't called myself.'

But Larry's anger would not be softened. 'Okay, give it all to me. What exactly have you done that you wouldn't want the bar association to find out, let alone the Commodities Futures Trading Commission?'

Peter's voice was barely a whisper, every word a physical pain. 'I falsified documents to set up illegal accounts. Every time you open an account with a commodities broker, they ask on their account forms if you have any other accounts elsewhere. I've always said no. Plus, we've used fictitious names for all our accounts.'

'How did you verify credit for all those accounts? Aren't there financial requirements? Don't you need liquid assets or collateral to buy on margin?'

Peter nodded. 'There's a bank officer at Union Commerce who verifies my grandfather's credit as applying to all the names.'

'How is Belson getting him to do that?'

Peter shrugged and glanced away guiltily.

'He's not paying him off, is he?' Larry yelled, and then lowered his voice as two women at a nearby table turned to look at him. 'He is, isn't he?' Larry asked. 'Jesus, are you involved in graft?'

'No!' Peter assured him. 'I have nothing to do with the banker. Belson takes care of that completely.'

'And how many accounts *do* you have?'

Peter couldn't meet Larry's eyes. 'As of our last pyramid transaction, we have thirty.'

'Christ!' Larry hissed.

Peter sat slumped in the booth, trying to ward off the self-hatred that flooded him, tasting acid in the back of his throat.

'What else is there?' Larry said, rapping on the table to get Peter's attention. The coffee in their cups sloshed over into the saucers.

Peter jumped as though he'd been struck. 'I've broken trading regulations too. There's a rule that you must report to the commission when you buy more than a certain amount of contracts, so they can keep track of such things as squeezes. I didn't report my buys over one hundred contracts and I opened other accounts to avoid detection. But I haven't been directly involved with the bank. I swear it. You've got to believe me.'

Larry gave a short, disgusted snort. 'You're only clean on a technicality. What a prince of a moral person you are, partner dear. If the ethics committee of the bar thinks you've been involved in a situation of graft, you'll be disbarred. On the other hand,' he added, 'they might not catch you.'

'I deserve to be caught.' Peter felt the hot sting of tears filling his eyes. He never realized what he had sacrificed when he agreed to help his grandfather. There was an emptiness inside that could never be filled again. And worse than his own self-loathing was the look of disgust he saw in Larry's eyes. 'I know you hate me,' he said. 'I wouldn't blame you if you disbanded the partnership.'

'Don't tempt me,' Larry snapped. 'The trouble is, it probably wouldn't do any good by now. They'll disbar me along with you. Who's going to believe I wasn't involved in all this too?'

'But you weren't!' Peter insisted, horrified at what he might have done to his friend. 'I'll testify to your innocence! I'll make them believe me. Even my grandfather will vouch for you.' He turned his head away in embarrassment.

'How could you have been so stupid?' Larry asked.

Peter blew his nose in the paper napkin off the table, waited a moment, and then asked, 'What do you think?'

Larry gave him a long, hard look, then he shook his head in exasperation. 'As far as disbanding the partnership, I'm very tempted, let me tell you. And I'll probably give it a lot of thought. But I'm not going to make a decision like that in a moment of rash anger. I know you've been under tremendous pressure. I've seen it all along. I just didn't know why. And frankly I don't know how you've lived with it all this time.'

Peter was grateful for Larry's understanding. 'You just can't imagine how rough it's been.'

'Well, I'm not the judge and jury of your stupidity. I know what Belson means to you, though for God's sake I can't imagine why you still give a shit about the bastard after all this.' He shook his head from side to side.

'I'm no one to cast stones at glass houses, Peter. My career isn't spotless and neither am I. But damn it, I'm pissed as hell because you kept me in the dark about this all this time. You knew what I stood to lose and you also knew I was tied to you whether I liked it or not. I'm afraid I'll be guilty by association. If only you'd have told me what was happening all those times I tried to get it out of you!'

'Lord knows I wanted to,' Peter said.

Larry gave a short, harsh laugh. He really did love Peter. His partner was as vulnerable as a puppy. 'Oh, what the hell. I'm no one to preach. We're all out for number one. I'm sure as hell more worried about my own skin right now than I am about yours.' He paused. 'But you're the one with the real problem.'

Peter nodded, but he couldn't speak. Larry's comforting words were a balm to his scorched soul. Finally the choking sensation in his throat subsided enough for him to ask. 'What do you think I should do?'

Larry's earnest answer came quickly. 'For God's sake, stop doing what you're doing. The longer you do it, the worse it is for you. Sell your contracts now and get out of the market. Then there won't be anything to investigate.'

Peter felt the torturer's rack pulling him again. 'I can't do that,' he said. 'My grandfather refuses. I've begged him myself.'

'Then you do it,' Larry said. 'If you have the power to buy and sell on his behalf, then sell out on your own. Don't listen to him anymore.'

'I can't go behind his back,' Peter exclaimed, horrified at the idea. 'If he ended up short of his goal because of me, it would kill him. He'd never understand why I'd betrayed him. I'd rather sacrifice myself than hurt him.'

'Well, that's exactly what you're doing,' Larry insisted. 'Don't you see? If the commission is on to you, they can suspend trading and the way you've leveraged everything will fall apart. That's what happened to the Hunt brothers. They were only allowed to sell silver and the market collapsed. Or they can make you pay back any ill-gotten profits and fine you a fortune. If that happens, the bar association is sure to find out. You'd lose everything anyway.'

'Maybe the man asking questions about me isn't from the commission.' Peter was grabbing at straws.

'Oh, where's he from? Disneyland? Come on, Peter. Of course it's the commission. Although I had no idea this was the way they worked.'

Peter was nearly in tears from despair and Larry seemed apologetic for his sarcasm. He reached across the table and patted Peter on the arm. 'Come on, kid,' he said. 'Don't do that. We'll find a way out of this. I'm sure we will. I'll do some research on Comex regulations and feel out some people on the bar association. In the meantime you pull yourself together and try to find a way to back out of the market gracefully. Maybe if you explain to your grandfather what an untenable position this has put you in, he'll understand.'

'No,' Peter said, his voice tinged with dejection. 'I've already told him that. It's no good. I can't pull out, and I can't expect understanding from my grandfather.'

'Why not?' Larry asked.

But Peter couldn't tell him. The truth was too painful to bear. His grandfather didn't care how much he was hurt by this scheme. Belson believed what he was doing was for Peter's sake and whatever inconveniences Peter had to endure were worth it. And Peter couldn't convince him otherwise. And the truth was that Peter did stand to benefit greatly. No. He would just have to continue on with the way things were until their contracts had risen enough for them to take the profit they needed and pray that the commission wouldn't be able to find enough evidence against them. (Or by some miracle weren't checking on him at all.) He turned his head away from Larry to hide the shame he was feeling.

'Try not to worry too much,' Larry said. 'I'll do what I can. At least you're not alone in this anymore.'

And when Peter looked up, Larry was gone.

The sick feeling inside of him was all-pervasive now, numbing his toes, driving shooting shafts of nausea up and down his guts. He wanted to crawl under the table and disappear. Slowly he got to his feet, left three bucks on the table for the coffee they hadn't touched, and headed back upstairs. But the roaring in his ears grew louder and louder until he had to clutch at the wall for support. A nearby waitress called out. 'You all right, honey?'

He nodded, hating the grating sound of her concern, straightened his shoulders, and assured her he was all right, then he made it up the stairs to the outdoor foyer.

The daylight was blinding after the darkness of the dungeon and he recoiled from its strength. *Please, God*, he prayed. *Help me through this somehow. And don't let Phyllis find out what I've done.*

BOOK III

The Ladies

Chapter 1

AT FIVE minutes after four Marla pulled her Audi into a corner parking space in the underground marina garage and glanced around the dark interior. There were several other cars, including his, but no other people, thank God. She reached under the seat for her makeup case, gave her mouth a fast Binaca spray, her neck a touch of perfume, and then a quick glance in the mirror told her everything looked fine. Her shoes clicked on the cement pavement of the garage and echoed in the large area, sending the same shivers of intoxication through her she felt every time she came here. How many times had it been? she wondered. But she knew exactly. Five.

The bright daylight of the breezy June day blinded her as she emerged up the ramp from the darkness of the underground garage; then the brilliant blue of the water came into focus along with the modern condominiums across the channel and the white rows of yacht sails docked aisle upon aisle. She loved coming here. Everything dazzled her, especially the crisp beauty of light against dark. She would really miss the marina when this job was completed—and that's not all she would miss. She let herself in through the locked gate at the head of a row of yachts and started down the wooden dock, aware that her heels were out of place here, but she wouldn't have worn sneakers with this suit. And she had dressed specifically for today. She wanted him to remove her clothes slowly, piece by piece, until he reached her sinfully rich silk teddy, because she knew he would take as much enjoyment from her lingerie as she did.

Vivaldi was playing on the stereo as she approached his yacht. She stopped a moment to listen and recognized the piece: Vivaldi's Concerto in G. Thank heavens, he might ask her.

The curtains in the salon were drawn; she hoped he had some chilled champagne today. It made things even more delightful. She came aboard and removed her shoes, crossing the warm wooden deck to knock on the door.

Felix opened it with a smile. 'Hello, beautiful,' he said. 'Right on time.'

Every time she saw him, it amazed that she was actually having an affair with the father of one of her closest friends. How shocking it was, how decadent, how delicious.

'You look wonderful today,' Felix exclaimed, taking her hand and drawing her into the salon. 'Those are just the kind of clothes I love to remove.' He reached for the bow on her blouse and she smiled at him. 'Today you're the proper career girl, aren't you? The sweet little wife and matron. But I know differently, don't I?' His voice was husky with intimate sensuality, and when the sensuality erupted, it would engulf her in hot passionate fire. She felt her heart thump excitedly. The lights in the salon were dim, the music soft, and he smelled so good. Felix did everything right.

He was wearing a silk shirt unbuttoned nearly to the waist and he was barefoot. The soft fabric of the shirt hugged the slight bulge around his middle. But for that tiny flaw, he was in excellent physical condition for a man of fifty-nine. Marla liked that bulge around his waist; even his tan leathery chest and the grizzle fur that grew there excited her. She loved to rub against him, nakedly, wantonly. Everthing about him was different from Larry, his scent, his taste, and especially his lovemaking.

He closed the salon door, cutting out the brilliant sunlight, removed her jacket, and kissed her lightly on the lips. He had been trying to stop smoking, but as she ran her tongue over his lips, she could taste the flavor of smoke and nicotine that lingered there. He grabbed her hips and pulled her close, showing her how she had already excited him.

'God, you're beautiful,' he whispered as he kissed her, exploring her mouth with his tongue.

She followed him down the narrow stairway to the bedroom below; he turned as soon as they entered the small, compact room and began unbuttoning her blouse one button at a time, lingering over the buttonholes, watching her face for signs of excitement. She felt her eyes glaze over as her pupils dilated with desire; she parted her lips, letting short bursts of warm air through her mouth. He removed her blouse, slid her skirt down past her hips, and caressed her lightly when she stood with legs slightly apart, breasts quivering under the silk of her underwear, nipples pushing through the fabric, reaching for him, wanting his fingers and tongue to suck them and engulf them. She was so excited it was all she could do to keep from grabbing him. He never took his eyes from her as he undressed, removing his own slacks and shirt and shorts; then he reached over and ran his hands over her body, touching her with the flats of his palms, rubbing her mound and hips and under her arms again and again while he stared into her eyes. She felt herself grow weak inside as his touch and his power took control.

His blue eyes were hard as they watched hers go soft with yielding, and her mouth filled with saliva that she almost let spill, but then swallowed for fear of staining her silk lingerie. But it was too late to save her clothes, the moisture from between her legs had already done it. Felix lifted her left leg and placed it around his waist then he reached his hand inside the loose opening of the panty and discovered the telltale liquids. Gently, firmly, he inserted a finger and moistened the outer lips, rubbing her in and out, around and around while he sucked on her throat and shoulders and massaged with a practiced touch on the core of her desire. Everything was pounding; her breath, her pulse, her entire body, responded to him. She was ready so fast she ached to have him in her and let go of him only to pull at the straps of her undergarment so that it fell in a whisper around her. Then she grasped his penis and rubbed it against the soft sensitive lips of her vagina, drawing in her breath sharply at the exquisite sensation.

'Baby, baby,' he murmured, as he placed her arms around his neck. Then he grasped both of her thighs and lifted her up above him until she slid into place around him, making short in-and-out movements with her hips. His rock-hard penis felt velvet smooth inside of her, increasing her pleasure as he moved backward to the bed, keeping her where she was with her legs wrapped around him until he could lie down and she was free to move above him. As soon as he touched her breasts with hot dry hands and then squeezed them together so that he could tongue both her nipples simultaneously, she felt a giant shudder overtake her. 'Oh, God,' she cried as violent spasms shook her. She had come too soon and was embarrassed that it was over so quickly, that her need for him was so hungry he set her alight with his expertise. Or that she had such a deep need for the affirmation of herself that only sex with someone who really wanted her could provide it.

His climax was quick and hard and violent and he reveled in his pleasure, abandoning himself to it, but he said his own satisfaction wasn't why he made love to her; it was rather to awaken her own potential. Well, he'd done a great job of that, she thought, an absolutely great job. And after he'd awakened her potential, then what? Would she be his slave forever, dependent on him to experience what he alone had taught her? She didn't want that to be true, though sometimes she wondered if it were.

Afterward she lay next to him, satisfied with herself; how easily she had climaxed with him and how difficult it was with Larry. And as she thought of Larry, that same old shyness began to return, to nibble away at the wanton freedom she'd so recently shown. Inhibition crept over her like a chill and she reached for the sheet to cover herself, but he caught her hand and then raised up on his elbow to stare at her, letting his eyes drift lazily over her body. She waited for what seemed a long time for him to stop and allow her to cover herself but he didn't; after a while a new emotion began to assail her—an overwhelming tension. Her mind felt squeamish, nervous, while her body fought not to respond to him. But she couldn't help herself. She flushed with warmth, felt her orifices fill with welcoming juices, his gaze made her want to open her legs, to lift her knees and pull them slowly back, all the way, until she was completely exposed to his unspoken suggestions, to the feelings he tried to evoke in her. She could tell he wanted that final surrender, wanted nothing left unexposed as though she ought to turn herself inside out for him. But in spite of the fantasies in her brain she did not move, except to lie there trembling.

He sighed. 'You're exquisite, Marla. Look at you.' His eyes traveled the length of her body and back again. 'You've worked hard to get into shape, why don't you enjoy it, glory in it? This moment will never exist again, you'll never be this age again. Let it happen.'

His eyes strayed to her ankles and calves and then slowly ascended, studying her knees, then her thighs, and then her vagina, where he lingered, examining, looking. She felt his gaze as a caress and her skin tingled in response. Her breathing became more heavy and the parts of her body came alive as he studied each of them in turn, creating miscroscopic excitement. Her stomach fluttered when his eyes rested there, her chest heaved as his gaze reached her breasts and circulated around each side; she felt her nipples come erect. It maddened her that he didn't touch her; his gaze was not enough. 'Please,' she whispered; and he almost reached out. She held her breath, longing for him, feeling every sensor in her body yearning, but he withdrew his hand just before contact and she nearly cried out in an agony of suspense. She could feel the heat of his body, of his hand above her, and she leaned toward his warmth as moth to flame, but he withheld his caress and instead brought his eyes to her throat, watching the pulse that pounded at the V of her neck. She felt her pulse quicken, her throat constrict, her mouth grow dry. He looked into her eyes and they stared at one another. She knew he could see how aroused she was—the yearning on her face said it all—yet still he didn't touch her. Try as she might, she couldn't form the words to ask him to relieve her though he alone could do it, as though she was holding on to the last vestige of her reserve. If she spoke the words he wanted to hear, she was afraid she herself would be lost, the essence that was Marla would be gone, plummeting over Niagara without even a barrel for protection and she would feel the force of a million tons of alien power inundating her. She couldn't breathe. She'd never seen anyone's face so naked with desire nor had she let her own be so blatantly expressive. And her body was filled with such needs, so many demands, *Touch me, lick me, puncture me, devour me, please, please, please!* Every rapacious part of her begged of its own volition. Her head pushed itself back against the surface of the mattress, whipping back and forth out of control, her chest thrust itself forward, her hips ground themselves around and around, trying to attract his touch, but all she received was his gaze on her—maddening, maddening. Finally at a fever pitch of yearning she grasped his hand.

But he pulled it away.

'Please,' she whispered, willing finally to abandon everything for his solace, 'do it, do it.'

But—'No,' he replied. 'Let it happen.'

Her body was burning, reaching, needing, wanting so much, that she finally reached that place where thought and guidance and censorship did not exist and rationale was even abhorrent and she began to caress herself.

Her own hands felt like fire and ice and she moaned to her touch, knowing how, showing him, feeling alight with a thousand tiny flames that were fed by his eyes on her and the glint of triumph in his eyes, the way a bundle of burning leaves is fed by a dry gust of wind. She was so transported by the sensuality of the moment that she was completely unaware of the demarcation between where she was and when he finally joined her; by then it was incidental. Suddenly his hand was there along with hers, probing inside of her, her anus, her vagina, his tongue in her mouth, his hand on her breast, rubbing expertly, wetly, every thrust exquisite pleasure. He removed her own hand and licked all her fingers one by one, sucking her own juices and adding his own before he placed her hand around his erect penis; it felt fiery hot to her touch. And then she felt the coolness of air as he pulled her knees up and gazed at her center, exactly as she'd so shamefully imagined only moments before, only this time she gloried in it, wanting him to see her and be inside of her at the same time. And then as she held her breath, he lowered his head and ran his tongue around the outer layers of her vagina as though conducting the orchestration of her needs in perfect synchronization, and then he dipped it into the hot wetness within, finding that core, that place that opened in her a floodgate and would not still the great waters of the falls. Her breath exploded out of her and she cried out again and again, 'Yes, oh, yes, oh, God, yes . . .' and wrapped her knees around his head as her hips shuddered up and down on the bed in uncontrollable transport, squeezing him between her thighs so hard she had no awareness of him at all.

Afterward she could hardly not do the same for him.

'Oral sex certainly breeds familiarity,' she said after she'd showered and used the contents of her makeup case to repair her indiscretions. She was dressing slowly, not wanting to end the afternoon.

'Oh, I don't know about that.' Felix watched her fix and fuss. He was sprawled out on the bed, sheets entwined between his legs, eating a bunch of green grapes. Every now and then he would toss her one.

'I'm certain you and Larry do it all the time and I don't think you know one another very well.'

Marla's gaze flicked away from him. Felix had a perverse side to him that she didn't like and that comment was a perfect example of it; she decided not to acknowledge it.

With Larry she had an emotional investment to offer a retort when he baited her: years of hurt needed to be avenged at every possibility, time after time of stab and thrust had to be parried and pushed home. And of course Larry loved her. He knew exactly how to hurt her. And she could hurt him back. There was no such advantage with Felix.

In spite of her resolve not to let Felix get to her, she asked, 'Why don't you think my husband and I know each other?'

He swept his hand to indicate the elegantly appointed cabin she'd worked so hard to design. 'You're here with me, aren't you? If you were my wife, I'd know what your needs were, I'd never let you get to the point of desperation or frustration so that you'd turn to another man for solace. Even if he is irresistible.' He grinned at his own compliment.

'Then why does your wife drink, Felix?' she asked softly.

His eyes grew flint hard, their sky-color blackened into dark storm clouds. 'Audrey's problems were hers before I ever came on the scene, before I married her.' He clipped off each word sharply. 'Perhaps being married to me has worsened her problems, but believe me I've tried with her. If she gave me half of what you give me, I wouldn't be here either. On the other hand, you and I should be grateful to her for her troubles. If things were different, I couldn't enjoy you so thoroughly.' His anger had softened a bit. 'You are truly delicious, Marla, do you know that? You taste so good. In fact, I'd say your bottom is tops.'

She started to blush and laughed at his outrageous comment. It was a nice compliment but one she could certainly never repeat. 'You make me feel that way.'

He beckoned to her. 'Come over here.'

She sat on the bed next to him and he stroked her hand, reaching up to caress her cheek. 'Has Phyllis ever said anything to you about us?' he asked.

She was startled, as though his innocent touch had just turned into a poisonous viper. 'No! Why do you ask? You don't think she knows about us, do you? Oh, dear lord.'

'No, of course not,' he hastened to assure her. 'I just wondered, that's all.'

But now she was apprehensive and moved away from him as though unseen eyes were watching them. 'I would never want Phyllis to find out about us. I don't think I could face her. She doesn't suspect, does she?'

'Phyllis doesn't suspect anyone, ever. She's the last of the pure innocents, like her mother.'

'You don't think it's possible Mrs Anhalt has ever had an affair?'

'Audrey?' The question stopped him. 'Who would want her?' He laughed derisively and then turned to her with that nasty teasing way of his. 'It's so cute the way you call her *Mrs Anhalt*, like a wicked little child who's trying to cover up that she enjoys pulling the wings off butterflies.'

She felt his hostility as something hard and ugly. 'Your double standard is showing, Felix,' she said. 'And don't attack me for your own guilts. I'm not cruel, although I know you can be. And I still think of you as *Mr Anhalt*, occasionally. A lifetime habit is hard to break.'

'You didn't call me mister when you were begging for it a little while ago.'

She felt tears of embarrassment ready to sting her eyes.

Felix moved her off the bed rather forcefully. 'You'd better finish dressing and then go.'

'How can you be angry with me, when it's I who should be angry with you for that comment?'

He stopped for a moment. 'Let's not either of us be angry.' But he smiled with only the lower half of his face. 'I want you to leave so I can fantasize about you. Half the fun of this affair is thinking about the things I'm going to do to you next time.'

'Did I surprise you today?'

'Actually, no, my dear. You didn't.

What a bastard, she thought. 'Do you plan all your other encounters in as much detail as ours? I know there must be others besides me.' Suddenly the truth of that hit her and she felt ashamed, cheapened. To be one of many made her feel so ordinary.

Felix chuckled. 'My dear girl, others?' Her question had really struck him as funny because he began to laugh. 'Of course there are no others, only you.' He was laughing very hard now. 'A man my age doesn't screw like an eighteen-year-old, you know.'

But she didn't believe him and her cheeks burned from humiliation. She imagined lines of girls waiting outside for her to leave, wanting to compete with her for the most exotic sexual contortions. 'Even if there are hundreds more, Felix, you don't have to rub my nose in it. I might have others too.'

But her bravado only made him laugh harder.

'I'm sure you do, I'm sure you do.' He laughed.

She hated him at this moment for laughing at her; he was laughing so hard that tears were streaming down his face, and each time he tried to stop, he was gripped by another gale. Finally it passed, and as he wiped his eyes, he said, 'I'm sorry. That was rude. And you've been so sweet. I'm beginning to treat you as Larry does. Or could it be that you invite such treatment?'

Jesus, she thought. *Another prick! I sure know how to pick them.* 'You give great head, Felix. Too bad there's not much in it.'

He seemed ready to laugh again. 'When will I see you?' he asked.

She looked at him standing there nude, his penis shrunken and vulnerable, the skin on his chest sagged slightly, and the lines in his face, which were permanently etched from an overuse of too many insincere smiles, seemed to have deepened by their afternoon activity, while she only felt vibrant and alive. *He's old,* she thought. *And I don't belong here.*

'Maybe we shouldn't see each other for a while, Felix. My husband is liable to get suspicious, or your wife.'

Felix seemed subdued by her statement. Perhaps she had surprised him after all.

'All right, my dear, if you say so.'

She finished dressing, watching her newly manicured nails as they pulled on her stockings, held the straps of her silk teddy for her to step into, zipped, arranged, and straightened her clothes. She was trying to control her panic. Could he be discouraged this easily? She was about to tell him to forget what she had just said, that she wanted to see him for as long as he'd let her, when suddenly they were startled by a loud knocking on the upper salon door. A man's voice called boisterously, 'Hey, Felix. Open up, Felix, I know you're there. Come on!'

Marla's face drained of all its color and even Felix looked scared. 'That's Larry,' she whispered, reaching frantically for the rest of her clothes. Felix grabbed a silk robe and thrust his arms through the sleeves, cursing because one of them was twisted.

'My shoes and my purse are upstairs,' Marla wailed. She'd never been so frightened in all her life.

'Stay here,' Felix commanded, 'and don't come up no matter what. I'll throw your stuff down to you.'

'Don't take too long,' she begged. 'Make him leave so I can get out of here.' *Oh, God, Larry*, she thought.

'Felix!' Larry was pounding on the door now. 'Wake up! I know you're there, I saw your car.'

Felix had started up the stairs. 'My car,' Marla said. 'He must have seen my car too!'

'Maybe not,' Felix whispered. 'But if he has, I'll tell him you were here and I missed you, that you left a note and walked over to the market.'

She nodded and waved at him to hurry up, as she locked the bedroom door after him. But then she had to open it again to retrieve her shoes and purse when he tossed them down to her. 'Oh, please,' she prayed, 'don't let Larry find me. I'll never do this again.'

Felix gave a quick glance around the salon, glad he hadn't served any champagne today. Everything looked in order. He mussed up his hair as though he'd been sleeping and called out with a fake yawn. 'Hold on a minute, I'm coming.' *When are you going to learn?* he asked himself.

You've just gotten caught shitting in your own bed.

Larry was leaning on the door frame when Felix opened it and he stepped inside, glancing around as though looking for something. 'So this is what you do in the afternoons?' he said. 'Come out here and nap? All by yourself? Where is my wife?'

Felix told him the story of her going to the market.

Larry was studying the expensive leather furniture, the chrome fittings, the built-in lighting, the upholstered walls. 'Did Marla do all this?' he asked. He was impressed in spite of himself.

'Of course she did it all, what do you think's been going on all this time?' Felix was washing his hands in the sink, working up a lather and rinsing them, then he dampened a paper towel, wiped his face, the back of his neck, and yawned for effect.

'Why don't *you* tell me what my wife's been doing here all this time?' Larry replied.

'Is that what you came to ask me?' Felix's reply was sharp. *Might as well get it over with,* he thought. But he abhorred being in a one-down position; he'd never been caught like this before; he'd deny everything.

They stared at one another for a moment while Felix prayed Larry wouldn't call his bluff. Finally Larry looked away. He seemed terribly uncomfortable, but still there were no accusations.

'What are you drinking?' Felix reached for glasses and ice.

'Myers's Rum?'

He made them both drinks. The ice tinkled pleasantly in the glasses as they lifted them in a silent toast.

'So?' Felix's tension level was subsiding. *If Larry was going to say anything about Marla he'd have said it by now.*

'I don't quite know how to begin this,' Larry said. 'I guess straight out is the best way.'

Here it comes, Felix thought, wishing he hadn't been so complacent and wishing he were dressed. He felt too vulnerable in his robe, at a physical disadvantage for being

306

nude under the thin silk fabric as though the only thing protecting him from bodily harm were the narrow cord pulled tightly around his waist.

'What can't you say to me?' he asked, innocence personified.

'I don't want you to think I'm ratting on a buddy,' Larry said. 'But you're the only person I could turn to with this. The only logical person, that is. You know Peter, you care about him.'

Peter? Felix thought. *He wants to talk about Peter and not Marla?* The relief that flooded through him was exquisite. 'Yes, of course I care about him,' Felix said.

'Well.' Larry sighed. 'Peter's in real trouble. He swore me to secrecy but I just couldn't keep that promise. Especially since I know how worried you've been about him the past few months. God, I never suspected a thing. I was so blind. And so were you. Maybe it's as much your fault as it is mine for not making Peter tell us sooner.' He paused and shook his head sorrowfully. 'No, it's not our fault. It's Belson's, the stinking bastard. How could he do such a thing to his own grandson?'

'Do what?' Felix asked. He was trying to remain calm but his blood pressure had just shot up over the cuff. All these months of detective work, and all the money he's spent to retain Bob Delman, and they still hadn't found out exactly what Peter and Belson were up to. And now, out of the blue, the answer might be falling right into his lap, gratis, without his making any effort at all.

'Belson has blackmailed Peter into ruining his life. The geezer's an old man, but he still wields so much power over Peter it's strange, fucking strange. And Peter does everything his grandfather asks him to do. The guy's a pussy. Jesus. I don't know how we can stop him. But we've got to try. If this keeps up, there could be a major disaster ahead for Peter. And that would certainly affect Phyllis. And me too,' he added. And then Larry told him about Peter and Belson, every detail he could remember.

'They're squeezing platinum?' Felix said in amazement

when Larry had finished his story. 'They'll never get away with it.'

'But they are!' Larry insisted. 'And talk about guts. That old man's balls are made of iron to do what he's doing. Christ. I almost wish they'd let us in on some of their action. Belson has accumulated nearly seventy million on paper so far. And they're going to reach their deadline soon. When they sell their current holdings, they'll have made over a hundred million in six months. Kind of makes you sick, doesn't it?'

Felix nodded. But he didn't feel sick, not at all. He was so elated he could hardly contain himself. No drug, or piece of tail, or deal in the world could have possibly given him a high as magnificent as this. *I've got you, old man,* he thought, wishing he could shout with joy. *I've got you.*

'And what do you want me to do?' Felix asked.

Larry seemed surprised by the question. 'You've got to put pressure on Peter to sell out his holdings now. If the enforcement division of the commission is on to him, he's going to be in worse trouble than he ever imagined. He could be facing jail.'

Felix nodded thoughtfully, assuming an expression of deep concern, but his mind was racing. He didn't want Belson to stop now. He wanted him to go on doing whatever it was he was doing so the old bastard would end up hanging himself in a noose of his own making. The deeper in trouble Belson got, the better. 'Didn't you explain to Peter how crucial it was for him to stop these illegal activities?' Felix asked.

'God, yes. I used every persuasive argument I could think of. Not to mention that he was jeopardizing *me* as well. He wouldn't listen. But you've got much more influence with him than I have. He thinks of you like a father. I know you could convince him.'

Felix shook his head sadly. 'I can't do it, Larry.'

'But why not?'

'Don't you see,' Felix said earnestly. 'If I go to him and

308

tell him you told me, first of all he'd know you betrayed his trust . . .'

'But it's for his own good,' Larry protested.

Felix held up his hand to silence Larry. 'And secondly, he'll think I don't trust him enough to run his own life, to make crucial decisions for himself.'

'No, no,' Larry protested. 'Belson's got Peter snowed. Peter thinks he owes Belson his integrity and his life. Only you can convince him he doesn't have to do this. No piece of property is worth all this.'

'You and I know that,' Felix agreed. 'But Peter doesn't. And besides, who are we to judge Peter's needs? Neither one of us has gone through what Peter has experienced.'

Larry looked at him with disbelief. 'You're just going to do nothing? And what about me? I can't just sit by and let this craziness continue.'

'You're going to have to, at least for the time being. But it will only appear as if you're doing nothing, while I'm studying every angle so I can be of assistance to him if he needs me. You check with the bar association as you told Peter you would, and speak to a good criminal lawyer, someone who knows about SEC regulations. In the meantime I'll be doing some checking on my own with my friends in New York. You say Peter thinks someone is already investigating him?'

Larry nodded, and gave him the description of the man who was asking questions about Peter in Phoenix.

Again Felix masked his emotions. It was an exact description of Bob Delman. Delman must have gotten a bit careless. God, it felt wonderful to be holding all the cards. 'Well, I'll check on that too. I have friends back East, also.'

'But don't give him away!' Larry insisted. 'That's the last thing we want. If Peter refuses to sell out now, we've got to see that he comes through this without getting caught. And if by some miracle he is able to avoid the consequences of his actions, he will end up with his grandfather's estate intact and a fortune besides. That won't hurt any of us. But if he's discovered, I don't have to tell you what it would do to all of our lives.'

'Please,' Felix said. 'You insult my intelligence. Phyllis is my daughter, after all. Do you think I want her name and my grandchild's name dragged through the mud?'

Larry stood up to go, apologies oozing out of him. 'I'm really sorry, Felix. It's just that I'm nervous about telling you all this. I guess I'm even more concerned about myself than I am about Peter.'

'It sounds as though you're pretty angry with him too,' Felix said.

'Yeah, well, it will take some getting used to.'

Felix led him to the door. 'Don't mention to Peter that you told me. And neither one of us will discuss it any further unless something happens.'

'You don't think anything will happen, do you?' Larry was extremely apprehensive.

'No, no,' Felix assured him. 'It will be all right. Just remember, if anyone asks, I'll say I never saw you today.'

'Right,' Larry said, gripping Felix's hand tightly before leaving. 'And thanks,' he added.

Felix closed the door and nearly leaped in the air from excitement. How amazing, how absolutely amazing. All this time he had been planting little seeds and out of those seeds gardens had grown. Now it was time to harvest his newly blossomed plants.

After many long minutes Marla's acute fear of being discovered subsided and a new fear took its place. She was very late. Leslie would become suspicious. She had to get out of here now, but Larry had been up there for ages. Why wasn't Felix getting rid of him? Frantically she searched for ways to get out. She considered crawling out of the forward hatch and coming around to the door as though she'd just arrived. And then she realized that she didn't have the courage to face the two of them together. She started to cry from frustration and fear—what a dumb idiot she'd been for being here at all. She didn't want Larry to find out about her, not this way. She did love him and she didn't want to lose him. Damn Felix. What was taking so long?

After thirty-five agonizing minutes where every second she felt her life might come to an end, she heard footsteps on the stairs and a light knock on the door.

'Marla, it's me,' Felix called. 'You can come out now, he's gone.'

She was so angry for being left here in terror, forgotten like some piece of stale cake, that she wanted to hit him. By now it was too late to go back to the office. Leslie would kill her for not showing up for the afternoon staff meeting. And now she'd be late for dinner too, and Larry would kill her. *It's what I deserve*, she thought, and not even Felix could console her. But Felix didn't try. He barely looked at her, gave her a peck on the cheek, and stepped into the head to take a shower, calling out to her, '*Ciao,* darling. See you soon.' He was whistling a Beethoven concerto so loudly he didn't hear her shout, 'Like hell you'll see me soon.'

She sneaked back to her car, petrified of running into Larry. And when she was locked inside with the windows secured and the comforting darkness all around her, she realized she was shaking with fear. *I've got to stop this*, she thought. *It can't go on. If only it wasn't so exciting.*

Exciting? a voice inside cried out. *Exciting. Is that what you call almost being caught by your husband in your lover's bed? What the hell's the matter with you?* And suddenly she was overwhelmed with self-loathing and disgust. She'd been taking the coward's way out. It didn't take courage to have an affair, to abandon herself to hedonistic pleasure; those were only the excuses she used to get back at Larry for infuriating her. She knew with certainty how much she wanted her marriage. It shocked her how desperately she'd wanted to keep Larry from knowing she was having an affair with Felix. Maybe it was because she was afraid of what he would tell her in return. *Larry and I have got to face each other with who and what we are,* she thought, *or there's no reason to continue with this marriage. But before I can face him, I've got to give Felix up.* At the moment that

311

seemed easy; but would it be tomorrow? She hoped so, but she didn't know. Dear God, she didn't know.

Chapter 2

THEY HAD been to see *Altered States,* and they left the theater holding hands. Neither of them would admit it but they were both threatened by the impact of the film's message.

'Good movie,' he said.

'Excellent performances,' she said.

'There was a bit too much psychedelia for me.'

'But I enjoyed it.'

'So did I . . .'

'What do you think it meant?' she asked.

'A lot of things.'

'Such as?'

'Such as . . .' He hesitated. 'Total intimacy and love stripped of pretense is all that really matters in life.'

'Yes,' she agreed. 'But that scientist with his brilliant mind certainly took a circuitous route in order to prove that to himself.'

He nodded. 'What do you think it meant?'

She waited a minute, pondering his question. 'Something similar to what you said. That it is more difficult to reveal one's inner self to another human being than it is to travel back to the moment of original creation.'

'And,' he added, 'if one could go back through the process of evolution to the very beginning, he would learn that the most important meaning to life is the combining of two souls in love.'

'Do you believe that?'

'Intellectually,' he replied.

'It's not easy to do.'

'No, it's not.'

Neither of them looked at one another, and Vicky sensed not for the first time that night that something was bothering Bob. She had a momentary pang of fear that maybe he was getting tired of her. But then he reached for her hand and she was reassured. Still, he wasn't his usual ebullient self. In fact this was one mood she'd never seen before and she thought she'd seen them all. They were practically living together. She knew which days he did his laundry, that he ironed his white ducks himself, that he loved liverwurst sandwiches with tomato and onion, that he snored (so did she), and that he'd kill for two kinds of food: Häagen-Daz's rum raisin ice cream and bittersweet Kron chocolate. He saw every movie of consequence, and some of no consequence; he was a musical comedy nut, a classical car enthusiast, could live without spectator sports, except for the World Series, the Rose Bowl, the Superbowl, and the Olympics, and he was a master at skiing, swimming, and screwing; but she also knew he was too bright to be really happy at what he was doing even though he said he was.

Vicky didn't mention his profession to him anymore because his lips drew into tight white lines when she did and his back stiffened and the veins in his neck stood out and his sweet scent seemed to alter subtly into sourness. She also didn't mention it to him anymore because she was in love with him. And being in love with Bob Delman was difficult because he was far from her ideal dream man except for the way he made her feel, all warm and melty inside, and as treasured as she had felt about her first cashmere sweater.

But the rest of her life wasn't going as well as her relationship with Bob, namely the book. Her fictional version of Leslie and Belson's lives had still not come to life. Each involvement she invented for Raymond Sinclair (her name for Belson) seemed false to her, hackneyed and artificial. Even Leslie's character, whom she'd named Andrea Belmont, only seemed to work because Vicky had more authentic nasty incidents about Leslie with which to pepper her fiction. What Vicky needed was more true-to-life information about both of them. If only Bob would reveal to her some real intimate details about Belson. But so far he'd only told her things she had already known from reading old fan magazines and clippings at the library. Sometimes Bob's reticence to talk about Belson was extremely frustrating, especially because she believed that Bob knew what she needed to know, and at other times it merely proved to be a challenge to her ingenuity to find clever ways to get what she wanted. It was her usual practice to let enough time go by between inquiries about Belson so Bob wouldn't think her too pushy. And even then he usually brushed off her questions with good humor and indifference. But time was going by; she was growing desperate. This book had to work and soon, or she would have to get a job and that wouldn't leave her any time to write. Tonight she would ask him, again.

An uncomfortable silence hung between them as they left Westwood and drove back to Beverly Hills after the movie. Again Vicky wondered what was bothering Bob, but she was unwilling to ask. Her own concerns at the moment were more important.

They stopped in at the Cultured Cow for soft-yogurt cones, an after-movie ritual with them, and then Vicky said, 'What do you talk about with your clients?' She was trying to skirt the issue and come in through the back door. 'Do your clients tell you intimate details about their lives once they get to know you?' The girl behind the counter handed her a mountain of strawberry swirl and she took a big lick, pretending to be much more interested in the cone than in her question.

'Not really,' Bob replied, exchanging money for his own mountain of carob and mocha. 'We discuss the weather, or their social calendars. Sometimes we talk about current events, politics, the price of oil. But mostly we're silent;

after all my massages are designed to help my customers relax; too much conversation would be a stimulant.'

'Well, what does Belson talk about: I know *he* confides in you.'

Bob's jaw was tightly clenched as they came out of the yogurt shop and turned west on Santa Monica Boulevard, strolling past the Rangoon Racquet Club and Carroll & Company. It was a warm June night, clear and star-filled, but Vicky felt apprehensive.

He fixed her with a stare and barely caught a melting rivulet of sweet fluid from dripping onto his red Merona shirt. 'I *told* you everthing I know about the man. And you also know he's a client. What I discuss with him is confidential and stays confidential, as in *secret*. You know what secrets are, don't you? They're what you keep trying to make of my profession every time one of your friends or family asks you what I do for a living. What are you going to tell them at Marla's party Saturday night, that I'm a temporarily unemployed atomic physicist?'

She was amazed at the fury of his sudden explosion and felt her cheeks burn with color. 'I invited you to that party, didn't I?' she said defensively, but again he'd touched her most sensitive place. 'And please lower your voice,' she said. They were standing on the corner of Rodeo and Santa Monica in the middle of Beverly Hills and he was nearly shouting at her.

'Why should I lower my voice?' he insisted. 'Do you think the books at Doubleday's across the street are listening? Or the chianti bottles at La Scala are bugged? Are they going to tell your society pals you've been slumming?' He turned his head and yellled directly into the street, 'Bob Delman is a masseur, everybody! Vicky Feinstein is going with a blue-collar worker who wears white duck pants,' he yelled at a passing Mercedes.

Vicky was humiliated and turned her face away from the headlights of the cars.

People walking by stared at them instead of in the windows on the only street in Los Angeles where glamorous merchandise was still on display. For a moment she was terribly embarrassed, but then suddenly she didn't give a damn who stared at her and she whirled around to face Bob.

'Why won't you just tell me what I want to know? What's so damned secret about the man, what are you protecting?' she demanded.

'And why do you have a vendetta against a sick old man?' he countered.

'If I tell you, will you tell me?'

He didn't reply, just waited defiantly.

'The man got me fired from my teaching job. He wrote a disgusting letter filled with lies about me to the board of my former school and they believed him. Or let's just say it was expedient for them to take his word over mine.'

Bob was caught for a moment by her confession and the look in his eyes told her how sick it made her feel. But when he stepped toward her to embrace her, she stiffened and that stopped him.

'That's really tough, baby,' he said, and she nearly softened. But then he ruined it by saying. 'But that's no reason to smear the man by using whatever inside information I can give you.'

'What's wrong with smearing him?' she said. 'He had no qualms about ruining my life.'

'But your life isn't ruined, is it? And if you used anything against him that *I* told you, it would be obvious where you got your information. Belson would sue both of us when your book was published.'

'From your mouth to God's ears the book should be published,' she said.

'Oh, it will be, Vicky,' he said. 'It will be a huge success. Books of that type always are, those roman à clef novels that exploit and denigrate people even though the only one who is really exploited and denigrated is the author. I'd hate to see that happen to you. And of course I'd be dead in this town. I'd never be able to gain the confidence of another living soul.' He paused to emphasize his next

316

words. 'The really sad part about this is, you're a good writer, a very good writer. You don't have to write this kind of book. Not when you have something real and meaningful to say. Why don't you leave this garbage alone and do what you're best at? Go back to your own book about the three women.'

Vicky felt the cool night air sting her eyes as she widened them in surprise. She blinked to moisten them. 'How do you know about that?'

He took a step toward her as if to ward off the blow he was about to deliver. 'I found the original manuscript in your office one night when I couldn't sleep and I read it. It's good, Vicky, damn good.'

'You read it?' She was furious, invaded, raped. '*You read it?*' she yelled. It was as if he'd said he'd been taking movies of her in the crapper. 'How dare you? . . .*Ohhh,*' she cried, stamping her foot, wanting to smash her fists into his chest.

'Wait. Stop,' he pleaded. 'I'm sorry. I didn't realize it was such a crime, such an invasion.'

'You didn't? You goddamned snoop. I'll bet you got your rocks off sneaking a peek. You just couldn't resist the temptation to sneak, is that it? If I'd wanted you, or anyone, to read it, I'd have shown it to you. But not you, you couldn't wait. Didn't have the decency to wait. What are you, some Peeping Tom or something, some hot-blooded Sherlock Holmes searching out other people's private thoughts and spreading them out for everybody to see?'

His face had drained of all its color, but he answered her. 'You're really amazing. You've just accused me of doing to you exactly what you want me to do to Belson McKintridge. Well I say, forget it.'

'Is that because I'm not paying you enough?' she said bitterly. 'If I pay you forty-five bucks an hour will you tell me what I want to know?'

He reeled as though she'd struck him and she was immediately sorry. But she couldn't back down. But then he pushed another sore spot again.

'You'd better give some honest thought to what you've chosen as your life's work,' he said. 'If you're not willing to have people read what you write, if you're not willing to bare your soul, to really tell what you're thinking and what dirty deeds you've done all on your own, you'd better not become a writer because all you'll be writing about is crap.'

'Thank you,' she snapped. 'I needed that from the super-sleuth.' He was staring at her, trembling. 'Well,' she demanded, wanting to hurt him. 'That's what you are, isn't it?'

'I'm sorry I invaded your privacy, Vicky,' he said tightly, skipping over her inference.

This was alien territory for them, much too wild a terrain for untried travelers. They were both drained and shocked by the anger they'd allowed to become unleashed and they had no precedents to show them the way back, no guideposts of past tiffs to assure them that this too would pass. And Vicky also wondered if she was actually fighting over what had infuriated her in the first place, or something else entirely, like the fear of intimacy she'd avoided thinking about since they came out of the movie. So he had read her manuscript, she thought, what was so terrible about that? But at the moment she felt it was terrible and she was grabbing on to the terribleness of it so as not to stay in love with a man who did not fulfill her fantasy. *He said I was a good writer,* she thought. But then her cruel self-critical voice asked her, 'What does he know?' She didn't dare ask him why he thought it was good.

Bob looked at that small face that had grown so dear to him, and he wanted to tell her the truth about why he couldn't reveal anything about Belson to her, but if he did now, it would only make things worse. For her to hear he was a private investigator hired by Felix Anhalt to investigate Belson McKintridge would be another major betrayal, and one night was enough. Maybe he'd been moving too fast with her. His life hadn't been his own lately, and tonight he felt like a real shit. He'd actually picked this fight with her so she would rescind her invitation to take him to her friend Marla's dinner party. There was no way he could show up there with Felix Anhalt and Belson McKintridge in the same room. He shouldn't have gotten so involved with Vicky when he was on this job, but she'd hit him right between the eyes, almost from the first minute he saw her. And if she reacted with such vehemence to his reading her work without permission, how would she react to his lying to her? He didn't have the courage to find out even though the job was now over.

The frozen yogurt lay like a cold lump in his stomach. He was sorry he'd eaten it, but at the moment five more cold lumps in his stomach would have been preferable to the look of sadness and disillusionment on her face.

She was more subdued when she said, 'You're right, Bob. I have to be willing to let everyone see me, or I'll never be a writer. And maybe that will never happen, at least not the kind of writer you think I should be. But I'm going to write *my* book, whether it's exploitive or not. I'll find out what I need, with or without you.' She heard a hard tone in her voice and hated it—it reminded her of her mother—but right now she used it defiantly and it served her well, giving her an impenetrable shield to hide behind.

'You're sinking to their level, Vicky,' he said sadly. 'You're demeaning yourself in the process. You're too good for that. It's disappointing.'

'Just look at who's calling who disappointing, "Mr Massuer". If that's the way you feel, maybe you'd better not stick around and watch me.' She was protecting herself from the pain of his pressing on her sore places again.

'I guess you're right,' he said. 'I have seen enough. You can go to the party Saturday without me.'

She lifted her chin defiantly, but felt as though she'd just taken a blow to the gut.

'Come on, I'll take you home,' he offered.

But she stuffed her hands in the pockets of her Windbreaker and looked down at her jogging shoes. 'I'll walk,' she said. 'I've walked home from dates over greater distances than this before and in much less comfortable shoes. So long.' And she turned away to hide the tears that sprang to her eyes.

And damn if he didn't let her go. She saw his reflection in the windshield of a parked car as she walked quickly away. He watched her for a while and she was sure he would come after her, but then he turned and walked the opposite direction toward where his car was parked.

Oh, Bob, she thought, holding on to the pain inside to keep it from exploding. But holding on to it didn't stop it and she could feel it radiating through her. *Well, Vicky old girl,* she thought, feeling the tears pouring down her face, *there goes love.* Chalk up another wipe-out notch on the barrel of Belson's six-shooter.

Chapter 3

GOD BLESS Dianna, Leslie always said, and her network of sleuths. Dianna Cunningham was one of the most controversial columnists in the country. She had unimpeachable sources feeding her gossip from the most unlikely places, though Dianna preferred to call what she wrote about 'social information.' But if there was anything to discover about anyone of interest in the public eye, Dianna found it. And the news was only acceptable to her if it crossed her desk much earlier than the subject wanted it released. Dianna was an expert at her job; she held a highly visible place in the limelight and she adored the homage she received from the publicity-seeking world in which she lived. Her loyalty to her friends, Leslie in particular, was legendary. Her friendships and her sources, often one and the same, meant everything to her and she would stop at nothing to maintain them.

But Diana was homely, tall and round-shouldred, her neck was too wide and her face too narrow, though she'd done the most she could with herself. And she had no appreciable talent, could never aspire to the kind of success Leslie enjoyed and was incapable of attaining it even if opportunities presented themselves to her the way they did to Leslie. She attached herself to people like Leslie, people with power, and lived vicariously through them, especially through Leslie's encounters with sexy attractive men who would never give Dianna a glance unless they had a new film being released or a business project under way that could use a boost in her column.

It was through one of those obsequious contacts that Dianna ferreted out the devastatingly interesting information that Felix Anhalt had employed Clarence and Kotlier, a private investigating firm, to provide him with information on Belson McKintridge. But why Felix wanted it was the multimillion-dollar question. What was there about Belson that Felix couldn't find out by merely asking his son-in-law, Peter? Of course Leslie was aware of the extreme animosity existing between Belson and Felix, but still it was one thing to hate a man and quite another to have him investigated. Leslie would have given Dianna's right arm to know if Felix had learned anything from his private eye.

'I could tell him a thing or two about the old goat,' Leslie said to Dianna. 'But I don't think Belson's sexual kinkiness is what Felix is interested in. No, it must be something much more intriguing.' And the best way to find out what it was would be to ask him, even though he might not tell her. But there was one particular thought that distressed Leslie to her very soul. What if Felix was gathering information about Belson so he could go after the McKintridge estate for himself? If that's what he wanted, she'd better move fast.

She called Mrs Murdock and set up an appointment with Felix for ten o'clock that morning.

321

'Leslie, come on in,' Felix's voice called from his inner office. Leslie crossed the custom-woven carpet and glanced around at the furnishings; how well everything had held up since she decorated these rooms five years ago in plum and russet tones and antique pine paneling.

'The place still looks good,' Felix said, reading her appraising glance.

'Yes,' she said, slipping into the persimmon glove-leather chair in front of his bleached pine desk.

'Are you here about the final payment on my yacht restoration? I sent a check for only part of the invoice because I'm still waiting for a few items to be completed. I haven't yet received the new lacquer night tables in the master suite that are to replace the ones that came in wrong. You don't expect me to pay for them in advance, do you?'

'That's not why I'm here, Felix.' She smiled, flashing him a knowing look.

'Well, I have no complaints about my decorator either. Marla's doing a bang-up job, if that's what you're here about.'

'I've noticed Marla's *bang-up* job,' Leslie said icily. Marla had been usurping much too much credit for Felix's yacht, and Leslie had been remiss in not putting her in her place long before now. Marla's proprietary interest in Felix Anhalt would have to be reduced to a minimum. And judging from the expression on Felix's face, Marla might have usurped more than credit for the job.

'I came to talk to you about another matter entirely, Felix. One that concerns us both.'

'What is it?' he asked, giving her a quizzical look. Leslie thought he seemed uneasy, as though he were holding rein on a guilty conscience.

'I need your advice and your help.'

Felix relaxed a bit. 'What kind of help?' He was at his best when he thought people needed him.

'I represent an anonymous buyer who is determined to acquire the McKintridge estate. He wants to purchase it

322

from Belson himself if that's at all possible, or his heirs at a later date.'

Felix started to interrupt but she held him off. 'Let me finish, all right?'

He nodded.

'This individual has enormous liquid assets and will even pay more than market price to get what he wants. But what I need to know from you is the best possible way this may be accomplished.'

While she was talking, she noticed Felix's reaction. Though he tried to hide his emotions he had visibly paled. When he tore his gaze away from her, it corroborated her worst fears. *Felix wants the estate too*, Leslie thought. *But he might not have the kind of money Banir does*.

'I'm assuming this is a man?' Felix asked; his eyes searched the ceiling as though he were unconcerned while he stalled for time.

'Not necessarily,' Leslie countered. 'But I'll refer to the buyer as "he" for simplication.'

Felix apparently gained control of his concern, for when he returned his gaze to her, it now held a hard, flat expression, and all pretense of conciliation was gone. 'What you ask is really impossible, Leslie,' he stated emphatically. 'Belson won't part with his estate. You of all people know what it means to him.'

'Perhaps he won't part with it willingly,' she said slyly, 'but there may be ways to persuade him. And if those ways exist, I'm confident you of all people will find them. Am I correct?'

He chuckled, momentarily lightened by her coyness. *He was always a sucker for flattery*, she thought.

'And what gives you such insight into my character?' he asked.

She took a deep breath and plunged ahead. 'It's come to my attention that you might be trying to acquire the McKintridge estate yourself.'

An oil slick of astonishment spread across the clear waters of his face. 'What are you talking about?' His voice had risen two octaves.

'About your contract with Clarence and Kotlier to search out the financial details of Belson's life, or any other kind of information concerning him, ostensibly to determine whether or not a joint venture between the two of you would be advisable. But anyone who knows the history of the two of you would realize you'd never go into a business venture with Belson.'

'How did you find out?' he demanded harshly.

'That's not important, and I wouldn't tell you anyway. What is important is that I know how difficult it may be for you to locate sufficient funds to purchase a thirty- to fifty-million-dollar property on your own with today's interest rates.' She pushed the advantage her surprise information had given her over him. 'I'm here to offer you sufficient financial clout to convince or coerce Belson to agree to sell you his estate after you've softened him up with whatever plan you've devised. If you have enough money behind you, and you're as clever as I think you are at getting your way, you're bound to succeed.'

He was still staring at her. 'And where do you come in?'

'Belson's property has to be subdivided, Felix. We both know that. Nobody can afford to hang on to fifteen un-developed acres in a prime Beverly Hills location in this day and age, except a fruitcake like Belson who has both feet in another era. And that means going to private capital to fund your scheme and in turn means splitting up your piece of the pie into less than fifty percent. But I'm offering you just that, half the deal. My client has enough cash to take the whole thing off your hands all by himself. He only needs you to get the deal for him.'

'Who is it? The King of Kuwait?'

'No.' She smiled. 'Not quite.'

Felix seemed to have regained more of his composure as he leaned his elbows on the hand-rubbed surface of his desk. Leslie noticed that the hunter green color of his tie against the pale green of his shirt was a wonderful com-plement with the plum and persimmon colors in the room.

'Your timing is amazing, Leslie,' he admitted. 'There just may be a way to pry Belson loose from his concrete citadel.'

'And have you been honing your chisel, then, Felix?'

He nodded thoughtfully. 'But this is strictly between us, you understand?'

'*Entre nous!*' she stated, leaning back to cross her tapered legs and align her gorgeous calves at a forty-degree angle. Felix didn't miss the view. Their eyes met and they both smiled pleasantly. He was relaxing more by the minute.

'Tell me something about your client.'

'Again, confidential?'

He nodded.

'It *is* a man,' she admitted. 'A man of international power and repute. He has extremely large real-estate holdings both here and in Europe as well as the Middle East and assets of close to a billion. And the only place he wants to live is in the McKintridge estate.' She shrugged in a mock display of surprise. 'I can't imagine why.'

Their mingled laughter crackled with conspiratorial humor, high and staccato, like wind blowing through tinkling glass chimes or Siamese temple bells.

'And where do you come in?' Felix asked.

'Oh, my rewards are strictly altruistic. You know how I feel about Belson. If I could deal him out, I wouldn't hesitate. Belson deserves every nasty trick coming to him. Of course I have nothing against Peter and your daughter, but they're not important here. It's *Belson* I want!'

Felix's head was bobbing up and down in agreement. 'Exactly,' he said, and gave a long satisfying sigh, as though the wind had finished with the chimes and the bells had grown strong enough to seal the door of Belson's tomb.

'My client, however, has some stringent requirements for the privilege of letting you use his money,' Leslie said.

'Of course,' Felix conceded.

'He wishes to purchase the house itself, intact, and several of the immediate surrounding acres, though he will not object to subdividing and sharing the outlying acreage with you or anyone else who brings this acquisition to fruition.'

Felix's eyes were steel hard again. 'Meaning, you think I'm not the only one with the potential to acquire the estate?'

'Not exactly,' Leslie hedged. 'You're just the first one we've approached.'

'I see,' Felix said. 'Then this is a bona fide offer and he's giving me right of first refusal?'

'Most definitely,' she insisted. 'But my client's identity must remain anonymous or others might begin to bid and drive up the price. Though he's willing to pay top dollar, he wouldn't appreciate being fleeced,' she said, a warning note in her voice. 'And he deals harshly with associates who get too greedy, if you know what I mean?'

Felix knew. 'But what if I just can't convince Belson?'

His question put her off balance for a moment; but then she detected that familiar Felix Anhalt glint in his eyes, the one she'd seen every time he tried to get her to sell him something for less than the quoted price. The man was an expert at bargaining, and though she may have caught him by surprise earlier with her bit of information, by now he had fully recovered.

'You'll find some way to convince him, Felix. I have the utmost confidence in you. But time is crucial,' she warned him. 'My client is extremely impatient and wants what he wants immediately, if not sooner.'

Felix was smiling now, a self-satisfied grin. 'Your confidence in me is well placed,' he said. 'It may happen even sooner than you think.'

Leslie was delighted that he was so agreeable. Evidently it wasn't the estate he wanted after all, but Belson himself. What luck! 'Will you act as our agent in this matter?' she asked.

He stood up and came around the desk, looking at her with sincerity etched in every line of his face. 'I'll be happy to,' he replied. 'If you'll tell me honestly what you want from me besides the satisfaction of revenge against Belson.'

She smiled and tossed her dark hair behind her shoulders. 'A five percent finder's fee and a guarantee of any design work that grows out of this union.'

'That's from my half. What is your client giving you?'

Her smile grew sweeter. 'Let us say his continued patronage.'

'Nothing like a wedding ring or anything like that?' he guessed shrewdly.

'*Moi?*' she teased, and they both laughed again.

All five of his phones were buzzing.

She took his hand in hers. 'I can't thank you enough, Felix. This means a great deal to me.'

'And to me,' he added, reaching for one of the flashing lights.

She turned to go.

'Leslie,' he called as she reached the door. She stopped and waited while he put three different calls on hold. 'About that confidential information concerning my hiring a private investigating firm. I wouldn't want my wife to hear about it at the beauty parlor, or read about in in your friend Dianna's column. In fact I don't want anyone to find out about it *ever*. If they do, I'm going to wring your attractive neck and the deal is off!'

She gave him a serious, wide-eyed look. 'I'm the soul of discretion, Felix. The very soul.' And she smiled happily as she waved. There was actually joy in her eyes as she went through the door.

So, the word was out, Felix thought, watching her leave before he went back to the phone. If Leslie knew about Clarence and Kotlier, others would soon find out. It was a good thing he had no more need for their investigative services. *An anonymous client, my ass. Leslie's representing Sheikh Ammani. It couldn't be anyone else. She's been doing business with him for months and fucking him too, knowing Leslie. He's got to have promised her a sizable*

*fee, or even an engagement ring, if she gets her foot in
between those huge oak doors.* Banir Ammani was a shrewd
man. Felix had admired the way he operated, even envied
him his success. But if Ammani thought he could horn in on
the plan that Felix had nurtured for so long, he was wrong.
I'll let them think they're getting what they want, he decided,
*that will neutralize them as a potential threat. And it won't
hurt to have someone with ready cash in reserve in case I
need it. But this is going to be my sweet success. Belson isn't
going to get away from me this time. Nor will Leslie and her
sheikh ever be able to buy the McKintridge estate out from
under me. I've got Belson exactly where I want him and the
screws have already been turned.*

Chapter 4

SOMETHING HAD happened to the platinum market. When
Belson awoke on Wednesday, June 11, at 6:30 A.M. and
called for his usual market quote, platinum had fallen 150
points; it was the largest downturn since he had invested in
the market in December. At first he didn't believe it. It just
couldn't be. And even though there had been a steady
decline over the past several days, it had not been enough
to panic him.

Now he was panicked.

Using Peter's code name, he called several of their
brokers to find out what was going on. Lou in San
Francisco, Abe in San Diego, Sam in L.A., and Buddy in
Carmel, all had different answers. 'The Russians decided
to hold back on their customary shipments.' 'There's a
rumor of political unrest in South Africa.' 'Detroit is
cutting back on their use of catalytic converters because the

government isn't requiring as many smog devices this year.'
'Nobody's buying platinum for jewelry because the price is too high.'

Any one of those factors could affect the price of platinum; but Belson read four papers a day, and there had been no mention of such occurences or any of those events, nor any hints of a potential decline in any of the recent market analysis sheets. But every broker he spoke to was concerned about his account and all told him he would have to come up with money for them by the end of the day.

He called Peter. 'The bottom just fell out of the platinum market,' he said. 'It's down a hundred and fifty points.'

Peter had just gotten out of the shower and this was the first he'd heard of it. 'Jesus,' he groaned. 'Are you sure?'

'What do you think this is?' Belson demanded. 'Kindergarten? Of course I'm sure. Get your ass over here and start calling around. I want to know what the hell's going on!'

'Wait a minute! Just wait,' Peter said, his voice registering alarm. 'We may still be all right even with such a huge drop in price.' He was whispering so as not to awaken Phyllis. 'Just let me check it out, Grandfather.'

But Belson slammed down the receiver in exasperation. Then he picked up the phone to call Henry in New York for the current totals of his accounts, but he put it down again. He could do his own calculations. His fingers felt achey and stiff this morning and he was so nervous he kept pressing the wrong buttons on his calculator. *I'm too old for this, just too old. I should have listened to Peter and sold out when we were ahead.*

He calculated the numbers three different times; it always came out the same. He was down seventy million dollars.

His beleaguered heart fluttered in his chest, which panicked him even further. He couldn't afford to get excited. Excitement could kill him. Right now he didn't care.

The phone rang. It was Peter calling back.

'Are you all right?' he asked.

'No,' Belson said wearily.

'I just spoke to Arizona,' Peter told him. 'Things don't look so good.'

'I know that!' Belson snapped, feeling rage at his helplessness. He wanted to fling it all at Peter.

'It's got to be only temporary, Grandfather,' Peter tried to soothe. 'A small downtrend in a steady upward movement. Platinum has been phenomenal all this time. It's just leveling off, that's all. There have been fluctuations before.'

'But it's never dropped a hundred and fifty points before.' His voice quavered. 'What could have happened?' He felt knifelike pains radiating from his stomach up through his chest all the way to his throat.

'Grandfather,' Peter insisted, 'you've got to get hold of yourself. Don't forget we've got that cushion in the bank of thirty million. We'll spread it around to all our accounts. Maybe we can ride this out.'

An hysterical laugh exploded out of Belson's constricted throat. 'Cushion? Cushion? We are down seventy million dollars. Our margin of forty million has been wiped out. And if we pay out every dollar in the bank we'll still be short five million as of today and it could go lower.'

'Then we've got to sell, right now.' Peter sounded more frightened than he was.

'No, no, no!' Belson said. 'We can't do that until I know more of what's going on. I have to know if this looks like it's a continuing pattern or a temporary one. Maybe I'll have some news by the time you get here.'

'But I won't be free until eleven thirty,' Peter said. 'I've got clients scheduled all morning.'

'Eleven thirty my ass!' Belson growled. 'This is an emergency. You get over here now!'

'Okay, okay,' Peter agreed. 'I'll be there as soon as I can. Just try to stay calm. And when I receive margin calls I'll try to stall them. We'll figure something out. And, Grandfather,' he added, 'I've got about thirty thousand in cash in T-bills. It's yours if you need it.'

Belson gave a short, derisive snort. 'My grandson, the

conservative wheeler-dealer. That's a riot. As of last week we were nearly eighty million ahead and you've got your piddly cash pittance stashed away in T-bills. It's too funny. Just too funny.'

Peter was silent and Belson could almost feel his hurt feelings radiating over the phone. He regretted his words, but he couldn't stop himself from lashing out at Peter. His desperation tinged with panic combined to throw him out of control.

'I'll see you later.'

By eleven thirty when Peter finally arrived, the metals market had closed in New York and platinum was up three points. They had gained back one and a half million, a drop in the bucket.

Peter had been able to calm the fears of his brokers, although he was exhausted from calling thirty different people in thirty different offices; just keeping them all straight was a monumental task. He had messengered cashier's checks to every broker within driving distance and had funds transferred to the out-of-town accounts, enough to satisfy everyone. Most of the brokers didn't press him too much and accepted partial payment on his deficit because he promised to pay them more in a day or two. He prayed he would have enough money in a day or two to fulfill his promise.

But the events of the day had taken their toll on Belson. He was physically ill, light-headed and nauseated. There were no definitive answers from Henry Cronyn, who was as shocked and dismayed as he was. But Henry was optimistic.

'He said we should sit tight,' Belson told Peter. 'Wait until it blows over because platinum is stable. There's no real reason for it to have dropped and it will turn around again.'

'God, I hope he's right,' Peter said.

But the next morning platinum had not recovered its previous losses and was holding steady at yesterday's close.

Peter and Belson were so tense they spoke in monosyllabic words and short sentences as though neither of them had the patience for conversation concerning anything other than the problem at hand.

Belson was waiting for Peter to arrive that morning when the phone rang. It was a Mr Lance Walker calling from Washington, D.C.

He debated whether or not to take the call or have Peter talk to the man when he arrived. It couldn't be a broker calling because none of them knew who he was or had his number. And then he figured it might be a friend of Henry's calling to give him some news.

He was wrong.

'Mr McKintridge? Belson McKintridge?' Lance Walker spoke with a Bostonian accent.

'Yes?' Belson replied.

'I'm with the Commodity Futures Trading Commission and there is a matter of importance I would like to discuss with you.'

Belson felt his body temperature suddenly plummet with every word the man uttered.

'First may I say, it's a great honor to talk to you. I'm quite an admirer of yours, never missed one of your films when I was growing up.'

Belson merely grunted, noticing with a kind of detached interest that his hands and feet were growing numb and tingly and the tip of his nose had gotten so cold it hurt. Even his earlobes throbbed with sudden chill. 'What do you want, Mr Walker?'

Walker had a well-modulated, low speaking voice but his politeness was just a veneer. 'It's become my duty to inform you that a complaint has been received against you by the commission, and they in turn have turned this over to us in the enforcement division. We are planning an informal investigation of these allegations and we'd like to talk to you about it.'

Belson had to force the volume of his voice to rise above a gasp. 'What kind of complaint?'

'You have been accused of trying to squeeze the commodity market in platinum and of trading under ficticious names. It's also been brought to our attention that you've not been making as many trader reports as are required by regulations.

Jesus, Belson thought. *How did they find out? How did they fucking find out?*

'We want you to consider this call a formal request that you come to Washington and provide us with all your records pursuant to the trading of platinum. At that time we might decide to take your deposition or it may turn into nothing. Of course you may be represented by counsel if you wish. But that's up to you. You would know better than I the advisability of such a decision.'

As Walker paused for a moment, Belson's mind traveled over the possibilities. All he could think was, *Stall, deny, object, and just don't panic.*

'You may take the rest of this week to gather together your dossier,' Walker continued. 'But there is some urgency to the matter because we suspect your involvement is ongoing and we would like to get to this as soon as possible. So we have scheduled a meeting for ten A.M. on Tuesday of next week. Do you know where we're located?' And he gave Belson the address. But Belson's hand was shaking so badly he couldn't write.

'Oh, yes,' Mr Walker added. 'There's something else I feel bound to disclose to you. There was a blurb in one of the Washington, D.C., newspaper gossip columns yesterday hinting that the CFTC was thinking of making inquiries into a high-priced metal commodity. Somehow there was a leak of our interest in platinum but I wanted you to know we didn't make that information public. In the interest of privacy, plus the protection of your rights, we don't condone public announcements by a securities commission. And if there was any fluctuation in the market due to that leak, I want to apologize to you. But often these things are beyond our control. When there's a party interested enough to inform the commission of a wrongdoing, often that same party leaks it to the press.'

Belson could not keep his voice steady; his extremities throbbed and ached from lack of circulation. He felt as though the walls were literally closing in around him. He cleared his throat before speaking. 'There is a minor matter concerning this request that you do not understand, Mr Walker,' he said. 'I cannot possibly attend any such meeting in Washington next week. My health is in an extremely precarious state and my doctor will not allow me to travel at all.'

Walker was silent for a moment. 'I see,' he said quietly. 'That does affect matters, now doesn't it? Well then, would you be so good as to give me the name and number of your physician? If that allegation is corroborated, something else may be arranged. We're most anxious to talk to you.'

Belson gave him the name and number of his doctor.

'I'll get back to you, sir,' Mr Walker said, all politeness and charm. And then Belson heard the click of a severed line.

His vision had become completely blurred and he was so dizzy he thought he might faint; at the moment unconsciousness was devoutly welcomed. Never in his life had he felt so overwhelmed with despair. And it was terrifying.

The first thing Belson said to Peter when he arrived at noon was, 'Did you ever tell anyone about our platinum investments?'

Peter stared at his grandfather, feeling shock waves reverberate through him. 'No,' he insisted. 'Of course not.' But it was the most flagrant lie he'd ever told.

'Well, they've found out,' Belson cried. 'The bastards found out.' His skin was as white and thin as tissue paper and Peter felt a terrible pang of fear grip him as he watched the old man 'Please, Grandfather,' he begged. 'Take it easy. Tell me what happened.'

When Belson told him about the call from Walker at the CFTC, Peter felt devastation sweep over him. He could not bring himself to contemplate the possibility of what would happen to them now. The shame, the legal implications—suddenly his head began to throb as though it were being pounded by a mallet. The events of yesterday coupled with this were just too much to take. But what really made the hammer pound was the idea that Larry might have been the one who turned them in. *No!* There was no way he'd ever believe such a thing about Larry. They were partners. Close friends. Yet somebody had found out. Unless it was the man asking questions about him in Phoenix. He should have told his grandfather about that. Now it was too late. 'Maybe it was your man, George Benning, at the bank,' Peter said, pressing his hands to his temples. 'The reliable credit verifier. Anyone who is willing to do what he's done could easily have informed on us.'

'No, I'm sure it's not Benning,' Belson insisted. 'He's too concerned about living the high life to chuck it all and go moral.'

'Maybe he was granted immunity.'

'I spoke to him, Peter. If he's an informer, he's one hell of a liar. The man's scared spitless that they'll trace everything back to him. After all he's the pivotal proof of my guilt. He's verified all those fake accounts. He could go to prison. No, I don't think it's Benning. And besides, finding out who turned me in is the least of our concerns at the moment. We have to find out what they know. We have to devise a plan and we have to know what we're going to do if the market continues to fall.'

'Can Henry Cronyn help you? Does he know someone who can get them off our back?'

'God, no,' Belson stated. 'As soon as the government steps in Henry is *out* with a capital O. I'm the one being investigated, not him, and he will want to stay in the clear. And lord help me if I snitch about what he's done for me. I have to cut myself loose from Henry so he can come up floating like a cork in a bottle of champagne. That's the unwritten code.'

'You don't think he turned you in, do you?'

'Stop asking questions along those lines. It's irrelevant right now.'

Peter felt tightening bands of pressure encasing his skull with deadly persistence. His grandfather was right. Partners in crime couldn't be depended upon to back up one another during hard times, and these were very hard times. 'Does the committee have any real proof?' he asked. 'Do they know any of the names you've been using? And if not, can't you refuse to tell them?'

'Sure I can refuse.' Belson's sarcasm was biting. 'But how long do you suppose it will take for the CFTC to check out the simultaneous purchases in platinum in the past six months, especially where there was only a broker report and no trader report accompanying it, and figure out that every one of those accounts was represented by the same man—you. And then they'll check the credit of all those different accounts and find they were verified by the same bank officer at one bank who issued all that credit. Jesus.' He sighed, despair etched into his expression.

'What will happen to our brokers, will they lose their licenses?'

'Who cares?' Belson stated flatly. 'They'll probably only receive a reprimand because technically they're not guilty of anything. Each one of them has fulfilled his obligations by filing his required reports. You and I are the ones who lied; the broker's only offense was in not asking enough questions.'

'But the CFTC probably won't do anything more to you than fine you,' Peter said, trying to offer some hope. *But there might be criminal charges for bribing a bank official,* he thought. The bar association would have his license in a minute.

'What kind of a fine?' Belson massaged his perspiring forehead.

'I *believe* it's a penalty of a hundred thousand dollars for every provable violation of a regulation, if it's a misdemeanor offense. And up to a year in prison,' he added. 'But nobody ever goes to prison.'

Belson's eyes were bloodshot as he gazed at Peter. 'You believe? You believe? And suppose they suspend trading in platinum and force me to liquidate? The price on the open market would collapse and I'd be totally wiped out. We'd lose the house and everything.' His voice cracked with emotion.

Peter came over and put his arm around his grandfather's shoulder, and for once Belson didn't pull away. Instead he leaned with a moan into Peter's embrace, the only comfort left to him. Peter's eyes filled in sympathy as he felt the warmth of his grandfather's tears spilling over onto his hand. Right now he was so concerned about his grandfather that he wasn't thinking about himself. But some part of him was scared to death, and his headache was getting worse by the minute, sending excruciating waves of pain through his body.

'I told them I couldn't go to Washington next week for a hearing,' Belson said, the words caught in his throat. 'I'm too ill to travel, too ill . . .' He was holding back the torrent of pain inside with such effort that Peter could feel his body trembling with it.

Peter hugged him with desperation. He wanted with his entire being to make things better, and not because of his own possible contributions to this disaster, but because there was very little on earth that meant more to him than earning his grandfather's gratitude or comfort.

'I'll go to Washington for you, Grandfather,' Peter said.

'Thank you,' Belson whispered, too exhausted to protest.

'I'll take care of everything. I'll find us the best securities lawyer in the country. And we'll come through this. Only don't worry. Please, just don't worry.'

'I won't,' Belson said, as though he were really taking Peter's words to heart.

And don't die, Peter prayed. *Not now, not yet, just when you've finally started needing me. Please God*, he prayed, *don't let him die, just give me the strength to help him. Give me a chance to show him how much I care.*

Chapter 5

ALTHOUGH PETER had taken a solemn oath to find some miraculous solution to his grandfather's disastrous dilemma, he had not been able to keep his promise. Not because he didn't want to, and not because he hadn't tried. He spent the rest of Thursday and most of Friday poring over law books and SEC regulations, looking for some way out. And the fact that he had found absolutely no way hadn't fully discouraged him either. What prevented him from continuing on in the face of this overwhelming impossibility was not the task itself, it was his body's physical reaction to it. He had so much despair and guilt to contend with, it had become a living presence. A steady pounding, a repetition that finally translated itself into a migraine so awful he was literally blinded by pain. He'd had migraines before in his life, but never this bad. He'd felt it begin when he'd heard the news that platinum had fallen 150 points and it had gotten worse when Belson told him of the impending investigation in Washington. He should have heeded the symptoms, but he'd ignored them and continued with his work until it got so bad that he couldn't work at all. And now his stomach churned ceaselessly, his body twitched with spasms, and his brain was on fire, alternating between rolling kettledrums of pounding pressure and electric jolts of ever-tightening metal bands that wrapped themselves around his skull. Phyllis didn't question him, only sensed his panic and pain. She offered her loving touch, provided compresses, ministered medications, called the doctor; but still the pain would not let go.

When he was lucid enough to have a cognitive thought, he speculated that he himself might not be letting go of the pain, as though it were a self-inflicted punishment for his mismanagement and stupidity. But then even that thought became elusive as the fleeting lucidity ended and the hammering began again blotting out everything.

Thoughts of betrayal tortured him. Larry couldn't have been the one who informed on them, could he? He was afraid to ask. He blamed himself utterly for his contribution to their situation, for choosing ficticious names that could be so easily traced, for not being more circumspect in his comings and goings. But the blame he heaped on himself for the state of this disaster was only a fresh insult to an old injury. He was an originator of sin; and his most awful one had occurred a long time ago. He'd locked it away in a dark part of his heart, blotted it from his consciousness forever, knowing that if he ever let it see the light of day it would surely destroy him.

Crack, crack, crack pounded the pain in his head while the activities of life revolved around him. He was only vaguely aware of the day going by, partly because the medication was very strong, and partly because he had a subconscious need to retreat from anything that might apply pressure to his already overstressed psyche.

One, two, three hours passed; and next Tuesday approached inexorably, but he could not function.

And then it was Saturday night.

'You go to Marla's party without me,' he told Phyllis. 'Give her my love, and tell her I'm sorry I couldn't make it.'

Phyllis protested. 'I don't want to leave you alone.'

But that only gave him more pain. Finally she agreed.

Later he felt her lean over him and kiss him lightly on the forehead; her lips were a cool breeze, a respite from hell. He heard the rustle of her skirt, smelled the mouth-watering, flowery scent of her perfume, and noticed for the first time in twenty-four hours that his senses hadn't caused him excruciating agony. Maybe the headache was diminishing.

'I'll be home early, darling,' she whispered. 'Call me at Marla's if you need anything.' And she left to go downstairs where Belson, his car, and his driver were waiting for her.

Peter's last thought before he slept was how ironic it was that his seventy-nine-year-old grandfather, who was near physical and mental collapse, who faced financial ruin, had been able to pull himself together tonight enough to attend this function, and Peter couldn't.

Everything was ready; the eggs for the roquefort soufflés had been separated, whipped, prepared, and were ready to be folded together and put into the oven during the middle of the cocktail hour; the baked Alaskas were in the freezer until dessert time when they would be browned for five minutes in a hot oven and doused with brandy for a flambéed entrance; the well-seasoned *gigot en croute* was succulent; and the Boston lettuce and hearts of palm *salade vinaigrette* was tart yet refreshing. There was a melange of fresh vegetables ready to be steamed and topped with herbed butter sauce and home-baked dinner rolls already in the oven. It was a rich menu, but Marla had wanted to go all out. And she was exhausted from cooking all day, even though she didn't look it in her new Saint Laurent outfit. She'd bought it especially for tonight and felt enormously guilty for spending fifteen hundred dollars on one suit. But what a suit it was. Black and gold brocade dinner jacket, wine-colored harem knee pants, and a handmade lace blouse.

The house looked wonderful: scented candles and votive lights flickered everywhere, hickory logs crackled in the fireplaces, David Jones's flower arrangements enhanced strategic locations, and Mozart on the stereo filled the air. The hired help were bustling about. Mark and Lori were in their pajamas, robed, bathed, and flushed pink with the residue of excitement they'd picked up from Mommy and Daddy.

Larry had stocked the bar, ordered the wine, and even made a salmon mousse hors d'oeuvre, one of his favorites. But though everything was under control, Marla was terribly nervous. It was one thing to give a party as lavish and detailed as this one, and it was another to have your lover and your husband soon to be seated at the same table. It made her feel faint with apprehension. True to her promise to herself, she hadn't seen Felix since their last encounter on the yacht. After all, his job was completed, and essentially so was the affair. But endings made her sad. And she was more than a little apprehensive about having Vicky here tonight along with Leslie and Belson McKintridge. But she couldn't have a party without inviting her best friend, Vicky, and Vicky, after a great deal of vacillation, had chosen to attend knowing who else would be there. If Vicky could handle it, she thought with a sigh, then so could she.

She took a final look around, fluffed her hair, applied some gloss to her lips. She checked the table, which was set with a Madeira cloth and gleamed with polished silver, her grandmother's cut crystal stemware, and her own Rosenthal china, and declared herself ready.

The doorbell rang just then and out of reflex she moved toward the door, but Conrad, the bartender hired for the evening, hurried ahead of her to answer it, straightening his tuxedo jacket as he walked.

Phyllis and Belson were the first to arrive and Marla greeted them with a kiss, exclaiming how happy she was to see Belson. But he looked awful. His skin was a waxy yellow color and his eyes seemed sunken in his head. She glanced at Phyllis with alarm but Phyllis's expression warned her not to say anything. Marla was even more alarmed when he took her hand to kiss it and she could feel him trembling. He was as dry and brittle as a winter twig in the snow and she feared just as fragile.

'How beautiful you look,' she exclaimed over Phyllis's lavender silk-jersey dress. It was the perfect color for her blond hair and enviable complexion.

And Belson beamed at Marla's compliment to Phyllis as if it had been made for him. 'She does look exquisite, as usual,' he said as Conrad helped him off with his overcoat.

341

Phyllis gave Marla's hand a squeeze. 'I'm afraid both the McKintridge men aren't feeling too well tonight,' she said. 'I tried to convince Belson to stay home with Peter but he wouldn't hear of it.'

'Damn right,' Belson insisted, making a brave showing of strength he obviously didn't feel. 'Spent enough time being his nursemaid. It's not every day I'm invited to young people's homes to dine, and certainly it's a rare opportunity to escort Phyllis out alone without the hovering presence of my grandson.' And he winked.

'How is Peter?' Marla asked.

'His headache is very bad,' Phyllis said. She too looked drawn and concerned. 'But if he feels any better later he'll join us for dessert.'

Marla nodded and made a mental note to try and figure out where she'd put Peter at the table if he should eventually arrive.

'May I show Belson around the house?' Phyllis asked.

'Of course,' Marla replied. 'But I can't imagine my home would interest you, living where you do.'

'But I am interested,' he assured her. 'I can see at a glance what a charming and original atmosphere you've created in this room. I notice "they're" back to upholstering walls again in the French tradition and using fine antiques in prominent places. And I like the uncluttered way you've mixed the old and the new. It reminds me of the philosophy of the Orient, the simplicity of design. Yet I see your own touches of modern eclecticism.'

He's charming, Marla thought as he and Phyllis moved away. *It's a shame Vicky dislikes him so.*

Leslie and Sheikh Banir Ammani arrived just then and Marla greeted them, stepping back to allow Leslie to enter. Leslie always swept into a room. Tonight her Guerlaine perfume preceded her, her jewels sparkled, and her sable stole was the softest fur as she flung it from her shoulders like the swirl of a matador's cape. Leslie's dress was also a Saint Laurent and her eyes appraised Marla's outfit. 'I must be paying you very well, Marla dear,' she commented.

Marla smiled, but she wasn't pleased by Leslie's obvious jealousy. For a moment she feared she'd made a mistake in buying Saint Laurent, like the vice-president of a corporation who disobeys the unwritten law and drives a Mercedes while the president of the company is only driving a Buick. One should not dare to assume the trappings of power until one had been crowned king, or in this case, queen. But then she decided not to let it worry her; it was only an outfit, after all.

Marla shook hands with the sheikh as Leslie glanced around the living room, then she tucked her arm possessively through Ammani's. 'The house is coming along, Marla. I see you've used the fabric *I* discovered for the Hamilton job. I've always loved it. It gives the appearance of elegance without costing full price.'

Marla colored slightly. Forty-eight dollars a yard, wholesale, had been price enough for her.

'Oh, I see Oswaldo finished your sideboard.'

'No,' Marla corrected. 'It was Jim Womack.'

'Hmmm,' Leslie said thoughtfully. 'He does good work for *you*.'

Leslie and Jim didn't get along, but Marla adored him and thought he was a master artist.

The doorbell rang again and they were standing nearby in the foyer as Conrad opened the door.

It was Vicky, wearing a red faille dinner suit trimmed with black piping and black frog buttons.

'I had no idea you were inviting *her*,' Leslie said, obviously annoyed as Vicky strode through the doorway on slim, perfect legs in black lizard pumps and stood defiantly in front of them. 'Hello.' She nodded coolly to Leslie, and Marla admired her control.

Leslie nodded back, trying to be unobtrusive as she guided the sheikh firmly away from the offending newcomer.

'Is Belson here yet?' Vicky asked, her voice betraying her nervousness. 'I saw the limo outside.'

Marla nodded.

'Oh damn,' she exclaimed. 'I thought he was sick and wasn't coming.' Vicky's hands were like ice.

'It's Peter who's ill,' Marla told her. 'A headache or something.'

Vicky sighed deeply, straightened her shoulders with resolve, and gave Marla a wicked smile. 'Well, it's now or never,' she said.

'Are you certain you want to stay?' Marla asked.

'Of course,' Vicky replied firmly. 'I wouldn't have missed this party tonight for anything, not even to attend my own wedding.' And she set her Charles Gallay clutch bag down on the entry table and walked proudly across the room to get a drink.

But Marla didn't have time to hover protectively around Vicky. It was eight twenty-five. Almost time to put the first-course soufflés in the oven. She went to inform the kitchen help.

By the time she returned, Felix and Audrey had arrived and were standing at the bar with drinks in their hands talking to Leslie and the sheikh. Audrey was effusive about the house and complimentary about the children. Marla could barely look her in the eye.

Lori and Mark had come downstairs to say good night and were sitting on either side of Belson dressed in their Carter's feet pajamas and gazing at him as though he were Santa Claus, while he told them the story of one of his famous westerns in which he single-handedly defended a mining claim against a gang of fifteen outlaws.

It was a beautiful tableau, the three of them, so many generations apart. Belson looked like a combination of Ronald Colman and Cary Grant with his thick white hair and still handsome face, even though tonight he didn't look his best, but he could still mesmerize an audience. Her children sat there all pink and cherubic and made her forget all their exasperating qualities, filling her with a rush of love for them. She went into the study for her Polaroid camera and took a picture of the three of them, warning the children they could only stay up as long as it took to develop the picture. Then she steeled herself for their protest, but evidently the earlier coaching she had given them about being good tonight worked, because they marched up to bed within minutes.

The dinner went smoothly; everyone raved about the food and she had to admit it was excellent, even though she was the only one who knew when the flavors were subtly amiss. And she also suspected that she was the only one who perceived the undercurrents ebbing and flowing among her guests. Unpleasant undercurrents. Earlier she had seen Felix standing with Belson and the two of them glared at one another, speaking in voices too low for her to hear, and when Larry interrupted them, they still continued to glare at each other.

Vicky was tense and nervous all through dinner in spite of her bravado and Marla noticed that she kept her distance from Leslie unless the two women were forced to look at one another across the dinner table. To bolster her courage, Vicky had drunk four glasses of wine.

Marla wished that Felix wouldn't keep staring at her with a look of proprietary pride every time a new delicious course was served, as though she had done all of this just for him.

Finally after the baked Alaska and coffee with brandy Marla's worst fears were realized. There was a lull in the conversation; everyone was satiated and lethargic, all except Leslie.

'So. You've been writing a book, Miss Feinstein, since you left Southwick School?' Leslie said. They were the first words she'd directed at Vicky all night. 'But then, isn't everybody?'

'Oh, no,' Vicky said, leaping to the challenge. 'I thought everybody was decorating these days.'

'And what's your book about?' Leslie asked, ignoring the zinger.

Vicky smiled sweetly. 'The ladies of Beverly Hills. And the men.' And she looked pointedly at Belson.

'What's that supposed to mean?' Leslie said suspiciously.

345

'I thought I might do an exposé on the behind-the-scenes intrigue that goes on in our golden ghetto. Fictional, of course.'

Leslie was not amused, and her face took on an appearance of wariness. 'What a silly idea.'

'I've always wondered what it would be like to write a book,' Larry said.

Vicky turned to him. 'Truman Capote says that finishing a book is like taking your child out in the yard and shooting him.'

'Good heavens,' Phyllis exclaimed.

'But I think it's more like giving birth to an elephant. The gestation period is just as long, sometimes longer than eighteen months, and the birth pains are enormous—you think it's never going to end. And once you finish, you have something that's not your offspring, but something that can grow to be bigger than you.'

'With galumphing feet, an ungainly trunk, and a god-awful smell.' Leslie laughed.

'I've imagined it would be more like an orgasm,' Felix said glancing slyly at Marla, who blushed.

Vicky smiled, '*Every* scene I complete is an orgasm. Pu-leeze. Do you think I could wait eighteen months for that?'

Everyone laughed.

She continued now that she commanded their attention. 'Although I will admit that some writers are so in love with themselves they come over their every sentence.' She turned to Leslie. 'You know about narcissism, I'm sure.'

Leslie almost blushed with fury and turned to the sheikh for comfort, but Banir was clearly enjoying the cat fight.

Marla gave Larry a desperate please-do-something look.

'Vicky,' he interrupted, 'I hear you've been seeing my old friend, Bob Delman. I was sorry he couldn't be here with you tonight. What's Bob doing these days?'

Both Belson and Felix stared.

'Your old friend?' Vicky said. 'Do you know Bob?' She was amazed, yet she wished he hadn't bought it up.

'Sure. But I haven't seen him since law school.'

'Law school?' she said. 'Oh, it must be a different Bob Delman. The one I know never went to law school.'

A look crossed Belson's face that was thick with animosity and sudden understanding.

'It must be the same man.' Larry described him. 'Curly hair? About my height, muscular, and a great smile. Knows a little about a lot of things?'

Vicky nodded in surprise. 'That sounds like him. But he's not a lawyer.'

'Yes. I'm sure of it. He graduated from Boalt when I graduated from S.C. Law School. His real name's Delmansky. I often wondered what happened to him. The guy had so much going for him.'

Belson interrupted. 'The gentleman you're speaking of might possibly be my former masseur. I had no idea he knew Miss Feinstein or that he was so well educated. I was sorry to lose him in spite of his "friendships".' Then his eyes strayed to Vicky but he looked right through her as if she were invisible.

Vicky wanted to reach across Phyllis on her left and stab Belson in his liver-spotted hand with her silver dessert fork. Maybe a puncture with silver tines would make him shrivel up and die like the Wicked Witch of the West. *Bob had quit working for Belson,* she thought. *But why? And why hadn't he told her?* She was dying to know, but she'd never find out from Belson.

'You say Delmansky is a masseur?' Larry exclaimed, turning to Belson. 'No way.'

'Yes, he is,' Vicky said in a small voice, and they all looked at her. So now they knew, they all knew. And suddenly she didn't care at all. It didn't make one damn bit of difference. All she knew was that a great weight had lifted from her shoulders. But she was confused about Larry's comments. Could Bob really be a lawyer and not have told her? That wasn't possible. Not after all their arguments over his dedication to his profession. He'd told her such authentic details about his year at Valley College,

347

about his trip to Katmandu. Had he been lying? But why? He knew how she felt. Maybe he had failed the bar and was embarrassed to say so. That must be it. That must be why he was so defensive about the subject of lawyers.

'I'd like to propose a toast,' Felix offered, hurrying in to fill the awkward silence that followed Larry's last comment. The one thing he didn't want was further discussion about Bob Delman's occupation. *Damn, this is such a small town,* he thought.

'A bit earlier we were speaking of completions. And I want to make a toast to our beautiful and talented hostess for the successful and magnificent completion of my yacht. That's what this party is about, isn't it? Well, you're all invited as soon as possible to see what this incredible young woman has wrought. Isn't that right, Audrey?' He turned to his wife, who nodded and gave Marla a proud maternal smile.

If only she knew, Marla thought, stabbed with remorse, and she glanced at Phyllis, who was staring at her with a strange look on her face.

But Felix didn't notice Marla's discomfort or the look on his daughter's face, and he went right on describing the details of Marla's accomplishments, how she cajoled the workmen to come and work under adverse conditions, how she always had an intelligent solution to every dilemma, how her talent shone, how lucky Leslie was to have her, and how she deserved not only a raise, but a piece of Leslie's business.

Belson looked at Marla with approval, but Leslie was hardly listening, turning to speak to Banir *sotto voce*. Marla could tell she was fuming.

'Felix, Felix, please,' Marla said hurriedly, afraid even to look at Larry. 'I didn't do as much as you seem to think . . . .' God, she wished he would shut up.

'Oh, yes, you did!' he continued. 'Now don't be modest.' And he continued describing how Marla researched yachts of his type and design so thoroughly that she could almost build one herself before she even attempted to begin any interior changes. But before he could finish his speech, Leslie abruptly stood up and excused herself from the table.

There was another awkward silence but this time Larry plunged in and offered a toast. 'To Marla's health and congratulations,' he said. And finally one by one the guests drifted away from the table and back into the living room.

Marla's stomach fluttered nervously as she searched for Leslie. She was in the foyer already wrapped in her sable cape, waiting impatiently for Banir Ammani—who was standing at the fireplace deep in conversation with Felix—to finish and take her home.

'Leaving so soon?' Marla asked.

Leslie whirled on her. 'It's not soon enough for me!'

'What's wrong?' Marla asked, knowing perfectly well what it was, and feeling as though the elevator soaring in her heart had just crashed into her stomach.

'What's wrong? You have the nerve to ask me what's wrong? How dare you.' She was speaking quietly but with harsh invective and every world seemed a bullet hurled toward Marla's heart. Yet no one within their sight could hear her.

'You ungrateful, two-timing cunt,' she whispered. 'You sly little weasel—you thought you could get away with shafting me, didn't you? Well, let me tell you, no one can do that to me, do you hear me, no one!' Her voice raised only a decibel but it was enough to send shivers down Marla's back. Marla's heart was racing and her hands were clammy, and where earlier she had felt a giddy kind of happiness, now she had only the most sickening feeling of fear.

'For God's sake, Leslie. What have I done?'

Leslie drew her rich chocolate brown fur around her in a regal sweep, pulled herself up to her full height of five feet nine in heels, and looked down at Marla as though she were a snail to be smashed to a frothy green puddle. 'You thought you could take credit for *my* job, with *my* client, while you worked in *my* company. Well, if you think that,

349

you're much mistaken. Nobody two-times me. I was the one who started with Felix's job. Those were my designs and my ideas; you did nothing but expedite them. And don't you ever forget it. You're nothing but a stupid little bore, and without my guidance and expertise you'd still be nothing. And you should have had the backbone and the good taste to admit it in front of your guests, and especially in front of my escort and client, Sheikh Ammani.'

'But, Leslie.' She was nearly crying. 'I had to discard every one of your original ideas, and Billy D.'s also. I started from scratch on Felix's job. I redesigned the interior completely by myself. And I did a first-rate job. One that upholds the LPW tradition.'

'Like hell you did. I consulted with you every step of the way. I studied your designs, and suggested changes.'

'And I never took one of them,' Marla said, suddenly feeling very possessive of her work. She had done that job alone and nobody was going to take credit for it, no matter who they were.

'If it weren't for me, you would never have had the opportunity for that job in the first place. I took a chance on you, and somehow you knew enough not to screw it up. But you'd still be a little nobody if I hadn't taken you in off the streets.'

Marla couldn't believe what she was hearing. 'Leslie,' she said with more calm than she thought was possible, 'I am not now nor have I ever been a nobody. Nor am I a two-timer, or any of the other names you've called me.'

In the nearby powder room a toilet flushed, breaking the silence with an embarrassing reminder of bodily functions.

'Well, if you think you're so wonderful, maybe you'd be better off on your own, or working for someone else whom you can stab in the back. Though I can't think of anyone who would hire someone with your lack of loyalty and appreciation. In short, I don't want to have anything more to do with you, even if you come crawling back. You're fired, Marla Gilbert. You and your snippy little low-class friend, Vicky Feinstein, deserve one another.'

Marla was staring at her white-faced, wishing she could throw her out of the front door. Phyllis was sitting on the sofa in the living room with Vicky and they had heard Leslie's last remark. They stopped talking to stare, and Marla felt humiliation and a fierce protectiveness for Vicky creeping into her body to attack her shoulders with sharp pincers. The word *fired* flashed in her brain over and over like a neon branding iron.

Banir started toward them, having concluded his discussion with Felix, and Leslie sped up her invective.

'Firing is too good for you, Marla. And don't ever get the preposterous idea that you'll ever be able to start your own business, because I'll see to it that no worthwhile client ever hires you. When I get through with you, no one will even let you design a kennel.'

The powder-door room opened nearby, and the last sounds of the water filling the toilet tank grew louder and then softer as the flushing cycle ended. Belson stepped out, took a long look at Marla and Leslie facing one another, and assessed them both. Then he stepped forward, came over to Marla, and put his arm around her shoulders.

'These walls are not very sound absorbent, ladies,' he said. 'I couldn't help overhearing.'

Leslie gave him a haughty look. 'Stay out of this, Belson.'

'No, I don't think I will,' he said, savoring the moment. He turned to Marla, who was even more humiliated, but at least in partial control, if only she could stop trembling. 'I understand you've just decided to open your own design firm, young lady, is that correct?'

She looked up into his sky blue eyes, topped with a glacier of hair, and felt nothing more surprising could possibly happen tonight. 'I don't know . . .' she stammered.

'And you may be specializing in animal compounds?' he teased.

She forced herself to smile at him, grateful for his humor.

'But that would be a waste of your talents, I believe. So how would you like to take on as your first client the

McKintridge estate now that you're free from the mother parasite.' And he looked at Leslie with an equal amount of hatred.

Marla gasped. 'Do you mean that?'

He chuckled. 'Yes, I'm quite serious. The place needs redoing badly. Why don't we draw up an agreement in the morning?'

Leslie's knuckles clutching her coat were alabaster white and her face was contorted with rage. Without another word she spun on her Charles Jourdan heels, grabbed Sheikh Ammani's hand, and fled from the house.

Marla threw her arms around Belson and hugged his thin body with all her might. 'This is a lifetime dream come true,' she said.

And behind her in the living room Phyllis and Vicky laughed with approval.

Belson preened with their attention. The encounter with Leslie seemed to have filled him with a burst of sudden strength; certainly he was exhibiting a greater degree of energy than he had all night. He looked positively healthy as he strode purposefully across the room and extended his hand to Phyllis. 'Are you ready to go, my dear?'

But Phyllis was not ready and stood reluctantly, glancing at Vicky.

'If you want to stay, I'll drive you home,' Vicky offered, noticing her reticence.

Phyllis wavered. 'I should be getting back to Peter.'

'But you spoke to him, didn't you?' Vicky asked. 'Didn't he say to stay and enjoy yourself?'

Phyllis nodded.

'Oh, stay a while,' Marla asked, approaching them. 'If only for a half hour. I'm so excited, you just can't go right now.'

Phyllis smiled and looked at Belson as if for permission.

He was still basking in the warmth of their approval and much too happy after besting Leslie to be grumpy. 'Do as you wish, dear,' he said.

'All right, I think I will stay for a while,' Phyllis said, taking Belson's arm through hers and walking with him to the door. Conrad helped Belson on with his coat.

'I'll call you in the morning,' she said. 'And, Belson, thank you so much for what you did for Marla.'

He chuckled. 'I figured you'd hire her one day anyway when McKintridge is yours. Never thought it would do me so much good to tell her now.' And they both laughed. 'It was a stroke of genius, wasn't it?' he asked. 'A moment of perfection right down to the timing.' And he laughed again. 'It feels wonderful to settle that old debt with Leslie, though; I never thought I would. Dear lord, the look on her face. I even think Peter's grandmother will rest easier in heaven from now on.'

Phyllis grasped his arm. 'You're terrific, do you know that?' And she leaned over and kissed him good-bye.

But he surprised her, no peck on the cheek for him: he gave her an open-mouthed kiss on the lips. If she hadn't been so shocked, she'd have returned it, he was sure of that.

Phyllis stood for a moment after the door closed, rather startled by Belson's behavior. But she chalked it up to the fervor of the moment. Over the years he'd sometimes taken liberties with her that were too familiar, such as the brush of his arm against her breast, a hand lingering on her thigh. But he didn't mean anything by it. It was his way of showing her that he was still a man in spite of his advancing age. And even though he was eccentric, she was terribly fond of him. And it looked as though whatever was troubling him lately and Peter too for the past week may have been resolved. She hoped so with all her heart, because that would mean Peter might start to feel better soon. And that's all she really wanted.

A crunching sound on the gravel startled Belson on his way down the drive to the street and he turned to see who it was.

'Leaving already?' Felix approached from behind a tree.

'What were you doing hiding behind there, Anhalt? Lifting your leg like an old dog?' Belson laughed at his own joke. How he had longed to let loose on Felix all night, but the bounds of propriety had kept him in check. Now there was no one around and he could say whatever he liked.

Belson's chauffeur was standing at attention on the curb. The door of the limousine opened when Belson stopped on the drive; the chauffeur made a move toward him. But Belson waved him away. He didn't want anyone overhearing this conversation.

'What *do* you want?' he asked Felix. 'It's too chilly a night for you to be out here for the air.'

'Very perceptive.' Felix grinned, enjoying the moment. 'You always had a small flair for insight. Too bad it's deserted you now when you really need it. In fact from the looks of things I'd say you were about to lose a great deal, and not in a blaze of glory either. No, I'd say you were going to go out like the sad, dying flicker of a sorry little match.'

'What are you talking about?' Belson asked, alerted by Felix's tone more than his words. Felix was being too cagey, too secure, too self-certain. Everything about him lent an aura of self-satisfaction: his golden tan; his straw-colored hair infused with gray, thick and coarsely cut; his beige cashmere jacket; his cream silk shirt; the hand-stitched slacks; and Italian shoes so comfortably worn and newly polished. Oh, yes, the dandy was cagey, and disgusting.

'I'm talking about your recent fiasco in the platinum market. I see there's been quite a drop in price in the last few days. Hurt you a little bit, didn't it?' A smile itched and pulled at the corners of Felix's mouth as he watched the cheer suddenly drain from Belson's face to be replaced by wariness and fear.

'Oh, I know all about it,' Felix gloated, puffing on his cigar, letting the smoke curl lazily from the tip. 'I know so much that I felt it was my duty to inform the CFTC that a certain ancient entrepreneur who's seen better days and whose last desperate stand to save his dwindling fortune has led him to defraud the commodity market. Tsk, tsk,' he said. 'Rather nasty business, don't you think?'

'So *you're* the one,' Belson said, trying to recover his equilibrium. The news hit him like a sledgehammer in the solar plexus and he stood there shaking from shock. But with all his might he would not let Felix know how he felt. It took every ounce of his strength to jut his chin forward and say, 'Well, stop toying with me, Anhalt; give it all to me. What exactly do you know, and how did you find out?'

Felix nearly exploded with venom. 'I've been covering you for months, you old windbag. Delman works for me.'

'I guessed as much tonight,' Belson said, expecting to feel weakness overcome him, expecting the same awful pain to radiate through his chest and terrorize him again. But none of that happened; there was no weakness, no pain. All he felt was a void, an emptiness inside so enormous that at the moment he would have sold his soul to fill it. 'Delman didn't know anything,' Belson said, nearly stammering, but recovering in time.

'He knew Peter was involved in something that had to do with you. Phyllis and I both could see how troubled Peter has been for some time. And so Peter became our pigeon; ultimately he became our informant. You know Peter, he could never hold his piss for very long, and so he finally unloaded the news about your dishonest dealings to his faithful partner and friend, Larry Gilbert . . . .' Felix turned his hands palms up, indicating the *fait accompli*. '*Et voilà.*' He was studying Belson for any indication of misery over which he could triumph, but Belson held on. 'It's too bad you won't live long enough.' Felix continued, rubbing salt into the wound, 'to see me acquire the McKintridge estate from Peter. I plan to subdivide all the acreage and knock that building down stone by stone until there's nothing left of you but the odor of flatulated gas.'

'Over my dead body, you will,' Belson said.

'Oh yes,' Felix smiled. 'I understand I won't have long to wait for that either. I hear your ticker is on its last tock. I had to laugh tonight when you so gallantly offered to hire Marla to redecorate the estate. You don't have enough cash to hire a two-bit whore off of Hollywood Boulevard. Besides, I think Leslie would do a much better job than Marla with the old place if I decide not to tear it down. She has a real feel for it, don't you think?'

Every word he uttered infused Belson with fury. His rage was so enormous and his hatred so strong that he thought the strength of it alone might be enough to kill. Every ounce of his being wanted to scream, *No! You can't have found this out. You can't.* He'd rather burn McKintridge to the ground than allow Felix to own it. But he'd never allow so much as an eyelash to blink if it would give away the torment inside of him to the man facing him. And right now it wasn't only Felix he wanted to murder, it was Peter too.

'I understand you've got a date with the enforcement division of the Commodity Futures Trading Commission next week? Give my best to Lance. Good man, Lance. He said my insider tip only corroborated some of their growing suspicions anyway.'

Belson's throat was an Arizona riverbed in August and he could feel the winds of time parching his dryness to a brittle edge. He forced a molecule of saliva through the dry canyon of his throat, willed his eyes to hold their steady gaze, pulled his atrophied lips into an idiot's expression, and let the shallow breath whistle through his paper-thin larynx as he spoke. 'You're really the one who told them? How could you do such a thing to Peter and Phyllis? Don't you know they're the ones who will pay for your vindictiveness if I lose the estate?'

'Don't give me that crap, old man.' Felix hacked some mucus out of his throat and spat it on the grass; Belson flinched. 'It's you I wanted, and you I've gotten. I've ruined you and I take great pleasure in it.' Felix's voice was an animal grunt. He exhaled his words as though they were the hot breath of the tiger and Belson almost sensed a fetid rotting jungle odor oozing out of him. 'Peter and Phyllis will recover from the loss of the estate,' Felix said. 'Besides, they'll inherit what's left of it from me someday anyhow.'

What's left of it? God. Felix would turn McKintridge into a rotting dinosaur among the garbage of modern life, a sore thumb on the hand of a leper. And now Belson felt an agonizing pain, but it wasn't the pain of his constricting cardiovascular vessels. It was a deeper, duller pain and it ached far more than something physical; the bitter bile of defeat felt more horrible to him than the thought of his dying. 'You don't have the kind of money it would take to buy McKintridge,' Belson whispered, trying for one last stand.

'Try me!' Felix said, grinning again.

And suddenly Belson's anger took over and swept away the bitter taste of bile in his throat. He wished with all his might he hadn't only been so vain tonight and had brought along his cane. If only he had a weapon right now, he would have cracked it across Felix's ghoulish face and smashed those white gleaming teeth down his throat.

'Mr McKintridge, sir,' the chauffeur called. 'It's very chilly for you to be out so long. Shall I bring you another wrap?'

Belson waved at him impatiently and then turned back to Felix. 'I'm not in my grave yet, Anhalt,' he said. 'Don't count me out until you see me in my coffin.'

'I'll see you in it, old man,' Felix replied with absolute glee. 'And I'll piss on it! Do you hear me? Before they cover your coffin with dirt, I'll piss all over it.'

'You're insane,' Belson said, backing away. 'You're fucking insane!' And he hurried toward the safety of his car, feeling as though the hot breath of Lucifer were breathing down his back. Felix's laughter echoed in his ears and he slammed the car door before the chauffeur could get to it. He had to shut out that demonic sound. If he'd had a gun at the moment, he would have shot Felix without a second thought. *It still isn't too late to kill him,* he realized.

I'd have nothing to lose by committing murder at this late date. Why not just take Felix with me? But he didn't want to spend the last moment of his precious life in prison, and he'd never find a way out of this mess locked in some jail. But could he find a way out? Oh, God, he didn't know. He only knew if there was one, he would find it, by saints, he would find it. Before tonight he had been determined to try; now he had even more reason. He couldn't let that man get the best of him. Never, *Never!*

But right now there was something he had to do.

'Take me to my grandson's house,' he instructed the driver. 'I want to see him now. *Right now!*'

'Yes, sir,' came the reply.

Dealing with that sniveling wretch of a man would come before anything else. *Wait till I get my hands on him,* Belson thought. *Just wait!*

Chapter 6

PETER HEARD the doorbell ringing through a cottony haze and with great reluctance came to consciousness. This was the first real sleep he'd had in three days and he hated to wake up. But the insistent sound of the doorbell clanged in his ears like sirens announcing a holocaust and started his headache pounding again.

He stumbled out of bed, staggered to the door of the bedroom, and flinched when the light in the upper hall shot needles into his eyes. Squinting and shading his eyes, he helped himself down the stairs, leaning heavily on the banister.

Where was Lupe? he wondered. Why hadn't she answered the door? And then he remembered that she couldn't hear it because he'd forgotten to fix the auxiliary switch that allowed the doorbell to ring near her room.

The incessant bell was interrupted by a frantic pounding that sent apprehensive jolts through his already beleaguered brain. Who could it be at this late hour? But when he glanced at the clock, he realized it wasn't so late; it only felt that way because he'd been sleeping so soundly.

'Who is it?' he called as he made it to the bottom of the stairs and approached the door.

'Open this door!' Belson roared.

The shock of hearing his grandfather's voice and the rage it contained stopped him in his tracks. Something terrible had happened, and whatever it was, he knew it would be his fault. He wanted to run, to hide, to disintegrate and be invisible, be anywhere but here at this moment. He was a shameful child again, the cause of everything bad in his life.

In slow motion he reached for the doorknob and opened the door. The sight of his grandfather was like having ice water thrown in his face. No fantasy could be as horrible as the intense hatred and fury that burned in Belson's eyes.

'So,' Belson said, pushing past Peter and slamming the door behind him so hard the whole house shook. 'It's finally come to *this*. THIS!' he screamed, whirling around to face Peter, his black overcoat flapping like a pair of raven's wings. Peter was terrified of the power of anger in his grandfather and by the thought of being enveloped in the evil darkness of those wings. 'You little *shithead*,' Belson said.

Peter had never seen him like this; his nose was white-tipped and pinched, drawn in as though he had sucked in all the oxygen out of the air. There were bright spots of unhealthy color on his cheeks, while his face was a pasty shade of gray. And his eyes—they blazed so with meanness that Peter could hardly look at them.

'You *cocksucker*! You *asshole*!' Belson sputtered. 'There aren't words fitting enough to describe what you are.' He was so overcome with fury that he reached out

359

with clawlike hands to choke Peter, but then stopped himself, realizing what an effort that would cost him. 'Ever since you were a sniveling little boy hanging on to your mother's knees, I knew there was no hope for you. But I denied what I knew. I refused to believe anyone with McKintridge blood in his veins could be as weak as you. I gave you every chance to prove me wrong: I took you in; I sent you to school. I suffered your boring presence on those endless vacations, forgoing my own holidays so you would have an example to follow. I tried everything, and now look how you repay me.' His voice raised to a murderous pitch as he fed on his own memories of disappointment. 'I came to you in my hour of need. I brought you my vulnerability and you said you would help me. I believed you,' he screamed. 'I believed you! And all the while it was you who stabbed me in the back.'

Every awful word scored Peter with a new wound. The pain was so intense he could barely ask, 'What is it, Grandfather?' though he knew exactly what his grandfather was talking about while praying he was wrong.

'You've ruined me,' Belson said, pointing a finger at him, reaching out with a hard bony digit and poking into Peter's chest, over and over, pushing as hard as he could, prodding, hurting, not stopping. 'You did it! *You*. Only you,' he repeated with each jab. 'You told your stinking rat of a partner what I've been doing in the platinum market and he ran immediately to Felix!'

'Felix!' Peter said in astonishment.

'Yes, Felix!' Belson said again, trembling, forcing the hated name out from between clenched teeth. 'That disgusting excuse for a human being, that rotten, conniving, miserable shit. Felix is the one who informed on me to the CFTC.'

'He wouldn't!' Peter insisted, completely shocked at the idea.

And Belson was so incensed by Peter's defense of Felix that he swung back his hand and slapped his grandson across the face. They stared at one another, each throbbing with overwrought emotions, while Peter burned with humiliation and cowered without protecting himself, awaiting another blow. 'Don't you dare defend that animal to me!' Belson yelled, his arm raised threateningly again. 'I've heard you spout that bastard's praises for the last time.' He was spitting as he screamed, almost out of control. 'He's lower than the lowest form of life. He told me himself what he had done to me and then he gloated over it. And you defend him?'

An eternity passed while they stared at one another, shaking with the pain of their discoveries, and then Belson finally controlled himself enough to lower his arm. But his look of disgust made Peter ache with shame.

'I can't believe it,' Peter whispered.

'Well, you'd better believe it,' Belson said. 'Because the truth of what that man is has been right in front of you all this time and you've refused to see it. Now look at what your blindness has cost me.' His moan of self-pity was heartrending.

Peter's mind raced, trying to find some kind of explanation, but there was none. He almost wished his grandfather would hit him again; anything was better than this pain.

'I know what you're thinking,' Belson said. 'That I could be wrong. You still don't want to recognize the truth. Well, I told you over and over not to trust him, not to confide in him. But would you listen? Not you! You think you know everything—well, you know nothing. And neither does your friend, Felix. He's never going to get the estate. Not from me! And he better not ever get it from you either, is that clear?' he shouted. And Peter nodded, not quite sure what his grandfather meant by that. 'He's not going to get it, because I'm going to save it. I haven't been sitting around waiting for your peanut lamebrain to figure out what we should do. I've got an idea I've been working on that might work. While you're here at home hiding under the covers, I've been looking for solutions. I've always known you were worthless, but I never knew until now just how worthless that was. But never mind. I don't need you. I'll do it all myself. I just have to get a postponement of the hearing next week, and convince the CFTC not to suspend trading in platinum. Then if I can find a way to hold off until the price of platinum rises again, I'll be all right.' He seemed to be rambling, making no sense at all. Peter knew a postponement of the hearing wouldn't do any good. Eventually they'd have to turn their records to the CFTC and those records would incriminate them. Nothing had changed; they still faced margin calls if the price dropped, and terrible losses. Platinum might never go any higher than it was right now, or it could take months to rise again. They didn't have months. Tears stung his eyes. Why hadn't he kept his mouth shut to Larry? Why, *why?* He knew how much Larry wanted to impress Felix.

'I can't believe Felix would do such a thing,' Peter repeated. But his misery over what Felix had done only increased his grandfather's anger. Belson's voice turned into a singsong mimicry. 'Are you sniveling again, like a little baby? Just because your hero has crapped all over you?' Then his voice shot through with venom again. 'You disgust me as much as Felix does. I can't stand the sight of you.' And he pushed past Peter, heading for the door.

'Grandfather, please,' Peter begged, grabbing on to him. 'Don't leave like this. I'm sorry. I didn't mean for this to happen.'

But Belson whirled around, pushing him off, his wrath reignited. 'You didn't mean to?' he yelled. 'You didn't mean to?' His fists clenched and unclenched; the veins in his temples were swollen and throbbing from exertion. Peter was terrified that he might drop dead right there and then.

'Please calm down,' Peter begged. 'I only meant that I never intended for this to happen.'

' "The road to hell is paved with good intentions",' Belson quoted. 'I'd like to know what you would have done if you'd really wanted to hurt me. You couldn't have done a better job if you planned this your whole life. And maybe

362

that's exactly what you did.'

He looked at Peter as though he were looking at a plate of rotting garbage filled with maggots. 'I'm through with you. I'm going to change my will in the morning and take you out of it. Only Phyllis and Jonathan will inherit anything from me. I don't want to be connected to you in any way whatsoever, even in death. Do you hear me?' he said.

But Peter just stared at him.

'Do you hear me?' he screamed again, until Peter nodded.

And then he left.

Chapter 7

'FOR ONCE in my life I actually felt admiration for Peter's grandfather tonight because of what he did for Marla,' Vicky said, following Phyllis into the house. 'Leslie finally met her match.'

'Shhh,' Phyllis cautioned as she closed the front door. 'Keep your voice down, Peter might be sleeping.'

'I'm not asleep,' Peter said from the living room. 'I'm right here.'

His appearance was shocking: he looked ravaged. He had the hollow-cheeked expression of a just-released prisoner of war and his eyes mirrored the tortures of the damned.

'How are you, darling?' Phyllis asked, going to him. 'Feeling any better?' But he stood there stiffly as she embraced him.

'What is it, Peter?' Vicky asked, as though sensing something in his expression that was more than the pain of his headache. 'What's happened?' There was a half-filled glass of Scotch on the table and a nearly empty bottle next to it. Peter seldom drank.

Phyllis followed her gaze and saw the liquor; she turned to Peter with alarm. 'You haven't been mixing drugs with alcohol, have you? That medication you're taking is extremely potent. It's terribly dangerous.'

'I know, I know,' he said impatiently. 'Just stop hovering and leave me alone, will you?'

Phyllis looked at Vicky as if to say, 'Do you see how he is? What am I supposed to do?'

'Peter,' Vicky repeated. 'Tell us what happened.'

'I can't,' he cried, sinking down onto the edge of the sofa and covering his face with his hands. Then from deep within him came the most terrible groan of anguish Vicky had ever heard. 'Oh, God,' he cried, 'I don't deserve to live.'

'Peter!' Phyllis cried out in alarm. 'Don't say such a thing.'

'I don't, I don't,' he said. And then in a voice full of despair, devoid of hope, he told them everything about Belson's visit, about the enormous financial losses and Belson's heart condition, about the platinum scheme to recover the losses, about the illegal acts he committed to help his grandfather, and finally about the Commodity Futures Trading Commission's discovery of Belson's duplicity and their impending investigation.

Phyllis was stunned, her mind rammed itself against the brick wall of what she wanted to believe and what she had just heard as truth. She alternated from rage to despair, from horror to sorrow, all in a matter of moments. It was an incredible story, each set of facts more damning than the preceding ones. *How could she not have known?* Questions fought to be asked. She felt as if she'd just broken out with a rampant case of allergic hives and she wanted to scratch and claw and tear at those hives until her skin was raw and bleeding, and then, just maybe, she could erase from her brain the awful things Peter had just told her.

Vicky was the first one to find her voice. 'Do you mean to say Belson has lost everything?'

Peter nodded, still not looking at them.

Briefly Phyllis thought of Marla. What a terrible disappointment this would be for her. She would certainly not be redecorating the estate now. 'Why didn't you tell me about this before?' Phyllis cried, unable to hold back any longer. 'How could you have kept this from me?' The enormity of it was more than she could comprehend.

'I couldn't tell you,' Peter whispered. 'My grandfather swore me to secrecy.' His voice was barely audible. 'I kept telling myself the scheme wouldn't last long because it wouldn't work, that it would be over in a short time. But it never was, it never was. And the lies and the secrets went on interminably. By then I was too ashamed to tell you.'

Phyllis was so furious with him for a moment that she wanted to strangle him with her bare hands. But as she stared at him the fury began to subside and then she found herself in a state of shock, numb, unable to think. Peter looked so miserable that soon her compassion for him became stronger than her anger. She reached out to touch his bowed head. 'How you must have suffered,' she said.

As she touched him, a sob caught in his throat and he fell into her embrace, sobbing uncontrollably.

Phyllis held him, crooning to him, soothing him, until his pain subsided a bit.

Vicky asked softly, 'Why is Belson so enraged with you, Peter? It seems to me you've done everything in the world for him. He should be eternally grateful to you for what you've sacrificed.'

The pain in Peter's eyes was inconsolable as he raised his tear-stained face. 'No,' he said. 'My grandfather has a right to hate me. I betrayed him.' Then he stopped for a moment, unable to go on. They waited until he gathered his courage enough to continue. 'After such a long time of keeping everything to myself, I had to talk to someone. But the person I chose to confide in gave that information to someone else who used it against us.'

365

'Who would do that?' Phyllis asked.

Peter glanced away and wiped the tears from his eyes. 'Just some business associates I know,' he lied. 'You don't know them.'

'But why didn't you come to me?' Phyllis asked, her voice as anguished as his. 'Why did you take it to some stranger? I don't understand that at all. You could have discussed it with Larry. Surely he would have helped you, and then you wouldn't be in these terrible difficulties.'

Peter started to cry again, more softly this time. His instinct was to protect Larry. 'I didn't want to involve Larry,' he said. 'I've already brought enough trouble on him by being an unethical partner. But I needed some professional advice.'

'Whom did you talk to?' Phyllis insisted. 'I'd like to wring his neck. What a terrible, terrible thing to do.'

'The man must hate Belson very much,' Vicky said.

'No, no!' Peter assured them. 'It was just one of those mistakes that happens. He mentioned it to someone, who mentioned it to someone else. You know, "loose lips sink ships". You don't know him, really you don't.'

'Well, there must be a way to find a solution for all of this before it goes any further,' Phyllis said. 'I can't believe the three of us can't come up with something. If not to save Belson's finances, at least to repair the breach between the two of you. It's not right for you two to be estranged, especially in light of Belson's condition.' She sighed, overcome with emotion. 'That poor man. I'm going to talk to him myself.'

'No,' Peter almost shouted, grabbing her hands. 'Don't do that.' But when she looked at him with surprise, he contained his agitation. 'What I mean is, let me try talking to him first. If I don't get anywhere, then you can talk to him.'

'All right,' Phyllis agreed, though she was bewildered by Peter's strange reaction. And then another thought occurred to her. 'Peter,' she asked, 'is there something else you're not telling me? Because if there is, I want to know it now! I'm not going to wait another six months to hear the truth. And I'm not as fragile as you think, I won't shatter into a million pieces like some china doll. Now tell me, what else is there?'

Peter looked at her with such sadness that her heart nearly broke for him. And then he sighed. 'You're right, there is more,' he said.

She took his hand in hers. 'Tell me, darling. Just say it,' she asked.

'I could be disbarred,' he said sadly. 'And then we would all be disgraced. Jonathan would have to live with the stigma that his father has committed fraud and been partly responsible for the loss of his inheritance. When Jonathan is old enough to understand all this, he's going to hate me.'

'Oh, no, Peter,' Phyllis insisted, greatly relieved by his confession. She'd thought he was going to say something much worse. 'Jonathan isn't going to hate you,' she assured him. 'How could anyone hate you, you're such a kind and gentle man. And as for the inheritance, Belson lost it long before you got involved in all his craziness. Besides, we don't need the money or the estate. We'll be all right without it. You'll earn a living at something, for heaven's sake. I can work. And as for the stigma of having a father who's made mistakes, lots of families live with that. Look at the Watergate conspirators—they're already out of prison, back in the mainstream of society; they're accepted, some of them even admired, and they've done much worse things than you have. Your mistakes are the least of our worries. What troubles me most is finding a way to reconcile you and Belson.'

Peter nodded and she put her arms around him again. 'You're right,' he said. 'That's all I care about. Grandfather has to know I didn't do any of this on purpose. He's got to forgive me. I couldn't bear it if he didn't.'

'He will,' she answered. 'We'll make him understand.'

Peter sighed. 'What would I do without you,' he said. But then sadness overcame him again. 'God, I'm so terribly sorry.'

'I know,' Phyllis said, 'I know you are.'

Vicky felt tears fill her eyes as she watched the two of them hurting so, yet loving and comforting one another. It made her think of Bob; she wished they could have that kind of love. And that thought brought a new wave of sadness to her heart. She stood up. 'I'd better go, you two. It's nearly one thirty.'

Peter untangled himself from Phyllis's arms and came over to her. 'As terrible as this has been for me tonight, Vicky, I'm glad you were here. At least now Phyllis will have someone to discuss this with, especially a loyal friend.'

Vicky couldn't help the tears in her eyes from spilling over as she hugged him. 'It's going to be all right,' she said. 'I know it is.'

But he didn't reply. Then he put his arm around her and walked her toward the door.

'I'll call you tomorrow,' Phyllis said.

Vicky opened the door, and then turned back. 'Who's going to tell Marla about Belson's losses?' she asked. 'Marla was so high tonight, thinking she was going to decorate his estate.'

But Phyllis's reply was interrupted by the phone.

The three of them froze for a moment, each feeling uneasy about a call coming at this late hour.

'I'll get it,' Peter said, walking back across the living room.

As he reached for the receiver, Vicky caught a glimpse of the back of his calves from underneath his bathrobe. They were pear-shaped and smooth and chalky white above the black of his stretch stockings. And for some reason during the rest of the night, through all the harrowing events, that image—the vulnerability of the back of his calves—stayed with her, seeming terribly poignant.

Peter picked up the receiver and listened for a moment, then he uttered a sound as though he'd been clubbed in the chest. His knees buckled and he clutched the edge of the table-desk near where he was standing.

'Peter!' Phyllis said, rushing to him. 'What is it?'

Vicky couldn't move. She felt the chill of night air from the open door against her back, tasted the acrid taste of fear in the back of her throat. Her toes were icy; her stomach fluttered.

'My grandfather's unconscious,' Peter said, turning to them in anguish. 'They think he's had a heart attack. Mr Albert was called an ambulance.' He was a frozen block of misery in a maroon robe and black stretch stockings. They stared at one another for a moment, nobody moving.

Then Vicky came to life. 'Wait here!' she commanded. She was shot through with energy as she raced up the stairs and into the master bedroom. Frantically she searched the dressing room until she found a pair of Peter's pants and his Adidas. Then she yanked open drawer after drawer until she found his sweaters while she tried to keep herself from speculating about Belson. What an incredible evening this had become. She'd found out more about Belson tonight than she'd ever wanted to know.

In a moment she was back downstairs, helping Peter into a sweater, waiting while he stepped into his pants.

'I'll call the house and ask for the car,' Phyllis said.

'No. We'll drive up,' Vicky said, taking control. 'It will save time.' Neither of them had moved since she'd commanded them to wait.

'He's got to forgive me,' Peter cried as the three of them ran out the front door.

'He will, darling; he's going to be all right,' Phyllis repeated over and over. 'He's going to be all right.'

The three of them jammed into the front seat of Vicky's 024 and she drove madly up the drive to the main house. It had only been three minutes since they'd received the phone call but every second counted.

There were so many lights blazing when they arrived that it looked like broad daylight; Mr Albert was waiting at the front door. Peter tore up the front staircase, leaping two and three stairs at a time with Phyllis close behind. Vicky hesitated only a moment and then followed them up the front stairs across the marble entry and up the main staircase; her heart was pounding. She was torn by two different emotions—her concern for her friends and her near obsessive curiosity over Belson.

The upper floors of the mansion were designed in an extremely ornate fashion. English linen-fold paneling was interspersed with antique paintings; there were rows of doorways up and down each side of the corridor and in between stood straight-back chairs and sofas. Other corridors, just as elaborate, led off in different directions. Vicky passed three different staircases, some leading up and some leading down, and of course there was the elevator, an elaborate, metal, see-through cage.

Belson's room was on the third floor. Phyllis and Peter ran down the long hallway to the double doors of the master suite past lines of servants crying and wringing their hands like peasants at a monarch's demise.

The light in the master suite was dim but Vicky could see one of the servants administering mouth-to-mouth resuscitation to Belson. It was a frightening sight, nightmarish and yet all too real. Belson's thin, pale chest, void of life, rose and fell only because of the infusion of foreign breath in his body. His eyelids were half closed, the eyeballs rolled back so the whites and only half of the irises were visible. The terrible tableau elicited a cry of anguish from Peter, chilling all their hearts.

'Grandfather,' he cried. 'Oh, God, no! Grandfather.'

Off in the distance, Vicky heard the sound of a siren, which meant the ambulance had reached Sunset Boulevard where it would turn and head up into the hills. But it could be another five minutes before it arrived. By that time Belson might be dead.

Vicky glanced around the dimly lit, cavernous room; the corners were obscured in the darkness. Odd triangular lights cast deathlike shadows on the walls; it was a gloomy place to live and an even gloomier place to die, obviously a room dominated by a formidable presence. Belson's bed was huge, set against an inlaid wood, Art Deco headboard that matched a pair of side tables and a twelve-foot-long

370

bureau on a nearby wall. The room was paneled in various shades of wood inlaid into fanlike Deco geometrics, austere and forbidding. And the furniture in an alcove across the room was huge—a sofa and two chairs—plump, round, and threatening; they looked like giant trolls ready to pounce. They made Vicky shiver.

A few servants high in the echelon of the staff and bold enough to enter the room hovered nearby. Vicky was amazed to see one or two of them tidying up at a time like this, or else they were checking around for out-of-place objects. One of the women, a young girl with long auburn hair, bent over to pick up something off the floor and Vicky caught a glimpse of a tiny, sparkling object before it disappeared into the pocket of the girl's uniform.

How odd, Vicky thought, moving nearer to that spot. And when she looked down, she saw three more green sequins lying on the floor before the same efficient hand reached down and snatched them away. Just then the servant looked up and met Vicky's gaze; Vicky was surprised to see the woman's olive skin blush and her dark Latin eyes glance away before she furtively turned and left the room.

Why was she acting so guilty? Vicky wondered. So secretive? She was actually slinking away. But then Vicky's attention was reclaimed by the tragic drama unfolding before her.

The resuscitation effort went on and on while Peter's state of agitation grew to a fever pitch. Every breath the servant breathed into Belson, Peter breathed with him. Peter patted and touched and caressed his grandfather's lifeless limbs, peering anxiously at Belson as though he were hanging over the edge of a precipice, which indeed he was, while he kept up a steady, repetitive dialogue, calling Belson's name, crooning to him, pleading with him to hang on. Mr Albert kept trying to get Peter to move away from the bed, but Peter wouldn't budge.

'Why doesn't the ambulance get here?' Phyllis cried. Vicky moved over and put an arm around her friend, who

371

was trembling with misery and praying with frantic concentration, as though her words had a direct connection with some being who could grant that her wish come true.

'Phyllis,' Vicky said softly, 'when the paramedics arrive, you and Peter go in the ambulance or else follow in my car, the keys are in it. I'll go back to your house and stay there so I can be with Jonathan when he wakes up in the morning.'

Phyllis nodded. 'Thank you,' she said. 'I'll call you as soon as there's any word.'

Just then the paramedics arrived and took over, clearing the room of spectators, continuing the mouth-to-mouth resuscitation, and applying electric pressure jolts to the heart. After a short time they brought in a stretcher, and as they moved Belson onto it, Vicky noticed he was nude. *How foolish for a man his age to be sleeping without any night clothes*, she thought. *He could catch pneumonia.* And then she realized how ridiculous that was under the circumstances.

And then they were gone; Phyllis and Peter rushed after the attendants, asking questions impossible to answer. An oxygen mask was attached to Belson's face, his heart had responded to the electric shock, but it was fibrillating and beating arhythmically. And of course he was still unconscious.

The room cleared out and Vicky found herself alone; but she couldn't bring herself to leave. The events of the past few hours had happened to quickly that there hadn't been any time to absorb them. Peter and Phyllis were suffering over Belson's condition, and she had to admit her heart had been touched by what she'd witnessed. But Belson's tragedy didn't change her opinion of him. He was still the same evil man who had once tried to ruin her.

She sat in one of the overstuffed chairs opposite the bed, trying to get her bearings, but her pulse was racing with excitement. To be alone in Belson McKintridge's huge bedroom was such an unexpected yet longed-for event, it was overwhelming to her.

She got up from the chair and walked over to the now

empty bed, a king-and-a-half. The beige sheets that matched the decor had been flung back by the paramedics and she ran her hand over the silky smooth linen; it was cold now.

Something caught her eye: a tiny sparkle glanced off the reflected glow of an overhead light. She reached over curiously and picked up another green sequin nestled among the sheets. Sequins, in bed? And then her attention was drawn to the top sheet on the bed; it had been pulled away to allow the paramedics to remove Belson and she noticed an area of discoloration; something dark was smeared there. It looked like blood. Not thick drops from a wound that would have soaked right into the fabric, but a paler smear that seemed rubbed in places. *Heart attack victims don't bleed*, she thought.

She heard someone coming then and just had time to duck back out of sight into the corner behind the open door before one of the maids entered. Vicky watched the girl walk quickly over to the bed and begin to strip the sheets. Then she gathered them up in her smooth, brown arms and left.

Vicky waited until she was gone before leaving her hiding place, then circled the room, examining everything more closely, looking at the art objects and memorabilia. There was nothing to explain the green sequins on the bed.

On her way back down the hall she stopped at each door she passed and opened them one by one, not knowing what she was looking for, but curious none the less. Each door opened into darkened, empty bedrooms. There were so many that it seemed like a hotel. And then she heard Spanish voices and footsteps approaching. She did not want to be discovered snooping around so she ducked into one of the empty bedrooms and waited until they passed.

'If someone does not get them out of here soon, we'll all be sent to jail.' A woman's voice spoke in rapid Spanish. Her accent, Vicky recognized, was Central American.

Vicky peeked through the crack in the door and saw the backs of two maids heading toward the master bedroom.

One was young, the other older; they were carrying a clean set of linens. 'It is very bad business,' the older one said to the younger, 'these little dolls.'

What is going on? Vicky wondered. Had there been foul play? Of course not, she thought. Her creative imagination was getting the best of her.

She left the safety of the darkened bedroom and continued on down the hall, opening doors, checking rooms, looking for anything of interest, anything that would give her a clue as to what happened here tonight.

She glanced at her watch. The ambulance had been gone fifteen minutes; they were probably arriving at the hospital by now. One of the servants, perhaps Mr Albert, might put two and two together and realize she hadn't left the house with the others. It wouldn't be long before they'd come looking for her.

She hurried down the corridor, away from Belson's room, and turned left into another corridor. Three steps up led to another long hallway. And if her foot hadn't slipped on the first step, she never would have looked down and discovered another green sequin. A chill ran up her spine, as though someone had left a trail for her to follow.

The hallway in front of her was empty. Dim, candle-shaped lights reminded her of a set from a Charlie Chan movie.

There were at least a dozen doors along this hall, six on each side. The hallway ended with a leaded-glass window and an antique chest beneath it.

She started opening doors one by one; each room was dark and silent. But when she closed the door to the third room on the right, she thought she heard a noise. It sounded like a sneeze. And then a rustling sound.

She let go of the doorknob as though it were alive; her heart froze and then started to pound so wildly in her chest she feared she might faint. She stood there for an eternity, listening, waiting. *Was someone hiding in there in the dark?*

Silence.

A floorboard creaked and she jumped; gooseflesh

prickled all over her skin, but the creaking floorboard was under her own foot.

Then she heard it again, another muffled sneeze.

Someone was there!

Without thinking she flung open the door and called, 'Who's there?'

The sound of three mouths gasping in shock scared her to death, even though one of those gasps was hers. She groped for a wall switch and then the room was flooded with light.

It was a guest room like all the others, double four-poster bed, French armoire, faded toile fabrics, a chair with lace doilies on its arms and back, and deteriorating swagged draperies above the windows. But this room was different; it was occupied.

Sitting on the planked wooden floor huddled together in front of the bed were two nearly naked children, little girls about ten or eleven, shaking from the chill. Their faces were absurdly made up like a younger version of Brooke Shields on the cover of *Vogue*, their bare feet dirty from a chronic lack of washing, and they held the remains of a sequined stripper's outfit clutched in their hands. In one glance Vicky saw it all: the blood smeared on the insides of their thighs, the streaked makeup worsened by tears, red gashes of lipstick across tender mouths on scared olive-skinned faces, the pitiful children's breasts pinched from the cold and covered with hickeys. Two pairs of eyes stared at her glazed in shock, black with fear and despair. Their stringy dark hair had been teased and sprayed in an obscene rendition of Brigitte Bardot when it should have been combed with pigtails and braids.

Both children started to cry when they saw Vicky; so did she.

So this is what killed you, Belson, you bastard, she wept. *You deserve to die. I spit on your grave.*

Just then someone came rushing past her into the room. A young Latin man, his arms filled with blankets, seemed shocked to see her. He glanced at the children and then started yelling at Vicky in Spanish. 'You want to stay alive, lady? You get out of here. You forget this. These girls have thirteen brothers and sisters. They will all go back to San Salvador and die there if you tell anyone about this.'

Vicky was shaking. 'Who are you? What are you doing with these children?' she demanded. But he didn't answer, just crossed to the children, put the large tattered quilts he'd been carrying around their shoulders, and picked them up in his arms. The children offered no resistance but curled up like pathetic little kittens, one head on each of his shoulders, and then they were gone, down one of the many back staircases into the bowels of the mansion.

Vicky felt sick. She could feel her stomach start to heave as the cold, clammy sweats engulfed her body. Waves of sickness came shooting up from her stomach, moving up in hot burning flames to her throat. But she fought it back with all her might. She couldn't give in to nausea and sickness now. She had to stay clearheaded, think of what to do.

Out into the night she walked, thinking that if she didn't get into a bath soon the filth around her would corrode into her like acid. It would take hours of scrubbing to get herself clean. And she had to think this through. She had to get a perspective on it. When she thought about those children, it filled her with an aching pain. She imagined what it would have been like to be in Belson's clutches at ten years old, the terror those children must have experienced tonight. And then the memory of Belson's display of righteous indignation when he'd caught her and Peter together that night so long ago overwhelmed her. Oh, God, how she'd suffered because of that man, and look at what he was!

It was halfway between Phyllis's house and the main house that her control broke and she burst into deep, wrenching sobs. The pain was so severe, she thought she'd never live through it. If Belson didn't die tonight, she was afraid she might actually kill him.

376

Chapter 8

LARRY HAD been waiting two hours for Peter and Phyllis by the time they came home from the hospital. Both of them looked exhausted; Phyllis was glad to see him.

'How good of you to be here, Larry,' she said, embracing him.

'Are you all right?' he asked, and she nodded.

'Peter?' he inquired. But one look at Peter's accusatory expression told him Peter wasn't all right, and Larry's heart sank. Peter's ravaged face was etched with pain over Belson's death but Larry could tell that Peter was angry with him. It was obvious that Peter didn't want to talk in front of Phyllis.

'I came over to help with the funeral arrangements.'

'That won't be necessary,' Peter said curtly. 'Mr Albert is coming down here in a few minutes to go to the mortuary with me.'

'Pete,' Larry said softly, 'I want to help.'

A flash of anger flared in Peter's eyes and then it was gone, suffocated by exhaustion.

Phyllis put her hand on Peter's arm and he turned to her. 'Let him help you, darling. You can't do it all alone.'

Peter gave a slight shrug indicating acquiescence and she kissed him on the cheek. 'I'm going to take a bath,' she said. 'Will you be all right?'

Peter nodded. 'Why don't you try and get some sleep?'

'Maybe I will,' she agreed, turning toward the stairs.

But as soon as she was out of sight, Peter turned to Larry, only this time the anger Larry had only glimpsed gathered up and exploded. 'You Judas!' he said. 'I swore you to secrecy. You gave me your word and it was worthless. Worthless! Do you realize what you've done? Do you know? Do you?'

'Peter, I'm sorry,' Larry began.

But Peter cut him off. 'Save it, you rat. Just save it. How could you do such a thing?'

'You mean because I told Felix about the platinum scheme?'

A terrible silence hung between them, and then Peter said, 'Felix went right to the CFTC and told them everything you told him. The bottom has fallen out of platinum and I think that shock is what killed my grandfather.'

'Felix did what?' Larry exclaimed with disbelief.

'Oh, what's the use?' Peter said, his eyes filling with tears. 'My grandfather's dead and it's *my* fault, not yours. I shouldn't have trusted you in the first place. I just didn't know you had such a big mouth.'

'Oh, Peter, I'm sorry,' Larry said. 'Please listen to me. I had no idea Felix would do that. He promised to help you. I was worried about you, that's why I went to him.'

'You were worried about yourself, and you wanted to make points with Felix,' Peter said.

Larry realized the truth in what Peter was saying. 'I guess you're right about that,' he admitted. 'But I was honestly worried about you too. God, I could kick myself for telling him. I never thought he'd do such a thing.'

'He's always hated my grandfather, but I thought he cared about me, that he wouldn't want to hurt me. I was very wrong.'

'Does Phyllis know?'

'No!' Peter said. 'And I don't want her to know. She'd only be hurt, and right now she's suffering enough because of me. There's no need to add to her burden.'

'How did you find out it was Felix who informed on you?'

Peter's hands were trembling so badly that he had to clutch them around his chest to try and control them. He could barely speak. 'Felix told my grandfather last night at

378

your party. My grandfather stopped by here on his way home and told me.' Peter's voice cracked.

'Jesus, God,' Larry said. 'That must have been rough.'

Peter looked away, his tears spilling over as he nodded. And then sobs overtook him. But he seemed almost too exhausted to cry anymore. 'He died hating me, Larry. He hated me so much, he said he was going to take me out of his will.'

Larry felt so helpless. He didn't know how to comfort his friend. And he felt terribly responsible. 'Have you spoken to Felix?'

'No. He and Audrey took their boat down to Ensenada late last night after your dinner party. We've sent word to them through the Coast Guard.'

'I can't wait to get my hands on Felix,' Larry said. 'What a liar he is! You should have heard him professing his deep concern for you, promising me he'd never do anything to jeopardize you or Phyllis. I'd like to wipe the floor with him!'

'No.' Peter shook his head. 'Stay out of it with Felix. This is something I have to do myself.'

'All right,' Larry said. 'And what about the investigation? What happens now?'

Peter shrugged, his expression helpless, beaten. 'I don't know.'

'I'll take care of it,' Larry insisted. 'You go to the mortuary with Mr Albert and I'll start calling people and see if we can come up with a defense. Was Belson using counsel?'

'Yes. Frank Wicks, but he's not a securities specialist.'

'I'll call him. Maybe he can recommend someone.'

Peter looked at him gratefully. 'Thanks,' he said.

'Please,' Larry replied. 'It's the least I can do.'

Chapter 9

MARLA HAD a sick knot in the pit of her stomach as she
closed the front door of her house and set out to walk to the
Episcopal church on Santa Monica; death had placed its
cold hand in hers and would not let her go. But she would
walk slowly to delay arriving at an event she didn't want to
attend. Funerals were like swallowing castor oil, bitter to
take even though it was for your own good, and afterward
you were proud of yourself for getting through the uncomfortable moments.

Her thoughts were of momentous things. How inescapable was death, how momentary and fleeting was life, and
how crucial it seemed to her to straighten out her own life as
soon as possible. She was embarrassed to admit it even to
herself, in view of the very great loss her friends had endured, but she was bitterly disappointed about losing the
McKintridge estate. It had almost been hers; she'd held
that wondrous palace in her hands before it slipped away,
the shortest dream-come-true in history. That dream had
lasted all of eight hours from the time Belson left her house
the night before last and she'd gone to sleep floating on a
cloud, until seven o'clock yesterday morning when Vicky
called to tell them the sad news of Belson's death and the
devastating condition of his finances. Marla had gone to
sleep believing she'd been given a crown of glory, a plum
that would make her world-famous, and awakened to find
she was only Marla Gilbert who'd been fired from her job
by a vicious, vindictive boss and there were no prospects in
sight. And yet her self-pity seemed indulgent in view of

Phyllis and Peter's plight. If it was a shock to her to lose the promise of the estate—and she'd never really had it— imagine how Phyllis and Peter felt about literally losing it. They were experiencing the Beverly Hills version of *Great Expectations*.

It was warm, she noticed as she walked, and a beautiful day, the kind that usually filled her with joy. But today's strong sunlight was harsh as it filtered through the thin layer of smog. And even though the edges of the bushy eucalyptus trees and the tall slender palms were softened by the mantle of unhealthful air that hovered over them, everything around her appeared in relief; the buildings, the trees, the cars, were etched sharply against a background of sadness. Belson McKintridge was dead and the beauty of life did not bring joy on the day of his funeral.

Two rows of limousines ringed the block around the church; police directed the heavy traffic crawling by as the curious craned their necks to see the famous mourn one of their own. Governors, former governors, movie moguls, major and minor stars, financiers, and even an ex-president mingled with one another, looking somber and sad. Belson McKintridge had known everyone.

'Step ahead, miss,' the guard at the door told her. But Marla looked around until she spotted a sign that directed her to the family room and headed in that direction. It was a small private alcove situated on the same level as the podium, separated from the clergy and the casket by a low wall and a sheer curtain. The casket was covered with a blanket of roses and surrounded by enormous baskets of flowers, their heavy scent slightly unpleasant.

Phyllis, seated in the front pew, turned and beckoned, smiling her soft, angelic smile. Marla came forward and was engulfed by the familiar aroma of L'Air du Temps. Even the somberness of today's event hadn't dimmed Phyllis's beauty, a young Grace Kelly at a state function, though her face was drawn with grief. Peter's face was pasty and gray, with none of his usual animation; even his soft dark eyes looked dead, ringed with dark circles and red from crying. But then Peter hadn't looked well in ages. Now they all knew why; he'd been going through the motions of living while covering up a deep despair. What a strain it must have been on him. Marla kissed him; his breath had that sickening sweet odor of someone who hasn't eaten lately. He needed a haircut—the delicate reddish-brown hair had grown slightly down over his ears and collar. But even more than his expression of pain, he seemed to be a vulnerable lost boy and she pitied that boy today with all her heart.

She looked around for Felix, wanting and yet not wanting to see him. 'Did your parents get back from their fishing trip?' she asked Phyllis, and then spotted Audrey Anhalt sitting at the end of her pew with two of Phyllis's cousins. Audrey gave her a brief wave.

'They docked early this morning,' Phyllis said. 'It was too bad they had to cut their trip short for such a sad occasion. No sooner did they reach Ensenada than they had to turn around and come back.'

'Where's your father?' Marla asked.

'Dad's out front checking on arrangements. He'll be in here later.'

Where else would Felix be but out front, Marla thought, where he would be the most visible, the most indispensable, and the least comforting to those who needed him. She was curious to know how Felix felt about the incredible events of the past few days. She was certain he hadn't minded cutting short his fishing trip with Audrey for the occasion of Belson's funeral. He would not have missed that.

Peter reached over and took his wife's hand. Marla saw tears in Phyllis's eyes. Belson McKintridge had been one of a kind. He was the most famous person she'd ever known and the world would never see the likes of him again. What was it he used to say to her? 'You're looking scrumptious, my dear.' And even at his age he'd made her feel scrumptious. Oh, she wished to God she'd never invited him to dinner two nights ago. Perhaps he'd still be alive today.

He'd been so happy that night, so vital, and so generous, giving gifts he no longer possessed.

Marla leaned forward and gripped Phyllis's shoulder in sympathy; Phyllis gave her hand a grateful return squeeze. Then the soft background organ music changed to something more salutatory and the minister stepped through a curtain onto the podium, taking his place next to the flower-covered casket.

A sudden burst of sunlight filled the family room as the door in the back opened and then closed. Larry slid in next to her, giving her a peck on the cheek.

'It's a madhouse out there,' he whispered, leaning over to kiss Phyllis. He and Peter grasped hands.

Marla felt better now that Larry was here, her anchor to reality, and she took his hand in hers, trying to make him feel the importance of their need for one another, if only for today. She was acutely aware of what a momentous event a funeral was: it underscored the banding together of human beings at an age-old ritual; the touch and embrace of those you loved held special significance and reminded you of their preciousness. But even a brief friendly truce between her and Larry did not mean a peace treaty had been signed, and he removed his hand.

'There are people on the sidewalks still waiting to get in, but the funeral people thought we should get started.'

'Have you been out there with Felix all this time?' she asked, feeling an acute loss at the withdrawal of his touch.

'No, I wasn't with Felix,' he snapped. 'He's your *friend*. Though I'd advise you not to have anything to do with him anymore.' His expression was grim at the mention of Felix's name.

'Why?' she asked sharply, her heart reacting wildly to his comment. Did he know? she wondered.

Larry leaned over and spoke close to her ear. 'It was Felix who informed on Belson and Peter to the Commodity Futures Trading Commission. If he hadn't done that, Peter wouldn't be in nearly as much trouble as he is.'

Her heart fell to her stomach and lay there like an injured

bird. 'I don't believe it,' she insisted.

He shot her a bitter look. 'It's true, damn it,' he insisted.

She felt sick inside from what he had told her. 'Does Phyllis know?' she asked.

He shook his head no.

Phyllis's back had stiffened at the sound of their bickering and Marla indicated it with a tilt of her head. Larry nodded and straightened up in his seat. She reached for his hand again and this time he didn't pull away. Instead he moved closer and put his arm around her shoulders. The significance of where they were had finally overcome petty considerations for him too, and in that moment she felt a rush of love for him, the kind she hadn't felt in a very long time. How could Felix have done such a thing? she wondered. And then she felt shame for having been the mistress of such a man.

A woman's voice singing a hymn interrupted her thoughts and she gave herself to the music. But just then the door to the family room opened once more, filling it with daylight, breaking her concentration as Felix took his seat at the end of the pew next to his wife. He nodded to Marla but she just stared at him until he looked away. She waited for that old familiar jolt of excitement to course through her as it usually did when she saw him, but this time there was nothing but disgust. *Am I over him?* she wondered. *Really through?* And then she looked at the back of Phyllis's head, saw Peter's profile as he cried for his grandfather, and knew that Felix held no special fascination for her anymore.

'Is Leslie here?' she asked Peter.

'Of course. She wouldn't miss gloating today. She and the sheikh are outside.'

'Oh, God, Larry. I'm afraid to face her.'

'Don't worry, baby,' he said. 'You haven't done anything; it's she who acted like a witch.'

Marla was grateful for his understanding. 'I wish things hadn't turned out the way they did.'

He nodded.

384

She leaned over and whispered in his ear. 'What is Peter going to do about the estate?'

'I don't know yet,' he whispered, indicating for her to be quiet, as the minister was about to begin. 'We're working on it, though.'

Larry and Peter had closeted themselves for hours yesterday trying to assess how Belson's death would affect Peter in light of the investigation. Larry had been studying alternative choices, gathering data, making appointments with brokers and market experts, and generally trying to be helpful. He was so devoted it was as if he were trying to make up for something. Marla suspected he was very worried about his own position. Yet he had not deserted Peter, nor had he criticized him for his gigantic screw-up, and this was one time Marla wouldn't have blamed Larry if he had. Peter's actions had placed Larry's reputation in jeopardy and it was magnanimous of Larry to stick by his friend under the circumstances. That more than anything else Larry had ever done endeared him to her.

Even on this day of sadness Marla was excited about going to the McKintridge estate, although she didn't want to run into Felix and hoped he wouldn't have the nerve to show up there.

She and Larry drove up the winding drive and parked where the attendant indicated, joining the crowd of people slowly approaching the front steps where Phyllis and Peter waited to greet everyone. The manor still evoked an aura of fairy-tale castles, knights and ladies, European royalty, and a life-style fit for the movies or heroines of romantic novels. And even though its master had died in debt, today the place shimmered with beauty and opulence.

Caterers had set up an enormous spread on the table in the dining hall, a room that duplicated the dining hall at Versailles and was nearly as large. A handwoven lace tablecloth made in Belgium expressly for this table lent a rich background to the cold meats, fruit, molds, hors d'oeuvres, sliced breads, cheese wheels, salads, and condiments arranged there. On a sideboard coffee, tea, and an obscene amount of rich desserts were arranged. Marla took a small piece of turkey meat and a thin slice of Swiss cheese and forced herself to leave the room. One more minute and the chocolate Bavarian or the raspberry tart topped with kiwi would have undone a week of starvation. A bartender approached her and she requested a diet drink, watching others tossing off salted nuts and sipping hugely caloric cocktails. It made her sick with envy.

Just then Felix passed by and winked at her, but she just glared at him. There was no thudding of her heart, no roller coaster drop of her equilibrium. The information Larry had told her about him had finally made her see the reality of the man, and the reality was much stronger than the fantasy. She remembered the last time she'd been with him, how used she'd felt, how discarded. His business deal with Larry had been far more important to him than her sensibilities, yet her entire life could have been ruined if Larry had discovered her on Felix's boat. And what he had done to his son-in-law and his own daughter turned her stomach. He was not one of the good guys, not at all. *It's about time, Marla,* she told herself. *It's about time.* And she broke out into a joyous grin. The relief was so great it almost made her cry, the magical lifting of a ton of guilt.

She spotted Vicky across the room, wearing an emerald green dress, looking like a femme fatale version of Peter Pan. But Marla turned away before Vicky saw her. For some reason she didn't want to talk to her right now. Vicky had a way of getting to the heart of a matter and Marla felt too vulnerable to be questioned. And besides Vicky hadn't been herself for the past two days. She wore a tortured expression on her face that was a cross between sickness and fury, as though she were about to explode. Marla had been so busy and preoccupied she hadn't really taken note of it. But now, seeing her across the room with that strange look in her eyes, Marla recognized it with a jolt. Vicky *was* tortured. And that was odd, because there had never been any love lost between her and Belson.

She saw Larry heading toward the front door and hurried to intercept him. She wanted him to stay and be with her. They had so much to say to one another.

'Where are you going?' she said, catching his arm.

'Back to the office. I have a meeting at four o'clock.'

'But . . . Peter needs you.' She was afraid he wouldn't stay just for her.

'That's why I'm having the meeting, for Peter. I can do more for him by trying to find a way to get him out of his mess than by sitting around here socializing. I hate these phony events anyway.'

'It's not a phony event, it's a funeral reception. People have a need to express their feelings of sorrow to the family when there's a death. It's comforting to everyone.'

'Sure. People like Leslie and Sheikh Ammani and Felix really need comforting, don't they? I'm telling you, Marla, very few of these people are sorry Belson died. They're here for a free lunch.'

'Well, I liked him,' she said defensively.

'You would.'

'Oh, please don't be sarcastic now,' she said.

'It just turns my stomach to see you fawning all over the man because he's dead,' Larry said. 'He was a *shit*, Marla. Just like your friend Felix. And if that's who you choose to like, then I don't want to stay around and see it, okay?'

'What's the matter, Larry?' she retorted, caught again by his baited hook. 'Aren't there enough contacts here for you today?' She swept her arm around, indicating a crowd of Beverly Hills's most prominent citizens. 'Isn't this what you're always looking for? New ways to make social inroads in today's upwardly mobile society?'

'You're really something, aren't you,' he retorted. 'I should think you'd be afraid to show your face around here. Two nights ago your majesty finally deigned to give a dinner party and what happened? The guest of honor went home and died of a heart attack.'

Marla stared at him, struck by the cruelty of his remark. What a low blow. How many times had she blamed herself since the awful news of Belson's death? And even though the doctors assured her that nothing he'd eaten at her home had caused his death, the thought gnawed at her constantly. 'You can really be disgusting sometimes,' she said, and turned and walked away. She was banking on the large crowd of people to prevent him from causing a scene. If they had been alone, this would have been an opening for hours of fighting. How much longer could they go on like this? She felt like crying. This wasn't a marriage, it was a battleground. And she'd been so hopeful, so loving, wanting to find a way to begin a reconciliation. Now that seemed impossible.

The door closed after him and she longed to call him back. They had to face what they were doing to one another. Enough of exchanging mortal wounds. She wanted to make a new start; she would tell him she loved him and wanted only him.

But, oh, that thought filled her with dread and a sudden chill of terrible fear.

What if she told him she wanted him, and he didn't want her?

Chapter 10

VICKY'S FEELINGS of fury and her state of misery hadn't dissipated one bit over the past two days; if anything she was even more agitated than she'd been the night Belson died. The knowledge of his disgusting acts preyed on her the longer she contained it, though she tried everything to forget. She'd kept herself frantically busy, managing to avoid Phyllis and Peter in the process with excuses like,

'I'm checking on the guest list,' or 'I have to play with Jonathan,' or 'I'm wanted on the phone.' Vicky thought if she were alone with Phyllis without telling her what she knew, she'd jump out of her skin. And it was all Belson's fault, damn his blackened soul. Whenever the minister spouted platitudes at the funeral today about how upstanding a citizen Belson had been, what a pillar of the community, what a revered family man, and how bravely he'd suffered so many personal tragedies and losses, she wanted to stand up and scream out the truth. That there were two children somewhere right now suffering irreparable damage because of the torture they'd met at the hands of Belson McKintridge. And she felt completely trapped in pretense and lies, damned if she told the world because of what it would do to Peter and Phyllis, and damned if she didn't because Belson would go off into history unsullied.

She wandered around the reception, gratified for the cover of people, avoiding those she knew, dreading the time when everyone would leave and she would be alone with Peter and Phyllis.

Deep in thought, she suddenly felt the touch of a hand on her shoulder and jumped with a start.

'Hey,' Bob said. 'I'm sorry if I scared you. I only wanted to see how you were.'

There was genuine concern in his eyes and she was so glad to see him she nearly threw her arms around him. But then she remembered what happened the last time they were together, and all the lonely days in between, plus the things she'd heard about him from Larry, and her gladness turned to pain.

'I'm all right, I suppose. But I can't say the same for you. It seems you've lost your patron and source of income. How will you ever support yourself now that Belson is dead? Join the law firm of O'Melveny and Myers?'

Bob just looked at her with that infuriating cool of his and said, 'I've missed you. Can we talk?'

'Certainly we can talk,' she snapped. 'The frontal lobe of the cerebrum conceives of word patterns, transmits them by electrical impulse to the section of the brain near the central fissure controlling body movements, which in turn transmits them to the nerve center in the medulla oblongata and then to our larynx, tongue, and mouth. We amazing humans, we advanced species of *homo sapiens* spend the early months of our formative years babbling gibberish and goo-gooing at everybody just so we can grow up and learn to say, *fuck you!*' She turned and walked away, dodging through the crowd of people around her.

He caught up with her at the door of the dining room and grabbed her arm. 'I want to apologize, Vicky. I know I owe it to you.'

'A smart lawyer like yourself, a graduate of Berkeley and of Boalt Law School, should be able to figure out a better way to do things than merely apologizing.' There were firecrackers of anger in her brain, exploding sparks that popped each time one was ignited, and the match that lit each fuse was every memory of him lying to her. And then, as fast as her anger flared it was gone. She felt burned out. 'A flash in the pan is all I am,' she said and shocked herself by bursting into tears. He put his arm around her and pulled her to him, holding her until it passed, until that tight knot of pain had unraveled inside. It felt so good to be in his arms she never wanted to leave. But then Bob took her hand and led her outside onto the terrace overlooking the outdoor pool. This was the exact place she'd come so many years ago with Peter. She remembered the way she'd felt the first time with Peter walking down these wide terrace steps, as though she were on her way to a bridal bower, for that's what she had believed that night, that she was becoming a bride in the biblical sense. How stupidly naive and romantic she had been. She turned away from the pool and leaned back against the balustrade, steeling herself for what was ahead, wishing his arms were still around her.

'Why don't you just start talking, and I'll listen,' she said.

He leaned forward over the balustrade next to her, his elbows supporting his upper body. He looked wonderful in his navy blue three-piece suit and wine-colored tie; his white duck's loss was the navy suit's gain, but she'd be damned if she'd tell him so.

'First of all, I'm sorry I hurt you.'

She didn't reply but it was a good beginning.

'I wanted to tell you many times what I was doing—you deserved to know—but I couldn't betray my client's trust. If I had, no one would ever hire me again.' He took a deep breath and let it out slowly. 'But I can tell you now that I was an investigator working undercover at the McKintridge estate. I was hired to find out anything I could about Belson.'

She looked at him in shocked surprise. 'You're an investigator? A private dick? But Larry Gilbert said you were a lawyer. I thought you might have failed the bar exam.'

He shook his head. 'No, I never took the bar.'

'But you did go to law school?'

'Yes,' he admitted.

She was ashamed of the sudden rush of relief that swept through her to find he was not a masseur, but shock waves still reverberated in her brain, questions bumped into themselves right and left like a Super Ball bouncing loose in a handball court. 'Why couldn't you have told me? I wouldn't have told anyone. I knew you were too smart to be a masseur. Something didn't jibe! If you hadn't been capable of more, I'd have understood, but you are capable, *too* damned smart.'

'The masseur part was a point of honor with me,' he explained. 'I didn't like it that you seemed to want me to meet certain economic and social criteria to fall in love with me. I really care for you, Vicky, but I don't want to be pigeonholed into your mold, the cute, Jewish lawyer, with a career in investigation. I'm still *me*. I've still done all the things I said I've done, and then some. I was in the Peace Corps, I was in Katmandu, I did some boxing. I just didn't go to Valley College.' He paused, watching for a sympathetic expression on her face, but she was still wary. 'I'm not practicing law because when I graduated I wasn't ready to settle into a dead-end existence. There were too many things I wanted to do and I was afraid if I went to work as a lawyer, I'd never be able to give it up. Yet most lawyers I knew were unhappy practicing law.'

'And now?'

'Now I'm back. I'm taking things slowly. I'm thinking of taking the bar refresher course and going for the next exam. But I like investigative work; maybe I should find a way to combine both careers.'

'An undercover narc who can defend the creeps he nabs and give them a rubdown at the same time.' She chuckled, and he laughed with her. 'But why couldn't you tell me?' she asked, growing serious again. 'I would have kept the secret. You know how I felt about Belson.' The statement made her shudder.

'You're Phyllis and Peter's close friend. I couldn't take the chance.'

She had to admire his high standards. 'You know what galls me is that you accused me of exploiting you, of trying to find out about Belson through your relationship with him when that's exactly what you were doing.'

He dropped his head in his hands. 'I know. That was a tough one. But I wasn't sure you cared about me personally. I was afraid you were only with me because of my place on Belson's staff.'

His words stopped her for a moment. Hadn't she started out that way? Tricking him into a meeting, trying to exploit him? But then he had turned out to be so delicious and all the other aspects became secondary. Yet he had known what she was after; she'd told him herself. No wonder he didn't trust her.

'Did you ever find what you were looking for in Belson's life?' she asked.

He straightened up and looked into her eyes. 'Are you asking for your sake, or mine?'

She flushed. 'I deserved that,' she said. 'But I was asking for your sake.'

'Yes,' he replied. 'I found out enough to make one hell of

392

a sundae, complete with hot fudge and whipped cream. Only someone else provided the cherry.'

All of a sudden it began to make sense to her, the things Peter had revealed the night Belson died. She didn't like what she was thinking. 'Was it you who Peter turned to for advice about Belson's platinum investments?'

'You know about that?' he asked.

She nodded.

'No,' he said. 'I never spoke to Peter, I don't even know him. But he's the one who inadvertently provided the cherry for the sundae by confiding in the wrong person.'

'But the information you obtained for the man who hired you was used against Peter at the CFTC.'

Bob glanced away from her accusing eyes. 'I would say that is partially accurate. I was after Belson and Peter unfortunately got in the way.'

'Unfortunately,' she retorted. 'Don't you feel guilty for what you've done?'

'No, Vicky. I only uncovered an existing situation. I didn't create it.'

'Can you tell me who your client was?'

He shook his head. 'No, I still can't tell you.'

She decided not to pursue it right now. 'I feel terribly sorry for Peter, but Belson got what he deserved.'

'I suppose so, but I never found Belson to be as bad as you thought he was.'

'That is so infuriating,' she said, almost shouting. 'You don't know, you just don't know!' She was shaking, so he put his arm around her again to calm her, but it didn't help.

'What is it, Vicky?' he asked. 'What don't I know?'

Her expression was a mixture of pain and fury. 'How can I trust you after all you've done? What's to prevent you from running to your client with this too?'

'I don't blame you for doubting me,' he said softly. 'But I'll keep your confidence. And I'm no longer employed by that person.'

There was something in his eyes that made her feel she could trust him. And right now she needed to feel that very badly. And so she told him about her experience the night of Belson's death.

Bob's face grew grim as he listened, interrupting every now and then with a question. When he had heard it all, he said, 'You poor kid. What a burden you've had to bear. And what a bastard that man was! It infuriates me.'

Vicky was grateful for his anger against Belson. 'I wish Belson had lived, just so he could have paid for his crimes.'

'But it's not too late. When you tell the police about what happened, they'll question Belson's servants and I'm sure they'll locate that child slaver who supplied the victims. At least the public image of Belson would be tarnished.'

'No!' she insisted, amazed that he would make such a suggestion, as if he hadn't been listening to her. 'Don't you see what that would do to Phyllis and Peter?'

'It would be hard on them, certainly. But you can't keep quiet about this just to protect them. A criminal will go free. You don't want that, do you?'

'I don't know what I want,' she said. 'This has been the most difficult decision of my life.'

'But the longer you wait, the better the man's chances are of getting away. Don't you know that?'

'I only know I don't want it to become public knowledge. Once the police know, the papers are certain to find out.'

Bob's eyes narrowed as he watched her. 'What are you really saying, Vicky? That you want this information exclusively for yourself so you can use it in your book?'

'What?' She was stunned by his accusation, wounded by his words. 'I would never do that,' she retorted hotly. 'I told you I'm protecting my friends. And it's even more necessary now because of what you've done to them with your investigations. So don't preach to me about ulterior motives.'

'Oh, come now,' he said. 'Weren't you a little bit glad to have this knowledge all to yourself? Isn't this exactly the prize piece of gold you've been looking for to shine up your book?'

Vicky could barely breathe. 'You unmitigated ass!

394

You've lied, and you've used people, and you've pretended to be somthing you're not, and you have the nerve to accuse me of feathering my own nest. Well, maybe I will use this piece of filth to my own advantage—and it is a piece of filth—and maybe I won't use it. But if I do, it will be a long time from now, after Peter and Phyllis have a chance to recover from your dirty deeds. And who would be more sympathetic toward them in revealing this information, me or the eleven o'clock news?'

They glared at one another until finally he said, 'You would, I suppose.'

'I told you I was in conflict over this, and I am. But, damn it, why shouldn't I want to benefit from my own experiences. It's my life too!'

'Because your values are still fucked, kid. You're fooling yourself if you think you're only worried about Phyllis and Peter.'

'No,' she insisted. 'You're wrong.'

'I don't think so,' he said, and turned to walk back to the house.

Vicky watched him go and felt the bottom drop out; disappointment flooded her. He'd done it again, shot her to hell. What a self-righteous bastard. How could she have thought she loved him? *love*—the mere thought of the word made her cringe. But why had he attacked her like that? Why had he been so bullheaded and unfair? It wasn't like him, not the Bob she knew. Maybe she didn't know him at all. Had she actually loved him? Yes, damn it, she had. And she still did. And for some reason they had alienated one another at the very moment they were closest to getting back together. He was no better than she, pushing away from himself that which he wanted the most, like the scientist in *Altered States*. And suddenly she hated him, and she hated herself, and she hated Belson, and she hated everyone else in the whole damn world!

Chapter 11

THERE WAS a cocoon of numbness surrounding Phyllis, an unreal state dulling her otherwise sharply focused awareness. But this morphinized desensitized condition was as uncomfortable for her as the full force of pain from which it protected her. Yet she knew that as soon as it was gone and reality flooded back again, she'd have to cope with so many issues she didn't dare contemplate them. Already the staff of the mausoleum Peter's grandfather had built were turning to her for answers, for advice, for instructions. She longed to shout, 'Don't ask me, I don't know!' But she was too well bred to display her temper to servants. So she did the best she could and coped. They were all in a state of distress about their futures. Many of the staff had been with Belson for years. Who else could they turn to but her? They were comfortable here, well paid, and not anxious to move on. But they would have to go, and soon. Yet they could postpone that reality at least for a short time, until it was less painful to absorb. She hoped Peter would do that too, and not be so hard on himself. If only he would let circumstances evolve as they must and not rush into the fray with his lance raised, especially since he'd just received such wounding blows. But Peter had not shown sensible behavior in a long time. And she felt helpless to do anything about it. If only she could help him bear his burden, share his pain. But he was overwhelmed by it and she was actually afraid for him. She didn't see how anyone could survive and still bear the kind of grief Peter carried; it terrified her to watch him.

She made her way through the public rooms of the mansion, accepting polite nods and pats on the back from their guests while she looked for Peter. She smiled and conversed and listened to condolence messages, but Peter was nowhere to be found, so she went to look for him upstairs.

He was in Belson's suite, sitting at the foot of Belson's bed, staring into space. It was the first time she'd been in this room since that terrible night and a rush of unpleasant memories hit her. The room had always depressed her, as though it were a forbidden lair, a vestige of the past containing a touch of malevolence.

At first she thought Peter was gazing at the family photographs on the bureau, but then she realized his eyes were focused inward on his own deep pain. The stylized portraits of family members twinkled in their ornate silver frames. There were pictures of Peter as a child with his sister and parents in front of the propeller plane that cost them their lives; one of Belson on a movie set; a lovely smiling portrait of Sherryn, gazing with a soft-eyed expression; and another of Belson's two daughters, Peter's Aunt Margie and Peter's mother, Jo Ann, whom they'd named Jonathan after.

Peter noticed her looking at the pictures. 'All dead,' he whispered.

'What?' he said.

'I said, they're all dead. I'm the only one left now.' His voice broke and he started to cry again, an empty, helpless sound. She sat down and put her arms around him while he leaned against her shoulder.

'Phyl, Phyl, I'm so alone. It hurts so much. He was so disappointed in me. Grandfather asked me to help him, he needed me and I let him down. He couldn't trust me. And he was so angry. Oh, God,' he cried with deep, heart-wrenching sobs, 'I want to tell him I'm sorry. But I can't tell him now. I want to tell him, please let me tell him.'

'Oh, Peter,' she cried. 'He knows how you feel. He knows you are strong, and trustworthy. He didn't mean the things he said that night, he didn't mean them.'

Peter pulled away, his eyes red and puffy, his face flooded with misery. 'You don't understand. He *did* mean them. He meant every word. And I'm finally beginning to realize why. He just didn't love me. I tried to do everything right my whole life. I tried to get him to love me, but nothing I ever did was right. Why didn't he, Phyllis? Did he blame me? Did he know? It wasn't my fault. He died before he knew how much he meant to me.'

'Of course it wasn't your fault, Peter,' she soothed.

'All my life I tried . . . but he didn't love me,' he repeated. 'And I don't blame him. He knew I wasn't good enough for you.' His last words trailed off into deep, wracking sobs.

Phyllis felt her heart wrenching at the sound of his pain. *Dear God,* she prayed. *It's not fair. He's so good, so dear. Let him find the comfort he deserves. Let him know how much I love him.*

She put her arms around his bowed shoulders again but he shrugged her away, too deep in self-loathing even to accept her touch. And so she sat waiting for his grief to subside, wondering what had happened to her perfect, idyllic life. Then gently she reached out and touched him again. This time he didn't pull away. *He'll be all right,* she thought. *Grief has to run its course and then he'll be all right.* But her confidence was badly shaken when she looked around the huge, oppressive room and realized what a legacy they had to contend with.

A few moments later they were interrupted by a knock at the door. Felix's voice called out. 'May I come in?'

Peter stiffened in her arms as though he were warding off a blow, but Phyllis called, 'Yes, Dad. We're here.' Eagerly she beckoned to her father to come into the room. Perhaps he would be able to help Peter combat this awful misery in which he was caught. She smiled at her father and he gave her a tilt of his head, indicating for her to leave him alone with Peter. She nodded and gave Peter a kiss. 'I'm going back downstairs, dear. But you stay up here as long as you need to.'

There was something in Peter's posture that almost kept her from leaving him as he clutched her hand, trying to keep her there; he looked as though he were about to face the devil himself. But she knew it was only grief making him so dependent and so she left him with her father.

Peter heard Phyllis leave the room and with his entire being he wanted her to stay. There was no worse time in the world for him to be alone with Felix than now. But here they were, just the two of them; he could not avoid it. So he searched himself for some inner strength with which to confront his father-in-law. But his body felt jellylike, empty and weak, and his heart held only sadness. There was no residual well of self-belief from which to draw, only a feeling of righteous indignation, and at this moment in his weakened state even that was deserting him. He was no match for the man standing in front of him in the gray worsted suit, even though he'd have to try to be, if only for his grandfather's memory. He clutched the edge of the coverlet underneath him as if to derive courage from the place where his grandfather had slept for so many years. And then he looked up, expecting to see the evil leer of a gleeful enemy.

But Felix's face was guileless. Peter saw only concern and sympathy. It was so unexpected that he was dumb-struck.

Felix spoke first. 'I'm so sorry for you, son,' he said with complete sincerity. 'I know what this loss means to you. I remembered how devastated I felt when my own father died.' And he reached out to touch Peter's shoulder.

Peter recoiled as if he'd been burned, finally finding his voice. 'I can't believe you are real. After what you've done you come here offering sympathy?'

Felix's expression was genuinely bewildered. And then he understood Peter's reference. 'Oh, you mean because I informed the Commodity Futures Trading Commission about Belson's activities?'

'You admit it?' Peter's voice was hoarse with incredulity.

'You're not even going to bother to deny it?'

'Of course not,' Felix answered gently. 'I was going to tell you what I'd done, only everything happened so quickly, there wasn't time. Are you very angry with me?' he asked kindly. 'I don't blame you if you are.'

Peter could only stare at him.

'But I had to do it, son,' he continued. 'I had to stop Belson's madness. Now I don't like speaking ill of someone who's no longer here, but what your grandfather was doing was unconscionable, especially what he was doing to you. I knew there would be no reasoning with him—there never had been—and so I did what I could to stop him. If I'd let it go on, it would have only gotten worse.'

'But you ruined him!' Peter cried. 'He was trying to save our heritage for us and you snatched it out from under him. He was almost there.'

'Oh, Peter, don't. Don't defend him. Can't you see, his megalomania is what drove him, not his need to preserve your heritage. He'd do anything, no matter if it was illegal, or foolhardy, or injurious to others, to keep his ego from tarnishing. How did he lose his fortune in the first place? Because of such a need. The man was crazy, absolutely mad.' He lowered his voice an octave. 'I know this is terribly hard for you to face. But if you search your heart, you'll find that I'm right.'

Peter was silent, trying to hold on to his anger and sense of outrage, but Felix's voice was insidious, whispering truths that his soul recognized in spite of a desperate need to deny them.

'If I had known what was going on long ago, I would have stopped it then,' Felix said. 'I'm only sorry you didn't come to me in the beginning.'

'No!' Peter insisted, trying to overcome that persuasive voice. 'You wanted to ruin him, and you did. And you didn't care what it did to me or to Phyllis or Jonathan. In a few weeks we would have sold our mature contracts. There would have been enough money to pay all the debts, all the taxes, and still maintain the estate. But you've made that impossible now.'

'You're so naive,' Felix said, his voice quiet and gentle. 'You were his perfect foil because you believed in a dream. The reality is, Peter, no one can predict from moment to moment what is going to happen in a situation as volatile as the precious-metal market. Any number of factors and permutations could have caused this recent downturn. You've been trading in commodities long enough to know that. Eventually you must realize that I saved you, boy, but you don't know it yet.'

'Sure,' Peter retorted. 'You saved me, and my inheritance.'

'But it's not lost, Peter,' Felix insisted, his expression saddened by being misjudged. 'Wait until you hear. I'm going to form a combine and buy McKintridge from your creditors. And then you and Phyllis and Jonathan will inherit it when I'm gone. You won't really lose it, it will merely change hands.' He was beaming with pride. 'It will truly be yours without any misdeeds needed to preserve it, and without any debts hanging over it. Of course I may have to subdivide some of the property, but it will still be McKintridge.'

'No,' Peter said. 'You can't!' He felt a horrible panic assail him at Felix's words, as though his grandfather's decomposing arms would reach out of the grave and pull him into the coffin for even listening to such an idea. He could barely get the words out of his throat. 'I promised my grandfather you'd never get the estate.'

'Of course you did,' Felix assured him. 'But that's one promise you can't afford to keep. Not if you care about your heritage, and your son's, and that of your unborn children.'

Felix paused to let Peter absorb these heretical yet logical concepts. And Peter's struggle was enormous. Warring factions pulled at him relentlessly. He felt as if he were being torn apart. The strength of his grandfather's hatred for Felix pulled at him from the grave while Felix's strong hold on him enmeshed him here.

Felix could see him wavering. 'It's going to work out for the best,' he said soothingly. 'You'll see. I'm going to make it up to you for what you think I've done. And someday you'll understand that I was right. It's the only way.'

Peter's sense of reason had exploded, leaving only fragments of his former self. There were bits and pieces of him scattered all over other people's lives and nothing of himself was left recognizable. It was an alien voice that answered Felix, an unfamiliar consciousness, but one that knew it was beaten. The only part of him that remained intact was the part that knew he had failed. He had promised his grandfather that Felix would never get McKintridge, and now, only days after making that promise, he was about to break it. But Felix was offering him a way to save the estate. Shouldn't that be the most important consideration? At this point he was so confused he honestly didn't know whether or not Felix had betrayed him after all.

He looked at Felix but his eyes weren't focusing. All he wanted to do at the moment was sink into oblivion. Everything was too much for him to assess. He reached out his hand to wave Felix away, but it fell helplessly back into his lap.

'Say you agree,' Felix said, his tone so friendly, so quiet. 'It's the only way you can save the estate.'

Peter just stared at him. 'What do you want me to do?'

'Instruct the banks to find only my bid acceptable. And don't worry, I'll pay anything that's fair, or ten percent above any other bid they're offered.'

Felix's face wavered before Peter's eyes as though it were disjointed from his head. 'Not now, Felix,' he whispered. 'I can't think now.'

'There's nothing to think about, son,' Felix persisted. 'Just say yes.'

And from somewhere outside of himself Peter heard someone else's voice saying, 'All right, if only you'll leave me alone now.' And then he lay down on Belson's bed and was asleep in seconds.

Felix covered him tenderly with the edge of the quilt and silently left the room. But there was a smile of immense satisfaction on his face.

Chapter 12

PETER SPENT the entire morning from 6:00 A.M. until noon on Tuesday the day after the funeral calling his brokers and having the remainder of the thirty million deposited in the various accounts. By the time he finished his final transaction, every account had been brought to a status quo position and nothing else was owed below the margin. But every dime of profit had been used up and he still had to decide whether or not to sell Belson's positions. As of the eleven thirty closing there was no change in the price of platinum, but any further decline would necessitate another margin call. And now he had no money left.

At one o'clock Peter met Larry and Belson's advisers at McKintridge so they could apprise him of his current financial situation and read him Belson's will.

The more he heard, the more depressed he became. The tax consequences were far worse than he'd expected. In fact the news was so devastating that its impact had only touched his consciousness and not penetrated his brain.

He had been named heir and executor of the estate; he had the right to draw at his discretion on any available funds to facilitate the current commodity maneuver still in progress, so at least the morning's activities had been within his legal right. There was a survivor clause that gave the estate equally to Phyllis and Jonathan without any additional tax event if Peter should not survive until the will was completely executed, and in that case Phyllis became executrix. But Peter felt as though he had inherited under false pretenses. If his grandfather had lived through Friday, he would have written Peter out completely, as he had threatened. That thought nagged at Peter all the time he was listening to the advisers describe his grandfather's litany of financial crimes against his heirs.

But in spite of Belson's careless financial dealings this room and everything in it intimidated Peter. The worn leather chair in which he sat, his grandfather's chair, held the scent of Belson's cologne; there were darkened patches on the arms and headrest from the oils in Belson's body. And the edges of the fine fruitwood desk were rubbed where Belson's decisive touch had been. Each reminder brought a fresh stab to this new raw wound. The loss was much more with him because of the feeling in his heart that his behavior had precipitated it.

Larry half sat, half stood, perched on the edge of Belson's desk at Peter's right; his arms were folded across his chest and he listened to the discussion, absorbing every word. Peter was grateful for his presence. He needed someone on his side in a roomful of all the 'I-told-you-sos,' as his grandfather called them. There was Thurston Duffray and Arnold Beckmiller, both wearing identical navy blue suits; Nathan McKinley, who had known Peter's parents; and Lester Abbott, who had been Belson's agent and was familiar with Belson's residual contracts. And of course Hugh Perkins, the only one of the bunch Peter felt remotely akin to. Every now and then Larry would catch Peter's eye and give him a nod of encouragement, but Peter could see his own face reflected in the silver cigar box on the desk; it looked completely colorless. But even as they talked of Belson, of his foolish, headstrong mistakes, Peter could hear in their voices the awe in which they still held Belson; his commanding presence still hadn't faded even in death.

Finally Hugh Perkins made his concluding remarks. 'Peter, if you sell out your commodity contracts at the opening of tomorrow's market, you will inherit an estate with the estimated market value of twenty-six million, minus the debt of three and a half million, and you would owe approximately eighteen million in taxes which you could obtain by selling the estate. But you must take steps immediately,' Hugh warned. 'It will take time to find a buyer and it will also take time to liquidate ten thousand platinum contracts without driving down the price; you can't dump them all in one day.'

There was a general murmur of agreement among the men in the room; they all concurred with Hugh's advice.

But Peter felt as if he'd been pierced by a volley of arrows and out of each wound poured his hope.

Then Nathan McKinley spoke. 'We know how important it was to Belson to retain his estate, but that is impossible now. The government shows no compassion for sentimentality. They are entitled to their taxes and that's all there is to that.'

Peter felt as though parts of his body were being torn off piece by piece; he couldn't hold back his anguish any longer. 'This estate means even more to me than it did to my grandfather,' he said. 'I cannot give it up. If I wait one more day before beginning to sell our commodity position, perhaps there will be a rise in platinum. I might still achieve what my grandfather set out to do.'

There was an almost unanimous roar of disapproval. 'There's no way.' 'It's foolhardy.' 'Unconscionable.' 'You must be reasonable.' 'You will end up with debts for the rest of your life.'

Tears of defeat rushed to Peter's eyes and his breath became lodged in his chest. They were right. Tomorrow morning he would sell, both the commodities and the estate. But the unfairness of it all overwhelmed him. They'd come so close, they'd tried so hard, only to have it end like this. 'Is there anything else, gentlemen?' he asked.

They were uncomfortable with his sorrow; no one had

anything more to say.

'Then I should like to be alone now, if you don't mind.' He wanted to show them to the door, but he knew his legs wouldn't hold him up, so he said good-bye still seated in his chair, Belson's chair, while he ached for the courage to go on.

'Please leave copies of your individual reports and a copy of the will on the conference table, gentlemen,' he instructed them. 'Plus whatever stock certificates, corporate papers, certificates of partnerships, anything pertaining to my grandfather's estate that I will need to study. And thank you all for coming. I know this wasn't a pleasant task for any of you.'

They filed out one by one. Most of them shook his hand; others came behind the desk to give him a comforting hug. But still he sat there as though drained of energy.

And when they were all gone and he was alone with Larry, he let himself go and wept. He felt so helpless. How would he ever pull himself out of this well of misery?

'I had no idea that inheritance taxes would destroy the estate,' Larry said in a subdued tone. 'I admit, I'm stunned.'

Peter wiped his eyes and stared off into space until the room seemed to recede and all he was aware of was the chair underneath him. A brief moment of peace descended on him. If only it could last.

'I think you've had enough for one day, don't you?' Larry said. 'Why don't you go on home now?'

But Peter's moment of respite had ended. 'Not yet. You still have to tell me what Lewis Cohen said about the commodity investigation.'

Larry walked around the desk and sat facing Peter in one of the Georgian chairs. 'Are you certain you want to hear this now? It can wait until later.'

'Might as well.' Peter sighed. 'No sense in avoiding it, it's not going to go away.'

'I suppose not,' Larry agreed.

'So?'

Larry shrugged. 'The man's a sharp lawyer, what can I tell you? He knows his business and I felt I was getting good advice.' He stopped talking for a minute, trying to assess whether or not Peter was strong enough to hear this.

Peter nodded for him to continue.

'In some ways it's to your advantage that it's you and not your grandfather facing the commission. After all, Belson is dead, which mitigates many of the sanctions they could have imposed. And he was the one who was guilty of possible criminal offenses, not you. But you have your own problems to face. Retaining your license to practice law, for one thing. That's uppermost in our consideration. How to preserve it for you.'

'I don't deserve to be a lawyer any longer,' Peter said. 'I broke the law.'

'Don't quote morals to me now, Peter. You're a good lawyer. Unfortunately, you were an even better grandson. Lew Cohen and I are looking for a defensible position here; let's leave the blame out of it, okay?'

Peter gave a slight nod.

'If there had been any illegal profit, we'd want to minimize what you'd have to disgorge, you know, pay back ill-gotten goods. But there weren't any, so our main concern is keeping you out of jail.'

'Jail? My God, is that possible?'

Larry looked straight at him. 'Lew Cohen says there's always that chance, but it won't happen, Peter. Believe me.'

Peter felt his hands and feet turning to ice at the idea.

'Now. Your offenses were not as serious as your grand-father's. You didn't conceive of the scheme, you didn't make payoffs or bribes, if any were made, and you did not profit directly from the transactions. It was clear to Cohen, and I think it will be to the commission, that you were acting on Belson's behalf. So the criminal proceedings against you may be easier to refute. But as far as the CFTC is concerned, you are in as much trouble as Belson because you broke their regulations and committed misdemeanor offenses.'

'There weren't any felonies?' Peter asked with relief.

'Not so far,' Larry said. 'Now Cohen feels, and I agree, the best way to go would be to try and make a deal with the CFTC whereby they would grant you immunity if you reveal what you know. Of course you'd have to liquidate Belson's positions as soon as possible, which you are going to do in any case.'

'What kind of information would they want?'

'Everything,' Larry stated bluntly. 'Details of your grandfather's scheme, names of his associates if any, and your testimony against Benning, the bank official who Belson was bribing. The case against Benning is a criminal matter and it's the most serious aspect. They would naturally want to catch anybody else who committed the more serious offenses. And if you co-operate, you might get them to agree not to refer anything about you to the state bar. Your license could be saved.'

As an attorney Peter could see the merit of what Larry was saying, but for him it was the worst possible choice. His insides felt as though they were being pulverized, as though sharp-edged beaters were churning inside, tearing him apart, and he cried out, 'You're telling me I should sacrifice my grandfather's name, destroy his reputation, and inform on the people who trusted him? I can't do that, don't you see?'

'Peter,' Larry said, 'the man sacrificed *you!*'

But Peter shook his head vehemently from side to side. 'No. He was trying to save my inheritance for me. For me!' he repeated. 'And you want me to throw him to the wolves.'

'The man's dead, for Christ's sake,' Larry exclaimed. 'What difference does it make, especially now?'

'It makes a difference to me,' Peter cried, hitting his chest with his fist for emphasis. 'I've got to live with myself. Can't you understand that? I won't do it, I just won't.'

Larry got up and came around the desk to stand next to him, placing a hand on his shoulder. 'I know it's tough, Peter. I know how you feel. Don't try to decide right now. You've got a few days till the inquiry.'

Peter looked at him warily. 'What do you mean, a few days? I thought you were going to request a postponement because of my grandfather's death.'

Larry's voice was filled with regret. 'All I could get was one day. They're extremely anxious to find out what's been going on. And they don't want to have to suspend trading in platinum. But they agreed to send a lawyer down from San Francisco so we don't have to go to Washington.'

Peter dropped his head in his hands in exhaustion. There was no escape from this torture, nowhere to turn.

'Felix told me you've agreed to let him buy the estate,' Larry said. 'At least that's one major worry solved, you've got a buyer. Unless you want to wait for someone who won't subdivide the property?'

But Peter wasn't listening. All he could hear was his grandfather's voice saying to him. 'I'm not surprised that it's come to this. I'd never expect anything better from you. All you've ever wanted to do was save your own skin. Isn't that the story of your life?'

No, Peter thought. Not again. *I won't save myself at the expense of others. I can't be the only one to survive when everyone else is dead.*

He could feel Larry's hands helping him to his feet, Larry's arms around him guiding him out the door, but Larry was a blur to him. The only thing that was clear was his grandfather's accusing eyes, the sound of his voice saying, *We'll just see what you're really made of. We'll just see.*

Chapter 13

PHYLLIS FOUND the bedroom dark, the blackout drapes drawn against the afternoon sun. She tiptoed in, closing the door behind her, shutting out snatches of the Spanish broadcast Lupe listened to while she ironed and the tinkling sounds of a music box coming from the nursery.

'Peter,' she called softly, switching on the bedside light.

He was sitting on the bed in his underwear, his knees drawn up to his chest, and he had stretched his T-shirt over his knees, clutching himself into a tight white ball.

'Are you all right?' she asked.

But he didn't seem to hear her. The tops of his knees and the T-shirt stretched over them were wet from his tears. 'I needed to talk to you,' he said, 'but you weren't here.' He sounded like a lost child.

'I was at a Helpers meeting, Peter. Remember? My finance committee was making their annual report. I told you I'd be home by three.' She smoothed his hair back from his forehead, trying to soothe her own dread as well. They had discussed at length where she would be this afternoon and both decided she ought to attend her own meeting, since she'd worked so hard on the recent fund-raising event. And now he'd forgotten. It was another example of the state of mind he'd been in since Belson's death. This morning he hadn't been able to decide what to wear, and he hadn't eaten a meal in three days. She was becoming more mother to him than wife; she had a nagging thought that he might never really be her husband again, in the full, equal sense of the word. But then she pushed those thoughts out

410

of her mind and clung to her usual optimism.

'Tell me what they said at the meeting,' she asked.

He put his head down on his knees. 'I'm going to lose it, Phyllis. I can't hang on. I haven't the strength to fight. You can't imagine how bad it is.' He couldn't even tell her about it; each time he tried, a new spasm of pain made him clutch himself for comfort.

Watching him, Phyllis felt like a moth caught in a jar, her wings beating against the truth of her own helplessness; she longed to be free, to fly around the room and find a way to ease Peter's tortured soul. But there was nothing she could do for him right now but give him love.

Finally he picked his head up off his knees and looked at her. 'I don't know if I can go on facing this loss, Phyllis,' he said. 'I don't think I can live with myself knowing how much I've let all of you down.' And finally he told her what went on at the meeting, the details of Belson's will, including the amount of inheritance taxes he would have to pay and his dilemma over whether or not to become an informant for the CFTC.

'It might be your only choice,' she said.

'I can't do it. I couldn't live with myself if I did. If Grandfather even knew I had considered it, he would have hated me even more than he did. That's why he was so angry with me the night he died. He knew I had let him down. I'm no good, I've never been any good.' His voice sounded empty and hollow. 'Keeping the estate means more to me than my life,' Peter said, 'and losing it proves how useless I am. Oh, God, I killed him!' he cried.

'No!' she shouted. 'Don't ever say such a thing. He was living on borrowed time, Peter. You did not kill him.'

But his expression told her he did not believe her.

'Don't you know how much you mean to me and Jonathan? More than any piece of property! As long as we have you, nothing else matters.'

He sighed, slightly comforted. 'Your father has offered to buy the estate,' he told her.

'What did you tell him?'

'That he could have it. He said he'd bring over a purchase agreement in the morning. At least that way the estate will stay in the family.'

'I don't know,' she said, suddenly doubting her father's altruistic motives. 'I'm not so sure he should be insinuating himself into this situation. And why is he in such a hurry? We have nine months before we have to pay inheritance taxes, don't we?'

'Yes,' Peter said. 'But your father's trying to help. It's a better solution than selling McKintridge to a stranger who might tear it down for a development.'

'Oh, no,' she cried. That was an unbearable thought.

She noticed that Peter was shivering with chill and she went to get him a comforter, but all the while her thoughts were racing. There was something terribly wrong about her father acquiring the McKintridge estate. She couldn't imagine Belson being happy about that, even if it did mean the estate would stay in the family. Peter and Jonathan belonged there, not her parents. And if her father had the money to acquire the estate, why couldn't he arrange for a loan so Peter could keep it, instead of trying to acquire it himself? That seemed to her a more logical thing for him to do than what he was doing.

The bright rays of the sun seeped in through the cracks in the curtains, making the shadows dance on the walls as though elves and fairies were leaping about, happily flirting in the corners. She wished life could be that innocent for her, that simple. Peter was watching her, more calmly than before, but still his eyes were so sad. She could feel his body warmth returning under the blanket.

'If you begin to sell the commodity futures tomorrow, doesn't that mean that you've lost the chance of preserving the estate?'

'Yes,' he replied.

'Then maybe we should wait one more day. Isn't it possible they could go up tomorrow?'

'It's possible,' Peter said, his voice losing the edge of despair. 'We lost a hundred and fifty points in one day; the market could reverse itself just as easily.'

'Well then?'

'But if the opposite happens and platinum falls again, we'd lose millions. And we'd be personally liable for such a loss. If the CFTC finds that I've committed sanctionable offenses, any debts I incur can never be written off. I'd have to pay on them forever. We'd lose our condominium, our cars, everything. We'd never get out of debt, and I wouldn't be able to earn a living as a lawyer.'

Phyllis took his hand, trying to show through her touch how much she loved him. 'Don't you want to give it one last try?' she asked.

'God, yes,' he replied.

'Then I'm willing to take the chance, if you are.'

He was fighting tears again, but his face was suffused with joy. 'I don't deserve you,' he said.

'Hush.' She put her fingers to his lips. 'No more of that now.'

'But I don't,' he insisted. 'You're the most wonderful wife a man could ever ask for. And I haven't even the courage to tell your father what we've decided. He'll think we're out of our minds. And he'll be furious too.'

'Would you like me to tell him?' she asked.

He nodded.

'Then I will,' she agreed.

He opened his arms with gratitude and she came into his embrace, hoping she had comforted him enough to ease his fears. 'I love you so much, Peter,' she said. 'You mean everything to me.'

Chapter 14

LESLIE'S JUBILATION was turning from frothy whipped cream into curdled milk. Where was Banir? Why hadn't he returned her calls? She was jumping out of her skin to give him the most important news of his life, and every time she called his suite, all she got was one of his flunkies. She still couldn't believe it was true; when Felix called to say that Peter had agreed to sell him the estate, the news had shot through her like two tracks of coke.

Ever since Felix's call she had not been able to contain her excitement and had literally danced around the room. But she knew her happiness wouldn't last forever, and while she was really up, she wanted to share it with Banir. She reached for the phone again but this time she dialed Dianna.

The whiskey voice answered on half a ring.

'Are you alone?' Leslie asked without preliminaries.

'Just a minute,' Dianna said, dismissing whoever was in her office. In a moment she came back on the line. 'What news?' Leslie heard that breathless yearning for undiscovered treasure that always colored Dianna's voice.

A torrent of words came tumbling out of Leslie. 'You won't believe it, Deedee, but Felix just called. We've got the house!' Leslie couldn't suppress a giggle. Damn being dignified at a time like this.

Dianna was gratifyingly stunned. 'I honestly never thought you would get it, Les. And I'm not being disloyal. But my gawd! McKintridge is yours? Actually yours? My gawd.' She pressed her buzzer. 'Can we still make next edition?' she asked her secretary. 'I have something to add to the details of Belson McKintridge's will.'

'Wait!' Leslie yelled in her ear. 'I haven't spoken to Banir yet. It's not official until he proposes. *Please*, darling, don't print it until I give you the green light.'

Again silence. 'Les, just the hint of a change in ownership of the McKintridge estate is vital news. I can't sit on it, it's a time bomb.'

'Twenty-four hours, pet. I'm begging on bloody knees. Tomorrow the story is yours; no one else can possibly find out until then. Felix, Larry Gilbert, Peter, and I are the only ones who know, so you won't be scooped.'

'If I am, darling, it's ta-ta forever.'

'Dianna, pet. I love you, but go to hell.'

'You too, sweet.' And they hung up, both smiling happily.

Where was Banir? Perhaps he'd gone off to Saudi Arabia without telling her. He'd been there twice in the last three months. He was involved in that new airport they were building in Riyadh. She called his hotel again; this time she asked for the French maid.

'*Monsieur Ammani est en conference, madame.*'

'But this is urgent,' she insisted.

'I yam so sorree, madame. *Mais, je* cannot disturb 'im.'

Leslie slammed down the phone. 'Maybe you can't disturb him,' she said out loud, 'but I can.'

She dressed carefully in a wonderful Gianni Versace outfit: khaki harem pants, a wrapped suede cummerbund, and a wraparound tunic top, finished off with lace-up suede sandals. Her homage to the Middle East, subtle yet deferential.

It was only a few blocks away to the Beverly Wilshire Hotel but by the time she got there, left the Rolls with the attendant, and took the elevator to Banir's penthouse, her excitement had lost some of its peak. Life was like that, she thought. When you wanted something to happen with all your heart, the way she wanted to share this good news with Banir, fate made you wait, held out on you without

415

granting your wish until you didn't care anymore, and then you'd get what you wanted.

The French maid answered the door.

'Oui, madame, Monsieur est trés occupé.'

Leslie could see over the shorter woman's head to the terrace beyond. There was Banir, in his favorite chair, sunning himself, surrounded by his entourage. They were all drinking tea (what else) and gossiping. Some conference.

She pushed past the protesting servant and strode out to the terrace. 'Good afternoon, gentlemen,' she said. They each gave her a nod. 'Banir. I've been calling you.'

He turned lazily to look at her, a laconic expression. She could see the Mideastern veil he'd drawn to obscure his emotions and she was slightly puzzled. But then this was his house where he was lord and master, the patriarch, and she was intruding. She smiled sweetly, 'I had something urgent to discuss with you. I'm sorry to interrupt, but it couldn't wait.'

He inclined his head for her to sit down with the group, but that wasn't what she had in mind. Those six pairs of black eyes were too public for the culminating moment when the engagement of Leslie Paxton Winokur to Sheikh Banir Ammani became official.

'May we speak privately, dear?' she entreated.

All eyes shifted to him and her heart skipped a little as she waited for him to decide. This battle they both waged for control would never be won during a lifetime together—she could see that now—and it frightened her as much as it excited her. Finally a man existed she couldn't dominate.

Slowly he got up from the table, brushed the pastry crumbs from his beige garbardine slacks, tucked his white handkerchief-cotton shirt more tightly into the waistband, ran his fingers through his thick, Semitic hair, and followed her indoors. She reached for his hand and led him through the living room, looking around for a place where they could be alone together, unseen and uninterrupted. She found it in the small study off the living room behind the staircase, and she led him there.

The room was overcrowded with furniture, dark corduroy walls, and an upholstered sofa to match. The bright light from the patio barely filtered in through the plantation shutters. She turned to face him, her eyes shining with delight. His back was to the door and she came up to him and ran her hands along his waist, up his rib cage, and over the fine muscles of his chest. 'I've wanted you.'

He waited, smiling that same laconic smile.

'Oh, Banir,' she burst out, unable to contain her secret any longer. 'I've heard from Felix. It's yours, the estate is yours. Peter McKintridge has agreed to sell it to Felix and he will sell it to you. Evidently Peter is quite bereaved over the loss of his grandfather and the circumstances of his inheritance. Do you believe it?'

Only the raising of an eyebrow showed his reaction, that and his smile. 'That's quite interesting,' he said. 'You look quite stunning today, Leslie. *Trés chic* and alluring.'

She was enormously pleased. The harem pants had turned out to be the perfect outfit for today. They made her appear more exotic, more the kind of woman he identified with. 'I wore this in celebration of our wonderful news. Do you realize what this means, darling? You will be living in the most magnificent estate in this country. A palace befitting a prince among men. I know you cannot be as excited about this news as I, because for you to acquire such a prize is part of your birthright, but for me it is a lifelong dream come true. And yet of all the excitement it brings to me, the best part is that we will be able to share it together. *N'est-ce pas, chéri?*'

He placed his hands on her shoulders. 'I too have spoken to your friend Felix. He was as happy about this news as you are. And well he should be, he got what he wanted. But for me it is not as satisfying.'

'Why not, my dear?' she asked.

'Because Felix has made the agreement with his son-in-law.' His hands pressed down hard on her shoulders so that her legs gave way under the pressure and she couldn't stand anymore. Soon she was kneeling on the floor in front of him.

Immediately she felt that unbelievable sexual heat that he evoked in her every time they were together. She never knew what he had in store for her, and whatever it was, she revelled in it.

'. . . And Felix has decided to demolish the main house. He has offered to sell me three and a half acres of the property on which I'm supposed to build my own Mid-eastern version of McKintridge. He suggested that you would be enormously helpful in such an endeavor.'

'Oh, yes! I would be,' Leslie agreed, still not under-standing, looking up at him. 'We two could build a Taj Mahal, a Brighton Pavilion, a Blue Mosque, all our own.' The disappointment of losing the McKintridge house itself to Felix was brief. She and Banir *would* build something more spectacular. Three and a half acres in the heart of Beverly Hills wasn't bad.

His eyes gazed suggestively down at her, examining the crease between her breasts where the wrapped tunic had fallen open; she felt her nipples blossom with response to his gaze like ripened berries longing to be crushed against his lips. She reached her long tapered fingers into the opening of her top and caressed her breasts, knowing he liked to see her do that.

His eyes narrowed seductively and he reached down and unbuckled his belt and unzipped his fly.

She closed her eyes and waited for the feeling of his groin against her face, his penis against her cheek; her mouth filled with welcoming saliva.

He moved closer and she reached out to find him, when suddenly she felt the shock of warm liquid splashing her in the face. For a split second she thought he had ejaculated too quickly and then she realized it wasn't semen she was feeling but urine. She sputtered and turned away, crying out, 'No, Banir, please, no.' She tried to protect herself and cover her face with her arms but she still felt the spray of his urine continuing to rain down all over her.

'I told you I wanted the *main house*,' he said, his voice hoarse with cruelty.

She was sobbing from humiliation. 'Banir, no. Please let me explain. Don't do this! Please.' It felt like it would never end. And when she tried to crawl away from him, he grabbed her roughly and pulled her back so he could continue pissing on her head and her arms and her legs. She thought she would die from humiliation.

And then abruptly he was through and she heard the sound of his zipper as he closed up his pants. His last words to her as he left her alone were, 'Now you know what I think of you, and always have.' And then he called for the servants to remove the garbage in the study.

Chapter 15

PETER AWOKE at 5:30 A.M., his shoulders in knots, his heart pounding. How was he ever going to get through this day? It was eight thirty in New York. He could call right now. Someone would give him a quote on platinum. But he didn't dare call. He didn't want to know.

Phyllis was sleeping peacefully beside him, her exquisite profile outlined by the early-morning light, but all he could see was the blackness of his future. He had barely slept all night, and now he was so tired that he thought he'd never be able to get out of bed. Every ounce of energy had been drained out of him, as though someone had pulled a plug at the ends of all of his fingers and toes and drained him of the will to go on. And yet he had to.

Wearily he swung his legs over the edge of the bed,

noticing that his thigh muscles quivered from weakness. How he longed to escape back to that black unconsciousness of sleep. His nightmares might torture him, but they were preferable to what lay before him in the day ahead.

Slowly he dressed in yesterday's clothes, wishing he could find a way to ease the pain in his heart, but the feeling of failure was overwhelming. By the time he made it downstairs it was six fifteen yet he still couldn't bring himself to call and check the price of platinum. None of the brokers had his home number, only the private number he'd installed in his office in Century City, which also connected to his grandfather's study. That way, if he received a call from one of the brokers, Belson could monitor the conversation and give him instructions on a separate line. He wished his grandfather were here to do that today.

He decided to drive up to the main house and use the phone in his grandfather's study instead of going all the way to his office. He would call for a quote when he got there.

The private phone was ringing when he entered the study, which only made him more apprehensive. There must have been a change in the price of platinum this morning; either it was up or down from yesterday's closing, or else no one would be calling.

He unlocked the desk drawer in which the phone was kept and with a trembling hand reached for the receiver. 'Yes,' he said.

'What do you want me to do?' It was Buddy Morris in Century City. 'Are you still in? Twelve points is a lot in your position.'

'A lot of what?' Peter asked, holding his breath.

'A lot of loss,' Buddy stated.

And Peter's heart fell into the pit of his stomach. 'Twelve points?' he whispered.

'Well, platinum opened down twelve today, but it's recovered nine already. So as of now it's only down three points. What do you want me to do? Sell some? Or are you going to send me more money?'

Peter's tongue was sticking to the roof of his mouth or he would have screamed. He'd promised Phyllis he'd place sell orders if the price was down today, but now he couldn't bring himself to give the order. 'Do you think the recovery of nine points indicates an upturn?' he asked.

'It might.'

He didn't know what to do. Selling was so irrevocable. 'I'll get back to you,' Peter said.

'Okay.' Buddy sounded cheerful. Peter had made good every margin call up to now. There was no reason to doubt his solvency. But Buddy had no idea of the broader picture and neither did any of the other brokers. To each of them a three-point loss meant Peter's client was down fifty thousand; to Peter it meant a loss of 1.5 million.

Suddenly he was too exhausted to think. He took the private line off the receiver so no other brokers could call him, laid his head down on the desk, and in a minute he was asleep.

He was making love to a woman. The touch of her skin was satin smooth. She had soft breasts and a young pliant body; there was the scent of musk about her and she was beautiful, enveloping him with desire. She was ready for him, beckoning to him to enter her, but he couldn't do it. He was not erect. He was not a man, he was a failure. And then he shamed himself even more by crying in front of her. He turned away and pressed his head against the table next to her bed so she wouldn't see him crying. Her doorbell rang. 'Next,' she called, pushing him away.

One of the other phones on the desk was ringing; the blotter beneath his cheek was wet with his tears.

Groggily he reached for the phone; for a moment he didn't know where he was.

'Have you begun to sell yet?' It was Felix. 'Platinum is down.'

'Not yet,' Peter answered.

'Well, what the hell are you waiting for?' Felix sounded both disgusted and incredulous. 'You can't afford a drop in three points, can you?'

Peter was silent.

'You've got to sign a purchase agreement with me today, Peter. I'll give you a deposit of fifty thousand, or even more if you need it. But if you wait any longer to sell your commodities, you'll piss away whatever profit you and Phyllis can still take out of the estate.'

Peter's own voice came from far away. 'Didn't Phyllis talk to you? She said she was going to tell you.'

'Yes, yes. I spoke to her last night. Something about you two waiting one more day to start liquidating the commodities and not being in a hurry to sell the estate. Well, all that's changed. You're going to have margin calls today. And I know you can't cover them. You've got to sign the purchase agreement with me today so you'll have some immediate cash. And for God's sake, don't wait any longer. Sell those damn contracts.'

But Peter was so tired, all he wanted to do was sleep. 'I will,' he agreed. 'You're right.'

'I'll give you twenty-seven million for the property, Peter. A security deposit today, six million down, and a thirty-day escrow. All right?'

No reply.

'That's fair, isn't it?' Felix sounded anxious. 'That's a million over the appraised value.'

Peter sighed, trying to keep the terrible sorrow in his depths from bursting forth. 'It's fair,' he said, feeling his eyes closing, his head nodding. He had to sleep or something terrible would happen. He could not stay awake.

'I'll bring over the papers later today,' Felix said. 'Where will you be?'

But Peter was already asleep.

When Phyllis arrived at nine thirty, both phones were off the hook and Peter was asleep at the desk. She tried to awaken him, but he seemed drugged. She helped him to his feet. 'I'm taking you home to bed,' she told him.

'I'm so sorry,' he mumbled, accompanying her without protest.

By the time she got him home, he was more coherent. 'Will you be able to call in all the sell orders yourself?' she asked. 'Or do you want me to help you?'

'I'll do it,' he assured her, trying to smile.

'I'm so sorry, darling,' she said.

He took her hand. 'I know.'

'There must be something I can do to help?'

He thought for a minute. 'You could go to the bank and close out our T-bill account. There'll be a penalty for early withdrawal, but that can't be helped. Put the money in our checking account, we're going to need it.'

'Do you want me to send some of that money to each of the margin accounts?' she asked.

He looked at her sadly. 'It's all the money we have, and it's only enough to send about twelve hundred dollars to each account.'

'But still, we should do that, shouldn't we?'

He nodded reluctantly. 'Please, don't be gone too long,' he cautioned. 'I need you.'

'I won't, darling,' she told him. 'And I love you.'

When Phyllis arrived home at one o'clock in the afternoon, Peter was asleep again.

She sat on the edge of the bed and smoothed his hair out of his eyes and kissed him on the cheek.

He stirred, but he didn't open his eyes.

'Peter,' she called. 'Did you sell any of the commodities?'

'Yes,' he whispered, turning over in his sleep.

Well, it's done, she thought as she tiptoed out of the room. And then she heard him cry out as he bolted up in bed and looked at the clock.

'What time is it? One o'clock! Oh, my God, I must have slept through it. I was dreaming that I sold out, but I don't think I really did it.'

Phyllis was startled, and then she grew angry. 'But you said you would. We agreed on today, Peter. We've lost enough already, don't you think?' She had just come from disbursing their life's savings and every check she wrote had saddened her, underscored their losses. She stopped being angry when she saw his face crumble with pain.

He fell sideways on the bed and pounded on the covers with his fist. 'Damn, damn,' he cried. 'I've done it again.'

She rushed to him. 'It's all right, Peter,' she said. 'We'll do it first thing in the morning. And this time I'll be there with you to help you. We'll do it together.'

And as he stared at her in gratitude, she saw his eyes drooping back into sleep again. 'I'm sorry,' he whispered. 'Please forgive me.'

'I do,' she said. 'You know I do.'

'How's Jonathan?' he managed to ask.

'He's still running a fever. I'm going to take him to the doctor this afternoon.'

Peter nodded. 'Don't leave me,' he begged.

'I won't,' she replied, alarmed that he would even think such a thing. But he was already asleep.

She looked around the room as though there might be some explanation for his strange behavior. And then she spotted a bottle of sleeping pills and tranquillizers on his bedside table. No wonder he was so groggy, she thought. But maybe it was good for him to sleep for today. Lord knew he needed a respite from all the pain he'd been suffering. But still she didn't feel safe, leaving all that medication nearby, so she took the sleeping pills and put them in her purse and left him only half the tranquillizers.

When Larry called at three o'clock, Phyllis had just left to take Jonathan to the doctor and Peter was feeling very tired again and very anxious.

'Everything's set for tomorrow morning,' Larry said. 'We're meeting with a lawyer named Talbot; he's on the enforcement committee of the CFTC. He'll be catching the seven o'clock plane from San Francisco and has agreed to meet at Lew Cohen's office. I thought that was considerate of him, don't you?'

'Uh-huh,' Peter answered.

'I've gone through the records of all your transactions. It doesn't look too bad to me,' Larry assured him. 'What you and Belson did was *malum prohibitum*, so they have to prove there was an intent to squeeze.'

'Who does?' Peter asked.

'The CFTC and the attorney general's office,' Larry said, 'for there to be any criminal action taken. It's just possible, according to Cohen, that you and your grandfather's investments never really constituted a squeeze because you lacked the volume, you never really influenced the price of platinum one way or the other. Of course, there is still the matter of falsifying records. And it's up to us to prove you had nothing to do with the bank fraud. But if we ask for a deal, like Cohen says,' Larry paused, 'and you give evidence, we might just pull through. Peter, are you there?'

But Peter wasn't listening, wasn't concentrating. 'I'll talk to you later,' he said, hanging up before Larry could even reply. And he fell asleep without noticing that he'd missed replacing the receiver back on the cradle of the phone.

Chapter 16

'I DIDN'T want to have any unfinished business between us,' Marla said, nervously taking a large swallow of the vodka gimlet she had ordered. She seldom drank during the day, in fact she seldom drank at all, but breaking off her affair with Felix required fortification. It was even more difficult than she'd imagined. Seeing him brought back all the conflicting emotions: his appeal, her embarrassment for being attracted to a man with such a blackened soul, and of course her need for the diversion of an affair in the first place.

Felix had reluctantly agreed to give her twenty minutes of his busy day if she'd meet him at the Hamlet, across the street from his office on Sunset, the most convenient place for him. His attitude toward her now only made her feel even more devalued.

'It's amazing how uninterested you are in me if you're not going to get laid,' she commented as he glanced at his gold Rolex for the fourth time.

He gave her an exasperated sigh and leaned back against the upholstered banquette, surveying her in the dim light. 'I'm not pleased by what you're doing. But I've always told you I'd never make things difficult for you, nor will I chase after you so you can get hysterical. If you want to call it off, then fine. It's just that you caught me at a bad time. I've got to take some papers over to Peter to sign.'

'Don't worry, Felix, I won't make a scene. I just wanted to make our parting official. We'll be seeing one another whenever we're thrown together by the peripheral aspects of our lives and I want to feel comfortable.' She kept her voice low, even though the bar was nearly deserted at three thirty in the afternoon. The lunch crowd had gone back to work and the cocktail crowd hadn't come in yet.

'You want to make certain there are no hard feelings so I won't tell Larry about us.'

'The way you informed on Peter and Belson? Is that what I can expect from you? Well, don't do it, Felix.' She was acting strong, but inside she felt very frightened. 'Phyllis and Audrey would be just as disappointed with you as Larry would be with me.'

He smiled and patted her knee. 'I'm not threatening you, Marla. In the first place, I don't care enough to want to hurt you. And in the second place, I don't think you mean it. You don't want to give up what we've had, you like it too much. Our kind of pleasure is addicting and we're not

426

hurting anyone, so why stop? You're just feeling remorse because of Belson's death. Funerals always make us assess our lives in view of our mortality. It's a perfectly common reaction for you to try and ease your conscience, rededicate yourself to marriage again and forget all about sin and seduction.' He leaned over and traced her fingers with his own. She jerked her hand away. 'Am I right?' he asked.

'No, you're wrong, Felix,' she stated. 'I've kicked my habit of you, and you helped me all the way. Even if you hadn't done that rotten thing to Peter and Belson, I would be through with you because you don't care about me or anybody else except yourself, and it shows. Your indifference to other people's pain is not just chilling, it's frightening.'

'And I suppose you think your husband is a real prince compared to me?'

'He'd never do what you did,' she said hotly.

Felix smiled an enigmatic smile, making her feel as though she were five years old. 'Why don't you ask him the reason he came to see me that day on my yacht and nearly caught us nestled in each other's arms?'

'Why should I ask him that?' she said, tension shooting through her head.

'Just ask him and see what he says,' Felix replied, signaling for the check while she glared at him. It was just like him to make up a story about Larry or even to tell Larry about them now that she was through.

'Poor little Marla,' he teased, 'bewildered by the games big people play. Don't you know you can't become a virgin again? Now that you've seen Paree, honey, the farm just won't keep you anymore.'

'No, Felix,' she said with determination. 'I'm going to try. What happens from here on in depends on Larry.' She stood as he paid cash for the drinks.

'He's got feet of clay, sugar,' he said.

'Do you think Larry plays around?' she asked, trying to appear unconcerned, but she was far from that.

Felix barely hesitated. 'Of course he does.'

Her eyes snapped to his face; he was grinning. 'Do you know for sure?' She was amazed at the force of pain in her chest.

'If you are, he must be.'

'But do you know?' she demanded. 'Have you ever actually seen him with someone? Has he ever told you?'

'Of course not. What do you think men do? Compare notes, like women?'

'That's exactly what they do, and you know it. And don't change the subject. Do you know for a fact that my husband has been unfaithful to me?'

'How can you even ask that question after the relationship you've had with me?'

'Because'—she could barely get the words out—'I want to know.'

'Then ask Larry.'

'Is that all you ever say?' she snapped.

Her eyes began to fill with tears and she cursed herself for displaying emotion, realizing that if Larry had been unfaithful, it would hurt her very much.

They came out of the restaurant into the bright daylight, both of them squinting against the glare that hit their eyes.

'Larry's a flirt, Marla,' Felix said. 'Flirts seldom carry through with anything. It's enough boost for their egos just to play the talking game.'

She nodded, overlooking the fact that Felix was the biggest flirt of all and he always carried through his flirtations.

'I think Larry would kill you if he knew about us,' she said.

'Don't flatter yourself, Marla. He wouldn't kill anyone. He'd divorce you so fast you wouldn't have time to take your jewelry out of the vault. And he'd glom on to every penny the two of you have and keep it all for himself, legally of course. Larry's as shrewd an attorney as they come.'

'Do you really think that little of him, Felix, that he wouldn't be fair with me? How disillusioned Larry would be if he knew what you thought. He used to really admire you.'

Felix was watching the traffic, waiting for the light to change on the corner so he could jaywalk across the street. After a Porsche 924 and a silver stretched limo drove by, it would be clear. He turned to her with a wicked look in his eye and said, 'Maybe I should test his generosity and tell him about you and me after all, then we'd both know exactly what his reaction would be.'

'You wouldn't,' she said, her voice betraying her panic.

'I might.' He grinned. 'Merely as an interesting experiment to see which of us knows your husband better. And I don't think you would retaliate by telling my wife and daughter because you care too much what they think of you, and I don't.'

And with that he blew her a kiss and dashed across the street, to the safety of his high-rise glass office building.

And Marla stood there in a daze, not even seeing her car as the attendant drove up with it. All she could see was her life falling apart around her. Maybe she should tell Larry before Felix had a chance. But that thought terrified her. She could never tell him. It would destroy their lives. And that thought made her literally sick to her stomach.

Chapter 17

HE HEARD a thumping. Someone was pounding. He was in the dorm back at school and he had overslept. He had to get up and get to class. Professor Willard would kill him for being late again.

'Peter!' It was Felix's voice.

He wasn't in the dorm at school, he was at home in his own bed. And then all the misery and self-hatred that had been mercifully postponed during the time of precious sleep came rushing back.

'Peter, let me in.'

Something about Felix's voice brought an immediate and unreasonable fear to him. And then he remembered: Felix had come with the deposit and the purchase agreement to buy the estate.

He would have to decide.

'Peter!' The doorknob twisted back and forth, the door rattled in the jamb as Felix shook it.

'Wait, wait,' Peter called, pulling himself out of bed. He was still in his jeans from this morning, hadn't changed. What was the point of changing? He wasn't going anywhere. He *couldn't* go anywhere. Every hour he had awakened, thinking he would get up and go to work, but he was unable to bring himself to wake up. If only he wasn't so tired, if only he wasn't so bone tired.

Why had he locked the bedroom door this afternoon? He couldn't remember, something about locking out his fears. It hadn't occurred to him in his stuporous state that he couldn't be separated from his fears by a locked door and so he'd gone back to sleep again, hoping for true unconsciousness, which to him was the same as a trunkful of the sultan's treasure to a beggar.

Peter unlocked the door and Felix burst into the room as though he'd been leaning against the door. 'What's all this?' he asked, surveying the dark room, the disheveled bed, the clothes scattered about. He fixed Peter with a judgmental expression. 'You're really wallowing in it, aren't you?'

'I w-wasn't ex-pecting you,' Peter stammered.

Felix looked concerned. 'Why are you letting yourself get like this, Peter? You of all people know what a no-good son of a bitch your grandfather was. Why are you allowing this maudlin behavior over such an unworthy man?'

Peter's windpipe began to constrict, cutting off the air to

his lungs. He turned away from Felix and gasped for air, reaching out for the bed, grateful to sink down onto it again.

'Why don't you open a window in here?' Felix asked, aware of Peter's distress. 'The room smells.' He strode over to the corner and yanked the drapery pull. Bright light flooded the room from the late-afternoon sun and Peter's eyes contracted painfully. He turned away from the light as Felix watched him. He felt like a specimen on a slide. A slight breeze fluttered the sheer inner drapes and Peter shivered. How he longed to climb back under the covers and go back to sleep.

'So what was the final outcome of the commodity sale? Were you able to dump everything today? Or are they selling you out gradually to minimize the loss?'

Peter could hardly speak, let alone tell him. 'I wasn't able to sell any today,' he hedged. 'But tomorrow for sure I'll give the sell order.'

'Why not?' Felix was amazed. 'How difficult is it to call a goddamned broker and say "sell platinum"? Jesus, Peter, what's the matter with you? You can't afford to wait any longer. I've been telling you that over and over. What is it? Do you need someone to take you by the hand and do it for you? Do you want me to do it? I will. I'll be here first thing in the morning and make those calls myself. You just tell me whom to call.'

He watched Peter, waiting for a reaction. And when there wasn't one, except for a slight shake of the head, he shrugged. 'Well, I'm here if you need me,' he said. 'And speaking of that. Here they are.' He advanced toward Peter, his hand outstretched holding a sheaf of papers.

The sound of the papers rattling was like firecrackers in Peter's ears.

'There's a check for fifty thousand up front, cash deposit,' Felix said brightly. 'And I'll release any amount of the down payment you need to pay off your debts before the close of escrow. After all, I do trust you. Go on, read it over, everything's there.'

Peter felt as though he were being pressed by an industrial steamer, as though Felix in his eagerness were as hot and terrible as the jaws of a steam press ready to clamp down on him and take out all his wrinkles with one searing hiss and a white-hot contraction of its iron claws. He put out his hand and pushed the outstretched papers away, then turned his head.

Felix stopped. 'What's the matter?' he asked suspiciously. 'Are you sick?'

It was such an understatement that Peter almost laughed. But instead of laughter he felt a pain of such intensity well up in him that he couldn't contain it. *Yes*, he wanted to shout, *I'm sick, with a sickness in my soul that cannot be cured. It has festered and contaminated me and everyone I love since the day I was born and now it's blighting everything around me with its noxious poisons. And the worst part of all, the very worst part, is that the disease is me.*

'I can't do it,' Peter whispered. 'I just can't. Please forgive me, Felix. I know you're trying to help me, but I just can't.'

'What are you talking about?'

Felix moved backward across the room, never taking his eyes off Peter until the back of his leg touched the edge of the ottoman in front of the chair. He sat down, he elbows on his knees, a fake concerned expression on his face.

'I believe what you told me the other day,' Peter continued. 'That you only informed the CFTC on our platinum investments to stop my grandfather from committing worse crimes than he already had and to save me from being compelled to help him. I can see that.' He spoke softly, gently, on the edge of tears, trying to make Felix understand, trying not to offend. 'And you've come here today with this money out of the generosity of your nature, to help me because I've done something so stupid that I need your help. And there is nothing more on this earth that I want more than to keep McKintridge in my family. You don't know how much I want it.'

432

'Well, then?' Felix asked.

'But I can't sell it to you,' Peter said. 'Not if I want to honor the memory of my grandfather. I think he would rather see McKintridge go to some stranger, to anyone, rather than to you because of the way he felt about you.' He couldn't hold back the pain any longer and the tears came. The look on Felix's face was so devastating. 'I'm so sorry, Felix. You've been wonderful to me and I'll be grateful for your offer for the rest of my life, but my conscience won't let me go through with my agreement with you. I'm going to put the estate on the open market and let the proceeds of the sale pay off the commodity debt. I only pray there's enough money to cover it all.'

There was a moment of excruciating silence. It was so quiet that Peter could hear his electric clock humming on the bedside table.

And then Felix spoke. 'No, you're not, Peter,' he said. 'No you're not.'

Something in Felix's tone obliterated Peter's sorrow and he snapped his head up to look at his father-in-law.

Felix was grinning, a broad, happy, terrifying grin, as though Mephistopheles had just captured another soul. 'You poor, soppy little pile of nothing. You think you can say no to me and that's all there is to that?'

'Please, Felix—' Peter began, sensing something untoward in Felix's tone, something almost vicious.

'Don't "Felix" me, you little worm. I didn't think I would ever have to tell you this, but now I shall, you and your misguided sense of loyalty.' And with that he threw his head back and laughed while Peter watched in bewilderment.

'Your signature on these papers is only a formality, only something that allows you to save face, that makes for a smoother transition of ownership. For it's I who really own McKintridge because I own all the outstanding paper on the property. I bought it months ago from the mortgage companies who loaned the money to your grandfather. I have the power to institute foreclosure proceedings against you at any time if your mortgage payment is one hour overdue. I know Belson reserved some cash to keep paying on his loans, but that cash will run out eventually and when you are forced to sell, I shall exercise something else I own, an option for "right of first refusal" for the McKintridge estate.'

'But why?' Peter asked. The shock of Felix's words was not nearly as awful as the tone of his voice and the hatred in his eyes. He seemed ready to explode with hatred, as though the fumes of his internal combustion were ignited and billowing forth into flames. He glared at Peter with such loathing. Peter recognized the expression immediately. It was the same look his grandfather had given him so many times before. But seeing it on Felix's face and aimed at him struck him as a fatal blow.

'You ask why?' Felix said. 'Because I want to destroy Belson and that's exactly what I've done and I don't want to wait any longer. I'm not going to be satisfied until I tear down McKintridge stone by stone; there's nothing you can do about it. So you can sign the papers or not, however you choose. But if you sign them you'll at least have access to some ready cash and it will save you the legal expense if I sue for specific performance.'

'What about me?' Peter whispered.

'It's just too bad about you,' Felix replied. 'Especially since you proved to be so helpful in getting me what I wanted. I used to wonder if all the patience I exercised with you, all the groundwork I laid, would ever pay off. Well, it finally did. I knew you would be the key to Belson, that through you I could pull him down. And that's exactly what happened. Of course anyone as loathsome as Belson would naturally sow the seeds of his own destruction.'

'You mean, you've only been kind to me over the years to get to my grandfather?'

Peter's vulnerability somehow reached beyond Felix's hatred. 'No, of course not,' Felix said with some embarrassment.

But Peter didn't believe him. He knew the truth. He had

434

aroused only ugliness in those he loved and that could only mean he was as disgusting as he believed he was. He leaned forward over his knees and clutched his arms around his body to contain the waves of sickness that shot through him. The pain was worse than dying; he felt he would ignite with it.

'Well,' Felix asked, 'are you going to sign, or aren't you?'

But Peter couldn't reply. All he could do was think about the years of devotion he'd felt for Felix, of admiration, of love. To know what Felix really thought about him was too much for him. Felix must know his secret too.

Felix was talking to him, but Peter couldn't hear him. He had retreated into his nightmare world again, where the screams of innocent victims and the smell of burning flesh rent his soul. But the more he kept silent, the more angry Felix became, until Felix's fingers were digging into his shoulders and he felt himself being shaken back and forth so hard his teeth clattered together top against bottom, all the while hearing Felix hammering at him to 'Sign—damn it—sign. I've waited long enough for this moment, long enough!'

'Nooo,' he said, over and over, until finally Felix stopped.

'All right,' Felix said. 'Suit yourself. But Phyllis will get you to sign it. I'm sure she will.'

Peter didn't hear him. Somewhere inside he had stepped into a dark cave and pulled the rock door closed behind him. He didn't even hear when Felix left. And this time he didn't even have to close his eyes to find the blackness of sleep.

Chapter 18

PHYLLIS WAS tired and discouraged when she drove into her driveway at five thirty after taking Jonathan to the doctor. He was hungry and cranky and his tears tried her patience, but at least there was nothing more wrong with him than a virus.

She glanced up at her bedroom window, wondering how Peter was; the window was dark but at least the drapes were open, that was a good sign. The front door opened just then and she looked up, hoping to see Peter standing there as he'd been a week ago, in slacks and a vest, his shirt sleeves rolled up, and a smile of welcome on his face for her. But it was only Lupe.

'Señor Anhalt was here,' Lupe said, opening the car door on Jonathan's side and unhooking his safety belt. 'He have *mucho* yelling with Señor McKintridge.'

Phyllis's silent alarm rang wildly. 'My father was angry with the Señor?'

Lupe nodded, full of importance for imparting this news, her eyes round with concern.

'How is Mr McKintridge?' Phyllis asked, lifting Jonathan out of his car seat and handing him to Lupe.

'Not so very good,' she pronounced with a negative assessment.

Phyllis raced up the stairs, wondering why her father had done such a thing when Peter was in such a delicate condition. He should never have upset him at all.

Peter was sitting on the edge of the bed, leaning forward with his arms wrapped around himself, staring at the floor.

436

He didn't look up or respond when Phyllis called his name. But when she touched his shoulder, part of him came to life, and he reached out his arms to encircle her waist. Even on this warm summer day his body was freezing cold, his hands and feet like ice. She stood holding him for a moment and then unlocked his arms and sat down on the bed to rub the circulation back into him. How long had he been sitting here like this? she wondered. 'What did my father say to you when he was here?' she asked. But he didn't reply, only reached out and put his arms around her again, clutching her silently. She held him for a while, not knowing what to do. There was a new element to his depressed state that she hadn't seen before. It was as if he weren't all there, as though part of him were gone, somehow locked away, and the rest of him acted only out of reflex.

'What happened, Peter, can you tell me? What did my father want?' She felt as though she were talking to a very small child or an injured animal.

At the mention of her father's name, Peter let go of her and turned away. She stroked his head, noticing that his hair needed washing. 'Would you rather I not talk about it?' she asked.

No reply.

'How about a nice shower?' she asked. 'Would you like that? You haven't had one today, have you?'

No answer.

She hurried into the bathroom, feeling as though she had to get him into the shower right away or something terrible would happen. She turned on the heater, took some bath sheets out of the cupboard, found his blue terry robe, and then back into the bedroom. He was sitting exactly as she left him; he hadn't even blinked.

She took his hand and led him into the bathroom; he followed her docilely, letting her pull off his shorts and T-shirt, adjust the water, and help him into the shower. But still he barely responded. 'Peter,' she called, trying to arouse him from his stupor. But it did no good. He just stood there. Since he wouldn't wash himself, she realized

437

she'd have to do it for him. She undressed quickly, tucked her long blond hair into a shower cap, and stepped in with him. It was the saddest moment of her life, washing him as if he were a helpless baby, turning him around to rinse the soapy parts, seeing his young, perfect body so deadened that even her presence didn't awaken him and he was unresponsive to the semi-erotic motions of her touch. She shampooed his hair and helped him to rinse it off. He wasn't protecting himself from the sheeting water of the shower and she had to move him out of the spray when he was rinsed. She shut off the water and wrapped him in a towel which he let hang around his shoulders while she dried and dressed herself again; then she dried him off, toweled his hair, combing it as she combed Jonathan's hair after his baths, and then helped him into his robe.

When he was all clean and combed and back into his slippers again, he finally came to partial life, turning and hugging her heavily with deep despair. The gesture had a finality to it and she felt like saying 'There now.'

'Would you like to come down to dinner tonight and eat with me and Jonathan?'

A fleeting look of panic dashed across his face but he didn't reply. 'It will be all right,' she assured him. 'I'll be there. I'll help you.' And when there was no further resistance, she took him by the hand and led him carefully downstairs.

Just get through this meal, she told herself, *get him back to bed and then you can collapse, or scream, or run crying out into the night.* All three possibilities drew her irresistibly.

By some miracle the sight of Jonathan in his high chair gnawing on a pretzel restored Peter enough to attempt to eat. He chewed slowly, carefully, only a few silent bites, as though the food were a curiosity more than a sustenance, and when he smiled at her, he didn't really seem to see her. If she asked him a direct question, he merely smiled. Phyllis found Jonathan's bewilderment over Peter's behavior the most heartrending thing of all. Peter always played games

438

with the baby when Jonathan was in his high chair and he obviously missed it. Peter's empty, nonresponsive expression filled her with dread.

As soon as dinner was over and she had him back upstairs in bed in front of the TV, she rushed to the phone to call Larry.

The sound of Marla answering the phone with such a calm tone of voice nearly made her break down. But she had to be strong for Peter's sake. After she described Peter's condition to them, they were as alarmed as she was.

'I'm calling a psychiatrist friend of mine immediately,' Larry insisted. 'Peter may need hospitalization.'

The psychiatrist's name was Dr Klein.

'Can you put my husband in the hospital, Doctor?' she asked after describing Peter's symptoms.

'No, Mrs McKintridge, I'm afraid I can't. The Lanterman-Petris-Short decision in California law prevents psychiatric hospitalization of a patient against their will unless they are acutely suicidal, acutely homicidal, or gravely disabled and unable to feed or clothe themselves. My strongest recommendation is to get him to professional help right away. There is a twenty-four-hour emergency psychiatric outpatient clinic at UCLA. If he won't see me or any other therapist, perhaps there is a family doctor whom he trusts.'

Phyllis thanked him for his advice and agreed to do as he suggested.

'Call me anytime tonight if you need me,' Dr Klein said. 'And try to impress upon him how important it would be to talk to someone. I'll make myself available for you, if you call.'

Minutes passed by, turning into a half hour and then an hour while Phyllis sat in the hall by the phone on a straight-backed chair, her mind searching, reaching, trying for possible solutions. Peter had always resisted seeing a psychiatrist before when she'd suggested he do so for his headaches, but now she would have to insist. *My darling Peter,* she thought, *how can I help you?*

Jonathan had his bath without her and was put to bed.

Lupe locked up the house and set the alarm. Still Phyllis sat. The sound of the TV upstairs was muffled and far away, yet unchanging. If Peter was watching it, he'd be changing the channels. She heard a toilet flush upstairs and was gratified to note that at least Peter was well enough to attend to his bodily functions on his own, and then she remembered how he'd been in the shower and she started to cry, a kind of helpless mewing sound that did not relieve her sadness but only underscored her fear.

Finally she couldn't put it off any longer; she would have to discuss his seeing a psychiatrist.

With every step he climbed, she felt as though a ton of pressure were forcing her back. Exhaustion dragged at her body as she placed one foot above the other.

Their bedroom was dark except for the flickering light of the TV. Merv Griffin was interviewing beautiful young fashion models, their faces alive with self-satisfaction and expectation. She remembered when she'd felt that way. A century ago.

Peter didn't look at her or acknowledge her presence when she entered so she changed into her nightgown and robe, avoiding as long as possible the conversation ahead. Finally she came back and sat beside him on the bed and was amazed to see him turn and look at her, really look. And then he smiled. It was as though someone had turned on a light at the end of a long, dark tunnel.

She cried out with joy, 'Oh, Peter, I've been so worried about you, so worried.' And she buried her head in his lap and cried while he stroked her hair.

'I know,' he said. 'I'm sorry. Please don't cry, I can't stand to see you crying.'

'I spoke to a psychiatrist a while ago,' she told him, her voice muffled by the bedding. 'His name is Dr Klein, he's a friend of Larry's. He sounds nice, darling. Will you talk to him? He said it was extremely important for you to talk to him.'

His hand, which had been stroking her hair, stiffened, and she picked up her head to look at him. His face was

440

twisted into a grimace as though he were fighting tears. But then he relaxed his expression. 'I'm okay now, Phyllis. Really, I'm okay, I don't need a doctor.'

'But it's *very* important,' she said again, watching for another blowup or a refusal, even for anger.

He looked away. 'If that's what you want,' he said resignedly. 'Maybe next week.'

She reached over and touched his shoulder and ran her hand down his arm. His hand was warm and so very dear to her. She picked it up in both of hers and kissed it. 'You must go right away,' she said. 'If we wait too long, you might change your mind.'

He stiffened again and she was afraid he would close himself off, but he said, 'All right, when do you want me to go?'

'Tomorrow,' she said firmly. 'I'll call in the morning.'

His eyes were filled with sadness and his voice caught in his throat. 'I'm afraid, Phyl. I'm so afraid.'

'I'll be there all the time if you want me to be, and I won't leave you.' And she squeezed his hand and kissed it again.

'I need you so much,' he said. 'I don't want to lose you.'

'You won't! I promise,' she insisted, feeling hope bloom once again in her heart like a sturdy flower pushing through the rocky crags of a barren landscape.

'I'm so tired,' he said. 'I want to sleep tonight. I don't want to have to think about selling the commodities in the morning or meeting with the CFTC lawyer or seeing a psychiatrist. Will you give me one sleeping pill tonight, and then will you hold my hand while I fall asleep? Maybe I will be able to rest.'

She still had his sleeping pills in her purse and she went and got him one with a glass of water, which she placed by his side of the bed. Then she took one pill herself and climbed into bed. It would be good to sleep, she thought, and just forget about everything for an entire night. He was going to be all right. She knew he was going to be all right.

They both fell asleep holding hands.

Chapter 19

MARLA SAT on the bed in her bedroom, listening anxiously to Larry's side of the conversation with Dr Klein. When he was through, she searched his face for some sign of hope. 'What did he say? Is he going to help Peter?'

Larry nodded. 'Mort is an excellent therapist. I've recommended several clients to him and they've all been satisfied. He's going to tell Phyllis that someone must intervene with Peter immediately.'

'Does he think Peter's having a breakdown?'

'It looks that way.'

'I had no idea he was so close to the edge, did you?' she asked. 'Did you see this coming?'

'No,' he said. 'I knew he was troubled, but not this badly.' Larry went into the dressing room and started to undress.

Marla followed him. 'Do you think we should go over there tonight?'

Larry shrugged. 'I don't think it would help. We'd just be in the way. I told Phyllis if she needed us, to call. I'm sure she will.' He turned to her. 'I hope he's well enough to go with me to that meeting in the morning. We can't cancel with the CFTC attorney; it would make Peter look too guilty.'

Marla reached into her closet for a clean nightgown. This crisis with Peter coming so soon after Belson's death made her feel very close to Larry. She wanted to tell him how much she cared, but she was afraid he wouldn't believe her. Love was something they hadn't discussed in a long time. And Felix's comments to her this afternoon about Larry were still gnawing at her. She had planned to discuss them

442

with Larry tonight, but now it didn't seem opportune. Larry's face in the bathroom mirror was tight with worry and her heart went out to him. She knew how much he cared about Peter and so did she. Peter's illness would affect Larry's career as drastically as his legal problems had.

They both came back into the bedroom as the phone rang again. Marla picked it up.

'Marla, it's Felix.' The sound of that voice shot sudden guilt through her. Was he calling to make good his threat to tell Larry about their affair? *Oh, please, not now,* she thought. 'Let me talk to Larry,' he demanded.

Every ounce of her being wanted to resist his demand and hang up. *Don't tell him,* she thought. 'Larry's very upset right now; it's not a good time to talk to him.' She forced her voice to remain calm. 'Have you spoken to Phyllis?'

'Yes, yes,' he said impatiently. 'I talked to her earlier. Now put Larry on!'

She stood there for a moment silently, pretending to be listening to Felix, though Felix wasn't saying a word, but she was stalling while her panicked brain tried to think of what to do. Should she pull the phone out of the wall and blurt out the truth, throw herself on Larry's mercy before Felix could tell him?

Larry was watching her and noticed her extreme agitation. 'What is it, Marla? Who's on the phone?'

She gave him a kind of sick smile and said, 'It's Felix.' But before he took the phone from her, she turned away and said into the receiver, 'For God's sake, Felix, *please!*' And then she handed it to Larry.

She kept her back turned, not realizing that her shoulders were tensed into knots while she waited for the explosion that would surely come at any moment.

'How's Peter?' Larry asked. And then he was silent, listening to Felix talk while Marla's pulse raced. She felt so helpless; there was nothing she could do but wait until it was all over and then see if there were any pieces of her life she could salvage. At this moment, if she could have, she would have erased every moment with Felix from her past.

'Yes,' Larry was saying. 'I know.'

She could hear Felix's excited voice through the receiver. He was shouting, speaking rapidly, insistingly, but she couldn't distinguish his words.

'No,' Larry said, and then repeated it again with great distress. 'Oh, no! You shouldn't have done that!'

Marla's head grew light and dizzy with apprehension. She clutched the edge of the bedside table where she was standing so hard that her whole body ached.

'I won't do that,' Larry said. 'I absolutely refuse. I'm sorry I ever talked to you in the first place. Peter is hanging on by an emotional thread and I feel partially responsible for that, Felix. I will not put any more pressure on him to sign that bill of sale for the sake of your impatience no matter what you say is at stake.'

Marla turned to stare at him. They weren't talking about her. What was he saying about pressuring Peter? That would be the worst thing for Peter now.

Larry had that sick, guilty expression on his face, the one she knew so well and hated as well as she knew it. *Larry was guilty of something. Of what?*

'All right, Felix,' he said. 'If that's the way you feel about it, it's your perogative. There's nothing more I can say, except I think your lack of compassion for a man in Peter's mental condition borders on the criminal.'

Marla could hear the sound of Felix's receiver being slammed down in Larry's ear.

Larry hung up the phone and looked away; his mouth was dry and he licked his lips. Then he sighed. 'Jesus, this keeps getting worse and worse.'

'Why did you tell Felix you were partly responsible for Peter's condition right now?' she asked, remembering Felix's sly innuendos today.

'Because I could have been a better friend to him these past months,' he hedged. 'I bitched and complained every time he wasn't in the office. I made it extra tough on him

444

when he was already in a terrible spot.'

'But you didn't know what he was doing, did you? How could you have been expected to be more understanding?'

He gave her one of his lopsided smiles, but something didn't feel right. 'I dunno,' he said.

'God, I hate it when you lie to me!' she snapped.

'What?' He was so injured. 'I'm not—'

'Don't, Larry! Just don't say anything you'll have to retract later.'

'All right,' he said. 'I won't.'

She followed him around to his side of the bed.

'Why did Felix imply to me that he wasn't the only one who had betrayed Peter and Belson?' She watched his eyes. If they narrowed to a normal position, he was telling the truth, but if they opened wider than usual, it meant he was lying.

He turned away from her and she couldn't tell. 'When did he say that?'

'This afternoon when I met him for a drink.'

'Why the hell did you do that, Marla?' he exploded, turning on her. 'The goddamned job is over. We gave a party last Saturday night to celebrate, remember? Why does *my* wife find it necessary to meet that lecher for cocktails? Or do you do it every day? Is that why you're never home till seven at night? Because you're out having drinks with your boyfriend?'

'Just answer my question first, Larry,' she insisted. 'Why did you go to Felix's yacht one afternoon two weeks ago? Was it about Peter?'

He looked caught, the wide eyes of a cat impaled in the headlights of an oncoming car. 'Yes!' he shouted. 'Yes. Felix told you, didn't he?' There were tears in his eyes. 'I've been such a schmuck.' And then he told her what part he had played in Peter's predicament, how Peter had confided in him, and how he had told everything to Felix. 'Felix asked me months ago to find out what was going on with Peter and his grandfather because Felix was so worried about Peter. And I was so blinded by my own greed,

445

thinking Felix would refer me business. I let him convince me he was really concerned about Peter's life. And besides I was pissed at Peter when I found out what he'd been doing. I wanted him stopped. I was thinking about myself.'

'Oh, Larry, how could you,' she said.

'I said I was sorry! What more do you want from me? I've been trying to make it up to Peter, I'm doing my damnedest trying to help him now. And he's forgiven me, why can't you?' He seemed on the edge of despair.

'Because I'm afraid to forgive you,' she said. 'If you could betray Peter for your own good, maybe you could do the same for me. Maybe Felix was right about something else he said.'

'What?' he asked defiantly. 'What else did that cock-sucker say?'

'That you're a player, Larry. That you won't turn down a piece of ass if it's offered to you.' She was guessing, only guessing and praying with all her might that it wasn't true.

'How the hell does he know what I'm doing or not doing?' Larry said. 'That bastard should talk, the way he's always sniffing around you like you were a bitch in heat.'

'Doesn't it take one to know one?' she retorted, feeling anger pulsing through her body. 'Why don't you deny it? Why, why?' she screamed, suddenly knowing where all her fits of jealousy came from. Why didn't he just say it wasn't true?

'All right, all right,' he said. 'So I've had a few meaningless screws in my life, had a few laughs that didn't mean a thing. Just someone to let loose with now and then, when you're too tired, or too frigid, or *faking* it again!' he yelled. 'You think I don't know when you do that?'

What was he saying? A molten rage roared through her and she couldn't contain it. 'Who else have you screwed, Larry?' she screamed. 'Were they all meaningless screws, just for laughs, or were there a few meaningful ones too? Like Sheila Conway. Have you been fucking Sheila Conway?'

It was almost imperceptible, but he nodded.

446

'No!' she screamed.

The explosion shocked them both when she hit him. She clenched her fists and hit him with all her might, over and over again on his arms and his chest, pounding, flailing, pounding again and again. She hated him with her entire being. The worst thing had happened and it hurt even more than she'd imagined. 'Who else?' she screamed. 'Who else, who else?' She remembered all the times he had denied it, all the lies he'd told her to her face. 'Not *me* baby, you know *me*, I only dig *you*. Sheila? She's too artificial, she's too hard. She doesn't appeal to me.' And she'd believed him. What a fool!

'There were others,' he said, trying to stop her, backing away to protect himself. 'I admit it. There were others.'

'How many?' She kept advancing; she wanted to tear his eyes out.

'I couldn't count.'

'Oh, God!' she moaned, stopping in her tracks, feeling as though all the wind had been knocked out of her. She gasped with the pain. And then the fires were stoked again and red-hot fury came whipping through her once more. 'Well, you're not the only one!' she said, thrusting out her jaw in bitter meanness, wanting to stab him as deeply, as painfully, as he'd wounded her.

'What are you saying?' His mouth was white around the edges, his eyes tight and wild. He grabbed her shoulders. 'What do you mean?' he cried.

'I've been having an affair with Felix!' She spat the words at him, unable to control her spite, her overwhelming spite.

'Felix!' he yelled. 'No! You're just saying it to get back at me.'

'It's true!' she said, defiantly wishing she could laugh in his face but the rage brewing in his eyes kept her back. 'I've been screwing him on his boat. And I was there that day when you came to tell him about Peter, you didn't even know it.'

Then he exploded, slapping her so hard it brought tears to her eyes. 'You filthy cunt, you bitch, you bitch!' he yelled, shaking her, slapping her, and she just hit him back with every slap he delivered. They were both enraged, out of control, crying, cursing, flailing at each other until she hit him so hard with the side of her hand she was afraid she'd broken it. A sharp pain shot up her arm and she cried out and bent forward, clutching her hand between her knees until the throbbing eased a bit.

Her injury shocked him into reality and they pulled away from one another, each turning into their own personal hell. Marla's guts ached and she hurt so badly both inside and out that she couldn't bear it. She started to cry. Larry was crying too.

'What have we done?' he said. 'I hit you; my God, I hit you.'

She couldn't reply, just shook her head, trying not to imagine him, her Larry, doing it with someone else. That most intimate, most secret sharing of oneself. It made her sick to her soul. And yet she had done it too. *She had done it.* How could she both minimize it in her own mind and yet feel it was the entire basis of her being, of their marriage?

'I'm sorry I hit you,' he said, his voice quivering. 'I thought I would never do that in my life.'

'I am too,' she whispered.

'Are you all right?'

But his question only brought her more pain. 'I may never be all right again.'

'How did it happen? With *him?*' He couldn't bring himself to say Felix's name.

'The same as you and Sheila, I guess,' she countered.

'I deserved that,' he agreed. And then he sighed and blew his nose. 'Now what?' he asked.

'Do you want a divorce?' she said, barely above a whisper.

'No,' he said. 'I don't think so, do you?'

'I don't know,' she said. 'I don't know.' And then she clutched herself and cried again. 'It hurts so much, Larry. I didn't know it would hurt so much.'

But he didn't reply. And then, 'Do you think there's a

chance we could work through this?'

She shook her head. 'I don't know.' She looked up at him. 'Have you been doing this for a long time?'

He nodded sadly.

'Oh-hh,' and her eyes spilled over again. 'Why, Larry? Didn't you love me?'

'It hasn't got anything to do with love. I love you too much. I've always been afraid this would happen. It's almost as if I drove you to it to prove that you didn't love me, or to justify my own need for other women. Oh, God, I've wanted to stop so many times but I couldn't, I just don't know.'

'You're exactly like your father,' she said angrily.

'Don't say that,' he cried, 'please don't say that. I don't want to be.'

She could see his pain and she was truly sorry. She reached out to touch him but she couldn't do it. Not yet. There was too much ahead of them to get through. Would they ever be able to?

'I'd go to a marriage counselor with you if you want,' he said. There was a sound of desperation in his voice. But as comforting as that thought was, it frightened her. Were they really that bad off? And wouldn't that really break them apart? 'Why?' she asked. 'Why now?'

'Because I want us to work it out,' he said. 'Do you?'

'I don't know,' she said. 'I just don't know.'

'Do you want me to go to a hotel tonight?'

She started to cry again. 'If you go, I'm afraid you won't come back. And you're my best friend. If you go, who will I have to tell how much you've hurt me?'

He reached to put his arm around and she let him. 'I know what you mean,' he said.

'Maybe we're the ones who should call Dr Klein in the morning.'

'Maybe we are,' he said, holding her lightly as a precious part of him. 'Maybe we are.'

They talked most of the night, confessing all their sordid

449

deeds and with each fresh confession came a torrent of pain and accusations and recriminations and fears. Larry had committed many more offenses, but hers was bad enough because of whom she had chosen. Sleeping with Felix was the ultimate betrayal. It made Larry squirm with frustration and fury.

But she felt he had driven her to it by his indifference ever since the early years of their marriage and by his roving eye, which she always knew was there. 'It hurt me so much when you'd flirt with other women right in front of me,' she told him.

'Your independence frightened me,' he said. 'I knew someday you'd walk out and leave me. You were so different from what I thought a wife should be.'

'Different from your mother, the kitchen aide,' she retorted.

He agreed without being offended. 'But that's why I was afraid to really care. Yet, I've always loved you.'

'And you're not my ideal of what a husband should be either,' she said.

'I've always known that,' he admitted. 'It's always made me feel inadequate.'

'Yet, I've always loved you,' she countered. Marla was so exhausted that her eyes were closing against their will. Nothing had been settled, but there was hope for their future. This was the first time in ten years of marriage that they had really talked. There was so much stale air to dispel. All the dried-up conversations of a lifetime. And just before she felt the heaviness of sleep overtake her Larry reached over and took her hand. For the first time in years she didn't pull away.

Chapter 20

PETER AWOKE at two thirty in the morning, aching terror
pressed in on him again. He could not breathe. 'No, no,' he
was crying, while voices screamed in his head. He felt the
sting of his grandfather's words like a whip lashing his body
raw, blow after blow; Felix hissed at him like an angry
snake whose venomous jaws were ready to strike with
virulent hatred; his parents and sister pointed at him,
damning him while their flesh disintegrated, seared by
flames. 'You did it, you did it all,' they accused him as they
cried.

He bolted up in bed, gasping for air, his heart pounding,
his body soaking wet. His heart was thumping like a giant
drum in his ears and his head throbbed with every beat.
Tomorrow loomed ahead like a terrifying beast. If he sold
the commodities, it would eliminate all chance of preserving his grandfather's estate; if he met with the lawyer
and it turned out as badly as he expected, it would tear out
his heart; and to confess to a psychiatrist would destroy his
very soul. *He could not do it.* He could not do any of it.
Phyllis would find out what he had done and he would lose
her too. She was all he had left, but she would end up hating
him more than anyone else hated him. It was too much to
face, too much, too much.

He could not live with this fear and self-loathing any
longer. It had been with him every day of his life since he
was ten years old and woke in the hospital still alive while
all the rest of his family was dead. The self-loathing had
never gone away and it never would.

Only his need to blot out the pain propelled him from the bed. He was tired, so very tired.

He walked quietly across the floor to the secretary against the wall. Inside was the letter he had written to Phyllis earlier in the evening while she was downstairs on the phone. He placed it on her bedside table. Then he went over to her purse lying on the chaise longue. His heart was still pounding. Foolish heart, it believed he still needed it. His brain knew he didn't. His brain was fuzzy, as though muffled in gauze.

Should he kiss Jonathan one last time? No. His resolve might crumble if he looked at that sweet face again in trustful slumber. He would not think about his son. Jonathan was better off without him; he was nothing but a weight of shame around his son's neck.

The bottle of Seconals in Phyllis's purse was nearly full; he did not pause, did not hesitate, swallowed them all at once, nearly forty in all, washing them down with the water at his bedside table. If only the ache and the pain would go away. Soon, soon, he wouldn't feel them anymore.

And he'd never have a bad dream again.

He got back into bed and leaned over to kiss Phyllis lightly on the forehead. A sob caught in his throat. 'Goodbye, my love,' he whispered. And then with unshed tears in his eyes he took hold of her warm hand in his and closed his eyes.

Chapter 21

SOMETHING WAS wrong. Phyllis sensed it the second she awoke. Peter's hand was heavy in hers; his fingers were chilled and hard. She let go of his hand and turned to look at him. He was asleep, his peaceful profile in the morning light calm and serene. He was so still and quiet. She glanced at the bedside clock and saw propped against it an envelope with her name on it in Peter's handwriting. And in that instant she knew; and she sat up in bed, horrified, screaming his name, *'Peter,* no!' But her voice only echoed in the canyons of her mind. He would never hear it again.

Phyllis could not screaming, though she tried to force herself to stop because of the baby. She was horrified, frozen, unable to move, to see if he was alive, even though she knew he wasn't, to try and help him, even though she knew she couldn't. If she moved one inch, she was afraid it would be to run across the room and throw herself out of the window. And then she saw the empty bottle of pills by his bedside, her purse lying open on the chaise longue and the dam broke; spasms of molten grief engulfed her so strongly that she wanted to die. *'Anything anything anything,* I'll do anything, but please don't let him be dead.' She was sobbing so hard that she could not catch her breath; she was unable to walk, so she crawled away from the bed across the room to the door to get help. Between spasms of grief she called for Lupe and finally she was so overcome that she was unable to hold herself up at all and fell on the floor, writhing in pain.

When Lupe found her employer dead in his bed from an overdose and her mistress lying in torment on the floor, she too was overcome with horror and grief. The two women held one another like flood victims grasping onto the branches of a tree, crying and crying as their sobs intermingled.

When Phyllis's brain was able to function above the pain, she realized she had to act and slowly she disengaged herself from Lupe. Then she pulled herself over to the phone and dialed the emergency number posted there. She could not look at Peter, could not turn around, look at him again. Using the table to help herself stand up and forced to stand upon her feet, she left the room.

The upper hall swam around her. Dizzy and dazed, her head spinning, her body in shock, she heard Lupe call her parents and then Larry and Marla. And then she remembered the note and turned back to get it.

But Lupe handed it to her at the bedroom door so she would not have to go in there again. Her hands were shaking as though she had palsy.

He has murdered me, she thought and then broke into heartrenching sobs again. 'Peter, no,' she cried over and over. 'I love you, I love you, don't leave me.' She heard the sound of tearing paper without even realizing she'd opened the envelope.

My Darling Phyllis,

What can a coward say to an angel? If I stayed with you, your beauty, your strength, your perfection would shame me evermore. I have basked in your golden glow too long, draining you for my sustenance. You have given me everything. The only moments of pure love I've ever known were gifts from you. But I did not deserve them and the burden of my debts grew too heavy to bear.

I always told you I was unworthy of you and now you have seen evidence of that. There is still more. I could not bear to see the look in your eyes when you learned the rest.

Forgive me, my darling, for never telling you my most shameful secret. But I never told it to a living soul.

I was at the controls of my father's plane when it flew into the mountain. I am the one who caused the death of my own family. I had been allowed to fly the plane several times before and that day I wanted to again. It was raining and Jack, the pilot, said no. But I begged and pleaded like the ten-year-old brat that I was and he let me. And then something happened, suddenly the mountain was ahead of us. Jack yelled at me to pull up, and I did. But it was too late, one of the engines had lost power and we crashed.

I should have died with them then; I've only been living on borrowed time ever since. I couldn't live with any of it any longer,

I love you forever,
Goodbye, Peter

Chapter 22

FELIX DROVE his golden Camargue at breakneck speeds over the mile and a half between his house and Phyllis's. Audrey was crying in the seat next to him.

'God, I wish you'd stop that,' he said through clenched teeth. 'That animal doesn't deserve your tears. How could he do such a thing to his own child and to Phyllis? How could he do it?'

'Where is your compassion, Felix?' she asked. 'He's dead. The boy's dead.' And she cried more deeply. 'So sweet, he was such a sweet man. And Phyllis loved him so, how is she ever going to get over this?'

'The shame of it!' Felix said, taking the corner of Foothill and Sunset with tires screeching. 'A suicide. Jonathan has to live with it the rest of his life.'

They passed Vicky Feinstein coming out of Phyllis's tree-shrouded driveway. Jonathan was in his car seat next to her. He waved to his grandparents and Vicky waved too, a brief, sad acknowledgment.

Felix pulled into a driveway and parked behind a City of Beverly Hills police car. Larry Gilbert's Mercedes was there too.

The front door of the house was open and they could hear voices coming from the living room. Marla was wearing a pair of jeans and a Lacoste shirt; Larry was in similar attire. Phyllis was still in her robe, her face red and swollen, her hair in tangled, damp clumps. Felix had never seen her like this. Two plainclothes investigators were just leaving.

'It's only a formality, Mr Gilbert,' one of them said to Larry. 'We'll see that the autopsy is finished as quickly as possible so the body can be sent to the mortuary.'

Larry thanked him. He'd been crying too. Larry ignored Felix but kissed Audrey quickly before she hurried to Phyllis's side.

'Mother,' Phyllis sobbed. 'I could have helped him. It wasn't his fault. He was only a boy when it happened. It was the fault of the airplane, not his. If only he had told me. Why didn't he tell me?'

'Mrs Anhalt,' Marla said to Audrey. 'Can you get her to take a sedative?' I think she should have something.'

'No,' Phyllis screamed. 'No pills. No pills!'

'All right, darling,' Audrey soothed. 'All right.' She looked at Marla helplessly.

'Phyllis,' Marla said softly. 'Would you come with me upstairs and put some clothes on? You'll feel better, I'm sure. There will be people coming over soon.'

Phyllis looked down at her robe; she hadn't realized what she was wearing. She nodded sadly. 'But we'll have to change in the guest room. I won't go in that room ever again.'

'That's all right,' Marla said, helping her up. Audrey supported her on the other side and the three women went to make the slow ascent up the stairs.

As soon as they were out of the room, Larry turned to Felix. 'I'd like to tear you apart, Anhalt, I'd like to rip you to pieces, and not just because of you and Marla—you didn't destroy my marriage—but you did a hell of a job on Phyllis's. I hope you're proud of yourself—you've made her a widow.' And he pushed past Felix on his way to the front door.

'Wait a minute,' Felix said, incensed at the innuendo. 'You don't mean I had something to do with this?'

Larry spun around, his fists clenched, his body rigid with fury. 'I don't have time to waste with you. No, I have to meet with the lawyer from the CFTC and tell him that Peter is dead.' Tears came to his eyes. 'And you're the one who crucified him, you *bastard*,' he said, spitting out the words. 'Belson was the one who condemned him, but you were his executioner. Well, now you've gotten what you wanted, the McKintridge estate belongs to Phyllis. I'm sure you can get her to sell it to you.' And then he left.

Felix watched him go. Larry was hurt and upset, he didn't mean the things he'd said. Felix didn't believe for one minute that he had anything to do with Peter's suicide. But Larry was right about one thing. Phyllis owned the estate now. That was the only bit of good news to come out of this tragedy; he hadn't even realized it until now. And of course Phyllis would sell him the estate. What did she care if he tore it down? As soon as she was feeling better, he would ask her. He could hardly wait.

Chapter 23

THERE WAS no antidote for the pain, no surcease: it was a state of continual physical torture at the hands of a sadistic enemy, but even a prisoner might pass out and escape for a brief moment the unbearable throbbing ache from burns and garrots, whips and beatings, broken bones and smashed teeth, crushed fingers, and mutilated parts. But Phyllis could not escape; even if she slept, the haunting knowledge in her subconscious would be worse than the waking knowledge: *I failed him, I failed him. He didn't love me, or he wouldn't have left me alone. Anything is better than this nothingness, and yet he chose this nothingness.* It was driving her insane. *Why? Why?* Would there ever be an answer? And then wave after wave of anguish would wash over her and she was again helpless against the tide of pain.

'His whole life he lived with the guilt that he had actually killed his family even though it was the plane's engine that failed and not a drop in altitude that caused the crash.' She sobbed after she showed Marla Peter's note. 'How he must have suffered with that.'

And with Larry she had cried, saying, 'His grandfather was one of the few people in the world Peter loved, but Peter couldn't save Belson's life or his fortune. It was a promise impossible to keep, like putting your finger in a dike and trying to hold back the power of Niagara Falls.'

'Belson was hard on Peter his whole life,' Vicky told her when she brought Jonathan back. Vicky stroked Phyllis's hands, put her arms around her, soothed her. 'I remember when we were kids how much Belson expected from Peter. And Belson was a more hateful man than any of us imagined.' For once Phyllis accepted that as true. 'He hurt you terribly, didn't he?' she asked. And Vicky nodded. 'Poor Peter,' Phyllis said.

But what was it that had pushed Peter over the edge?

Phyllis finally swallowed a sedative; one pill did not mean she was committing suicide. She spent time with Jonathan, telling him about his father, establishing a precedent for the day Jonathan was able to ask her about him. It was a dialogue that would never end for them throughout their lives and it exhausted her to contemplate the number of times Peter's death would affect them all. Her friends had cried with her briefly, deeply, and then gone to other concerns, Marla to check on her own children, Larry to the meeting on Peter's behalf. She knew they would come back to the pain with her again, deeply, briefly; it was the lack of Peter that would cause them all unalterable changes, especially Jonathan. 'We think we are all so strong,' Phyllis said to her mother. 'That our roots are imbedded in rock, when really they are planted so shallowly, we can be uprooted by a breath of air as small as a kitten's sneeze; our entire lives can be annihilated in a moment.'

What had pushed him over the edge?

The coroner's office called to say Peter's body had been

taken to the mortuary. She chose a suit and a shirt and tie for him to be buried in, the ones he'd worn to Belson's funeral. 'No shoes,' they told her, his feet wouldn't show in the open casket. Reverend Fields visited; kindly, compassionately, he listened to her description of her love. She cried as she told him, trying to distill Peter's essence into words.

Why, Peter, why?

It would be a private funeral, only the immediate family and friends. She couldn't endure a major spectacle. Her slender hold on life was pulled taut; it could snap at the tiniest yank. How could she strengthen it? She wondered. What could she do to hang on, to hold on to what they had without hating him? She didn't want their love to die with him; he couldn't take her life with him to the grave. She had loved him, still did, always would. There had to be a way to go on, to wade through the muck of fetid swamp he'd left her in.

Peter, why?

Another day until the funeral. One more day to find an answer she could offer to him while he was still here, before she had to say good-bye forever. She'd put it off, the taking leave of him, until those final moments when she was forced to. Until then she wouldn't think about his face, so dear and gentle, his arms around her: And yet all she wanted to do was talk about him. 'He was fine in the evening. He fell asleep holding my hand. He knew I was going to make things work for us.'

Why didn't he wait? Why didn't he let me help him?

Death is so final, there's no going back again, no second chance. And that's what she wanted with her entire being: a second chance. A way to show him he could have trusted her to help him, proof that she was strong enough for both of them, that she would have made it work. If only he had let her. She had to find her second chance.

She still had to face her first night without him. Soon it would be years without him.

'Phyllis, I'd like to talk to you about something.'

'Yes, Dad. What is it?' It was mid-afternoon and there was a lull in the steady stream of visitors who had been crowding the house all day. Phyllis had managed to eat a piece of coffee cake and a glass of milk. The food had regenerated her briefly. Now she could face life for the next ten minutes at least. She was in the breakfast room; yellow and green and white surrounded her. The sunny decor could not cheer her. Her father took a chair opposite her.

'Tomorrow is the funeral,' Felix said. 'And then after that, when you've had a chance to recover from this shock, you're going to have to face some difficult decisions. The same ones Peter would have faced concerning Belson's estate. I imagine there'll be some new additions to the problems since you are now Peter's heir.'

She stared at him blankly.

'What I'm saying, dear, is that my original offer to buy the estate from Peter still goes, but I want to add to it. You mustn't be burdened with any more than you've already had to bear. So I'm going to take care of everything for you. I'll handle the liquidation of the estate, all the assets, see that you and Jonathan are well provided for with the pro-ceeds that are left after the government takes their share. There should be enough money for the two of you, at least for a while. You just give me power of attorney and you won't have to worry about it ever again.'

She brushed the idea away, swatting it like a pesty fly. 'We'll talk about this later, Dad. I'm not certain what I want to do yet.'

'Yes, of course, dear,' he pressed. 'But later will be even more difficult for you. You might want to go away for a while, travel—you'll need to be free of these problems. This will be best for you. Trust me.'

She looked at him, alerted by his tone, by the way he was leaning toward her, too eagerly, too hopefully, too kindly. 'No, I don't think so, Dad,' she said. 'No decisions right now.'

'But why?' he asked, his eyes widening in surprise.

And she looked at him again, only this time she saw another element in his face that she'd never noticed before. It was rage. He was covering up the rage, but it was there just below his soft, solicitous smile. *My God, he was enraged.*

She shrank back imperceptibly, wishing she could run out of the room. But there were questions she had to ask him. Some she had wondered about over the past day; others she'd wanted to know for her whole life. 'Can I trust you, Dad? Will you tell me what I want to know?'

He nodded, spreading friendly calm over ugly rage. She shuddered.

'The other day when I spoke to you on the phone and told you Peter and I had decided to postpone selling the estate, that there was plenty of time to do it later, you agreed. I told you how terribly hurt Peter was, how wounded, and that I was very worried about him. You said you wouldn't press him, wouldn't discuss any business with him at all. And yet you came over here. Lupe told me she heard you yelling at Peter. Why did you do that? He was extremely unstable. Didn't you realize you could have hurt him badly, enough to make him want to kill himself?'

She was crying again because she wished she could go back and protect Peter from that encounter. If only, if only. 'What did you say to him, Dad? He was so much worse after your visit. What did you talk about?'

Felix was indignant. 'Oh, come now, Phyllis. You don't expect me to remember our conversation, do you? Peter always talked in inanities anyway.'

'No, he didn't,' she snapped, feeling her own anger surge forward. 'And you weren't supposed to be there. You must have had a reason to come, and I damn well want to know what it was.'

'Don't swear at me, Phyllis,' he said huffily. 'We only discussed the McKintridge estate. I brought him the escrow papers to sign.' Felix appeared to be injured by her outburst. 'I know you both decided to wait, but platinum had fallen badly that morning and I knew he would need im-

461

mediate cash. That's what I was doing here; I brought him a check. I thought that would ease his mind, not upset him. And that's what I want to do for you, the same thing I offered to do for him. Ease your burden.'

Was that all it was: she wondered. There had to be more. That wouldn't have caused the reaction in Peter she'd seen when she came home that night. He had been in a mental collapse. She'd had to call the psychiatrist. She wished to God she'd taken Peter to the emergency room.

'Dad, it's good of you to want to ease our burdens. And I need your help. But I'm not sure what I want to do about selling you the estate right now.' He started to interrupt her but she stopped him. 'This is a decision I must make for myself. I cannot remain a sheltered child and let Daddy take care of me. I'm a grown woman, with a child, and I'm a widow.' It was the first time she'd ever used the term before about herself, and it made her sound so old. *Her husband was dead*. She felt that searing pain erupting inside again but she forced it down. It was true that this decision about the estate was crucial. Someday, maybe a long time from now, her pain might ease, a life would beckon to her again. And the decisions she made now would have an impact on that life.

'You're right to go slowly, dear,' her father said, taking her hand. 'And I'm proud to see you taking such command of your life. but one thing has nothing to do with the other. Peter saw the wisdom of my purchasing the estate, even though he wasn't able to see other things as clearly, such as the way his grandfather took advantage of him and what his cowardly death would do to your life.' He shook his head. 'But then he just wasn't worthy of you.'

Her head snapped up and she stared at him. 'That's not true.'

'It is true,' he insisted. 'And I told him so!' He saw her expression and stopped.

Phyllis was shaking. 'You told him so? When did you tell him? Yesterday? Did you tell him that last night when he was in the worst emotional pain of his life? Is that what you did? Did you come over to my house when I asked you not to and tell my sick husband he was unworthy of me? There was never a worthier man on this earth than Peter. How could you? How could you do that?'

Felix's face was drained of color so that his gray-blond hair blended with his skin. Except for the brilliant blue of his eyes he appeared almost colorless. 'Phyllis, be careful of what you are saying. Don't jump to conclusions you may regret.'

'Regret!' she shouted. 'I'll tell you about regret. I shall regret bitterly the rest of my life that I left Peter alone that day, that I ever appealed to you and told you how vulnerable he was, that I didn't get home in time to save him from encountering you. You yelled at him? I can't believe you did that. Did you yell at him that he was unworthy? A man who suffered so from feelings of failure that he was in a state of near collapse. Did you pile more agonizing torment on his head under the guise of helping him, of setting him straight? Oh, my dear lord, tell me you didn't, please tell me you didn't!'

Her shouting had carried to the next room where shocked family members and friends heard them arguing and moved to the kitchen, wondering what all this was about.

Felix looked up and saw Marla and Audrey standing in the doorway and Vicky nearby. 'Phyllis, not now,' he said. 'We'll talk about this later.'

But Phyllis didn't care who heard her and she spoke with a sudden strength that surprised her. 'My husband is lying across town in a mortuary dead from committing suicide and you tell me not to talk about what put him there? I want to discuss it now,' she said. 'And since you've brought this up, I want to tell you how I feel.' Her eyes filled with tears again. 'I don't think I could bear having you own the estate and live in the house that meant so much to Peter. Especially since you think he was so unworthy. God only knows Belson would have hated the idea.' Her tears spilled over and she wiped them with her hand. 'I just don't think it's right. If the estate cannot belong to me and Peter and our son, maybe it's better then that some stranger have it. If you lived there, it would always remind me of the tragedy of Peter's death and what he lost. It meant so much to him to keep it.'

'But, Phyllis,' he said, hastening to assure her, 'you don't have to worry about that, I'm not going to live there. You won't be reminded of it at all. I have plans to demolish the main house. It's much too large and unwieldy. No one wants a place that enormous anymore. So you see, your memories will be safe . . .' He stopped because she was staring at him, horrified.

'Demolish it!' she screamed. 'You want to tear it down? To desecrate Peter's memory? I don't believe you. I don't!' She felt anguish overtaking her again. 'Did you tell him that yesterday too? That you were going to buy his home, the one place in the world that he cherished, and tear it down? No wonder he was so desperate. That would have been the worst thing in life to him. And he must have been so torn. He wanted to please you by selling you the estate because he loved you, and look at how you rewarded him.' She pressed her fists against her temples as if to press away the awful thoughts in her brain. But they wouldn't leave her alone.

'I won't let you do it,' she said. 'Unless you promise me you will preserve the estate, put it in writing that you will care for it, and leave the house intact, then by God, I *will* sell it to someone else.'

They heard Audrey gasp, 'Phyllis, this is your father you're talking to.'

'He wants to destroy it, Mother,' she cried.

But Felix held up his hand to his wife not to interfere. 'Phyllis,' he said softly, 'you have no choice in the matter.'

'What do you mean?' she asked incredulously.

'I hold all the outstanding mortgages on the estate. I bought them months ago. I have the right to foreclose if the mortgage payments are late, and I have the right to buy the estate before anyone else's offer is considered.'

Phyllis just stared at him as though she were watching a horrible transformation of a man into a demon, as though his flesh were crawling with disease. 'I don't understand,' she whispered. 'How? Why?'

'I only had your best interests at heart,' he swore.

'You're a liar!' Marla said, pushing her way into the room past Vicky and Audrey Anhalt.

'Marla!' Felix cautioned.

But Marla would not be deterred. She came over to Phyllis and took both her friend's hands in hers, then looked directly into Phyllis's eyes. 'Do you want to know why he's a liar?'

But even as Phyllis nodded, Felix shouted, 'Marla, you'd better stop right now, if you know what's good for you.'

'No, you stop!' Phyllis said, glaring at Felix. 'I want to hear what she's going to say.'

'She doesn't know anything!' Felix insisted, his voice rising in panic.

'Yes, I do,' Marla said, never taking her eyes from Phyllis. 'I know that Peter loved you more than life itself; he was a true and faithful husband. And mine wasn't.' Marla's stricken face told Phyllis the truth of that statement. 'And neither was your father. He has been trying to ruin Belson McKintridge for years and he never gave a damn what his lust for revenge did to you or to Peter. It was your father who informed on Belson and Peter to the CFTC. If he hadn't done that, they might both still be alive.'

Phyllis moaned in anguish and Marla waited a moment before continuing. 'Did Peter know?' Phyllis asked.

'Yes. But he wanted to spare you that pain. Belson blamed Peter for the whole failure of the scheme. And Peter accepted the blame. He was so tortured by what your father had done, and yet he forgave him and agreed to sell him the estate, thinking Felix would pass it on to you someday, and to Jonathan. But Felix never intended to do that. In fact he was so bloodthirsty for Belson's destruction, he couldn't even wait a decent amount of time to get the estate. He had to have it now! Destroy it now! And that's why he went to Peter yesterday, to pressure him again about selling. He backed Peter into a corner and then told him what he just told you, that there was nothing Peter could do, Felix had the right to buy the estate and would destroy it.'

'That's not true!' Felix insisted. 'I went there to help. I offered him money when he needed it.'

Marla turned to him. 'Then why did you call Larry last night and ask him to pressure Peter into selling right away? Why not just loan him the money if he needed it so badly, if you really wanted to help him?'

'Shut the fuck up, Marla,' Felix snarled. 'You've had it, you're dead in this town. There is someone who's going to be very interested to learn what I know about you.'

'There's nothing you can say or do that can hurt me anymore, Felix, because Larry knows everything. *Everything,* do you understand? So just watch it!' Marla and Felix glared at one another.

'You're so honest, aren't you, Marla, you Judas.' Felix's fury cut the air like a knife. 'Haven't you left something out? Why don't you tell Phyllis about your loyal husband?'

'I will,' she replied, turning back. 'Phyllis,' she said. 'Larry is the one whom Peter confided in, and Larry, for his own selfish reasons, went and told Felix. But he honestly believed your father would try to help Peter, not destroy him.' She had tears in her eyes. 'I don't think Larry will ever forgive himself.'

'He must,' Phyllis told her. 'Life is too precious to be spent in self-recrimination. Look at what it did to Peter.' She turned to her father; her expression mirrored her heartbreak. 'I want you to get out of my house. And I don't want you to ever come back here unless I specifically ask you. You are not to see my child, you are to divest yourself of any interests you are handling on my behalf immediately. And don't call me! Now please, leave!'

'Phyllis,' her mother said. 'Are you sure this is what you want? Do you want to hear his side of it?'

'No, Mother,' she replied. 'You listen to him if you must, but I never will again.'

Audrey stared at her daughter, absorbing the impact of her words, and Phyllis stared back, willing her mother to understand, to derive strength from her own determination, to join in her rebellion.

Audrey's struggle was apparent from the expression on her face and after moments that seemed interminably long, she crossed the room and came to stand behind her daughter. Finally, she had declared her long-desired independence. She turned to Felix, raised her own chin in defiance and stared at him.

At that moment both Marla and Vicky moved to Phyllis's side, put their arms around her, and the three of them wept together.

Audrey watched Felix go, his haughtiness annihilated by this rejection.

Chapter 24

THE ENCOUNTER between Phyllis and her father left Vicky shaken to the core. But as much as Phyllis needed her right now, and Marla too, there was something she had to do for herself before another minute went by.

She left Phyllis's house and drove directly east on Sunset Boulevard to Laurel Canyon, cursing the heavy rush-hour traffic that moved at a snail's pace. By the time she turned left on Laurel and then left again on Kirkwood toward Bob's house, she was praying out loud that Bob would be there.

When she saw his Volkswagen and motorcycle in the

garage, she breathed a prayer of thanks. But then as she got out of the car and climbed the long steep staircase to his front door, her knees began to shake. Nightmare visions of beautiful blondes lounging in his bed haunted her; after all it had been ten days since Belson's funeral. 'Okay,' she said out loud. 'If there are any blondes in there, I'll kick them out.' His bed was her territory and she was about to claim it. She knocked on the door loudly, but her knock was worse than her bite, for when Bob opened the door, bare-footed and wearing only shorts, his body wet with perspiration, she couldn't say a word. He was panting and she could see a set of barbells in the middle of the living-room floor.

Finally she found her voice. 'Hi, Tarzan,' she said. 'Me Jane. Wanta swing?'

He laughed and stepped aside for her but as she came into the room, her heart sank. For sitting on the sofa with her back to the door was a blonde with long silky hair. 'Oh, excuse me,' Vicky stammered, her resolve melting like snowfall in summer. But when the blonde turned her head Vicky saw that it was a full-grown Afghan.

She whirled around to Bob. 'Who's that?' she demanded. 'In my chair!'

'That's Princess.' He laughed, seeing her expression. He was still panting from exercise. 'Princess,' he said. 'Meet the queen.' And he leaned forward and planted a wet kiss on Vicky's mouth. Then he shooed the dog off the sofa and out the front door. Princess looked at them haughtily before she lumbered away. 'Princess lives down the block and comes to visit on occasion. She knows how to be kind to a lonely bachelor.'

'So do I,' Vicky said, gazing at him, and then her eyes filled with tears. He grabbed a towel and wiped his arms and upper body, and then wrapped it around his shoulders before he came over to hug her.

'I heard about Peter McKintridge. I'm really sorry. What a terrible shock. Phyllis must be sick with grief. I know how close you were with him.'

Vicky cried silently against his chest, drinking in the odors of him, the alive, hard muscular feeling, the beating of his heart, the breathing of his lungs. He was alive! She clutched him tightly.

'I've been an idiot,' she said. 'And I wouldn't tell you because I was so angry with you. But life is too short to hang on to anger, especially when we belong together. I love you. I love you, Bob. And it doesn't matter what you are, it's who you are that matters. If you want to be a masseur, I'll buy the oil; if you want to be a lawyer, I'll help you study; if you want to be a guru in Katmandu, I'll shave my head.' She paused. 'Well, maybe I'd only cut it, but I'll go with you.'

He laughed, a deep chuckle way down in his throat; she felt it vibrate happily against her.

'But I love you and I want to be with you. You were right about everything. It's wrong to exploit others' misfortunes even if they are despicable. Leslie Winokur and Belson McKintridge are not worth honoring with the written word, not while I still long for revenge against them. Maybe someday I'll have perspective enough to treat them objectively, but I can't right now, and that means I shouldn't write about them. It would be immoral.'

He kissed the top of her head and held her closely, and she felt as though she'd come home, really home, where there was a safe haven, and someone knew her as she really was. He saw the best of her as an inspiration for her capabilities and the worst of her, and yet forgave her for it.

'I owe you an apology too,' he said. 'The day of Belson's funeral I attacked you unfairly. I've had a chance to think about it and I realized I was trying to keep us at arm's distance; I was afraid of getting too close.'

'And now?' she asked, her heart pounding as she waited for his answer.

He hugged her more tightly. 'Even this isn't close enough,' he said.

'I'm brokenhearted for Phyllis,' she said. 'She's lost so much. I never want to lose you!' She pulled away to look at him. 'Phyllis has always lived an ideal life. I never really believed it could shatter in a moment. She was Snow White in the castle, Cinderella with her prince. And look what's happened. Everything is gone, all at once.'

He was looking at her tenderly, a smile playing in his eyes.

'Well, don't just stand there all musclebound and tongue-tied. Say something,' she demanded lightly. 'How do you feel? And don't say anything flip, because I'll flip you. I have a black and blue belt from Jack La Flame and I'll grab you between my teeth and swim sixty miles pulling you behind me.'

'You're a real tough lady, aren't you?' he said.

'Well?' she said, her eyes filling with tears again.

'I love you, Vicky,' he said. 'I love you very much.'

And then he kissed her and she sighed with relief.

'What do we do about Belson and those exploited children?' Vicky asked after they'd made love, and made dinner, and made plans.

'I was going to call you tomorrow and tell you what I found out,' Bob said. 'The police caught the man who supplied the child prostitutes to Belson. His name is Raphael and he was into drugs, smuggling, child prostitution, as well as exploiting illegal aliens. They have enough on him to finish him for good.'

She shook her head. 'So there's no point in revealing what we know about Belson since he's dead and can't be a corroborative witness.'

'It would only hurt Phyllis and Jonathan now that Peter is gone.'

'I couldn't do that to her,' Vicky said. 'Though it kills me not to have Belson pay for his crimes in some way.'

'You'll find a way,' Bob grinned. 'I know you will.'

'Maybe,' she replied, reaching for a dish towel to dry the salad bowl. 'But it's not important to me anymore. What is important is my work, doing good work, and being with you.'

He put the wine back into the refrigerator and turned to her. 'Will you marry me?' he said.

She nodded thoughtfully. 'In time.'

'How much time?' he asked.

'Are you in a hurry?'

He shrugged. 'A man likes to know.'

She thought a minute and then shifted her weight from one hip to the other. 'How about eighteen minutes?'

'Make it seventeen,' he said.

'You're on!'

Chapter 25

THERE WERE no cars parked in Phyllis's driveway when Larry arrived and he thought it was strange. It had taken him all morning and most of the afternoon to try and straighten out Peter's affairs and he'd only just scratched the surface. But only that most pressing business would have kept him from being at Phyllis's side at a time like this. The pain in his heart over Peter had been eased slightly because of the positive events of the day and the significant part he played in them.

Phyllis and her mother were alone in the living room with only Marla to keep them company.

'I'm so glad you're here,' Marla said, giving him a welcoming embrace. He could tell how sincere she was and it was a new sensation for him to trust her, to believe she was really glad to see him. But then he had finally allowed himself to see how much she meant to him too. He clung to her for a moment before breaking away, aware that the display of their affection might point out to Phyllis what she had lost, but he really didn't want to let Marla go.

He turned to Phyllis. 'You shouldn't be alone like this,' he said. 'Where is everyone?' There were black circles under her eyes and an aura of defeat about her that alarmed him. He needed her to be strong right now. If she had been defeated by Peter's death, she never would be able to accomplish what lay ahead of her. Perhaps his news would give her strength.

Phyllis held out her hand to him and he came and sat beside her. 'I sent everyone away, Larry.'

He glanced at Marla as if to ask, 'What's going on?'

'Marla told me about my father, that he was the one who informed the CFTC about Belson and Peter. I know all about his schemes and what he did to Peter yesterday.' Her eyes held a sadness so deep that it made a mockery of fairness. 'I know everything,' she repeated dully. 'I've told my father to get out of my life. I never want to see him again.'

'Felix has lost a great deal today,' Audrey said.

'Did they tell you about my part in all of it?' Larry asked.

'Yes,' Phyllis answered still as sadly, but she held on to his hand, conveying her understanding.

'I'm so sorry, Phyl,' he said. 'Peter knew how badly I felt about it. But he forgave me. The day Belson died we had a talk, he told me then that he knew what I had done.' The pain of that memory deepened the furrows between Larry's eyes.

'It's over now,' Phyllis said. 'It's over. Why don't you tell me what happened today?' But before Larry could reply, her eyes suddenly grew wide and her pale face drained of all its remaining color. 'My God,' she exclaimed. 'The commodities! I forgot all about selling Peter's holdings this morning. He was going to do it today, and I didn't remember!' A fresh wave of pain assailed her, but she didn't break. 'What happened with the market? I'm afraid to ask how much we lost.'

'You didn't lose.' Larry said. He'd been so involved with details of his meeting today he'd neglected to call and tell

472

her. 'Platinum shot up today, there was a gain of ninety points.'

'But how could that have happened?' Phyllis's voice quavered with disbelief.

'There are often large fluctuations in commodity prices; ninety points isn't even that much of a gain. We just didn't know if it would happen. And we've been so distracted by the events of the past week we overlooked the fact that although platinum fell, gold did not. It kept climbing. Platinum almost always rises higher than gold as gold rises. In the past few days gold has been going through the roof. So it was only a matter of time before platinum reversed its downtrend. We just couldn't predict when.'

Marla stood up and came over to Larry. 'What are you saying?' she asked with growing excitement. 'That Phyllis might be able to keep the estate after all? That she won't have to sell it to Felix, or anyone else?'

'If platinum keeps rising,' he said, grinning at them.

'But isn't it too risky to wait?' Phyllis asked. 'Shouldn't I sell now, while I've recovered some of our loss?'

'It's still a gamble,' Larry agreed, 'but there's a damn good chance platinum is going to keep rising. The prediction is in a couple of days it might be over a thousand dollars an ounce.'

'But what about the debts and the sanctions of the CFTC?' Marla said. 'Won't the commission make her liquidate her holdings now?'

Phyllis chimed in, 'And don't I have to forfeit this profit because it was gained illegally?'

Larry held up his hands to stop their questions. 'Wait, let me explain. I spent the entire morning with Lew Cohen and the lawyer from the CFTC, then it took me the entire afternoon to talk to every one of Peter's brokers plus the New York enforcement division of the Futures Trading Commission. They've all concluded that Belson and Peter were not guilty after all of squeezing the market. Platinum is priced unusually high this year and there has been such a large volume of contracts sold this year, their holdings were

473

not significant enough to affect the price either way, up or down.'

'Even though they owned ten thousand contracts?' Phyllis asked.

'That's right,' he said.

'But what about the huge drop in the price that occurred last week?'

'It was one of those fluctuations that simply occur and are unpredictable. It just happened to coincide with the CFTC's call to Belson and he correlated the two events; actually they were unrelated.'

'What about the criminal action?' Marla asked. 'The bank official, and all that?'

'Belson was the one guilty of bribing an official. And he is dead. He can't be punished any more than that. After all, death is the ultimate sanction. Of course the bank official has been indicted, but that doesn't affect Phyllis's holdings.'

'I can't believe it,' Phyllis said, her voice revealing how this news had stunned her. 'Just like that?' And then the reality of her loss etched her face with agony. 'If only Peter had lived one more day. One more day,' she whispered.

Larry squeezed her hand. 'You mustn't torture yourself like that.'

'But things could have been so different,' she cried. 'I almost wish this hadn't happened today. It's just too cruel to bear.'

'Phyllis,' Marla said, 'Larry's right. You're torturing yourself with what might have been.'

'I always will,' Phyllis said to her. 'Always.'

'But you're forgetting that Peter would still be suffering, Phyllis,' Larry said softly. 'He would have had to face serious consequences of his actions. The committee only decided not to inquire further into his case because of his tragic death. But they would have expected him to inform on his grandfather's associates and on his grandfather. That choice was unbearable to him. There would have been heavy fines to pay, and they may have forced him to liquidate immediately so McKintridge would have been lost in any case. You know how he felt about that. Then there was the question of the bar. He might have lost his license to practice law and had to live with that failure. There would have been months, maybe years, of added stress for him to endure.'

'He was in such pain,' Audrey said.

'Felix would not have let up on him,' Marla added.

'But we would have faced it together,' Phyllis cried.

'Don't,' Larry said, putting his arm around her. 'He couldn't take the pain any longer, honey. He just couldn't. And he would not have told you about his part in the plane crash. He'd still be carrying that burden.'

She knew the truth of that statement. She had seen the extent of all his suffering. But still her loss was so great. If only Peter knew how great. Finally she asked, 'What do I do now?'

'Wait a few days,' he told her, 'or a week, to see what happens with platinum. You are Belson's heir and Peter's now too. You have the same rights and powers that were granted by the terms of Belson's will. And if you make enough money on your holdings to keep the estate, then you can decide to do with it whatever you choose.'

'Will the brokers allow me to keep all the accounts open that long, even though Belson is dead?' she asked.

'Yes,' he told her. 'We can arrange that.'

She shook her head, trying to absorb the enormity of what he had just told her, and everyone was silent, watching her struggle. This news would mitigate some of her problems, but it would hardly begin to minimize her suffering.

'I'm glad for you, darling,' Audrey said, finally breaking the silence.

And Phyllis smiled at her mother, a sad, tremulous smile. 'I'll have something hopeful to tell Peter at the funeral tomorrow when we say good-bye.' And then she turned to Marla, her smile a bit stronger. 'I hope there will be enough money for me to hire a good decorator when I move into the estate. McKintridge can really use you.'

Marla moved over next to Phyllis, put her arms around her friend, and the two women wept together.

Author's Note

For the purpose of fiction I have altered the dates of platinum's rise and fall during the time period of this novel. However in the pursuit of accuracy the changes were minimal and in fact it would have been possible, from September 1979 to June 1980, for an investment in platinum of two million dollars to be pyramided into a net gain of $100 million over a six-month time span.

TIMES OF TRIUMPH
by Charlotte Vale Allen

Spanning more than three decades in the turbulent history of our century, Charlotte Vale Allen's magnificent saga traces the life and loves of a woman born to struggle against every adversity with dauntless courage and unflinching love.

Leonie came to New York with all the world against her and built her tiny eating-house into a mighty business empire.

Gray, the London journalist who followed her across the ocean, was the father of her children and the love of her lifetime.

Through the First World War, the hard and hungry years that followed, through love and pain and bitter sadness, through the growing years of their son and daughter destined to retrace their mother's footsteps into a Europe once again torn apart by war – Leonie's life was a time of triumph.

NEW ENGLISH LIBRARY

MEET ME IN TIME
by Charlotte Vale Allen

Meet Me in Time is a story about love, its intensity and destructiveness, its needs and satisfactions. It is also the story of the Burgesses, a brilliant, tormented family.

Gaby : bitter and unstable, cheated by the failure of her marriage and resenting the child she never wanted . . .

Dana : a talented playwright who recoiled from the truth about himself . . .

Glenn : the artist, haunted by her mother's death, expecting more love than anyone could humanly give her . . .

All three had dreams of fame, and passions that demanded fulfilment. All three shared the bittersweet inheritance from their mother, whose need to love had been overwhelming, and whose need to be loved was an inescapable legacy to her children.

POST A LITTLE HAPPINESS

Post·A·Book

A Royal Mail service in association with the Book Marketing Council & The Booksellers Association.

Post-A-Book is a Post Office trademark.

NEL BESTSELLERS

T51277	'THE NUMBER OF THE BEAST'	*Robert Heinlein*	£2.25
T50777	STRANGER IN A STRANGE LAND	*Robert Heinlein*	£1.75
T51382	FAIR WARNING	*Simpson & Burger*	£1.75
T52478	CAPTAIN BLOOD	*Michael Blodgett*	£1.75
T50246	THE TOP OF THE HILL	*Irwin Shaw*	£1.95
T49620	RICH MAN, POOR MAN	*Irwin Shaw*	£1.60
T51609	MAYDAY	*Thomas H. Block*	£1.75
T54071	MATCHING PAIR	*George G. Gilman*	£1.50
T45773	CLAIRE RAYNER'S LIFEGUIDE		£2.50
T53709	PUBLIC MURDERS	*Bill Granger*	£1.75
T53679	THE PREGNANT WOMAN'S BEAUTY BOOK	*Gloria Natale*	£1.25
T49817	MEMORIES OF ANOTHER DAY	*Harold Robbins*	£1.95
T50807	79 PARK AVENUE	*Harold Robbins*	£1.75
T50149	THE INHERITORS	*Harold Robbins*	£1.75
T53231	THE DARK	*James Herbert*	£1.50
T43245	THE FOG	*James Herbert*	£1.50
T53296	THE RATS	*James Herbert*	£1.50
T45528	THE STAND	*Stephen King*	£1.75
T50874	CARRIE	*Stephen King*	£1.50
T51722	DUNE	*Frank Herbert*	£1.75
T51552	DEVIL'S GUARD	*Robert Elford*	£1.50
T52575	THE MIXED BLESSING	*Helen Van Slyke*	£1.75
T38602	THE APOCALYPSE	*Jeffrey Konvitz*	95p

NEL P.O. BOX 11, FALMOUTH TR10 9EN, CORNWALL

Postage Charge:

U.K. Customers 45p for the first book plus 20p for the second book and 14p for each additional book ordered to a maximum charge of £1.63.

B.F.P.O. & EIRE Customers 45p for the first book plus 20p for the second book and 14p for the next 7 books; thereafter 8p per book.

Overseas Customers 75p for the first book and 21p per copy for each additional book.

Please send cheque or postal order (no currency).

Name ....

Address ....

....

Title ....